PURSUING FLIGHT

A DRAGON SPIRIT NOVEL: BOOK 4

C.I. BLACK

Gryphon's Gate Publishing

Gryphon's Gate Publishing

550 King St. N.

PO Box 42088 Conestoga

Waterloo, ON

N2L 6K5

ebook ISBN978-1-988115-47-4

Print ISBN978-1-988115-46-7

PROLOGUE

Becca drew her knees tighter to her body and squeezed her eyes shut. She didn't care how vulnerable the position made her look. It only mattered that she hold onto herself, and *please*, somehow let her physical grip strengthen her mental grip.

Just hold on. That was all she had to do. Hold on. Her name was Becca Scott. Captain Rebecca Ann Scott. Not Lash or Kopis or Styx.

Rebecca Ann Scott.

She was a soldier, a granddaughter, a friend. A human.

God, she was human!

Dragons weren't real. Magic wasn't real. And she wasn't losing pieces of her soul, everything that made her *her.*

This was a nightmare. Just a nightmare. If she could just wake up, she'd be back in Kandahar with her brothers-in-arms, exhausted and wound tight, gathering intelligence on Taliban positions—

Except that wasn't right. She'd gone home. One tour as a peacekeeper in East Timor and almost two in Afghanistan, and she'd had enough.

No. It hadn't been the tours that had ended her military career. It had been a teen with a backpack full of explosives, a crowded village market, and a tent being used as a makeshift school. The ambush on her unit, with RPGs tearing into both her light tactical transport vehicles and a sniper picking them off as they scrambled for cover, might not have pushed her over the edge. But she could still hear those people in the market screaming and the kids in the school tent wailing after the explosion—timed just before the first RPG hit her first transport—and there hadn't been a damned thing she could have done about it. They'd walked into a trap. Someone had tipped off the Taliban that she was planning on convincing the village chief to share intel, and they'd retaliated.

Right. She'd gone home to Toronto…

Had she?

She couldn't remember. Monsters had ripped through her soul, tearing at her essence with an agony that made the shrapnel, burns, and gunshot wounds from that ambush pale in comparison. She was helpless to stop them, just like she'd been helpless to stop that teen.

Everyone in position around the feast hall, a masculine voice growled. *The voice.* Somehow, in the unreality of nightmares, this monster was different from the others. He wasn't inside her body, clawing at her soul. He was in her head, talking to the devil and ordering kidnappings and assassinations.

Diablo, get eyes on Zenobia. Incapacitate if possible. Regis will want to sentence her himself.

Yes. Make Zenobia pay. She was the monster queen the others—the ones who tore at Becca from the inside out—obeyed and feared.

Except Zenobia wouldn't meet justice. That didn't exist, because this wasn't real. It was a dream, a nightmare.

It *had* to be a nightmare. PTSD. Something. Anything. It couldn't be real.

Life would be normal. Fine. If she just woke up.

God. Please. Wake up.

She jerked awake. Pain snapped through her skull, but the nightmare didn't vanish. Her pulse raced and the vise around her chest tightened. She was still trapped in a dimly lit, fifteen-by-fifteen foot cell, with an impossible stone lattice blocking the entrance. The semi-catatonic man who'd been in the corner since her arrival was still there, in a puddle of his own filth, still rocking back and forth and still softly weeping. The nine others—seven men, two women—also remained—

No. One of the men was missing.

She tried to think of his name but couldn't remember it and couldn't remember if she'd ever learned it. All she remembered was his starvation-thin features and the haunted, empty look in his eyes. The haunted guy was gone. The big guy in the corner, with shaggy light brown hair and a bushy beard—Werner—had said the haunted guy had arrived just before her, but with their inability to tell time in the cave and the missing time during the worst part of the nightmare, no one seemed to know how short or long 'just' was.

Except a part of her *knew* how long it had been. If she believed the *truth* of the nightmare, it had been almost six years since she'd been taken, and her dragon hosts had yet to awaken the magic promised within her aura. She also *knew* she was one of the lucky ones. If her aura hadn't held such promise, she would have been killed and thrown out like trash. A vessel without magic was a waste of time.

But that didn't make sense. That was the nightmare, the mess of thoughts and emotions that weren't hers... couldn't be hers.

Remember, the masculine voice said.

Becca's breath caught in her throat. *No. No no no.* She was still dreaming. The devil's master never spoke to her when she was awake. But she was still in the cell. She had to still be asleep.

Capture Zenobia.

"Make the bitch pay," Becca hissed into the shadows.

"Another dream?" Werner asked, his voice low and difficult to understand with his thick German accent.

"The devil's master is going after Zenobia in some feast hall."

Glenn—a twenty-something who also looked like an island castaway and who claimed he'd been stolen from the jungles of Vietnam —barked a harsh laugh that made the weeping man in the corner moan. "Wouldn't that be something."

"I want your dreams," the blond woman beside Werner said. "I'm always at the center of a—" She groaned. "In the center of a— a tornado." She screamed, and a gust of wind exploded through the cell. It slammed Becca against the wall. The air burst from her lungs and the whirlwind whipped it away. The guy in the corner wailed, the five on the far side hit the floor, two others were wrenched to their feet and pinned to the ceiling. Werner shoved against the impossible tornado, seized the front of the woman's soiled T-shirt, then froze.

Light flared around him and everyone else, except the weeping guy in the corner, and a weight filled Becca as if she was so exhausted she couldn't move. Her thoughts muddled and a command within the core of her being to stand jerked her to her feet.

The tornado vanished, dropping the two against the ceiling to the floor, and in unison, with a glazed look in their eyes, everyone turned toward the entrance as the stone lattice melted into the floor.

This was it. Her chance to escape. But, like all the other times the lattice had impossibly vanished, she found herself frozen, unable to move, controlled by a monster in her head.

The vise around her chest squeezed tighter, and she fought to breathe. They were going to try to awaken her magic again. Someone was going to invade her, seize her body, and tear into her.

Wake up. Please, just wake up.

They weren't going to activate some strange magic within her. She didn't possess magic. Magic was impossible.

Across from them, the lattice over the other cell also melted away, and the queen monster—Zenobia—and her lieutenant strode into the hall from the far end. The lieutenant hissed a guttural word and everyone but Becca, weeping guy, and Glenn stepped into the hall, joining the others from the other cell.

Everything within Becca screamed to run. Just run. It was a dream. If she concentrated hard enough, she could escape. Or better yet, wake up. But her body wouldn't obey. She could barely get the thought to form before it turned into mindless howling... or was that weeping guy still howling?

Zenobia flicked her wrist and the lattices swept back over the two entrances. The others marched like well-trained soldiers out of sight, and the force possessing her let go and dropped her to the floor. The weeping guy turned silent, but his rocking picked up, and Glenn moaned, his eyes unfocused...

Or was it Becca who was unfocused? Her pulse sped up, and she clung to that sensation. She lost time when she felt like this. The monster in her head thought of that time in terms of months and years. But that was the nightmare. Not reality. Not truth. Not—

Agony exploded in her head and shot like lightning through her limbs. The weeping guy screamed. His eyes rolled back and he collapsed, while Glenn howled and gripped his chest. His breath came in fast gasps like he'd been shot and was clinging to consciousness.

"Something's happened," Glenn said.

Someone in the hall roared. Someone else started yelling for help.

A black vortex erupted against the wall beside Glenn, and Werner leapt out as the impossible vortex vanished. He grabbed Glenn's arm and helped him stand. "It was the Asar Nergal."

"They know about us?" Glenn's eyes widened. "They're after us, like the dragons knew they would."

"But you—" Werner's gaze jumped to Becca and bore into her. "You knew they were going after Zenobia. You heard them."

"I didn't hear anything." Because it hadn't been real. *This* wasn't real. But she couldn't control her racing pulse. The monsters who'd been in her head knew that even trying to awaken her magic meant death for both of them. The Asar Nergal—whatever the hell they were—were merciless. They eliminated threats with extreme prejudice. And she was a threat.

"You did. We attacked the other dragons in a feast hall. But they were waiting for us, just like you said." Werner pressed his hand against the stone wall and another vortex burst to life. He shoved Glenn inside and held out his hand to her. "Let's get the hell out of here."

Round up all the humans, the masculine voice said.

But she was certain what he really meant was *kill* all the humans.

Nightmare or not, there was no way she was sticking around for that.

She grabbed Werner's hand and plunged into a black, consuming nothing.

1

White lightning snapped across Nero's sight and seared through his head. He shifted in the tub chair across from his imposing office desk, the leather squeaking with the movement. But nothing eased the agonizing magic that made him the dugga of the Asar Nergal and warned him about a human mage threat. Except his magic was wrong. It wasn't a human who endangered his people, his coterie, and more importantly, the members of his *puzur*, his secret coterie—and if he was being honest with himself, his hoard since he didn't collect anything else but these misfit humans—it was him.

And if he didn't do something about it soon, it might be too late.

It could already be too late.

He was the reason Diablo hadn't been able to capture the last of the mages created in Zenobia's coup and why Capri's Clean Team was working overtime to cover up any instances of magic to keep the human world oblivious to the truth that magic and dragons were real.

The last time humans had known about them, they'd cast a spell and destroyed dragonkind, and it had only been through the sacrifice of their goddess that dragons had managed to survive—albeit in a weakened spirit state, forced to inhabit human vessels.

Another flash of lightning in his head. He ground his teeth, knowing the magic would take him back to the woman in the hospital… yearning to go back to her.

Yes, he needed to deal with her. Killing her was the most expedient solution.

But he wasn't that drake anymore. He didn't just kill humans because they *might* become a danger. This woman needed help. If she hadn't gone insane, unable to accept the truth about the world—or because she'd been forced to share her body with a dragon's more powerful spirit—then she'd need help. She didn't have to become the danger dragons feared.

Except she *was* a danger. She could highjack his mental connection to his Asar Nergal soldiers and warn other mages they were being hunted. As well, from the flash he'd gotten last night, whatever facility she was in, the doctor had seemed to know she could hear him. Which only complicated the situation.

Yes, that explained his lack of action—aside from the fact that he didn't know where the woman was—there were just too many unanswered questions.

He needed more information—like, did the doctor know the truth, or was she assuming this woman suffered from auditory hallucinations? How many people knew the truth about this woman's ability? How many people would he have to neutralize? How much of a mess would Capri and her team have to clean up? How many loose ends were there?

It was all about the logistics and nothing to do with the pain and fear and confusion that had seized him when he'd connected with the woman. He couldn't just send in his whole team, even if the medical facility was in a secure prison lockup. Word that he was weak might make those few ambitious members in the Asar Nergal challenge him for the position of dugga. And he didn't have the time for that.

Over the years, he might have changed how he and the Asar Nergal dealt with some of the mages they hunted—saving who they could instead of killing them—but the directive remained the same. Protect dragonkind.

Except above that, he had to protect his *puzur*, those humans he'd saved, and those dragons who'd embraced them as kin. And those dragons included the members of the Asar Nergal who—all who remained—had willingly broken their king's directive, saving innocent humans instead of murdering them. If any of them thought he was weak or endangered their cause, they'd kill him and claim his rank.

This was a situation that needed to be carefully dealt with. Nero needed more information, and if he were smart, he'd deal with it himself, eliminating any chance of anyone finding out that a human could highjack the telepathy the Handmaiden had given him, which she'd sworn could only be heard by other members of the Asar Nergal.

Which only gave him more questions. Was it him? Or was the Handmaiden's magic failing? And if the Handmaiden's magic was failing, what did that mean?

More light seared pain through his skull, and his every muscle tensed. He fought to breathe and keep his consciousness within his body.

Not yet. Just. Not. Yet.

He needed to figure out what he was going to do. And no, it had nothing to do with the fear that once he released his magic and it connected to the woman, he'd be caught in her nightmare again.

Mother, he'd never feared that before. But then, his magic had never trapped him *inside* a mage's consciousness, either. Usually he was a disembodied essence seeing the mage from afar, but last night—

Last night had shaken him more than he wanted to admit. Somehow he'd managed to keep himself mostly together in front of Raven and during the mental connection with Diablo, but he had no idea if he'd be able to do it again.

His pulse throbbed, radiating agony through his head and slicing flecks of white lightning across his sight.

Something beeped and someone moaned. His office flashed into a sterile hospital room and the beeping grew faster.

No. He wrenched the image of his office into his mind's eye.

Someone said something, the voice muffled and tinny, as if coming from a speaker.

Not. Yet. He concentrated on his bottle of scotch, sitting on the edge of his desk. Half empty—and most of that consumption had happened last night.

Another voice. Then laughter.

The bottle snapped into focus.

"Get a room, you two," a feminine voice said.

The hospital room vanished, and he sat gripping the arms of the chair so tight his knuckles had turned white and the muscles in his forearms cramped.

Another woman laughed. They had to be in the hall. From their footsteps, it sounded as if they were drawing closer to his study.

"We have a room, Capri," Grey said. "And so do you. You know you're going to get caught by one of the kids if you keep making out in the solarium."

"They already have," Tyler said, his reedy tenor thick with disgust. "It's like catching your parents doing it."

"What's that like?" Ivy asked as the group strode past Nero's partially opened office door.

"They say you can't remember things," Tyler said.

"Who says that?" Grey asked, a growl in his voice, his inamorated bond to Ivy making him overprotective.

Tyler snorted, unaware of the potential danger—still too new to the *puzur* to fully understand dragon behavior. "Be glad you can't. I need to wash out my eyeballs after what I saw those two doing."

Their voices carried down the hall toward the back of the house and the enormous kitchen. It seemed like at least one of his kids had accepted Ivy into the family. She hadn't even been there a full day, and the *puzur's* newest human member, Tyler, didn't seem worried about the newest dragon member. Of course, that might be because Tyler still knew next to nothing about how dangerous the world actually was. Nero might have trusted Raven's decision to tell Tyler the truth about how his father had gone crazy and killed people, but, knowing Raven, that information would have been crafted into the gentlest of blows.

Laughter burst from down the hall—the opposite direction from where the others had gone—and three of his youngest kids raced past his office. It had to be mealtime.

His gaze slid to the window and the night sky beyond.

Dinnertime?

He'd been sitting in his office all day?

He rubbed his aching temples, but the movement did nothing to ease the pain.

Mother of All, he'd been sitting there since the early morning—since the latter half of last night, really—and then the entire day. He hadn't checked up on Raven and their new intake—a human whose pain and blazing aura promised a dangerous and powerful earth magic—and he hadn't checked to see if Grey and Ivy had been assigned a suite and duties and been properly included in the *puzur*.

At the very least, he should join everyone for dinner. Even when things had been difficult, he'd always tried to participate in the evening meal. It might have been a weird human custom when he'd first tried it with the human members of his *puzur*, but now it was the part of the day he looked forward to.

He sat forward to rise out of the tub chair and his cell phone rang.

For a moment, he contemplated not answering, but too much was happening in the Dragon Court with Regis for him to be out of touch, and he didn't doubt there'd be fallout from the latest mess. Hell, there was still fallout from the messes made by Zenobia and Katar over the last four weeks.

Besides, he'd never been the kind of drake to hide from his problems, and he wasn't going to start now.

He pulled his phone from his pocket and checked the call display. Not a number he recognized. Which meant it could be anyone. "What?"

"Permission to enter your house?" an unfamiliar voice asked.

White light sliced across his sight and through his head.

No… wait. Nero did recognize that voice. "Hunter?"

"Yes. I'd like permission—"

"Your inamorata is here. I'm pretty sure I couldn't stop you from entering my house if I wanted to." In fact, Nero was surprised Hunter hadn't been by already. The initial bond between inamorated souls was often overwhelming. It explained why Capri and Ryan spent every night in the solarium and why, if Raven were smart—which she was—Grey and Ivy would have been given a suite in the wing opposite the kids' wing. The need to be with your inamorata or inamorato consumed a dragon's thoughts, made them irrational, and made them dangerous to themselves and everyone around them. Nero knew first-hand. He'd found his soul mate before the Great Scourge and had been overwhelmed with rage and grief when she hadn't survived.

Another slice of light.

"Is that a yes?" Hunter asked.

Even with Hunter in a new body and without the agony screaming through Nero's head, he wouldn't have tried to stop Hunter. One, a dragon would fight to the death to protect his inamorata, and two, Hunter was and had always been a more powerful drake. Face to face, Nero's chances were slim.

"Nero?" Hunter growled.

Shit. Right. This was bad. He was losing his concentration just trying to function past the pain. "It's a yes."

The black vortex of a gate formed in front of the office window, and with a whoosh of air, Hunter emerged. The red drake, in his new lean-muscled body with dark eyes and a dark buzz-cut, had an all-too-familiar aura that radiated more strength and power than it had the last time Nero had seen him—which had been when he'd quit his position as the prince's assassin after Zenobia's failed coup. It shocked Nero how fast Hunter's earth magic had developed, and how it had grown stronger in only a few weeks. It was terrifying to think how powerful the red drake would be in a few years, let alone a few hundred.

Another snap of light.

Hunter's eyes narrowed, his expression worried. "You all right?"

"Grey made it a very long day."

"Not Grey's fault." Hunter's tone darkened.

"Didn't say it was." Best to change the subject. Grey might have become an unofficial member of Nero's *puzur*, but he was without a doubt a member of Hunter's, and—if Hunter was even a fraction like Nero—the red drake would protect his unofficial coterie almost as aggressively as he'd protect his inamorata.

Nero jerked his chin to the open bottle of scotch on his desk. "Drink?"

Hunter's gaze slid to the bottle and the single glass beside it, amber residue dried at the bottom.

"There's a clean glass in the middle drawer." Nero shifted, about to stand and get the glass, but more lightning blazed through him and he collapsed back, struggling to not look like he was in agony. "I'm surprised you're being so formal," he forced out. Maybe if he addressed the obvious, Hunter would go find Anaea, and Nero could get back to figuring out what the hell he was going to do.

"Grey said for a Traditionalist you were surprisingly loose on tradition, but..." Hunter gave a half-shrug that exposed his tension.

"But there are drakes calling for you to revive the Red Coterie and be doyen."

"And a doyen doesn't enter another doyen's house without an invitation," Hunter said. "Not that I'm a doyen."

Nero snorted. "You might not have a choice in that."

"I really hope you're wrong."

"And for the sake of everyone, I hope your return means you've found the Handmaiden." But Nero could tell from Hunter's grim expression he hadn't. Which only made the situation worse, since she was the only one who could fix whatever was wrong with his dugga's magic. It was her God damned spell in the first place, not an earth magic ability. His human body could free gate and control wind. That was it.

Hunter crossed his arms and the muscles in his jaw tensed. "I thought if I stayed away, I could focus on finding the Handmaiden."

"But you can't ignore the bond." Nero hadn't been able to either when he'd been first inamorated. "I'm surprised you lasted as long as you did."

Hunter snorted. "Two weeks. I lasted fourteen whole days."

"Without any contact with her. Trust me, that's hard."

"Trust you?"

"And trust me when I say spend all the time you can with her." They might be spirits now, trapped for eternity in human bodies, but that didn't mean they couldn't be killed. And with the Handmaiden missing, if anything happened to Anaea—the only full sorcerer currently around—dragonkind was at greater risk of becoming extinct, since they needed a sorcerer to cast the rebirth spell—

Except that wasn't true anymore. Grey had the rebirth coin. When joined with the medallion, which was enspelled to temporarily absorb and protect a dragon's spirit, the coin helped place that spirit in a new vessel. But if the wrong dragon got his hands on the coin, he could force any drake to be reborn—a process that stripped a dragon of everything but his core essence, essentially killing him.

Jeez, he'd thought things were complicated before.

"That's the other reason I couldn't hold out," Hunter said. "Grey says things at Court are a mess. If I can't find the Handmaiden, I need to have a plan to protect Anaea and Grey and—"

"Careful, you're sounding like a doyen." Nero tried to smile, but the best he could manage felt more like a grimace.

"Yeah, well, I'd swear my allegiance to you if that didn't mess you up."

"Please don't. I'm not sure I can handle another ancient drake in my coterie. Grey is more than enough."

"Ha. And here I thought you were worried I'd jeopardize your position with Regis."

"I think me just existing jeopardizes my position with Regis." Pain sliced through his skull and for a heartbeat, the office turned into the hospital room.

"You think he suspects you're not a Traditionalist?"

"I think he's on the verge of going insane, like his father." A heart monitor beeped and someone moaned.

"That's blunt."

Nero yanked his attention back to Hunter, but the red drake now stood with a semi-transparent hospital wall in front of him. "And dangerous, I know."

"Any move against Regis without the Handmaiden's backing will destabilize Court."

The white wall turned opaque, obscuring Hunter.

Son of a—

"Court is already destabilized," Nero said, fighting to keep his consciousness in his office.

The beeping picked up.

Not. Real, the woman's raspy, broken alto said. *I'm Becca Scott. Captain Rebecca Ann Scott. Not Lash. Not Styx. Not Kopis. I'm Becca.*

Nero clenched his jaw. He had to get back to his office—although if he'd wanted proof whether this woman was a natural mage or a byproduct of Zenobia's coup, he now had it. Those were dragon names. Which meant she'd been unnaturally created and was clinging to herself, fighting the soul sickness that threatened all mages created by unnatural means, holding on by her mental fingernails.

Becca. Scott, she growled.

"Nero?" a masculine voice asked. Hunter. In his office. Where Nero sat. Where he had to yank his consciousness back to.

I am Becca.

God, he couldn't help her. Not right now. No matter how much he wanted to. He needed more information. He needed a plan.

Well, I didn't ask for your help, and I don't need it. Fear, determination, and pain roared through Nero. All hint of his office vanished, and he was wrenched into her body. Her pulse raced. The heart monitor's beep turned wild. Her gaze slid down her arm to a wrist captured in a leather cuff, securing her to the bed. *I don't need your help. I'm not anyone else. I'm me. God, please. I'm me, and this is a nightmare. It isn't real.*

Footsteps clattered toward her, and Becca's gaze jumped to the door. The woman in the doctor's coat and the dark-rimmed glasses rushed to her side.

"What do you hear? What's he saying?"

"He's not saying anything," Becca said.

More lightning, more blinding pain.

Where are you?

"He's not saying anything," she gasped.

I can't help you if—

"You're not real. You can't help me."

Pain exploded through him, and she screamed. The hospital room shattered in shards of crystalline light that sliced into his soul. He couldn't catch his breath—

She couldn't catch her breath?

He had no idea where he ended and she began.

Becca Scott. Becca Scott. Becca Scott.

She fought a sob—

He fought a sob?

Light and darkness battered him. He had no idea where he was or who he was.

Crack.

His head jerked back, pain bit his cheek, and the office crashed back into existence.

Anaea, her bright blue eyes wide with concern, stood in front of him, her hand raised to strike him again. Close behind her was Hunter, his expression hard.

"I'm fine," Nero growled.

"You don't look fine." But Anaea dropped her hand and stepped back into Hunter's embrace without looking for him, the action instinctual, as if they hadn't just spent two weeks apart and were still fully connected to each other. "Raven said—"

"Raven and I are going to have a conversation about sharing personal information."

Anaea cocked an eyebrow and glared at him. "She's worried, and she's busy with the new mage. I said I'd help."

"What the hell was that?" Hunter asked. "You were convulsing."

"Another good reason to find the Handmaiden." Nero rubbed his cheek. He needed to do something about that woman—Becca Scott—soon. As much as he was pissed that Raven had told Anaea about his problem, he was grateful she'd been around to snap him out of it. Next time, he could be on his own, and there was no telling if he'd be able to break free or not.

"Raven says it's getting worse."

"What exactly is getting worse?" Hunter asked.

"The problem with my magic that makes me dugga. It connects with human mages and lets me communicate with my team to deal with them. And it's currently on the fritz."

"Wonderful," Hunter said, his voice dark. "We can't afford to have you incapacitated like that. Not with everything going on at Court."

"Well, I've looked, but there isn't anything in the Handmaiden's grimoire about it," Anaea said. "I think we have to go to the Handmaiden's secret residence and see what we can find."

"You've looked for answers in the grimoire?" Which meant Raven had told Anaea everything. He really was going to have to have a talk with his third-in-command.

"The Handmaiden's residence is huge," Hunter said. "Unless you know what you're looking for, you're never going to find it." His grip around Anaea's waist tightened.

"I'll take Ivy. Maybe her magic will help narrow down the search." Anaea ran her hands over Hunter's forearms and tilted her head back against his chest, her pixie cut brushing his jaw. Her words said she was leaving, but her body clearly wanted to stay. Nero remembered those early days. It was as if his body and soul had had a mind of their own and it hadn't mattered what was logical or smart.

"With Ivy goes Grey," Hunter said. "It'll be a four-man team, then." His embrace around Anaea tightened. "I'll tell Grey, and we'll head out in the morning."

This was getting out of hand. He hadn't asked for help, and he damned well didn't want anyone to risk themselves for him. No way would he allow himself to become a liability.

Except he already was.

His phone rang and he pulled it from his pocket. Tobias.

Wonderful. The last time Tobias had called had been to tell Nero his cousin was a traitor, had destabilized Court even more than it already was, and Grey had killed him.

"Yes?"

"Regis has called the Council for a meeting," Tobias said. He sounded angry and exhausted. It couldn't be easy right now, being the Court chamberlain.

"When?"

"Now."

Swell. Nero hung up and stood, the ever-present pain in his head throbbing.

"The prince calls." And if he wanted to maintain his position in Court as prince's favorite, he had to keep himself together. If Regis suspected Nero was weakened or disloyal, he was dead. And so was everyone he cared about.

2

B ecca Scott. *Becca Scott.* She was real. She *was* the right soul in the *right* body, and this was just a nightmare. Just a nightmare.

But the pain in her cheek and the agony in her head made it feel all too real. Her whole body still trembled, convulsions snapped through her muscles, and she fought to catch her breath and steady her pulse. Yet even with all that, and with the connection severed between her and the devil's master, she felt like her tenuous hold of herself was slipping through her fingers.

Becca Scott. Becca. Human. Herself.

The connection with the devil's master had never been that strong before. Even last night, when, for the first time, his presence— powerful, dangerous, and seductively masculine—had overwhelmed her and burned through every cell in her body, it hadn't been that consuming. It was as if talking to him, making contact instead of just eavesdropping, had solidified something between them. As if it had created a connection that called to her and terrified her at the same time, and now he had the key to get inside her and take over, just like the other monsters from the cave.

Doctor Stanbury, with her dark-rimmed glasses and hair pulled back in a severe chignon, stood at her bedside and stared at her. With a *tsk,* her dark gaze jumped to the monitors beside the bed, and she made a note on a chart secured to a clipboard. "Lost the connection again."

Thank God.

"You should attempt to reconnect."

Hell, no. Please. Don't make me try.

"There's no connection." The words jumped out before Becca could stop them. Arguing, denying, saying anything to her captors was pointless. She'd learned that from the cave. Besides, they weren't real, and this wasn't happening. Clearly, Stanbury was a part of the dream... hallucination... psychotic break? Whatever the hell it was, since she wanted to know what the devil's master was saying. God only knew why Becca wasn't just telling her.

Except she knew that, even in this nightmare, if she gave in to her captor's demands, she'd be lost, her body imprisoned, and her soul just as trapped as it was now. Freedom didn't come from giving in. It came from fighting.

Which meant she really had to be crazy, because there was nothing to fight. This wasn't real. She wasn't feeling what she was feeling, and she wasn't hearing what she was hearing.

"There's no point in lying," Stanbury said, her smile so cold it could freeze fire. "Tell the truth and your... situation will become more comfortable."

Yeah, because grabbing me off the street and strapping me to a bed makes you trustworthy. Thank God, it was just her wrists and not her legs as well. At least the monsters in the cave hadn't tried to manipulate her. They'd just invaded her head and tried to brutalize her mind into submission. That was the kind of fight she preferred. Head on. None of these games.

But maybe that was why her nightmare had changed and become manipulative. She feared she wasn't mentally strong enough to survive. It hadn't been the attack on her men... her friends... her family at the market that had made her leave the armed forces. It had been the look on the face of the boy with the bomb. The certainty and fervor in his eyes. It had been the wails of a bleeding toddler, tugging at his mother's body, and the cries of the children in the mangled school tent. It hadn't mattered what Becca had done then. She hadn't been able to save everyone.

And it didn't matter what she did now, because this *was* a nightmare. It wasn't real. She was herself, Becca Scott. A human. Dragons and magic didn't exist.

Maybe if she thought it hard enough, said it enough times, it would be true, and she'd wake up.

Stanbury tapped her pen on the clipboard, the ticking a counter-rhythm to the beeping of the heart monitor. "If you're going to beat this, you need to confront it."

"And telling you I hear voices is confronting *this*?"

"It would indicate there's still a part of you resistant to the delusion." Stanbury pursed her lips. *Tap. Beep. Tap tap. Beep.*

Yes, that was what it was, a delusion. Except—

"It would mean," Stanbury said, "a part of your mind can detach itself from your condition and examine the situation dispassionately."

Except that would mean Stanbury wasn't a part of the nightmare?

Becca's chest tightened, and the beeping of the monitor picked up. If Stanbury wasn't part of that nightmare, that meant not all of this was in her head.

Tap. Beep. Tap tap. Beep.

Surely being trapped in the cave, having monsters invade her mind and tear into her soul to awaken an impossible magic, was the nightmare.

But when had she regained consciousness? When Werner had created that vortex and dumped them in a deserted playground in... she had no idea where. It had been freezing, and there'd been modest-sized mounds of snow. Or had she still been captured by the hallucination when she'd figured out they were in Newgate in the USA—only God knew why her nightmare would toss her into a foreign country. Or had it been when they'd found an abandoned warehouse, dumpster-dived for food, and stole clothes from a bag abandoned beside a clothing-donation drop box? Or had it been sometime when the devil's master had been after them and the others, and they'd fled, hiding in a different abandoned warehouse or then the abandoned house or when in the park or—

She didn't know what was real. If *anything* was real. Was Stanbury? The hospital?

All she knew was that she couldn't stay like this. Every instinct she had screamed Stanbury couldn't be trusted, but that could be part of the dream. If she was losing her mind, she couldn't trust anything she felt or thought.

"The voice—"

"The devil's master?"

"Yes." Heat flushed Becca's face. She really was crazy. Last night she'd said he was sending the devil after her. It had felt so real, and the devil had been so angry.

When she'd first heard the voice of the devil's master, it had been a growl in her dreams. The night she'd escaped from the monsters and their cave had been the first time she'd heard him while awake, and now—

Now he was inside her. Not just a voice, but a presence, filled with agony and rage and heartache and determination.

"I think he's looking for me."

"I see." Stanbury adjusted her glasses and jotted something on the chart. "Does he know where you are?"

"*I* don't even know where I am." *Or if any of this is real.*

"You're in a private facility." Something flashed across Stanbury's expression, but Becca wasn't sure what it was. It seemed like hope... or satisfaction. That had to be it, because Becca was opening up—a move that made Becca's insides squirm.

Hadn't she just decided fighting was best?

Hadn't she just thought a thousand crazy thoughts before that?

God. Please. "What kind of a facility?" And who was paying for it? She didn't have a lot of money and didn't have any family left to help pay for a private facility. She doubted the government would cover something private... and this wasn't her country, so not her government—

Jeez. The point was, the lack of details only added to the evidence that this was still part of the nightmare.

"You've made good progress today, Rebecca." Stanbury slipped her pen into the side pocket of her lab coat.

She was leaving? But she'd promised to make the situation more comfortable. Surely that meant removing the cuffs.

Becca flexed her wrists against the leather securing her to the bed, hoping Stanbury would realize what she'd forgotten.

The doctor's gaze dipped to the restraints and the ice returned to her smile, making Becca's heart stutter and breaking the monitor's steady rhythm.

Stanbury's attention jumped to the screen.

In that heartbeat, Becca knew Stanbury wasn't going to remove the cuffs. Ever.

Stanbury's smile bled from frozen to satisfied. *So soon. The dugga must know who she is and be desperate to find her.*

Becca's pulse leapt again and she fought to steady it. She hadn't just *heard* that—

No, she *had*, and she was still trapped in the nightmare. A nightmare with a monster so terrible, even the monsters from the cave had feared him more than their terrifying queen. They knew if the dugga had discovered them, he'd kill them all, monsters and human prisoners alike. If the devil's master was the dugga, she had to find a way to get him out of her head.

Her pulse beat faster.

He was coming for her. He'd wanted to know where she was.

She had to get out of there, hide, and then come up with a plan.

"What's he saying?" Stanbury asked.

Becca's throat tightened. Her first instinct had been right. She couldn't trust Stanbury, and there was no way in hell she was staying there.

"Tell me, Rebecca." Stanbury leaned closer, the lab coat brushing Becca's knuckles. "What is he saying?"

"Saying—?" Who was saying what? Did Stanbury think Becca was hearing the devil's master right now?

"Rebecca," Stanbury said, her tone too sweet as her gaze returned to the heart monitor and Becca's rapid pulse.

"He's saying—" God, she had to get out of those cuffs. She had to lie, say something to convince Stanbury to release her, or—

The pen in Stanbury's pocket bumped against the back of Becca's hand, and her heart jerked again.

Escape. She could use the pen to undo the buckle on the cuffs.

"He's talking to the devil," she lied as she shifted her hand, straining to grab the pen without Stanbury noticing.

"Diablo?"

"Yes."

"I see." Stanbury drew the pen from her pocket and made a note in the chart.

Shit.

Becca's pulse beat faster.

God damned shit.

Confirmation of the black dragon Diablo, known member of the Asar Nergal. Confirmation she's attuned to the dugga.

Becca gasped and fought to concentrate on her thoughts instead of Stanbury's.

Come on. Get the pen. She couldn't hope someone would accidentally loosen the cuffs. The pen was her only way to freedom, and, even if this was just a nightmare, she sure as hell wasn't going to remain a prisoner. She was going to fight with everything she had.

3

F*ight*. That was what Becca needed to focus on. *Getting free, getting safe, and fighting—*

But was there really anything to fight?

She didn't know.

No. Get the pen. Get free. Figure the rest out later.

"The devil's master." Stanbury checked her watch. *Duration until convulsions...* "What's he telling the devil?"

"The devil?" Right, she was lying to get Stanbury to step closer. *Crap. Think of something.* "They're looking for me."

"Are they close?" Stanbury glanced at her watch again. *Convulsions could start in thirty seconds. I have to get her to maintain the connection longer.* "Concentrate on what they're saying."

"It's not clear," Becca gasped. If Stanbury would just put the pen back in her pocket. *Come on.* There had to be a way to get the woman to stop taking notes.

Convulsions in fifteen seconds. "Really concentrate, Rebecca." Stanbury held the pen close to the clipboard, ready to write the instant Becca said something.

"He—"

The pen dipped to the paper.

Son of a—

This wasn't working. She had to find another way to get the God damned pen.

Five seconds to convulsions, and she'll stop talking. Say something, Rebecca. Tell me where the dugga is. Tell me who the dugga is.

Becca ground her teeth, and a ripple of pain flashed through her chest, reminding her that moments ago her body had been wracked with a seizure. And that seizure had severed the connection with the devil's master. That was her only way out of this mess. If she couldn't get the pen, she had to regroup, figure out a new plan, and that was best done without Stanbury standing over her. But God damn it, she wanted that pen. It was the fastest, easiest solution to her problem.

She jerked, and the heart monitor screamed in time with a pulse racing half in desperation and half in fear she'd get caught.

It's worse than before. Stanbury shoved the pen into her pocket and hit a red call button on a panel above Becca's head.

A nurse... orderly?—Becca wasn't sure. The guy wore nurse's scrubs but had a shaved head and the build of a linebacker. He rushed into the room, along with a woman with brilliant white hair and dark skin dressed in a pale blue pantsuit and a white lab coat.

Stanbury glared at the woman. "I don't need your help."

"She's convulsing again," the woman said.

"I have this." Stanbury nodded at the nurse and stepped back. *It's too often in too short a time.* "Secure her so she doesn't hurt herself against the restraints, and I can get the connection back."

Becca jerked harder, straining to hear anything from Stanbury's thoughts indicating how long she was supposed to be seizing.

"Twice within the hour," the other doctor said. "We need to sedate her."

Becca's heart stuttered and her chest tightened. If she was unconscious, she couldn't escape and she couldn't come up with an alternate plan. She had to get that pen, now, hide it in the blanket, and pray it was still there when she woke.

"He's saying—" Becca gasped. *Come on. Get closer. Give me that pen.*

Stanbury leaned forward. The pen brushed Becca's fingers.

Yes.

"15 ccs of Versed, Lenard."

Lenard, the nurse, turned to a small cabinet beside the bed and opened the door.

"No," Stanbury said, and Lenard stopped, his hand poised to take something off the middle shelf. He glanced from her to the other doctor. *God damn it, Koehn, I have this.* "She needs to be conscious to reconnect with the dugga."

"She might not survive if we don't get these seizures under control," the other doctor, Koehn, said.

"We won't survive if we can't learn the dugga's identity." *Keeping her alive would be nice, but knowing the dugga's identity is better.* Stanbury grabbed her pen and leaned closer to Becca. "What is he saying? Concentrate, Rebecca."

Shit. Just one fucking pen. That was all she wanted. Becca rolled her eyes back in her head and jerked again.

"Six ccs of Versed." Koehn raised her chin, as if daring Stanbury to disagree.

"Six is still too much."

"The connection has gotten stronger in the last twenty-four hours. Six might not be enough to control the convulsions and prevent brain damage."

"Fine. Six ccs," Stanbury said, her tone sharp, and she jotted something on the chart.

Becca strained to breathe against the panic screaming at her to fight, survive, even though it was hopeless. There was no way she was getting that pen and no way she was getting out of there. But that was exactly how a nightmare worked. There was a hint of hope, but no matter how hard she tried, she'd never find an escape.

Koehn drew close with a needle. Lenard's grip tightened as he leaned over her and held her down.

Something hard and cold from Lenard's uniform bumped against Becca's hand. She bucked Lenard back and loosened his grip for a second. A pen. Another pen. In his pocket.

Lenard shoved her back against the bed, his fingers digging into her shoulders. Koehn shoved up the sleeve of Becca's gown and jammed a needle into her biceps.

Last time the Versed took two minutes, Stanbury said... thought? Becca wasn't sure anymore what she heard or what she imagined. All she could think about was getting that pen.

Lenard started to ease back, taking the pen with him.

Grab the pen.

The monitor screamed her racing panic.

Grab the pen. Escape.

She jerked one last time, straining against the restraints to reach it. She caught the tip between her first two fingers and yanked it down. It tumbled out of her fingers, bounced on the blanket beside her arm, and she wrenched her body over it to capture and hide it.

"The other one said the dugga could change. That it was a position, not a person, and could be given to another dragon," Koehn said. "If you kill her, we'll lose our chance of keeping tabs on whoever becomes the dugga."

The pen tip dug into Becca's wrist, but there was no way in hell she was moving. If she could keep it hidden, she could escape.

And she had to escape. Kidnappers weren't this open about their plans if they were going to release their captive. Yes, they'd needed to reveal their faces to convince her they were doctors in a hospital, but outright discussing what they wanted made it clear that, if they weren't holding her forever, they were going to kill her.

Becca jerked once more—keeping her arm pinned against the pen—to sell the last of her fake convulsions and not give them a reason to suspect anything. Her pulse stuttered, an uneven thump within her and beep on the monitor, as a weight wrapped around her with sudden, consuming exhaustion.

Stanbury glanced at the monitor, checked her watch, then wrote on the chart. "The Versed has kicked in. You'd better hope if she connects again, she'll be conscious enough to communicate."

Koehn huffed and stepped close. "Rebecca, can you hear me?"

The weight increased. It crept over her face and into her head, and the need to close her eyes and melt into the bed overwhelmed her.

"Rebecca." Koehn's cold hand pressed against her cheek and forehead, and she forced Becca's right eyelid open and flashed a light in her eye.

Becca winced, the movement two seconds too late to protect against the light.

"Rebecca?" Koehn moved to the other eye.

"Yes?" Becca's mouth responded of its own volition... or had she actually thought the response first?

Responses slow. Too slow, Stanbury thought. *I should have stopped Koehn and risked the damage.*

"If the dugga reconnects, the heart monitor will pick it up," Koehn said.

"You better hope he does." Stanbury straightened, and the doorway behind her tilted, shuddered out of focus then snapped back into sharp reality... Except this was still all a nightmare?

"You said yourself you think he's looking for her." Koehn glanced at Lenard and jerked her chin toward the door.

His gaze slid to Stanbury then jumped back to Koehn, who glared at him until he rushed out of the room.

"He will," Stanbury said.

Right. The devil's master was still after her. If she stayed there, she was safe... no, she was a prisoner. No...

God, it was so hard to think... and keep her eyes open... and...

"—sedation will only last a few—"

The room grew dark, and the weight warmed like a too-heavy blanket, binding her arms—

Binding... her arms...

Bound!

She was cuffed to the bed.

She wrenched her eyes open.

"We have unfinished business with the other—" Koehn said, now standing in the doorway. "—he'll be more forthcoming, like—"

Something clicked. The door? Something else? Becca floated, yet sank deep into the mattress at the same time. The heart monitor's slow chirp jarred with each beep, yet lulled with its steady rhythm.

If she just closed her eyes, she'd fall asleep... except darkness surrounded her, and she was pretty sure her eyes were already closed. But if she could just fall asleep, she'd wake free from the nightmare.

A jolt snapped through her, and the rhythmic beeping stuttered.

She was in a nightmare. She couldn't forget that. Ever. Not until she was free.

She concentrated past the fuzz in her head to her arms. They were so heavy, she didn't know if they'd move, no matter how hard she thought about the action. The leather cuffs pinched tight around her wrists, and the metal pen dug into her skin.

If she could just grab it, she could use it to slide the strap free of the buckle.

She forced her eyes open.

Darkness still surrounded her.

No, her eyes were still closed.

God, she was never going to make it like this. She should wait until the sedative was out of her system.

Except she had no idea how long that would last, or if Stanbury would come back and find the pen, or if they'd decide she was no longer useful and kill her.

Her pulse stuttered again.

Shit. They were monitoring that. She needed to control herself. Needed a plan. Needed to open her eyes and stay awake.

She strained past the weight dragging her into the mattress.

Just open her eyes.

The heart monitor beeped, and her muscles twitched, jerking for a second past the sedation.

Open.

Another beep. Another twitch. She clenched her jaw and concentrated.

Please. Open.

Chirp.

She could do this. Fight through it. She was stronger than some drug—and she was not going to acknowledge how impossible that actually was. This was just a dream. She could God damn open her eyes if she wanted to.

Chirp.

She *would* God damn open her eyes.

Chirp.

Come on. Wake up.

Chirp.

Wake. Up!

Someone gasped. A tremor sliced through her, and the heart monitor squealed. Her eyes flew open, and her gaze jumped to the monitor. She didn't know how fast was too fast, but this was clearly a change. She drew in a quick breath, but it was too ragged to slow her pulse. If she couldn't get her heart rate under control, she was going to have to be ready to fight her way out of there.

4

She wrenched her attention from the monitor to the pen and twisted her wrist to pin it between her first two drug-numbed fingers.

Another tremor sliced across her chest. The monitor chirped and her body tensed. She tightened her grip on the pen and slid it closer to her thumb to get a better grip. No way was she twitching and tossing her only means of escape to the floor. She was stronger than that. If she'd managed to keep her head while pinned down by sniper fire and with her light tactical transport vehicles lit up with flames, she could hold her shit together now.

The pen tip brushed her thumb, and she changed her grip, pinching the pen between her thumb and forefinger, and pushed the end under the tongue of the cuff at the buckle.

Just shove the tongue back. Just an inch.

The drug's weight buffeted her senses, dragged her toward a darkness that threatened everything. Her vision tightened to just the pen's tip against the cuff. The rest of the room blurred and dimmed. Even the chirp from the monitor faded.

Just enough to release the buckle. One step at a time. One step to freedom. One—

Darkness bled over her hand, the cuff, then the pen. She was floating and melting and—

Someone groaned, but she had no idea if it was her or someone else.

Another tremor sliced through her body, this one stronger. It jerked her awake, stole her breath, and made her pulse leap again.

The pen flashed back into focus, thankfully still under the cuff's tongue. She pushed it deeper, the tongue slipped, and the buckle's prong jumped a grommet then caught again. She tugged, but the leather rubbed against already raw skin. It was still too tight.

Crap. She shifted her grip and fought to adjust the pen's tip back against the catch. One more grommet. That was all she needed.

Darkness swarmed across her vision and the exhaustion dragged at her muscles. Her fingers twitched, but the pen didn't move.

Come on. What she wouldn't give for a pulse-jerking tremor. *Stay awake.*

The pen tip bled back into sight, and she tightened her mental grasp on her consciousness. Her hand trembled, but the damned pen didn't move. She ground her teeth, willing everything she had into pushing the pen the necessary fraction of an inch to the prong.

Another tremor sliced across her chest.

Holy Mother.

Her thought? Not her thought? God, it was so hard to think.

Her hand twitched, and the pen jammed against the prong as something clicked. Logically she knew the sound had to be quiet, but it roared through her, setting her on high alert. The click meant something important. Except she couldn't make her mind work past releasing the cuff's buckle to figure out why the heart monitor screamed and adrenaline shot through her. No—

She could.

Danger.

The click meant someone was in the room.

She dragged her gaze to the door—

The cuff shuddered into focus.

No, she had to look at the door. It was important.

She rolled her head to the side and focused on Lenard, standing in the doorway. Everything was in stuttering slow motion. She wasn't just thinking through water. Thoughts were being ripped from her head before she could fully think them.

Lenard's attention was locked on her hand. The one holding the pen.

Oh, shit. She heaved her attention back to the pen and shoved at the tongue. The heavy leather shifted, but the buckle didn't release.

She shoved again as Lenard materialized at her side and snatched the pen from her fingers.

"Looks like extra precautions will have to be taken," he said.

And then she'd have no hope of escaping.

Lenard shoved the pen into his pocket and reached to tighten the cuff.

She couldn't let him secure her. It was now or never and never wasn't an option. She heaved her legs up against the drug-induced weight of the blanket and rammed her feet into Lenard's chest. He staggered back to the foot of the bed, and she yanked her hand against the loosened cuff. The leather ground against her skin.

Lenard grabbed an ankle restraint at the foot of the bed and shoved the blanket up, exposing her legs. She kicked at his face and yanked harder at her wrist, squeezing her thumb as tight to her palm as possible.

He snagged her foot. She kicked at him with her other foot and cracked her heel against his temple. His head snapped back, but his grip didn't release.

Shit. She kicked again and missed, her leg suddenly heavy, as if her desperation to flee was only strong enough to survive a few seconds against the sedative.

Lenard secured the cuff around her ankle then shifted to seize her hand again.

Her chest tightened and another blast of adrenaline sliced through the sedative. With a scream, she wrenched her wrist against the cuff, and her hand slipped free. Lenard scrambled to get a hold of her, but she jerked out of the way and rammed her fist into his throat.

He gasped, his eyes wide, and staggered back. She heaved against the drug slowing her limbs and unbound her other hand.

Lenard drew in a ragged breath and reached for her again. She sat up, punched him in the face, and snatched the pen from his pocket. He lurched forward, and she jammed the pen into his neck. With a howl, he staggered back and grasped at the pen.

Becca undid the ankle cuff and rolled off the bed, but the sedative slammed into her, sweeping into her head, making the room twist and the muscles in her legs give out. She grabbed for the bed to keep standing, but didn't have the strength to hold herself up and sagged to the floor. *Come on. Get up. Get out of there.*

Someone groaned—

She groaned? The out-of-focus room spun. Lenard screamed, the pen clattered to the floor, and he staggered toward the bed. The heart monitor wailed, wrenching her attention toward it, and for a second she couldn't remember why that was bad.

Because they're monitoring it.

Shit. Right. Whoever her captors were, they had to know something was happening. She had to get out of there. Now. It didn't matter if this was a dream or not. This was her one chance to escape, and she sure as hell was taking it.

Lenard staggered to the edge of the bed. He was going to cut her off, and then she'd have to fight both the sedative and him to get out the door.

She tightened her grip on the bed and hauled herself up. The world twisted and darkened.

This was not how it was going to end.

She ripped the heart monitor leads from her chest. The machine's wild beeping turned into a grating squeal. Lenard, with one hand clamped against his neck, blood oozing between his fingers, lunged for her.

She lurched toward the door, but as soon as she put weight on her leg, her knee gave out. A pressure swept through her and darkness flooded her vision. She grabbed at the closest thing, a trolley with medical stuff on it. Her hand bumped the silver tray on top, knocking it and the contents to the floor.

Lenard lunged at her. She twisted out of the way, but couldn't keep her balance and collapsed to her hands and knees.

"You can't fight it," Lenard said. "The sedative is too strong."

Except she had to fight it. If she closed her eyes, she wouldn't get up, and she'd never be free.

Her hand bumped the tray.

Lenard seized her shoulder.

Grab it.

Her fingers clenched around the tray as Lenard yanked her around to face him. She swept into the movement, using it to propel her around, and smashed the tray against the side of his head.

He jerked back, and she bashed the tray against the side of his head again. He screamed and crumpled to the floor. The room darkened and the drug's weight billowed within her.

She clenched her teeth and wrenched her attention to the door. If she could get her brain to work faster, she would have taken a second to look for a better weapon, a scalpel or pair of scissors, but it took everything she had to stand, let alone lurch to the door.

Her shoulder hit the wall beside the door and she grabbed the handle. She couldn't remember crossing the room. And it didn't matter. The only thing that mattered was escaping.

She eased the door open and glanced into a brightly lit, institutionally beige hall. She strained to hear anyone coming but couldn't hear past the screaming heart monitor.

Her thoughts stuttered and her heart pounded with a heavy thud that shuddered through her, darkening her sight and weakening her limbs.

She couldn't just stand there. She had no idea how long she'd been standing there. Lenard was going to get up any minute. Stanbury and Koehn were going to come back.

Keep moving.

Yes. Just keep moving.

She staggered out the door, her shoulder against the wall to keep standing and the tray clutched in her hand. *Just keep putting one foot in front of the other.* But her insides churned, howling that she wasn't moving fast enough. They were going to capture her. The nightmare would continue.

No. She squeezed her consciousness, tightening it into a pinpoint, and focused on the hall. She could do this. She *had* to do this.

She pushed her legs to go faster until she managed a lurching jog and reached another hall. A split-second pause to peek around the corner confirmed no one was in sight, and she forced herself into the other hall as footsteps pounded from somewhere behind her and someone yelled.

Her pulse thrummed faster, each beat dragging against the weight of the sedative. They had to have seen her. If she didn't get moving, they were going to capture her.

She half-staggered, half-ran down this hall to a T-intersection and stumbled around the right-hand corner. Here the wall on the left side was lined with windows looking into rooms. The first room was empty, but the second had a woman in it, huddled in the corner opposite the bed. The next room held Werner, who lay on his bed.

She stumbled to his door and wrenched on the handle. The door swung open. Werner's head jerked up and his gaze jumped to her.

"Becca?"

"Come on." Darkness shuddered around her and the room twisted. She clung to the door to keep standing. She had to keep moving. Had to stay awake.

His gaze dipped to her side as he rushed from the bed. "A tray?"

Becca glanced at the tray, still clutched in her hand. "Only weapon available."

He wrapped an arm around her back and they hurried to the next door. Inside, Glenn was strapped to his bed. His eyes widened when he saw them, and Werner leaned her in the doorway and raced to his side.

The weight in Becca's chest flared and she fought to stay awake.

She concentrated on the hall, looking for trouble, and realized—in slow motion—there were more window-rooms in the hall.

She staggered toward the closest door, threw it open, and moved to the next one before registering if anyone was inside. Behind her, a surprised woman—she looked familiar, but Becca couldn't make her mind work enough to remember—darted into the hall.

"Help the others," Becca said, not knowing if there were others or not. She stumbled to the third door and shoved it open.

Werner and Glenn materialized at her sides. She hadn't noticed them approach, as if time had stuttered—and she wasn't going to consider that it could have been the impossible vortex that Werner could make.

Behind her, someone barked something, and others started yelling and screaming.

"They found us," Glenn said, wrapping an arm around Becca and taking some of her weight.

Werner pressed his hand against the wall then swore. "I can't make a gate. Something is blocking me."

"Then we run. I'm not staying here," Glenn said.

Werner glanced at him. "Agreed."

They ran down the hall, Becca half-running, half-carried by Glenn. She fought to keep her balance and the darkness from her vision and consciousness. The hall shuddered. No. Time did, slicing sections from her awareness. One minute they were in the middle of the hall. The next around a corner. The next at a metal security door with a glowing exit sign hanging above it.

Werner opened the door, revealing a plain stairwell, cinderblock and steel. Someone yelled, and Glenn slammed to a halt. A large man in tactical gear, complete with helmet, held Glenn's arm. Glenn yanked against the guy's grasp, the movement making Becca jerk, her body too heavy for her muscles to properly balance.

Glenn's grip across her back loosened and she staggered into the doorway, clutching the frame to steady herself. Werner rammed his elbow into Tactical Guy's arm. With a grunt, he released Glenn but twisted to punch at Werner. Behind him, at the end of the hall, more people in hospital gowns hurried toward them, followed by men in full tactical gear and a few in scrubs. People screamed and begged, growled and swore. The sounds roared through Becca's head and pressed against her senses in a heavy, all-consuming weight.

Werner seized the front of Tactical Guy's vest at neck and crotch, and shoved the man down the hall into another guy with tactical gear. Glenn grabbed her again, but two more guys in tactical gear rushed around the two toppled-over guys and drew their Tasers.

Becca opened her mouth to yell, but time slowed, drawing a delay between thought and action.

Both men fired. One barb hit Werner in the arm while the other bounced against the wall, while both Taser barbs from the second man hit Glenn in the back. Searing agony sliced through her and all her muscles contracted. Glenn screamed and shoved her. The agony vanished, but so did the floor. She dropped to the first step of the staircase, off balance, and grasped for the railing, but she was moving in slow motion... or was that thinking in slow motion?

Her hand brushed the cold metal railing, but she tumbled away before she could grab hold. Her shoulder slammed into the concrete step, exploding pain through her neck and chest, then her hip, other shoulder, other hip, back, shoulder. Her head smashed against the cinderblock wall and sharp flashes of light snapped across her vision, biting through the enveloping darkness.

Get up.

She fought to catch her breath. Above her, someone yelled.

Run.

A hint of sight broke through the darkness. Two guys had Glenn pinned to the ground, and another one was punching Werner in the face.

"Run," Werner screamed. "Becca. Run."

5

Nero clenched his teeth and fought to concentrate on Regis yelling at the doyens of his Counseling Coteries. The prince's face was crimson and spit flew from his mouth with every word, but his voice was ghostly, barely there, compared to the woman, Becca Scott, screaming in Nero's head. She had to get up and save her friends... no, run... concentrate... wake up—

Run!

Her will squeezed so tight around his essence he could barely breathe, let alone focus on Regis. He had to get out of there, find wherever the hell she was, and deal with her. He couldn't let anyone know about his weakened condition, especially not the other doyens and certainly not his prince. Definitely *not* his prince.

A tremor lanced up his arm and across his chest, threatening to send his body into convulsions, and he bit back a moan.

Regis's wild-eyed glare jumped to him. "You have something to say?"

"Only my hearty agreement." Mother, what the hell had Regis been ranting about? Nero wasn't certain he'd heard the prince's last few statements.

"We can't control everyone in our coteries," Barna said. He was the next eldest drake after Nero on the council and controlled the second largest coterie. "That's impossible."

Regis glared at Barna. "Then maybe you shouldn't be doyen. They're your drakes. You're responsible for what they do. Everything they do."

Get up.

Get up and run.

"You should be a better example for them, instead of hosting charity events for the very humans intent on making us extinct," Regis said.

Barna clasped his hands in front of him on the table. The motion was relaxed, although the rest of his body was anything but. "If I'd canceled the event at the last minute, the humans would have been even more suspicious."

Another tremor rippled over Nero, and the council chamber faded into darkness then flashed into a hall? ...stairwell?

He stood— no, was *sprawled* on his back in a gray concrete stairwell with agony shooting up his neck and chest—possibly from a broken collarbone?—while a lesser agony throbbed through the rest of him, churning with a massive weight that dragged at his thoughts and muscles and—

Except it wasn't him. It was Becca, and his dugga's magic had thrown his consciousness back into her body again.

Shit. The convulsions would follow soon if he didn't break free.

"Dragonkind must be protected at all costs," someone said— no, that had been Regis. Back in the council chamber.

Focus on Regis. On the room with the other doyens. On how dangerous it was to expose such vulnerability to any dragon.

But the stairwell remained. Heavily armed security men at the top of the stairs yelled. A large bulky man with shaggy hair and a bushy beard fought with two others, while another man was pinned to the floor by someone else in tactical gear.

"Your drakes step out of line, you've stepped out of line," Regis said, his tone dark.

"It's more important now than ever," Maize, doyen of the Major

Yellow Coterie, said, her gaze sliding to Barna's. "We can't risk having another disaster like the one at your human fundraiser."

"Run, Becca," the man with the bushy beard yelled from the top of the stairs. Werner. His name flashed into Nero's mind. "I. Said. Run."

He— *She* lurched to her feet. The stairwell twisted and darkened, and the weight within her swelled until it felt as if he was running and thinking through water.

More agony seized his chest. *Mother, just break the connection.*

Run. God, run. This was her only chance. There was no hope of the nightmare ending if she didn't escape. But God, it hurt to leave everyone behind. She hadn't done that in Afghanistan. She didn't want to do that now.

But she was helpless. She couldn't fight. She could barely walk. It was taking everything she had to get down the stairs. Regroup and return was her only option.

Another snap of lightning. Nero couldn't tell if it was his or her pain, only that it burned through his head, threatening to overwhelm what little connection he had left with his body.

His body!

Shit. He was going to lose it in front of everyone and endanger his *puzur.*

"Any drake steps out of line, he gets a date with Odyne," Regis said, sounding miles away.

Nero mentally grasped onto the prince's voice again, determined to drag his essence back to the council chamber.

"The Handmaiden banned using Odyne's magic for a reason," Lothair, the doyen of the Major Orange Coterie, said, his form materializing through the stairwell railing as he leaned forward against the council table, placing his bony elbows on the polished top. "Is the situation so dire we need to ask your father's torturer to return to the Royal Coterie's service?"

"Are you saying it isn't dire?" Maize crossed her arms under her ample bust. "One of our own thought she could break our highest laws and make human mages." Her attention jumped to Pike, the new doyen of the Major Green Coterie and former third-in-command to Zenobia—the doyen who'd broken those laws.

"I've already sent two dozen from my coterie to Odyne for their participation in the... *events* perpetrated by the former doyen," Pike said.

"I'm still not convinced you didn't play your part in that." Barna cocked an eyebrow, accentuating the lines in his forehead. His human vessel was twenty years Nero's senior, with more gray in his dark hair and his face more weathered and lined. "You *were* her Third."

"By rooting out and sending traitors to Odyne, he's more than demonstrated his loyalty to the Royal Coterie," Regis hissed.

The stairwell solidified around Nero again. Shit. He wasn't going to make it. His only way to keep this problem under wraps was to get away from the other doyens and Regis and get the hell out of Court.

Nero stood and slammed his palms against the council table, wrenching the room back into focus. "This isn't up for debate. His Highness, Prince Regis, has spoken. Keep your coterie members in line, or they'll face the prince's torturer. Anything else endangers dragonkind."

Barna glared, a clear attempt at proving his dominance, but Nero glared back and flashed his teeth, revealing a hint of the monster curled tight within his human vessel. Barna's body might be bigger, but he didn't have an earth magic as powerful as Nero's. No one on the council did.

Maize and Lothair nodded, while Pike met Nero's gaze for a heartbeat then slid his attention to the wall behind Nero's head. Tobias, the Court Chamberlain, watched, his posture neither aggressive nor submissive, while Regis smirked—he always enjoyed it when Nero revealed his ancient dragon spirit to the younger doyens, albeit some of them were only marginally younger.

Run. Come on. Run.

Nero ground his teeth and forced his attention back to Barna, who raised his chin. He'd been on the Counseling Coteries when Regis had proclaimed his father, King Constantine, unfit to rule, and taken the throne. Barna was fully aware Nero had ambushed the previous doyen of the Major Yellow Coterie—and staunch supporter of King Constantine—in the arena and forced the doyen's rebirth, thereby removing him from his position as leader of the Major Yellow Coterie, to ensure Regis's succession.

Nero cocked an eyebrow. He'd do the same to Barna if it suited his needs. He'd force rebirth on all of them if it meant protecting his *puzur*, and he let that resolve seep into his expression.

Barna's eyes widened, and his gaze leapt to the wall.

Lothair gave a tight nod, the movement so slight Nero would have missed it if he wasn't in the middle of trying to glare down all of them. The elder drake—not ancient like himself, Regis, or Tobias—was smart enough to know he wanted Nero as an ally.

God. Please. It wasn't real. But even knowing that, all she could focus on was escape.

Pain slashed through Nero's head, and he deepened his snarl to hide the agony. He had to get out of there, had to figure out where she was and—

What? Save her?

She thought she was in a nightmare, and he had no idea if he could convince her any of it was real. He had no idea if he should. Her magic endangered his *puzur*. Besides, she was clinging to her soul by her mental fingernails, and soon she'd lose her grip. So very few human spirits could handle the truth about the world, and even fewer could manage that after being invaded by a dragon's spirit. In the two thousand years since the Great Scourge, there'd been less than four dozen humans who'd body-shared with a dragon and kept their sanity—and one of them was currently living in his house. No matter how much, since having to clean up Zenobia's mess, he'd hoped the odds would be in the human's favor, Becca wasn't going to be another case like Anaea. God damn it. Being inside her head and knowing she was falling apart, the only realistic kindness he could offer her was an end to her suffering.

Just stay awake. Come on.

The stairwell flickered over his sight.

And an end to his suffering as well.

"It's been commanded." He shoved away from the table and stormed to the door. As much as he wanted to just gate out of the room, doing so broke protocol. A drake didn't summon a gate near the prince unless he wanted to be arrested for endangering Regis. A gate wasn't just an exit. It was a portal that allowed others to enter as well as leave.

"Nero," Regis growled. "A word."

Shit.

God damn shit. He couldn't afford to lose it in front of Regis, but he couldn't afford to disobey his prince's summons, either.

6

Nero wrenched around to face Regis and managed to force his gaze to the wall beside the prince's head before he thought Nero was challenging him. "Your Highness?"

"I said, a word."

No way in hell. He had to get out of there before the convulsions overwhelmed him.

He fought to keep his expression neutral. "Of course."

"So?" Regis glared at the other drakes.

"Your Highness?" Lothair asked, his gaze dropping to the floor.

"So?" Regis asked again, red sweeping over his face and his eyes narrowing, as if the other doyens were supposed to have known what the first *so* had meant. "Out! All of you, out! Now. Or the last one to leave goes directly to Odyne."

Maize sneered, but leapt from her chair and rushed to the door. The other doyens scrambled for the exit as well, and Nero pressed tight to the wall to keep out of the way. Barna—closest to the door—was out first. Maize shoved Lothair behind her to get out next, which blocked the path for Pike, forcing him to be last.

Regis threw his head back and laughed.

The color drained from Pike's face. "Your Highness, I—"

"Pike," Regis said with a dark chuckle, "keep cleaning up Zenobia's mess, and I'll give you a reprieve from meeting Odyne."

"Yes, your Highness." Pike bolted into the hall.

"Oh, and Pike," Regis said, stopping the green drake mid-step, "I think you owe a report to my chamberlain about the state of your coterie."

"Of course, my lord." Pike's gaze jumped to Tobias, who still stood in the corner, somehow making his massive body and radiant aura unobtrusive. "I can do that right now."

"In my office," Tobias said as he stepped away from the wall and strode out the doorway.

"They need to understand," Regis said as Tobias and Pike walked away. "We can't be exposed. Every time a drake goes into the human realm, he risks revealing us to the humans and then they'll destroy us for good."

"Your Highness," Nero said.

Someone yelled, and lightning shot through his head.

Five flights down. Looks like a door. Please let it be the way out.

"Every drake must be recalled from the human world. They can't be allowed to leave Court again."

So that's what Regis had been ranting about. No wonder Barna was so upset. His coterie's wealth had grown to enormous proportions because of dragons going into the human realm. His whole business was designed to cater to drakes living and shopping and being entertained outside of Court. If Regis recalled everyone, that would mean the Major Brown Coterie would take a financial hit and could lose its position in Court. As well, Nero's *puzur* would be nearly defenseless, and his most valuable member, Raven, would be trapped in Court, since she wasn't a member of the Asar Nergal and therefore wouldn't have permission to be in the human realm.

The bottom of the stairwell flickered into sight, and a heavy metal security door materialized in the middle of the council table.

Nero ground his teeth. *Just get the hell out of there.*

Yes. Get out.

Of the stairwell. Of the building—

No. Out of Court.

Nero yanked his attention to Regis's jowls, dangerously close to making eye contact, which could be misconstrued as a challenge for dominance. "I'll let Tobias know."

"Tobias?" Confusion flickered over Regis's expression. "My father's chamberlain?"

"Yes." A chill fluttered through the pain. Regis was regularly demanding, sometimes even cruel—they were after all a spirit race of predators and aggression was part of their nature—but lately he was becoming more and more confused. Just like his father when his soul sickness had started to overwhelm his spirit.

Regis's confusion melted into rage. "My father," he said, his tone dark. "You must deal with my father, Nero. He can't be allowed to hold the throne. It puts us all in danger."

"He can't." Mother, Nero had no idea what to say to that. He could barely think past the pain and see the council chamber through the semi-translucent stairwell, but this was the same conversation he'd had with Regis five hundred years ago, before they'd imprisoned Constantine in his suite.

"Yes." Regis bared his teeth and hissed. "And I want to see the heads of Hunter and the sorcerer he created at my feet within the week."

Nero's brain stuttered at the sudden jump in topic.

"Within the week," Regis growled.

"Hunter is a resourceful drake." Shit. How was he going to get out of this? Even if he wanted to kill Hunter or Anaea, they were too powerful for him or any of his soldiers in the Asar Nergal. "It might take more than a week. Hunter has gone into hiding."

"You're the dugga. She's a sorcerer. You know exactly where she is. Isn't that how your magic works?"

The simplified version. Yes. "She's—" *Come on. Just think of something.* But even just concentrating on Regis's words was difficult. "They're—"

Regis's eyes narrowed. "This should be an easy answer. Do you need Odyne to jog your memory?"

"That won't get you Hunter's head any sooner."

The red fury swept over Regis's face again in a giant wave, rushing from his throat to his forehead. If the situation weren't so serious, Nero would have laughed at how close to a cartoon it was.

"You can be replaced," Regis growled.

"I can. But do you trust any of the other doyens?" Nero's pulse pounded. Confronting the prince was a risk, but he didn't have the time or ability of thought to be delicate. He needed to finish this conversation and get the hell out of there, deal with this Becca Scott, then figure out what to do with a prince whose mental state was even less stable than Nero had feared.

"I can't trust anyone."

"You can trust Tobias, and you can trust me." A tremor raced through Nero's chest.

"I've yet to decide that," Regis said. "You still haven't killed Hunter or his sorcerer."

"She's hiding herself with magic. But when I find her, I'll kill her." Just let him go. Please. "I'll kill Hunter, too." And when he had a moment to figure out how to deal with that, he would. One problem at a time.

"You'd better." Regis stormed away, his two-man guard—who'd been standing discreetly a dozen feet away—falling into step behind him.

Another bolt of pain shot through Nero's head, and the muscles in his chest spasmed. He pressed a hand to the impossibly smooth granite wall—shaped by the Handmaiden's powerful magic, like all the halls in Court—in part to summon a gate to get the hell out of there, but mostly to keep standing.

He'd known keeping a *puzur* of natural human mages—in direct defiance to dragon law—would eventually become a problem. Even as the dugga of the Asar Nergal, he'd known he wouldn't be able to keep his kids a secret forever. But he'd hoped, from the depths of his soul, that dragon attitudes would have changed by the time his secret coterie was discovered.

Except Zenobia and her coup, using unnaturally created mages, had once again swung popular opinion among leading dragons away from openly co-existing with humans. While there were few drakes who remembered the first couple hundred years of chaos after the Great Scourge, and even fewer who remembered the Great Scourge and the time before, it was as if the fear of being wiped out of existence was written in the DNA of half the dragon population, whether they remembered those times or not. The fear even defied logic, making drakes kill other drakes in order to seize leadership—marching them closer to extinction.

It made no sense. And yet the need to do anything to protect his *puzur* strained against all logic. It was as if his bonds of family—even if it was an unusual family—were stronger than the bonds of species. Like a miniature insanity, a ghostly reflection of the insanity that captured the newly inamorated.

And Regis wasn't helping by demanding all drakes return to Court. That would only fuel the fear as well as the divide between those drakes who were afraid and those who weren't. Hiding wasn't going to help. Getting information. Making informed decisions. That was their best recourse. Not all humans wanted to finish what their ancestors had started. The kids in his house and those he'd raised and taught over the centuries were proof of that. No one would win in an all-out war. Only a minute fraction of the human population even knew the truth about magic, and even fewer knew about the existence of dragonkind. The only conflict dragons were involved in was one of their own making and imagination.

Another slice of agony burned through him, and the muscles in his chest tightened. He gasped, fighting the convulsion. He needed to hold it together long enough to get out of Court. He could give in to the pain back in the privacy of his room—and he wasn't going back to his office. Someone still might find him and he didn't want to terrify any of his kids. Once he'd pulled himself back together, he could find Becca Scott, deal with her, then deal with Regis and the rest of this mess.

He subvocalized his power word and summoned a gate. A speck of darkness, the heart of the gate, flared to life against the wall, then whooshed into a man-sized vortex. He concentrated on his bedroom at his house in Newgate. A simple room, decorated by Raven in black, white, and burgundy, with a king bed and an en suite bathroom. Since Zenobia's coup, he'd been spending more time than usual in Newgate. As dugga, Newgate was currently where the greatest gathering of human mages were, and even with the ability to free gate anywhere in the world, it helped if he wasn't juggling too many time zones. But if he wasn't careful, the other doyens—who didn't know he was the dugga—could become suspicious, and then this mess would get worse.

The image of his room wavered, and a heavy security door appeared, semi-transposed over his bed.

Almost... there, Becca thought.

A weight flooded his limbs and he stumbled.

Shit. Except he had no idea if that was his thought or hers.

The world darkened and twisted— no, he'd stepped into his gate —? No, he'd...?

His chest heaved, each breath an effort, each step a marathon. He had to get free. Had to get out of there. Had—

Had to control his gate, or—

His foot hit something hard and the world lurched into focus. Shadows surrounded him and a freezing wind stung his cheeks. He faced a brick wall with a rusted fire escape bolted into it beside a barred, grimy window. To his right, across a street edged with filthy small snow banks, was some kind of square, with half a dozen leafless miniature trees in massive concrete boxes, a wide set of curving steps leading up to the front of a high-rise, and some kind of sweeping metal modern art installation with metal umbrellas hanging from it.

Something crashed, and Becca's metal security door flickered into sight over the brick wall. The door swung back toward him... her... and she staggered through, clutching at the frame to get her bearings. Across a small patio sat two picnic tables surrounded by piles of snow, and on either side of her stretched an ice-slicked walkway. The path to her right was shorter than the left and had more light. There'd be people there. Help. She just had to make it along the icy walkway, up those stairs to that... arm of metal with two umbrellas hanging from it?

Shit.

The muscles in Nero's arm and chest seized. He'd gated right to her, without a weapon or a winter coat, and barely in control of his body, let alone his magic.

7

More pain lanced through Nero's body, and he clenched his teeth, fighting the impending convulsion as he forced his focus from inside Becca, on the walkway, back into his body, standing in the alley. He needed to get his bearings so he could gate home, grab a gun—humans didn't panic as much if it was a gun instead of a sword—and return. Back in two flashes—

Except his last gate hadn't sent him where he'd wanted to go. There was no guarantee he'd be able to manage gating home and back.

Mother of All! He was just going to have to make it work. He couldn't let Becca continue to endanger his *puzur*. And the one horrible option, of leaving her to whoever was attacking her, wouldn't work since they were trying to capture and not kill her.

Not that killing her was an option. She didn't deserve any of this—

Except she endangered everything.

God damn it. Make up your mind.

Someone yelled and his sight jumped back into Becca as she glanced over her shoulder toward the security door. She'd gotten farther than he would have expected, given the pain and weight dragging at her body and thoughts. Almost thirty feet from the door —and toward him.

A man in full tactical gear rushed out of the doorway and pointed his Taser at her. If he hit her, she'd go down, and then Nero would have to figure out how to break into the facility to get her out.

If he was smart, that was what he'd do.

But Becca's essence dug deeper into his. She wasn't going to remain a prisoner. There wouldn't be another opportunity to escape this place, this nightmare, this... this everything.

Another tremor clenched Nero's arm and chest.

"I'm not going back," she said.

The guy—he looked more like a soldier than a security guard—holstered his weapon and sneered. "How are you going to stop me, little girl?"

"Little girl?" Did she look that helpless? God, she *was* that helpless, and she was sick and tired of it. Dream or no dream, it was time to fight back.

Her rage at being a prisoner in a nightmare swept through Nero. She growled, the sound surging through the mental connection and igniting a growl within Nero, then she lunged at the security guard.

Nero's mind stuttered, his vision half in her, half in himself. She could barely stand, let alone fight. There was no way she could win this—and it didn't matter how impressed he was at her tenacity.

God damn it. Going home and returning was no longer an option.

He hissed his power word and summoned a gate, praying that even though it was still early evening, the dark and cold would have kept most people inside, and they wouldn't notice it. He leapt through, concentrating on the wall behind the security guard, but the gate tossed him out in the middle of the square, materializing in the base of the metal umbrella art.

The muscles in his chest seized and his knees buckled. He wrenched forward, forcing his legs to hold him. The impending seizure must have screwed up his gate again. At least he hadn't accidentally jumped to the other side of the world.

Adrenaline roared through the pain and strange weight that

dragged at Becca and him. The security guard's eyes flashed wide, and he reached for his weapon, but Becca slammed a hand against his wrist, impeding his draw, and rammed her other hand against his nose.

His head jerked back, but he didn't fall, and dove in with his own strike to her ribs.

Nero yanked his mind back to his body. Teeth clenched against the threatening tremors, he raced across the square to the three wide steps leading up to the front of the high rise.

Pain exploded through his side— Becca's side, and the burn in his chest grew into an inferno. Her ribs were broken. The fall down the stairs had cracked them, and the security guard had finished the job. He was going to capture her, and the nightmare would never end.

It will end. I promise. And killing her was no longer an option.

You're part of the nightmare. You'll promise anything to keep me trapped.

Except killing her was the best option.

Everything else aside, he had to ensure the safety of his *puzur* and his position as dugga and doyen of the Major Black Coterie. Killing her was the *only* option.

Nero reached the top step and the sizzle of a powerful gatelock rushed over him, making the hair on the back of his neck stand up.

Becca's thoughts stuttered within his. *What the hell was that?*

The security guard grabbed for the front of her hospital gown and she jerked back, barely escaping.

A gatelock. Which meant whoever was holding her had to be a dragon with a sorcerer's magical ability.

Dragons aren't real, Becca hissed, the force of her determination making Nero's knees buckle, and a tremor threatened to burst into full convulsions. *You're not real. There is no devil, you're not his master, and I'm getting the hell out of this nightmare.*

She screamed and punched at the security guard's face. He side-stepped her attack, exposing his side, and she seized the tactical knife at his hip, drew it, and rammed it into his thigh.

He howled and staggered back as Nero ran around the building's corner and stumbled to a halt. A red aura blazed around a stunning, emaciated woman with pale, almost luminescent skin and long wild black hair. For a second, Nero had no breath or thought. There was only her, with her ferocious power, a power so strong that if her aura hadn't been flickering, indicating she was a human mage, he would have assumed she was an ancient red drake, old enough to challenge Hunter for seniority. She looked like she'd barely eaten in months, and while her skin was clean, her hair looked like it hadn't been combed in months, either. She hadn't deserved this. Any of it.

Behind her, the security door crashed open and the bulky man with the bushy beard bolted out. He also wore a hospital gown and had a wavering aura, although it was half as powerful as Becca's and yellow instead of red. Another human mage.

"Werner—" Becca took a staggering step toward him.

"Run." Werner rushed to her and rammed the security guard into the wall. He crumpled to the ground.

"Glenn? The others?" Becca gasped.

"We'll have to come back for them." He grabbed her arm to steady her, but his gaze jumped over her shoulder to Nero. "We have to go. Now."

The security door banged open again and five more men in tactical gear stormed out.

"Shit." Werner released her and leapt at them, shoving them back toward the door. "Run. I'll catch up."

"But—"

"I can handle them." He grabbed at the closest guy, who scrambled out of reach.

"Don't let him touch you," one of the other men said, drawing his Taser.

"Yeah," Werner said, a wildness lighting his eyes, "don't let me touch you." He lunged in again, yanking one of the men between him and the guy with the Taser.

A flicker of hesitation flared within Becca. She didn't run from a fight. But the weight dragging at her thoughts and body consumed the hesitation, and darkness swarmed at the edge of her vision. She was a liability. All Werner needed to do was distract them enough for her to get away, then he could run, too. It was a terrible plan, but it was the only one they had.

She turned to run up the path toward Nero.

"Not toward him," Werner yelled.

Becca's gaze jumped to Nero's. Heat fluttered in his chest, followed by searing agony and a tremor threatening an overwhelming convulsion.

"You," she gasped, her shock snapping through Nero and wrenching his gaze back into hers. "You're the devil's master." For a second, he saw himself as she saw him, a man with a square jaw and dark, intense eyes who exuded lithe danger. His posture, ready for battle, promised a honed, muscular body, and the sense of surging darkness clinging around him—which had to be her not quite seeing, but sensing, his dragon's aura—promised efficient death. He knew he wasn't the biggest drake around—Grey and Tobias both had human vessels that made him look small, and even Hunter's new vessel was still bigger than his—but he'd always had a hardened presence that he'd never been able to hide that made drakes fear him. "Dugga."

"I'll make a path this way," Werner yelled, jerking her attention back to him. He grabbed one of the men and slapped his palm against the man's cheek. The man heaved against Werner's grip and screamed as Werner rammed him into two of the other men.

The security door flew open again, and three more men stormed out between her and Werner. She wasn't going to make it, and even if she did, that wouldn't help Nero deal with her.

And above all, he had to remember he *had* to deal with her.

The new men barreled toward her. Another flicker of hesitation.

Fight or run? Run. One unarmed guy was better than three who are armed.

I'm not your enemy, Nero thought at her.

I don't believe you. She bolted toward him, and the men in tactical gear followed.

Nero subvocalized his power word, outstretched his hand, and shot bursts of wind into their chests, slamming them against the wall.

Becca's eyes widened. Her thoughts stuttered, making Nero's thoughts stutter and his muscles tremble. *You have magic, too?*

Footsteps clattered behind Nero. Two more men in tactical gear rushed toward him from the front of the high rise. None of them had an aura, but that didn't mean the dragon who'd cast the gatelock on the building wasn't using humans for security.

He had to get out of there before he was recognized, and he had to take Becca with him.

He sent another blast of wind toward the new assailants, but white lightning sliced through his head and his magic faltered, knocking only one of them to the ground.

Shit.

More pain burst through Nero, sweeping through his chest. His attention jumped back to Becca, too slowly, as if he were somehow being mentally dragged down by whatever was affecting her. One of the men had shoved her against the wall. The pain in Nero's chest was from *her* broken ribs.

Jeez. He had to sever their connection before he completely lost it. And to do that, he needed a moment to catch his breath and concentration—something that wasn't going to happen right then.

She slashed at the security guard's face with the tactical knife, but couldn't get the leverage for any kind of strength, and he batted her attack away. "You're coming with me."

Nero rushed toward them.

"I'm not going back." She rammed her knee into the guard's groin. His grip weakened, and Nero shot a blast of wind at him. It shoved him back a step, onto a patch of ice, and he lost his balance.

Nero grabbed Becca's arm. "Come on."

She wrenched from his grip. "I'm not going back *there*, either."

"I'm not here to hurt you."

"Becca," Werner yelled. His aura flared as he captured the face of one of the men, who went rigid and screamed.

The man she'd kneed drew his Taser and fired. Nero whipped out a thread of wind, but the muscles in his chest seized. His magic faltered. He wasn't going to stop the attack, and with their strange mental connection, he had no idea if he'd go down when she did.

He lurched in front of her, and the barbs bit into his back and shoulder.

8

E very muscle in Nero's body jerked taut, and the white lightning shooting through his head engulfed his whole body. Time stuttered. People around him yelled, fought, ran closer, but he was frozen, locked tight, only his thoughts whirling as if making up for the rest of his enforced stillness.

Werner shoved a guard into another one, making a hole in the chaos for Becca to slip through. She bolted, but the guard who'd been shoved lurched forward and grabbed her arm.

Darkness billowed across Nero's senses, but he didn't know if it came from within him or her.

She staggered.

Her. The weakness was hers.

She slashed at the guard's wrist with her knife, but he wrenched her off balance and the cut went wide.

Every muscle in Nero's body went slack and pain returned to just screaming through his chest and head. Time lurched back to normal. His knees buckled, and he yanked his wind around him before he could fall.

Becca slashed again at the guard holding her wrist, but her attacks were weak and growing weaker. The adrenaline that had burned through the haze was waning, and she was going to collapse.

Her weight crushed within him and her thoughts narrowed to one focused word: freedom.

The man who'd shot Nero with the Taser rushed toward him. Nero knocked him back with a blast of wind and staggered toward Becca.

The extra men from behind were almost on them, and he had no idea if he had the force of will right now to cut deep enough with his wind to stop them. Three of the original five were on the ground, and he couldn't tell if Werner had killed them or not—or even what type of magic the human mage had used to subdue them—but that still left five remaining, and the two more who were fast approaching.

"There are too many," Nero said. "We have to get out of here."

Werner's gaze snapped to him. "*We're* not doing anything." He jerked his attention back to the fight and rammed an elbow into the gut of the closest guard.

The man grunted but didn't go down, and another guard raised his Taser and aimed at Werner.

Nero shot wind into Taser Guy, slamming him over the picnic tables and snow bank and into the high rise wall on the other side of the patio.

"You can argue semantics after we've escaped." And once they were out of the gatelock. Hopefully, Werner couldn't summon a gate, and Nero could at least control where they went. Whether Werner was another product of Zenobia's coup or not, it didn't matter. He was a mage, which meant Nero was going to have to deal with him. Hopefully *dealing* would mean staying sane and joining the *puzur*.

The guard on Becca grabbed for her other wrist. With her weakened muscles, if he captured both her hands, she'd be lost. She heaved to the side, her foot hit ice, and she slipped. Her will snapped tight around Nero's essence and shot another blast of agony through his skull.

With a gasp, Nero whipped a thread of wind against the guy's hand, making him release Becca, then drew more wind to shove the guy back, but the muscles in Nero's chest clenched. Becca groaned.

Her eyes rolled back and the tremor snapped taut, lancing through Nero's body. She was going down and taking him with her.

The guard who'd had her before lunged in, reaching for her knife.

Nero's wind stuttered. Darkness rushed around his vision, razor sharp, with every muscle contracted. He couldn't help her, and while one of the men on Werner had dropped unconscious to the ground, the other had scrambled out of reach and drawn his Taser. They weren't going to get to her in time.

Fight, Nero barked, half to Becca and half to himself, to break through the convulsion.

Becca's eyes flew open. "Get out of my head." She slashed her knife at the guard's hands. He dodged the attack but stepped in close enough to grab her.

Fighting wasn't working. Their only option was to run.

Nero shot another blast at the man on Becca. It lurched halfway to the target, threatening to vanish. He ground his teeth, forcing more of his will behind his magic, and it gained enough strength to shove the man out of reach.

Becca leaned against the wall, the knife still held ready but the rest of her body sagging with exhaustion. Her lids dipped as if she was about to lose consciousness, and the weight within Nero swelled.

"I said fight." Nero slammed wind into the next closest guy, tossing him over the picnic tables and crashing into the wall of the opposite high rise with a sickening crunch. He forced a third gust at the two on Werner—his power stuttering out halfway and only managing to shove them back a few feet—and reached for Becca. With a lasso of wind, he captured her knife hand, steadying it long enough to hold it in place while he snaked his other hand across the back of her waist, pulled her against his side, and took her weight.

"Let go." She wrenched against his grip but didn't have the strength to break free.

"Not going to happen."

"She said let go." Werner jerked toward them, but one of the guards dove at him. He stepped into the attack, letting the man grab his arm, and slapped his palm against the guard's cheek. The guard screamed and thrashed against Werner's grip.

Another man fired his Taser at Werner. Nero swept a gust of wind and knocked the barbs off target. "I'm not your enemy."

"You're not my friend," Werner growled.

"I won't go back." Becca wrenched harder, her rage and fear giving her power.

"You're not going back." He had no idea where *back* was, but he had the distinct impression it wasn't the facility she'd just escaped from.

That's a lie. You're one of them. You're the devil's master, you're—

Another blast of pain shot through him and her exhaustion weighed down his muscles.

Shit. He couldn't fight all of them. He had to get out of there, with Becca, and—

And what?

Mother, he had no idea. He couldn't think straight, and he'd never not been able to think straight.

He tightened his grip on her and bolted down the walkway. Becca twisted in his grip, the pain from her ribs and cracked collarbone screaming through him. They reached a narrow street with vehicles parked on one side, leaving enough space for a single one-way lane. The sizzling magic of the gatelock flickered, indicating he was drawing close to the edge.

"Let go," Becca hissed, her tone dark. The tendons in her knife hand and up her forearm flexed with the effort to rip free from his grip. She wasn't going to go with him, and she wasn't going to abandon Werner.

Another guard screamed and dropped while two more lunged for Werner. Nero shot a blast of wind down the walkway and shoved one of the men on Werner into two others. If Werner could escape, Nero could go after him later without having to deal with a dragon-controlled facility. Once he'd dealt with Becca, of course.

One more gust, and Werner could run.

Nero shot another blast, but a snap of agony exploded through him and his power faltered. The wind capturing Becca's knife arm vanished, and she wrenched free.

"You're not taking me back." She lunged at him faster than he would have thought possible, given her injuries and exhaustion.

He leapt back, his foot hitting the icy curb, and stumbled into the road to catch his balance. The sizzle of the gatelock vanished as if he'd stepped from one room to the next. Becca glared at him, her eyes wild and hard with determination and her breath misting around her head as if she really were a red drake from before the Great Scourge. She was mesmerizing, everything about her capturing him, breath, body, and soul.

His thoughts stuttered. He'd been there before. Had experienced this moment before... not this moment but this... sensation?

Another man screamed. Nero's gaze jumped past Becca's shoulder to Werner. Bodies littered the ground around him. Whatever his earth magic was, it was powerful. He'd incapacitated half a dozen men within a handful of minutes.

Shit. Yes, ideally Werner needed to escape as well, but there was no way Nero would be able to deal with both him and Becca at the same time. Not without help. And there was no way in hell he was letting anyone, not even Raven, see how Becca affected him.

"This is my nightmare, my brain. I control you." She lunged at him.

He heaved to the side and whipped a lasso of wind around her knife arm. She kicked at his knee, but he yanked his wind and jerked her to him, her back to his chest. With a hiss, he summoned a gate under their feet—please, Mother, let it take them to the safe house—and shot a final gust of wind at the three remaining men on Werner.

Becca wrenched against the wind holding her, and the black nothingness of the gate enveloped them as the three guards on Werner were shoved five feet back. Werner glared and yelled at him, then bolted toward them as the world turned black.

Heavy, consuming darkness pressed against Nero's senses. Up and down vanished, the weight emanating from Becca dragged at Nero's muscles. Then his foot hit solid floor and the gate released them into the front room of what used to be a convenience store, on the main floor of a converted house, and now was his secondary safe house.

Thank the Mother his gate had taken them where he'd intended and had positioned him a few feet from the side wall, with him between her and the way out. Everything would have become more complicated if he'd gated them to Raven and the new intake.

Becca gasped, and a flash of pain cut into him. His wind vanished and she ripped free of his grip.

"I'm done being a prisoner." She lurched away from him, stepping into a beam of streetlight cutting through a crack in the boarded-up windows, away from the door. Her dark eyes were too wide, her heart-shaped face too pale, and her black hair was matted and hung at uneven lengths, adding to her feral look. It hurt looking at her. No one deserved to have suffered like that.

"You're not a prisoner." But she was probably crazy, which meant—

"And I'm not crazy. This is a nightmare. It isn't real." Her gaze jumped over his shoulder to the door, and her eyes narrowed. "You're not real."

"I am real." Was there even any point? He'd thought trying to convince her of the truth was the right answer. Everything... *almost* everything said working with her was the best option, but he could feel her confusion whirling with the exhaustion and knew it was only a matter of days, if not hours—if not already—before the soul sickness consumed her mind. The greatest kindness he could offer her was a quick death. And now his chest hurt even more.

She widened her stance, ready to fight. "I won't make it easy on you."

"Nothing about this is easy." Mother, this was why he'd created the *puzur*. She was innocent. She hadn't deserved what Zenobia had done to her. None of the mages the Asar Nergal had been forced to kill in the last couple of weeks had deserved that fate. But if he let her live, the sickness would consume her soul, and her magic could endanger others and would certainly endanger his *puzur*.

"I'm only a danger to the monsters in this nightmare."

"But this isn't a nightmare." Why was he even trying? What was wrong with him? She'd had a dragon's soul inside her and couldn't accept it was real. She'd seen his wind and felt the woolly darkness of a gate. If that didn't prove the truth, then just telling her it was real wouldn't change anything.

"You honestly expect me to believe those monsters, those... dragons—" The hand holding the knife trembled and her will clenched tighter around his essence, slicing agony through his head. "It wasn't real."

"It was." And he was so sorry it had happened.

"You can't be sorry. You're one of them—" *This isn't real. It can't be real.*

Her trembling increased, physically and mentally. Her thoughts were shards, disjointed, fracturing and refracturing, cutting into both of them.

"I'm Becca Scott! I am Becca."

"You are." If only he could fix this. Mother, he *wanted* to fix this. But what had been done to her couldn't be undone, and if he let this go on any longer, she was going to take him and everyone he cared about down with her. He was stronger than this. He was the dugga, doyen of the Major Black Coterie, and an ancient drake. He'd do what needed to be done. He always had.

"Get out of my head!" She lunged at him, her essence surging stronger through him, a whirlwind of broken glass.

He jerked to the side, caught her wrist with a wind rope, and wrenched the knife from her hand. With a roar, he swept the blade toward her heart, and an inferno exploded in his chest. His muscles froze, clenched in place, the knife a hair's breadth from the front of her hospital gown, and every cell in his body screamed to protect her.

Protect.

The fire in his chest grew, searing over his limbs and into his skull.

Protect her. With everything. To his last breath.

Mother, no.

It wasn't possible. He'd felt this before, welcomed the elation, the resolve, and the surety of soul. And he'd been crushed by it two thousand years ago. But that time before hadn't felt as if every nerve had been touched with acid, or as if this resolve was encased in iron and unbreakable. It had been hot, sultry, and quietly certain. He'd known the truth in the core of his being. It had been strong and solid, but this... this was as if an unrealized missing connection had suddenly been completed, and all the world's electricity was raging through him, wild and out of control.

Except there was only ever one. That was the way it worked.

Only one.

He'd already found her, and his inamorata was already dead.

Becca scrambled back. "I said get out."

The exhausted weight emanating from her surged, and the fire in his body froze into agony. The muscles in his chest and left arm seized and the tremor swept through him, beginning a convulsion.

"Get. Out!" Desperation filled her expression, her body taut and trembling. The impending convulsion threatened to consume her, as well.

Nero's knees buckled, and he couldn't focus long enough to summon even a hint of wind to hold himself up or break his fall.

Inamorated. He was inamorated again. To a human.

A soul-sick human.

She punched at his head, her will squeezing both of their essences tight. He raised a hand to block her strike, but his thoughts muddled between brain and body. Her fist slammed into his cheek. Something cracked. The room twisted and the threatening darkness rushed around him.

His other cheek hit the floor before he knew he was falling. Becca grabbed the knife from his hand and bolted to the door.

"Wait—" His vision blurred and darkened. He was going to pass out. He had to stop her, had to protect her, had to—

Mother. Inamorated again. It wasn't possible.

9

Becca bolted out the door before the monster, with his dangerously alluring presence and impossible magic wind, could grab her again. Her movements were jerky as she fought to run against her spasming muscles, and the cold stung her cheeks and bare arms and legs. On either side of her stretched an abandoned street with tired, three-story brick stores crowded close to the edge of a sidewalk that was half broken concrete and half snow bank.

Left or right? She couldn't see a light in any of the nearby buildings, and the store across the street from her had a broken sign and boarded-up windows.

She ran left, as fast as she could, ignoring the cold, the agony of her seizing body, and the bite of ice and broken sidewalk on her bare feet. If this was still a nightmare, she couldn't give in and stop, and she couldn't risk banging on doors and begging for help. That wouldn't work. Of course, just running wouldn't help, either. The prison was her mind, and she couldn't escape from herself.

But a part of her wasn't sure anymore. That monster— no, the *devil's master*—God, she'd recognized his thoughts and essence the moment she'd seen him and hadn't been surprised he'd exuded intense, raw masculinity. A part of her had sensed that the moment his thoughts had appeared in her dreams. He'd been determined to convince her this was real. And God help her, a part of her wanted him to be real.

But wasn't that just part of the nightmare?

Except—

Her throat tightened and she fought back a sob. She needed a safe place to get her bearings, but the shock and fury from the monster's thoughts still raged through her. It wasn't possible. None of this was possible. But she no longer knew what was possible and what wasn't. And what about Glenn and the others? What about Werner? Were they creations of the nightmare, or were they real? Stanbury? The facility?

No, they had to be figments. It couldn't be real. But the devil's master had said it was. And he was sorry. They'd ripped into her soul, tore at her essence, determined to ignite the impossible hiding dormant within her, for hours, days... years?

She stumbled, shooting pain through her chest and shoulder from her broken bones, before the drug-induced weight from the Versed swelled, dimming the agony and weakening her muscles enough that the convulsions didn't overwhelm her.

It couldn't have been years. It *wasn't* years, because it wasn't real.

She should have frostbite on her bare feet by now. Surely that meant it was a dream. She couldn't remember when she'd last eaten. She should be starving... she was starving. But did that mean—?

God, she couldn't think straight... no, that had been the devil's master. He'd been worried about not thinking straight. Except—

God damn it.

Someone said something, too softly to make out the words, and her heart skipped a beat. She wrenched her gaze up then down the street. It was help? Danger?

No one was there. Which meant it had to be the devil's master waking—

Except the essence inside her was different. She couldn't explain it, only knew on an instinctual level that it hadn't been *him*.

Most likely her imagination and just another figment from the nightmare... if this was a nightmare... which it had to be? How would she even be able to tell?

No. Shelter and clothes first. Determine reality second. And not even think about how hot the devil's master had been in person. Jeez, why did this have to be a nightmare? He was as attractive as his presence had felt. Except that was just part of the horror, another torture to add to all the others.

God, if he'd heard that— But thank goodness, his thoughts were still quiet. They'd gone quiet the moment she'd hit him and reached the door. She prayed that meant he was unconscious, and when he woke, he wouldn't renew the connection—because any kind of connection with him was a bad idea.

Escape and regroup. That was what she needed to focus on. Werner had established an emergency meeting place almost two weeks ago, when their first hideout had been raided by the devil. If Werner had escaped Stanbury's men, he'd be there. And it had looked, with that parting glimpse she'd gotten before the devil's master had jerked her away, that Werner had escaped. That's where she needed to go. Werner knew more of the others who'd been prisoners in the cave than she did. They'd create an assault force and get Glenn and anyone else back.

And she wasn't going to acknowledge how those thoughts fit in with the nightmare versus reality. Right now, the thoughts steadied her, gave her a purpose, and that was the only thing holding her together.

Before Stanbury had dragged her off the street, she'd had a ten dollar bill stuffed in the toe of her boot for emergency transportation and food. What she wouldn't give for those boots now, with or without the money. What she wouldn't give for summer weather. It'd be too much to ask for a clothesline filled with clothes hanging nearby, but she wouldn't turn down an open window, either. That at least would indicate if any of these buildings had occupants, which in turn would mean clothes and shoes.

She reached an alley that ended forty feet down with a brick wall that was too high for her to climb with her cracked collarbone, but she slipped into the shadows anyway and pressed her back against the wall. A moment to catch her breath and think. That was all she needed. She strained to hear sounds of pursuit from the devil's master.

Someone said something again... no, a few someones, whispering, but she couldn't tell if they were having a conversation or how many there were.

Her pulse beat faster, and she glanced down the street again. Still no one following her and no sign of the devil's master. It had to be the Versed. It made her dizzy, dragging at her senses, and everything was getting muddled. Even with the adrenaline from the fight helping to burn through the drug's effects, she couldn't shake it. There wasn't anyone around. It was her imagination or the nightmare. She just had to keep in mind her priorities: clothes and shelter, and thank God, across from her in a large, clean storefront window stood a mannequin wearing a beaded embroidered full-skirted wedding gown.

Finally, something was going her way. She wasn't going to hold her breath the gown store had anything practical to wear or even pantsuits in impractically thin fabric, but hey, it might have shoes— and she'd take unpractical footwear over no footwear any day.

The cold seeped through the thin hospital gown, making her teeth chatter. At least she was dressed in something that wrapped around her body and attached at the hip and shoulder, and she wasn't running around with her ass hanging out. It surprised her the nightmare hadn't stuck her with that, and soon, if her luck stuck, she'd be in something warmer.

She groaned—

No... wait...

Her pulse stuttered. *This wasn't possible, this—*

Aw, shit. She hadn't groaned. *He* had. The devil's master was waking and she could still hear him.

"God, just get out of my head."

That's what I've been trying to do— When he'd gone after her at

Stanbury's facility and then again in the abandoned building she'd just escaped from.

Yeah, right. He'd only rescued her from Stanbury's men because she could tell Stanbury his every order to the devil and the others. If Stanbury's men had been trying to kill her, he would have sat back and watched.

That's not tru—

Don't even try. I'm not an idiot.

A flash of pain cut through the Versed, more voices whispered at the edge of her hearing, and the muscles in her chest tightened. Shit. She had to get him out or she was going to collapse, and then he'd find her.

How about a truce. We meet and work this out. He almost sounded sincere. If he hadn't just tried to stab her, she might have believed him.

You're a monster. Like the others. Oh, God. What if the voices were the monsters still in her? But that didn't seem right. They were... she couldn't explain it and didn't have the time to figure it out. All she knew was the devil's master was different. He wasn't inside her like the others had been and neither were the voices. Those monsters—

Dragons. They were the spirits of—

Monsters. After what they'd done to her and the other captives, giving the monsters a name didn't make them less of a monster. They'd been *in* her, tearing at her from the inside out. They'd—

Another slash of agony cut through her and made both of them groan.

But this monster, the devil's master, was different. He wasn't inside her, fighting her soul for her body. He was—

Still a monster. The monster the other monsters feared. He—

Nero. He sounded exhausted. *My name is Nero.*

I really don't care what your name is. A gust of wind swept into the alley, making her teeth chatter and her heart skip a beat. Was that him controlling the wind? But she didn't see him, and the gust vanished. She needed to put more distance between them and get away. It was her only hope. She had to end this conversation and get across the street to the—

Where? His thoughts in her head tightened, as if trying to focus.

There. That? He was stuck, merely a passenger. Did that mean she had control over him?

Mother, that was the truth... Except she was pretty sure he had thought that and not said it directly to her.

In fact, if she thought about the last few minutes, they'd been half responding to thoughts spoken directly to each other and half to just thoughts.

Oh, God. If he could hear thoughts she wasn't thinking at him—?

She needed to be more careful. The monsters from before had made it clear. If the dugga —the monster she now knew was the devil's master—got a hold of them, both monster and human would be killed without a second thought. He'd already tried to kill her once. She couldn't let her location or where she was going to meet Werner slip out. Hell, she didn't even know if she could control that.

The drug-induced weight in her limbs flared and her heart leapt into a rapid tattoo. She had to get him out before she did anything. *Out. Get out.* He had to get out now.

I'd love to, he growled back, but a sense that he couldn't let her go seeped past his mental words and tone. She endangered everything.

I'm not a danger to you.

You're the greatest danger I've faced in recent history.

Yeah, right. That was just more proof that this was a nightmare. Sure, she'd been a competent soldier and risen to the rank of captain before retiring, but she was still only one person. This monster controlled the wind and the other monsters feared him. She couldn't possibly be a danger to him. Besides, it was just a nightmare.

It's not a nightmare. Although it was certainly becoming one for him. Mother, he had no idea how to make her accept this was real.

It isn't real. And she was shutting him out. She concentrated on the essence within herself, that part of her, her soul, that the other monsters had forced into a tiny mental box. She was stronger than some nightmare monster, and she would kick him out.

Her muscles trembled, shooting agony through her chest and shoulder. The monster, Nero, groaned.

Becca, please.

That's Captain Scott to you. It was her mind. She was in control.

Nero's essence gasped as if fighting for breath. Her trembling increased, but the Versed, still coursing through her veins, dulled the edge of the pain and the convulsion. She was kicking him out and taking charge. Her nightmare. Her mind.

Another blast of agony shot through her, and Nero screamed.

Son of a— His essence snapped tight into ferocious primal rage, his murderous intent clear, making her pulse race faster.

This is my head. I said get out.

And I said I'd love to. But there was nothing in the raging emotions indicating he wanted out or had any intention of letting her go. He wanted her gone, wanted the danger she presented to be eliminated, and he'd stop at nothing to end her.

Fuck you. She tightened her will on him and imagined a solid metal box. If those other monsters could lock her away in her own head, she could lock him away.

Another blast. Nero screamed again. Something squealed. But it wasn't his essence being forced into the box. He was still too big for her to mentally hold on to. She had to crush him down, had to—

A thunk. Heavy metal? Voices? Whispered voices…? No, not whispered—

She blinked, not realizing she'd been so focused inward that she'd stopped paying attention to her surroundings. A black van, like the van Stanbury's men had driven when they'd first picked her up a few days ago, had stopped at the alley's mouth, and two men in tactical gear rushed out while two more stayed in the van, the one on the right aiming a Glock—not a Taser—at her.

How the hell had they found her?

But it was a dream. Of course they'd found her.

"Get in the van," the guy on the left said. His hand dipped to the sidearm holstered at his hip, and he squared broad shoulders almost twice the width of hers.

"I'm not going back." Not to the devil's master, not to the monsters in the cave, and not to Stanbury. Becca tightened her grip on the knife and widened her stance. The whispers grew louder, pressing against her senses. She darted her gaze down the street, but knew, with gut-churning certainty now, that the voices were inside her.

Becca. Nero's essence flared, cutting through the other voices and straining against her mental grip. *What's going on?*

With the Versed still dragging her down there was no way she'd win a fight against one of these guys. But they had her cornered and fighting until she could get past them was her only option. God, it'd be so much easier to concentrate if the voices would just shut up.

Becca—? Four of them? Nero swore and groaned. *Holy Mother, that hurt. Hold on. I'm coming.*

I said get out of my head.

And I said I'd love to, he barked back at her.

The man on the left jerked his chin at the other guy—a smaller guy with a fist-sized welt on his cheek, probably from the fight at Stanbury's hospital. Welt Guy lunged at her, reaching to capture her arm. She leapt into his attack, sidestepping his grab, and thrust the knife blade under the bottom of his Kevlar vest and into his gut.

He screamed, and the first man seized her other arm and yanked up. Pain exploded through her shoulder, across her chest, and over her neck.

Nero howled in her head and a thick darkness swept around her. The whispers grew louder, turning into the roar of a crowd, the words still unintelligible and grating against the inside of her skull.

Welt Guy seized her other wrist and snatched the knife from her hand. They heaved her to the van's door, and the man with the Glock jumped out to cover them. The fourth guy set a phone on the floor by his feet and twisted his fist into the front of her hospital gown.

She wrenched against his grip. No way in hell was she getting into that van. There'd not be another opportunity to escape if she let them capture her again.

One of the men behind her shoved her forward, smashing her

face and chest against the van floor. Van Guy bumped the phone with his foot. It skittered closer and the screen flared to life. A stationary green dot flashed on a map, and the words at the top read: Subject 147006 – Rebecca A. Scott.

What the hell? She wrenched again, fighting to get free.

The first guy leaned against her. "Go ahead. Fight all you want. Even if you manage to get away, we can still find you."

Van Guy chuckled. "Yeah, you're low-jacked."

"Like a criminal on house arrest," Welt Guy said.

But she wasn't wearing an ankle or wrist bracelet. It had to be in her clothes—

"More like an expensive car." Glock Guy sneered. "And the tracker is implanted under the hood."

Her breath caught in her throat, and the crowd's noise thundered in her head. "Implanted?" Now she knew it had to be a nightmare, but if it wasn't—

God, she didn't want to think about that. All the things she'd survived, and the hopelessness of this reality. Even if, against all odds, she could escape Stanbury's hospital again, they'd always be able to find her.

Hold on, Nero growled. Pressure filled her head, and the sense of an enormous power rushed over her.

"Holy shit," Van Guy said, his gaze locked behind her, and his grip on her gown loosened.

Becca twisted enough to see. A black hole swelled to man-size against the front of the closest building and Nero leapt out. His expression was hard, his eyes filled with a deadly calm, and he looked every bit the monster the other monsters feared.

The man with the Glock fired two shots. They slammed into Nero's chest near his heart, drawing a roar and a ferocious wind that ripped Glock Guy from the van and tossed him against a streetlight pole with a sickening crack. Blood rushed over the front of Nero's pale blue dress shirt, and the muscles in his jaw clenched. His pain burned past the Versed and across Becca's chest, but the man— the *monster* didn't drop.

"Get her in the van," the first guy said. He released her and drew his Glock from his hip holster, but Nero flicked his hand and another blast of wind smashed the guy through the boarded-up window of the store beside them. Another flick and a whip of wind sliced deep into Welt Guy's forearm. His hold on Becca's wrist loosened, and she wrenched free from both his and Van Guy's grips. She punched Welt Guy in the face. His head snapped back, and the knife he'd taken from her fell to the van floor.

She seized it and slashed at Van Guy. He staggered back, scrambling to draw his Taser, but another gust of wind smashed him against the van side and shoved him and the vehicle into the center of the street.

"Come on." Nero grabbed her forearm. "We have to get out of here."

She jerked around and rammed the knife into his gut. "I'm not going anywhere with you."

His wind snapped around her, yanking her closer to him and pinning the knife in his body.

Holy God, how is he still standing? Shot twice and now stabbed. His agony radiated through her, churning with the screaming crowd in her head, and the Versed.

"I'm not letting them take you again." A black vortex formed under their feet, his power straining, as if the pain, controlling the wind, and now summoning the vortex were too much.

Please let it be too much. Please let his wind falter when they stepped through to the other side, and please let there be a way to escape. It was her only hope. Stab him again and run like hell—

Except he was still in her head, and it seemed he could find her as easily as Stanbury's men could with the GPS tracker embedded in her body.

10

Nero staggered through the gate, pain screaming through his body from the gunshot wounds in his chest and the knife in his gut. His foot hit solid ground, his wind stuttered, and Becca wrenched away, taking the knife with her, just like she'd planned.

Raven dropped her book and stood. She'd been sitting in a chair beside the cot with the new intake—a young man whose yellow aura burned Nero's eyes just glancing at him. They were in the *puzur's* primary safe house, the secure set of rooms in the back of a warehouse held by one of Nero's many anonymous holding companies. It had been fitted with a bathroom, two hospital cots, basic medical supplies, a kitchenette stocked with food, and a monitor with the feeds of two security cameras trained on the areas outside the front and back doors. Everything Raven needed to help the humans they rescued stay sane and safe during the awakening of their earth magic.

What? No, I— Becca gasped. Something rushed across Nero's mind. It felt like a blast of mental wind, howling with sudden force, then vanished. She jerked back, putting both Nero and Raven in her line of sight, as if she'd sensed Raven's presence behind her. Which meant there was a possibility her mental abilities weren't just connected to him.

"I said, get out." Becca's gaze jumped to the man in the cot. "And let me guess. This is how you plan to help me?" *Torture first, then kill. That's what the other monsters did.*

"I'm not the other monsters."

Raven frowned.

One of the bullets—one that had gotten trapped in his body—popped from Nero's chest and clattered to the concrete floor.

Becca's eyes flashed wide. *Oh, my God.* She tightened her grip on the knife, even though her thoughts recognized stabbing him wouldn't kill him.

"You've been shot?" Raven's frown deepened.

"Already healed." Mostly. He raised his hands, palms up, the universal sign of harmlessness. "Becca, we need to disable that implant."

"There is no *we*."

The mental wind swept through his head again, and he gasped. So did Becca.

"Nero?" The muscles in Raven's jaw tightened.

"I said I wasn't going back. Not there, not to the hospital again, and not with you." She lurched toward the man on the cot. "And I'm taking him with me."

"They'll find you. Let me at least deal with the implant."

"Like you'd actually help me." She staggered another step toward the cot.

Raven tensed and her mouth opened—likely to hiss her power word and summon her wind magic.

Nero gave a tight shake of his head. He needed Becca calm, needed her to see reason. Mother of All, needed *her*.

She barked a harsh laugh. "There's no reason in a nightmare. It doesn't make sense. Just like popping a bullet out of your chest."

The mental wind swept through him again. She groaned. Pain burned over his face, down his neck, and into his chest. This wasn't the pain of the gunshots. That was mostly healed. This was her pain, her broken bones and the shattering of her mind.

How the hell was he going to convince her this was real? How could he convince her he wasn't going to hurt her?

You can't. "You've already tried to kill me. You shouldn't have hesitated."

I had no choice. Mother, it hurt just thinking he'd tried.

"Bullshit." Becca inched back another step. The back of her thighs hit the cot and she glanced down.

Nero followed her gaze. Ah, shit. The new intake had been restrained. With how ferociously his power had been threatening to manifest when he'd sent Diablo to bring him in, it wasn't a surprise. Earth magic often required a word and a gesture, and only a few highly experienced drakes managed to eliminate the need for one or both. Restraining the young man helped ensure Raven's safety when his magic fully appeared, in an attempt to eliminate the gesture aspect of summoning the power.

Another blast of mental wind and another groan in unison.

"What's going on?" Raven asked, her body tense, ready to attack.

"Your boss here thought I'd be an easy target."

Now, that doesn't make sense. "I'm trying to help, and if we don't deal with that implant, those men from the facility will find you again. I don't know how much time we have." *If their dragon master can create a gatelock, that dragon can make a gate, as well.*

"Gates and locks?" The agony swelled, and she pressed her palm to her temple. "I said get out." *No, I'm getting out.* "And taking him with me."

She yanked open the restraining cuff and grabbed the young man's wrist as his aura flared blindingly bright. White lightning shot through Nero's head and Becca screamed. They dropped to their knees. The muscles in his chest seized and people, a horde of people, yelled, screamed, howled, whispered, hissed, roared in his head— no, *her* head.

Raven rushed toward him. "No, Becca. Sedate her." It was the only solution. Knock her out, deal with the implant, then deal with her... somehow.

"I'm not going back. I won't be your prisoner again." *Never again.*

The last words pounded into him, crushing his essence with their force.

Raven snatched a pre-loaded syringe from the drawer in the cot. She hissed her power word and snapped a lasso of wind around Becca's arms, pinning her to the floor.

"I won't go back!"

Raven shoved the sleeve of Becca's hospital gown up and jabbed the needle into her biceps.

"Half dose," Nero gasped. "Already been dosed with something."

Raven bared her teeth in disagreement but obeyed. Thank the Mother. He didn't know what he'd do if he lost another inamorata. He didn't even know Becca, and with her stabbing him, she clearly wasn't inamorated back—she'd have hesitated like he had—but a second loss would surely shatter his soul. The Mother only knew how he'd survived that first loss.

Becca wrenched against Raven's wind and screamed. Her agony, physically and mentally, seared through him, stealing all breath and thought, and then, between one heartbeat and the next, a weight flooded her and she collapsed.

Raven glared at him. "What the hell was that?"

"Complicated and not anywhere out of the woods." He pulled his phone from his pocket and dialed Capri.

"Anaea said Tobias had called you into Court," Raven said.

"He had."

"What?" Capri asked over the phone.

"Where's Gig?" He was the only drake Nero could think of who, with his ability to magically control technology, would be able to quickly deal with the tracker implanted somewhere in Becca's body.

"Gig?" Capri's tone turned wary.

Raven glared at him.

"You owe me." He didn't want to get Gig involved with his *puzur*— the fewer drakes who knew about it, the better—and he had no idea if he could trust Gig. But Grey had said the young silver drake had stood by him and Capri to help Hunter, even knowing Hunter had broken dragon law and body-shared. With luck, Gig wouldn't have the rare ability to see the difference between human mage and dragon auras and everything would be fine.

"Is this coterie business or Court business?"

"I'd go through the proper channels for Court if it was. Where is he?"

"Here, at headquarters, in the communal living room."

"Is Swipe there?" The other member of Capri's team.

"No."

"Good. Tell him I'm coming."

"Nero—"

He hung up before Capri could argue and summoned a gate underneath him, so he wouldn't have to stand. His power swelled, burning with mental agony, and enveloped him. God, even with Becca unconscious, his head still hurt. He straightened, using the woolly black weightlessness to help him stand, and staggered into the communal living room of the North American Clean Team headquarters.

Gig, a drake in a vessel barely twenty years old, the youngest vessel the Handmaiden would ever put a drake's soul into, stood on the other side of the room. He wore a black, blue, and silver T-shirt with the depiction of a dangerous-looking dragon curled on a bed of human skulls, and his eyes were wide, as if he hadn't expected a gate to materialize in the middle of the living room wall. Capri stood beside him glaring at Nero, her phone still in her hand.

"Less than two minutes, and I'll return him."

Gig flashed a goofy grin and strode toward Nero. "Cool."

"He's not some tool you can borrow from your neighbor." Capri's expression darkened. As team leader, she was responsible for him, and while she might be caught up in Nero's *puzur* because her inamorato was human, Gig had nothing to do with this mess. A mess that was surely going to get them all on the prince's wanted list sooner rather than later—especially if Nero couldn't figure out what to do about Becca.

"Less than two minutes. I promise." Nero summoned another gate without waiting for confirmation of Capri's permission, Becca's pain straining his ability to control his unanchored magic. Now he knew how Grey must have felt when he'd staggered into Nero's living room yesterday, barely having survived a grenade explosion... God, had that only been yesterday?

They lurched back into the safe house. Raven was propping Becca into a sitting position against the foot of the cot and had handcuffed her to one of the lowered guardrails. The knife lay forgotten on the cot beside the young man's knee. Here was hoping everything was mostly dealt with and the cuffs were removed by the time she gained consciousness. There'd be no way he could convince her he wanted to help her if she woke while still cuffed.

Mother, it hurt to just look at her. Unconscious, the woman looked even more vulnerable and fragile than before. The ferocious adrenalin that had to have been keeping her upright during the fight outside the facility was gone, and now the horrors of what she'd experienced were clear in her gaunt features and matted hair. He ached at the idea of how much she'd suffered and boiled with the need to fix this, protect her, bring her meat, so she was strong enough to properly rage her defiance against those who'd wronged her.

Gig shifted away from Nero, his attention sweeping over the room. "What is this place?"

Nothing anymore. Nero was going to have to destroy this safe house as well as the other one, to keep his activities secure. Even if he thought he could mostly trust Gig, he couldn't risk the young drake accidentally saying something to the wrong dragon.

"Over here." Nero strode to Becca and knelt. The aura on the new intake flared, and Gig's eyes widened. "Watch the yellow drake. Don't touch him. He's... sick and having trouble with his earth magic."

"And the red drake you've got handcuffed to the bed?"

"None of your business," Raven growled.

Gig raised his hands. "Hey, no need to get all angry. You invited me."

"The red drake is the job." Nero knelt beside Becca and fought the urge to brush her hair back from her face. Any sign of tenderness could expose his unwanted condition. It was bad enough Raven had probably already figured out Becca was the source of the convulsions he'd been suffering the last few days. It could only get worse if she knew not all options to deal with a soul-sick human mage were on the table. "She has a GPS tracker implanted somewhere on her body, and I need it disabled."

"Who the hell would implant a tracker on a drake—?" Realization flashed across Gig's expression, and for a second he looked more like the ancient drake Nero had known before the Handmaiden had rebirthed him and unexpectedly shoved his soul back into the same human vessel. "I knew it'd come to this. Hunter has—" Another flash of realization and Gig snapped his mouth shut before he could utter treasonous words in front of the prince's favorite dragon.

Nero cocked an eyebrow, testing Gig's recovery of the situation.

The color drained from Gig's face. "Well, you know... Hunter has created a real problem. Yes, he has."

"Mother of All." Raven rolled her eyes. "That was pathetic." A hint of wind flickered around her hand. "I think he should never return to Court."

"I think Capri and Tobias would have something to say about that," Nero said.

"And Capri knows you took me. She—" Another flash of realization across Gig's face that turned to horror. "She let you take me."

"Just deal with the tracker, and I'll get you back to the Clean Team's headquarters." Nero would deal with the fallout from Gig later. Hopefully much later, although he had a sinking suspicion that everything was going to come to a head soon. "Can you fry the tracker or something? I don't want it to work again, not even accidentally."

"Pinpointing where it is would be nice, too." Raven tipped Becca's head back and brushed her hair from her face—the move Nero yearned to make. "Even if it's broken, I'd want it out."

"Well..." Gig crouched beside Nero and placed a hand on Becca's ankle. His gaze grew unfocused, and he tilted his head to one side. "The implant is in the back of her right shoulder, just under the skin. Nasty place to put it. Hard to see and get out by yourself. And—" His attention jumped to the door on the other side of the cot. "It's talking to a smart phone that's approaching fast."

11

S hit. Nero glanced at the monitor. Men rushed to the outside of both doors, moving with the efficiency of an experienced combat team. These men had breached buildings before, and more than half of them carried sidearms and not Tasers.

Nero stood and faced the front door. "I can't gate us out of here until that tracker is disabled."

He hissed his power word and summoned his wind. Raven stood, woke her magic, and turned to the back door.

"Sure." Gig said. "Just—"

Agony sliced through Nero's head and someone— no, *Becca* gasped behind him, awake.

Raven's wind stuttered and vanished—she still needed to concentrate to hold it at the ready. "How the hell did she burn through even a half dose of midazolam?"

"Gig, that tracker," Nero growled.

A *crack* erupted from the back door. It crashed off its hinges, and four men stormed into the tiny room. Another *crack* from farther away, the other team breaching the front of the warehouse, and on the monitor, they stormed into the empty main room of the building and headed toward the smaller safe house room.

"Let me go." Becca wrenched against the handcuff, making the cot jerk forward, the feet squealing against the floor.

Raven barked her power word, reviving her wind, but the men in the doorway had already raised their sidearms to fire.

Nero shot his wind into the first two, but a slash of pain from Becca made the gust sputter, and it only shoved them back into the doorway. "The tracker?"

"Working on—"

Becca kicked Gig in the chest. He fell back and cracked his head on the floor.

"He's trying to help." Raven slammed another blast at the men at the door, pushing the first two farther than Nero had managed and into the two behind them.

Becca yanked harder against the handcuff, her expression wild. "I said I'd never go back. And I'm not."

One of the men in the doorway fired at Raven. Nero swept his wind up, but the bullet skimmed her shoulder. With a roar, she lassoed the guy with her wind and tossed him against the far wall.

The front door crashed open and more men rushed inside. Nero strained against the agony and roar of voices in his head and sent another gust into the guys at the back door.

Gig groaned and squeezed his eyes shut.

"Get up and deal with that tracker," Nero yelled.

"Dealing with it, and I'm staying the hell away from her."

Two of the guys at the front heaved themselves out of the doorway to make way for the other two, and the biggest guy managed to wrench his Glock up and fire. Two bangs erupted, and blood sprayed from the back of Raven's shoulder. She screamed and her wind vanished, but she remained standing—thank the Mother her healing was fast enough that it would take more than a bullet to the shoulder to incapacitate her.

Nero tore his wind in half and sent blasts at both doors. Becca's agony flared and the muscles in his chest seized. His knees buckled and he dropped to the floor. Mother of All. He had to gate them out of there, but he couldn't risk moving them until the tracker was disabled.

"Tell me it's dead."

"Almost," Gig said.

Get out! Becca screamed. *Just get out. Please, get out. Please, God, please.*

The roaring inside him increased. Every nerve had ignited into an inferno. Now. He had to gate them away now, or it was never going to happen. Raven and Gig couldn't free gate. Nero was the only one who could get them out of there.

More gunfire exploded. Pain ripped through Nero's chest.

"Got it," Gig said.

Nero yelled his power word, forcing his magic to form a gate past the agony and whirlwind in his head. Becca screamed, yanking on the handcuff, as if hoping she could break free. Raven dropped to one knee, another spray of blood exploding from her side. She grabbed Gig, his eyes wide, and shoved him to the side of the cot, while the young man still restrained in the cot started to howl. His aura blazed as Nero's gate formed beneath all of them, the cot included, and the gate enveloped them.

Power surged through Nero, burning with agony and threatening to consume him. He grasped onto the one safe place he could send them that was close, and the gate shoved them up through another concrete floor into a dark room. With what little strength he had left, he snapped a tendril of wind to the light switch and turned on the overhead light.

Raven gasped. "You brought us home?"

He pressed his forehead to the concrete floor of the biggest room in his house's transition suites, a series of underground rooms built two hundred feet from the main house, used to help those humans Raven believed were safe to join the *puzur* but who were having trouble controlling a dangerous earth magic. Both the door to the hall and the en suite bathroom stood open, and the cot sat beside a bed, crammed against a lounge chair and the bedside table.

"We can argue about this later," Nero said.

The whoosh of air from a gate gusted behind him.

"What the hell?" Diablo growled.

"Hey, Diablo," Gig said.

"Diablo?" Becca's fear and agony jerked taut within Nero. With a roar, she heaved at the handcuff, wrenched the guardrail from the cot, grabbed the knife forgotten beside the young man on the bed, and leapt at Diablo.

E verything within Nero froze. Becca growled like a dragon while holding the guardrail in one hand and the knife in the other. Then she slashed at Diablo.

"If I'm going down, I'm taking the devil with me." Her eyes were wild, as if her reality had fully shattered, and her thoughts were jagged shards slicing through Nero's head in a whirlwind of a roaring crowd.

Diablo shifted to the side, letting the knife skim the front of his T-shirt, then seized Becca's wrist and twisted, driving the blade toward her heart in one swift movement.

"Stop!" Nero snapped his wind at Diablo's arm and yanked the knife off course. "Don't kill her." *Please, Mother. Don't.*

The knife sliced across her bicep, drawing a howl, and she swung the guardrail, smashing it against Diablo's side.

"What the hell—?" Diablo batted the railing aside, rapid free gated behind Becca with a whoosh, wrapped an arm around her neck, and captured her head.

"Full dose this time." Raven snatched another preloaded syringe from the cot's drawer, jammed it into Becca's shoulder, and plunged in the entire contents.

Becca jerked against Diablo's grip, clawing at his arm, and

screaming gut-wrenching feral sounds. She rammed her heel on the arch of his foot, making him wince.

"Mother above, this one is soul sick," Diablo said.

The whirl of her incoherent thoughts in Nero's head faltered and a massive weight rushed over him. He sagged forward into his hands.

Raven crouched beside him.

"Are you okay?" he managed to ask, his gaze jumping to the blood on her shirt.

"Already healed. You?"

"Fine." Except he wasn't, and it was so hard to focus.

"I won't go back. I won't—" Becca slammed her head back and cracked it against the bridge of Diablo's nose.

"Ah, fuck." Blood oozed over his upper lip, but he held tight.

"I won't. I—" Another swell of heavy darkness, she went limp, and the roar in Nero's head vanished.

"One of—?" Diablo glanced at Gig. The silver drake didn't know Nero was the dugga or that he rescued as many human mages as he could, instead of murdering them.

"Yes," Nero said.

Diablo let her sag to the floor, grabbed his nose—his rapid healing already setting the bones in their broken state—broke it again, and reset it. "The one you mentioned earlier?"

Last night Nero had tried to communicate with Diablo using their mental connection, but Becca's powers had hijacked it. "Yes."

"She's not coming back from that. She's hanging on by a thread," Diablo said.

"She'll have to come back from it." The quiet in Nero's head made him shiver. He hadn't realized how loud she'd been—and constantly, for hours... maybe even the last few days.

Gig's gaze jumped from Nero to Diablo, surprisingly without adding a comment. Maybe the silver drake could be discreet. He hadn't revealed much about Hunter other than his hero-worship of the red drake, and Gig had had that before Hunter had broken dragon law.

"Gig." He needed to get the silver drake out of his house before he learned anything else. It was bad enough Raven had let their location slip. "I appreciate your help. Time to go."

"That's it?" Gig asked.

Nero glanced at Diablo. "If you would be so kind. Clean Team living quarters."

"Sure." Diablo grabbed Gig's arm, summoned a gate under their feet, and they vanished with a whoosh of air.

Raven sagged onto the edge of the bed, the young man unconscious again, not having fully wakened during the fight and his aura still bright, but no longer blinding. Her gaze slid from Nero to Becca and back to him, as if trying and failing to figure out what had just happened. Nero wasn't even certain he knew. A few days ago, everything had been fine. Now—?

A black gate formed against the wall, and Diablo returned.

Raven drew in a breath, but Nero wasn't sure if it was to gather her thoughts or steady her nerves. "I know you want to—" Her expression tightened. Ah, not to steady her nerves. It was to tell him a hard truth she didn't think he'd want to hear. "You can't save all of them."

So far, they hadn't been able to save any of Zenobia's victims, and he knew that hurt her more than it hurt him.

"When have I ever made you think I believe they can all be saved?" Except this one, he had to save. Every cell in his body screamed at him to protect her, bring her shinies, kill her enemies, return with meat. The compulsion was a hundred times stronger than the first time he'd been inamorated... but maybe that was time having weakened the memories. Surely, there wasn't anything more powerful about this soul bond than his previous one. Being inamorated was the most powerful connection a dragon could form with another. There weren't degrees. It was once, all in, and forever.

But God damn it, this was *again*. Mother, he couldn't lose another one. He'd die with her. His heart would just stop when hers did. And that terrified him.

Diablo's expression darkened, but he crouched and picked up Becca before Nero could fully read what the change meant.

"Let's get her to a room." He carried her into the room across the hall, flicked on the light, laid her on the bed, and reached for the restraints.

Nero staggered to his feet and followed. "No restraints."

"I'm not sure that's wise," Raven said from the doorway of the first room.

"She was a prisoner when Zenobia had her, and I recovered her from a facility where she was being held against her will. It's dangerous for her if she leaves, but if she wants to, I won't stop her. I won't be what she fears the most." Even if he already was.

Raven frowned. "Are you okay?"

Shit. That was too much. He should be focusing on protecting his *puzur*, not one soul-sick human mage.

"I'm fine. How's the new intake?"

Raven glanced over her shoulder at the young man in the bed. His dark hair was tousled and his brow furrowed, as if even in sleep he was unsettled. Which, given the continued pulsing of his aura, was probably true.

"Do we know what his earth magic is yet?" *Do we know what he hit Becca with—and without uttering a power word or using a gesture?* When she'd touched him, the roar of voices in Nero's head had exploded into a raging storm, but he had no idea if that had been because of the man's power or Becca's.

"I don't even know his name." She glared at Diablo. "D knocked him out, and he hasn't woken. I'm just glad he didn't turn her into ash or something when she grabbed him." She jerked her chin at Becca.

"Her name is Rebecca Scott." *Victim, mage, soldier.*

Diablo cocked an eyebrow. "When the hell did she tell you her name?"

"It's complicated." Nero rubbed his temples. Yeah, the silence in his head was deafening, but hints of her pain still remained and all he wanted to do was take that pain away.

"Well, if we're going to be here now, I'm going to get some supplies." Raven drew in a quick breath and squared her shoulders.

Back to business, even if Nero could still see concern in her eyes. "Do you think you can hold down the fort long enough for me to get a few things from the house?"

She took a self-adhesive bandage, a package of disinfectant wipes, and a suture kit from the cabinet in the hall, shoved them into Nero's hands, then headed to the kitchenette /communal living room— much like the set-up the Clean Team had—and the long under-ground passage back to the house.

Diablo leaned against the wall and crossed his arms. "So what the hell? You show up with all this emotional energy, and Anaea nearly takes out the living room with half the kids in it. They're pissed they're going to have to watch the last ten minutes of the game on playback."

"It couldn't be helped." This wasn't a conversation he wanted to have with Diablo. He'd known bringing Becca here could affect Anaea, with her unstable sorcerer's ability, but he hadn't had any choice. He pulled the lounge chair to the side of Becca's bed and set the medical supplies on the nightstand. Hopefully the bandage would be enough, because he had almost no experience suturing flesh—and he wasn't going to think about her broken ribs or collarbone until she was awake and Raven was around to help.

"What about the baby silver drake?" Meaning Gig.

"That facility implanted a GPS tracker on her and had men after her that were too well-trained for some hospital. And no—"

Diablo opened his mouth to say something.

"It wasn't a prison, unless there's a special operations black site in the middle of Newgate with a gatelock on it." Nero pushed the sleeve of Becca's hospital gown back and dabbed at the knife wound with a wipe. It didn't look deep and was already starting to scab over.

"A gatelock?" Diablo's tone turned dark.

"Yeah." The implications weren't good.

"Grey just dealt with a drake with more sorcerer ability than first believed. Could it be something he'd done?"

"Doubt it." From what Nero had learned of the facility, it hadn't felt like Servius's style, which meant there was another drake out there strong enough to create a gatelock... unless the lock was the Handmaiden's handiwork, but that didn't fit with what he knew about the Handmaiden.

"And her?"

Nero's gaze slid to Becca. Her matted black hair covered most of the pillow, and her features were too delicate from hunger and too pale. It was astounding she'd managed to fight the sedative the doctor in the facility had given her, as well as the dose from Raven, with so little body weight.

Of course, maybe that had something to do with enhanced soul magic. It wasn't common in human mages, but during the hundreds of years he'd had his *puzur*, he'd encountered a few with strong enough souls that they could heal wounds faster and, as a result, metabolize drugs faster.

He applied the bandage. That healing was nothing compared to a drake's, but it did extend their lives. Maybe he'd have a century with her before her too-short human life ended.

A vise seized his chest at that thought. Mage or no, exceptional soul magic or no, she was still human. She wasn't a sorcerer like Anaea and hadn't been reborn like Ryan. In a blink of Nero's dragon eye, Becca would be dead and he'd have lost a second inamorata.

Mother of All. One problem at a time. He wrenched his emotions into a mental box. There were other, more dire problems that needed to be dealt with first. How he felt was a luxury he couldn't afford. He might be unable to kill Becca as common sense demanded, but he still needed to protect his *puzur*.

"I need you to take a team to both the primary and secondary safe houses and clean them out."

Diablo rolled his eyes. "You burned both locations."

"I did." Nero let a growl escape. It had been a long, painful twenty-four hours, and if he couldn't convince Becca this wasn't a nightmare, it was going to get longer. "Deal with it."

Diablo's eyes narrowed and the muscles in his jaw twitched, as if he wanted to fight Nero but had somehow found his restraint. "What about the facility with the gatelock?"

"The safe houses are the priority."

"I'd say another dragon with sorcerer ability who's implanting chips into human mages is a problem. Even if it isn't somehow connected to Zenobia's failed coup, it means there are drakes still active and flying under our radar. That's dangerous."

"And if they can tie a safe house to us, that's even more dangerous." Nero glared at Diablo. "Go." *Or I'll make you.*

Diablo huffed. "Fine."

He stepped toward the door but disappeared with a whoosh of air as one of his unique rapid free gates enveloped him.

Nero sagged back into the chair. He should get up, get clean, get back to work. There wasn't time for... *this.* There would never be time for this. His love, his *true* love—he couldn't even pronounce her name with his human vessel—was dead. Fate couldn't just replace her. Dragons communicated in roars and growls and clicks with complex body language and a psychic connection similar to a mix of telepathy and empathy. When a dragon was inamorated, that psychic connection grew deeper, wider, stronger. How could he have anything like that with a human? But that wasn't the problem. His psychic connection with Becca was stronger than anything he'd had in his dragon form, even with his true love. He'd never seen through his love's eyes or experienced her pain.

Of course, maybe he was wrong.

Maybe he wasn't inamorated, and it was his broken dugga's magic making him feel like he was.

That had to be it.

A gust of wind swept down the hall, and a feminine voice said something too quiet for Nero to make out. Diablo must have gated to the kitchen in the main house first and helped Raven return with the supplies, since she couldn't free gate. Hopefully the younger black drake would then do what Nero had asked and deal with the safe houses and not turn the order into a fight.

Actually, it was kind of surprising how little a fight the whole request had been. In the past few weeks, Diablo had fought him on everything, as if he wanted to be put in his place. The fact that Diablo hadn't demanded Nero kill Becca—or tried again while Nero was down—was a stark change in character.

Raven eased into the doorway. "You can go get cleaned up now."

"Yes." He should. But he couldn't make himself get up and leave Becca. He had to be near her, bathe in her aura, touch her, kiss her, solidify the bond between their souls.

"I can handle her if she wakes and becomes violent again," Raven said.

He had no doubt his Third could.

He flexed his fingers, but still couldn't turn the thought of leaving into action. *Solidify the bond.* Except that wouldn't work, because there was no bond. He was *not* inamorated.

"I won't handcuff her this time. I promise." Raven's expression remained worried.

"I believe you." *Come on. Get up. Jeez. It shouldn't be difficult.*

She pursed her lips.

His gaze slid back to Becca. *Stand up. Come on. Leave her.*

Raven shifted in the doorway. Nero tugged his attention back to her. If he couldn't pull himself together, he'd be the danger to his *puzur* that he feared. Hell, he already *was* the danger he feared and couldn't seem to concentrate long enough to figure out what to do about it.

"How did the Council meeting go?"

"Worrisome." Which was an understatement. And something else he needed to have a plan for. He had to get Regis to rescind his order for all drakes to return to Court or he'd lose Raven's help with his kids here in the human realm. And just adding her to the Asar Nergal when she hadn't publicly announced her combat abilities would draw suspicion from Regis and Tobias and anyone else who suspected Nero was the dugga.

"Mother of All," he growled, and used his frustration to force himself to his feet. "I'm getting cleaned up."

"I'll call you if anything changes."

He opened his mouth to summon a gate but couldn't say his power word, could barely think it.

God damn it. It looked like he was washing up here.

13

D iablo paced the kitchenette, his insides writhing. His beast, curled tight within him, raged at the danger that woman, Rebecca, presented, and the emotional and physical agony radiating off Nero. It hadn't just been Anaea whose empathy had been slammed the moment Nero had gated into the transition suites, and now Diablo's beast wanted a fight.

Mother, he needed to hit something, break something, release the pressure. But if the dragon who ran wherever Rebecca had been kept knew about the safe houses, they had to be dealt with immediately. It wouldn't stop the inevitable discovery of their *puzur*—something Diablo was certain was one of the many worries clinging to Nero's emotions lately—but it could put it off until they had a plan.

And he had to trust that Nero could come up with a plan, because right now the only plan Diablo could think of was the one his beast wanted. Fight and kill them all. It didn't matter the *them* was his own kind or that dragons, even in their spirit state, were an endangered species.

Raven stepped out of the room Rebecca was in and headed into the room with the other intake, but stopped, her gaze jumping to him. Her eyes narrowed, the line of her jaw hardened, and his beast readied in expectation of the impending fight.

Not fucking now. And not with my sister. He mentally shoved at it but knew there wasn't really a way to control it. Not since his best friend's murder. Not until he managed to steady the emotions from him and everyone else churning within him, and that, without Andy's stalwart confidence in Diablo, might never happen again.

He bit back a growl as Raven stormed toward him, half in part because she was marching and the other half because there were blood and holes in her form-fitting sweater—and even though she could heal almost as fast as he could, it still should have been him getting shot because of Nero's mess.

"You don't have to hang around." She shouldered past him and opened the fridge, as if trying to disguise confronting him with getting something to drink. "I've got this."

"I know you do," he said. She was just as capable as him, even if she was now the younger sibling by a good couple hundred years. And while her emotions revealed she still didn't fully trust her earth magic in a fight, that would disappear with a bit of time and experience.

"So?" She took a single serving bottle of orange juice from the fridge and shut the door. "What is wrong with the both of you?"

"You know what's wrong with me." He forced a wry smile, unable to fully commit to the lie. She only knew half of what was wrong with him—how powerful his beast was—and only knew of a fraction of the power of his empathic earth magic. That wasn't her burden to carry.

"I said I could handle them and I will. But Nero is cleaning up in the bathroom off her bedroom and you're still here."

"I'm waiting on Asma to call me back and giving Terry time to pick up supplies before heading to the safe houses."

"And you just decided to wait here?" Her tone was clear. She didn't believe him.

"Well, what if I was hanging around to watch your back?"

She sliced a thread of wind across his cheek with a stinging snap. "Well, stop."

Blood had oozed to his chin before the cut sealed shut, and his beast howled to be released.

"If that woman wakes and sees you, you might have to kill her. No matter what Nero wants." Her expression darkened. Raven had seen the horrifying reality of what Zenobia's dragons had done to those humans they'd kidnapped, and there was a chance she had two of them on her hands now, although the last time they'd talked she'd been pretty sure the young man who remained unconscious was a natural human mage. And while she hadn't been the one to kill any of those too soul sick to save, she knew what had happened to them and knew that was a possible outcome for their new intake if he wasn't a natural human mage, and definitely the outcome for Rebecca if Raven couldn't pull off a miracle.

Except the emotions blasting from Nero to protect the woman were so strong even Diablo's beast had hesitated. It was the only reason Nero's wind had managed to deflect Diablo's knife strike to Rebecca's heart. The emotions weren't even weak or concealed. They were certain and horrified, and Diablo feared them as much as Nero did. His doyen was inamorated, shockingly, suddenly, in the blink of an eye, and if they couldn't save this human, he'd lose his mind, as well.

"You have to save this one." As much as Diablo's beast yearned to challenge Nero, the *puzur*, the Asar Nergal, and the Major Black Coterie needed its leader—and Diablo could never hope to replace Nero as doyen. He didn't want to, either, no matter what kind of fight the beast craved.

"I don't know if I can. I haven't been able to save any of the others, and those have been the ones you've convinced to meet with me." Raven glanced down the hall to the two open doors, where Rebecca and the new intake lay. "She doesn't want to be here, and I'm not sure she wants to believe this or believe what happened to her was real."

The memory of the woman's terror and ferocious determination made him shudder. He wasn't sure he'd want to believe those feelings were real, either. "Doesn't matter. We save her."

"And by *we*, you mean me."

"You're the one with the gift." Perhaps not a proper magical gift for helping those humans with earth magic—he really didn't know— but still something with a hint of power. Maybe because they were siblings, they both had empathy, but that wasn't how earth magic worked. Earth magic came from the human vessel. Before the Great Scourge, dragons had a magical essence in the core of their soul that helped them communicate and, in the end, helped power the spell their Goddess had sacrificed herself to create to save them. But earth magic—controlling water, creating gates, manipulating the earth, summoning wind—that was a dormant ability within humans acti- vated by the dragons' more powerful souls.

His phone chimed. Someone had texted him.

"Asma or Terry?" Raven asked.

Eva. His new neighbor and... girlfriend? They'd already had coffee together earlier that night and while there was attraction in her emotions—blazingly hot attraction when she thought he wasn't looking at her—there was also hesitation, which was completely understandable since they'd only met about a week ago. The attrac- tion, however, was starting to burn away the hesitation, and if he wasn't careful, he'd give in to temptation and see what other sultry emotions he could inspire within her.

But before he did that, he needed to get his God damned beast under control. If he didn't, he risked terrifying her, or worse, hurting her.

"Oh ho! Not Asma or Terry."

Crap. He'd stared at the phone for too long and hadn't answered.

"The new girlfriend, I see," Raven said.

"She's a human. It's a fling." It couldn't be anything but a fling, given how short a human's life was.

"You've never had problems with flings before."

"And I don't have a problem with this." So long as he controlled his beast and didn't accidentally maim her. "But don't call her my girlfriend and don't expect me to bring her home for dinner to meet the family."

Raven snorted. "You haven't met any of mine. I wouldn't expect to meet any of yours."

"You have a boyfriend?"

She flashed a hint of teeth, a mix of aggression and wicked sibling playfulness. "Do you honestly think I've been celibate for the last two hundred years?"

"A brother can hope." He bared his teeth back. "Of course if you're dating, that means I get to threaten someone." His beast loved that idea.

"You're not going to threaten anyone."

"Oh, come on. Isn't that a rite of passage, for the older human brother to threaten the younger sister's suitors?"

She rolled her eyes at him and headed back to the rooms with the mages. "They're not called suitors anymore."

"And I don't have a girlfriend." He dropped his attention back to his phone. Except he did, one he didn't want to scare away when his beast seized control.

14

Sensation returned to Becca, oozing out of a clinging dark haze. Warmth surrounded her, softness lay beneath her, water—it sounded like a shower—ran nearby, and a soft feminine voice in the distance said something. No beep of a heart monitor, no acerbic reek of harsh cleansers, and—so far—no voice over a tinny speaker. The hospital was gone, and, from the lack of cold and dampness, the nightmare hadn't returned her to the cave, either.

She fought the urge to open her eyes and see where she was, afraid that if she did, she'd learn she was wrong and still a prisoner.

In that moment, she felt safe. She couldn't remember the last time she'd felt that.

Except that was part of the nightmare. She *was* safe, home in her bed in Toronto after an evening of dropping off coats, sleeping bags, and food to the homeless. The new kid had called in sick, so she'd gone alone, but that hadn't been a concern. She'd been volunteering for almost a year now, and the locals knew her. Even if there was trouble, she wasn't completely helpless. She could handle herself in a fight and likely more than a few people would jump in and help her if she needed it.

But there had been trouble. Monsters disguised as men had

impossibly appeared out of whirling shadows, seized her along with two others, and the nightmare had begun...

No, the nightmare started before that? Men couldn't just appear. She'd—

God, why couldn't she remember how the night had ended?

The image of the devil's master, Nero—God, he had a name—his dark, imposing figure standing three stairs up at the end of the walkway, jumped into her mind's eye. His essence had captured her soul with a seductive strength and masculinity and called to something within her, and his thoughts had burned through her head. She was dangerous. He had to control the situation. He had to protect her.

She trembled. He'd tried to kill her. Then the devil had tried. Then...

No, just a nightmare. Just—

She jerked up, eyes open, to find herself in a strange, stark bedroom without any windows. An unopened suture kit sat on the nightstand beside her, and a beige and teal lounge chair had been pulled up close to her bed. A bed that had restraints only they weren't in use. Thank God!

Across from her, through her open door, she saw a woman in another stark bedroom, sitting in another lounge chair—a match to the one in Becca's room. The woman had her waist-length brown hair drawn back in a tight ponytail that trailed over one shoulder. She said something to the unconscious man in the bed, her voice too low for Becca to make out the words, only the tone of encouragement and concern, then the woman sat back, turning her attention to a book in her lap, her expression tight.

Becca had seen that look before, in the army hospital after the ambush on her unit. This woman was sitting a vigil, waiting to help the moment there was a problem and praying for recovery. This wasn't a guard who was bored or anticipating danger. This was someone genuinely concerned about the person in the bed. Becca didn't know how she knew this, but something whispered at the back of her mind saying it was true.

Just like she knew this bedroom was real and—

Except it wasn't real. It couldn't be. Which meant her sense about the woman wasn't real, either. Nothing was real, and she wasn't safe. She might not be able to see the devil or Nero at the moment, but that didn't mean they weren't nearby. For all Becca knew, she was back in the hospital and Stanbury would storm in.

She needed to get out of there. If she was quiet, maybe she could sneak out the door. But how long would she have to run until she felt safe or Nero found her again? Somehow he'd found her at Stanbury's hospital. He'd find her again and kill her this time.

Except he'd saved her twice from Stanbury's men—getting shot in the chest for his trouble—and again when the devil had tried to kill her. Not to mention that, mere minutes before those hundreds of people had started screaming in her head, his thoughts had changed from her being a danger to him needing to protect her and needing to convince her this was real.

Was it real? "How can I tell?"

The woman in the chair glanced up, her gaze locking with Becca's.

Shit. Had she said that out loud? *No chance of sneaking out now.* Her thoughts were muddled, flickering from normal to loud, with whispers—but thankfully no one screaming—constantly in the background.

"Do you need something?" The woman set the book on the nightstand, stood, and eased across the hall into Becca's doorway. A hint of something—warmth? calm?—joined the whispers for a second, then vanished. "Are you hungry? Thirsty?"

Not the questions of a captor. But this could be a new trick, a new torture from the nightmare. "I'd like to go home."

The woman's expression remained calmly concerned, no hint that Becca's request would be refused. "I can make that happen."

"But?" There was always a but. That was how the nightmare worked... except the more she pushed at that thought, poked and pulled at it with mental fingers, the less real it felt, when it should have been feeling stronger.

Unless, of course, that was the nightmare, too.

Jeez. At some point, she was just going to have to decide on something, and God help her, she was leaning toward reality and not a nightmare.

But then those monsters—

Her pulse leapt into a roar, and she fought to slow it back down. *Not going to think about that.*

"There's no but. Although—" The woman's gaze dipped to Becca's torso. "I might recommend a change of clothes."

"And the others?" Maybe if she was vague, the woman would tell Becca if Nero or Stanbury had her...

No, wait. She knew who had her, because she recognized the woman. She'd been at that second location Nero had taken her to. Which meant the guy in the bed across the hall had to be the guy in the bed from there.

"You mean Nero or—"

"The devil?" Becca asked.

The woman frowned.

"Diablo?"

"Oh, my brother." She rolled her eyes. "He picked that name a long time ago, and I can't tell if he regrets it or not."

"So he's just a person?" That didn't make sense. He had magic. They all had magic. Which was impossible. Magic didn't exist. It wasn't real, it—

"He's a person, but not a human." The woman's expression grew serious and more warmth seeped into Becca's head. "But you know that."

"He's a monster?" A shiver swept through Becca. They'd torn into her soul, boxed her up until her mind had screamed itself into confusion.

"You know that isn't true, either." The woman shifted, as if she wanted to go to Becca and offer her comfort. *But I need her to hold it together first. Please, Mother.* The woman's mental tones grew strained, as if she was fighting to concentrate while looking outwardly calm.

"I am holding it together."

The woman's eyes flashed wide, and the warmth within Becca vanished and cold panic flooded in.

Becca's throat tightened and her pulse roared louder. *Keep it together. Just for a little while.* "Or at least I'm as together as I can be, given what—"

God damn it. Not going to think about *that*. She was sick and tired of feeling helpless. She wasn't helpless. She'd proven that when she'd attempted to escape from Stanbury. Jeez, just for the next ten minutes, she was going to hold her shit together.

The warmth returned, bolstering her determination. Yes. She could do this, face whatever this was.

"Those who did that to you were monsters, but not all of us are."

"Sure. That's why Nero and your brother keep trying to kill me." But Nero had protected her from the devil.

The woman raised an eyebrow, as if she could hear Becca's thoughts as well, but Becca had no sense the woman was in her head, not like Nero had been. Maybe she just knew Becca's statement was wrong... because it was wrong.

"Fine. Nero only tried to kill me once."

He had to have thought he was ending your suffering. Sudden telepathy only increases the risk.

"The risk of what?"

"Excuse me?"

"Sudden telepathy only increases the risk of what?"

"We need to teach you to control that." *If she can conquer the soul sickness.* "It's rude to listen to someone's thoughts."

But *they* had listened to her thoughts, dug into her soul, laughed at her screams, all to awaken— "Holy shit! *This*, being able to hear other people's thoughts, is what they wanted."

"They wouldn't have known your ability was telepathy, but yes." Raven offered a sad smile. "My name is Raven. If I come in and sit, will you attack me?"

"Do I need to protect myself from you?" Yep, Raven had confessed to being one of those monsters, but nothing about her set off alarms within Becca. Not like the devil, Diablo, had, and not like the bells that were still alarming but also different for Nero.

More warmth spread into Becca's head, and her thoughts glommed into it. The warm calm had to be Raven's magic—and she wasn't going to dwell on the magic part for fear she'd start screaming. It was soothing her… manipulating her—

No— Well, yes, she did get a sense of being manipulated, but there was no feeling of malicious intent.

Could she trust that? God, she wanted to. She was so tired of being afraid. If this was still a dream, at least it was a reprieve from the terror.

"You need to be very gentle with yourself," Raven said.

"Because of the soul sickness?"

"Yes. Unless you're a child or someone who's already sensitive, the human brain has trouble accepting the truth about the world." Raven eased into the room, pulled the chair back from the bed, and sat. Becca wasn't certain if the distance was to put her at ease or Raven. Even with the space between them, though, Becca could see the strain in Raven's eyes, and—Becca concentrated on the warmth— she could feel the determination behind it and confirmed the sensation came from Raven.

"Magic is real," Raven said. "And so are—"

"Dragons." The word rushed out of Becca with the release of an emotional weight.

The warmth chilled, then the muscles in Raven's jaw tightened and it flooded back in. *You can handle this. Diablo says you have to handle this for Nero's sake, but I need a win, too. I don't want to lose anyone else. I can't, please.*

"Oh, don't worry. I'm a fighter," Becca said, her voice low. She didn't care if she was being rude by responding to Raven's thoughts. In that moment, she recognized a kindred spirit, someone ready to fight with everything she had to save innocent lives. She had no idea how this woman, this *dragon*, had ended up with the monster the other dragons feared or why her brother named himself after the devil, but the warmth radiating from her and the whisper of her thoughts solidified Becca's certainty. She could trust this woman.

But that only strengthened the sensation that this was real, that what had happened to her—

Not going to finish that thought. Her body trembled, and a cold sweat chilled her skin, defying her determination.

Not. Going. To think about. What they did. What—

"We are spirits of dragons." Raven captured Becca's gaze and held her steady, seeping more warmth into her head. "You've got this." *You need to handle this.*

"And Nero and your brother kill them?" Except Nero had been sending Diablo after those humans who'd been prisoners as well.

"Think of them like the police."

Becca cocked an eyebrow. "Seems pretty extreme that killing someone is your first choice for law enforcement."

Raven matched Becca's dry look. "You've had one of us in your head. You know we're predators."

"I've had three, actually."

Three? Oh, Mother. "I'm sorry."

"Yeah, that's what Nero said... thought?" She wasn't sure anymore if he'd said it or thought it. The escape from Stanbury's facility was starting to blur, and there was something she was forgetting, something important, but she couldn't remember what and had a feeling part of Raven's warmth was dulling her memories. At the moment, she wasn't sure it mattered... which wasn't like her at all, but—

Focus on holding it together. Focus on the conversation. Deal with everything else later. "So Nero and your brother killed them? The ones who had me?"

"Yes." The warmth chilled for a second, and Becca got the impression what had happened to the monsters who'd tortured her was more complicated than that.

"And those of us who were kidnapped?"

So far no one's made it. They've all succumbed to the soul sickness.

Which meant terrible odds for Becca. A tremble swept through her again, and she hugged herself and fought to cling to the soothing warmth in her head.

Raven's eyes flashed wide. *Shit. She heard that.* "I'm sorry. I'll try to control—"

"Your thoughts?" Becca asked. "You're telling me the impossible is possible, but I'm not even sure controlling your thoughts is possible."

"I've never worked with a telepath before."

"Neither have I." Becca flashed a hint of a smile. *What the hell, might as well go all in.* "I'm pretty good at beating terrible odds." And if she held onto that thought, and Raven's calm, maybe… just maybe?

Another shiver.

Come on. Hold it together. You've gotten through at least ten minutes. Now try for ten more.

"All right, then." Raven stood. "I brought you down some clothes. They're on the shelf in the hall. Nero is still in your bathroom, but you can use the one next door to clean up, then we'll get you some food." *And if you haven't gone crazy, we'll move forward.*

"Baby steps." Sure, she could handle this, except—

Realization snapped through her, and her pulse leapt back into a rapid tattoo. "Werner. Glenn. The implanted tracker."

Raven sat forward and her warmth surged through Becca. "I don't know about those people, but the tracker has been disabled."

"I have to save them. If Werner got away, I have to warn him about the tracker." But all logic screamed that with a tracker implanted in his body, Werner wouldn't have gotten away. Still, she had to hope, had to go to the emergency meeting place. He and Glenn hadn't left her behind in that cave, and they easily could have. She owed them.

"Get cleaned up, grab something to eat, then we'll find your friends." *I just hope they're not soul sick. Please don't let her be soul sick.* Raven offered a soft smile that, if Becca hadn't just heard her worries, would have been convincing, then stepped out of the room. She glanced into the other room at the still unconscious young man before heading down the hall, taking her warmth with her.

The cold seeped into Becca's skin and her teeth chattered. *Fine or not, she had to get Werner and Glenn out of Stanbury's hands.*

God, she wanted to be fine, but with Raven gone the harsh truth crowded in her thoughts, slashing at her insides and trying to rip her apart again.

She gripped the blanket beneath her. *Beat the odds. Hold it together. Save Werner's ass and return the debt you owe him.*

The whispers in her head grew louder.

She shoved at them, trying to push them farther away, but they didn't budge. At least this time they were soft and she couldn't understand them.

She can do it. Raven's thoughts whispered through her. *D says she has to for Nero's sake.*

Nero. Becca's gaze jumped to the other door in the bedroom, where the sound of running water emanated. The door stood partially ajar. If she was at the correct angle, she could see in. Nero had tried to kill her. Then he'd saved her. Raven had said— no, she'd *thought* Nero had been trying to end Becca's suffering. No one else's mind had survived the torture from the cave. He'd probably thought she was going crazy, too. Maybe she already was.

Another shiver rushed over her, and she yearned for Raven's warmth in her head, any warmth, really. A shower might be the best place to start.

She hung her legs over the side of the bed, her gaze locked on the space between the door and the frame. This new angle gave her a perfect vantage into the bathroom and the glassed-in shower stall. Nero stood in a stream of water with his shirt off, pants on, and head bowed. Water sluiced over his muscular physique, the powerful muscles in his back and shoulders bunched with tension, accentuating his sculpted lines and swarthy complexion as well as the stiffness in his body. The sense of danger and strength now visibly radiated around him in an intense black aura, reminding her of the ferocity that had been in his gaze when he'd looked at her. Even just standing there, his eyes closed, he looked like he was about to face the fight of his life and had to figure out a solution before it was too late.

All that worry. All that pain. It made her chest ache. How had she not noticed it before?

Maybe because she'd been running for her life?

Or maybe because he'd been hiding it, and there, in the shower, where he thought no one could see, he'd let down his guard. Raven was worried she wouldn't be able to save Becca. Did Nero worry about that, too? It was hard to believe a man, or rather a dragon, as hard-edged as Nero would worry about saving the life of one person. No, it had to be with his need to protect, not himself but others. Yes, that had been the driving fear screaming the loudest in her head before she'd been sedated... the second time.

She could relate to that, as well. She'd joined the army to help and protect those who couldn't protect themselves. That, however, didn't mean her goals were aligned with his or that he wouldn't use her in order to protect those he cared about. If she was smart, she would go next door, clean up as fast as possible, eat Raven's meal, and then get the hell out of there. To hell with Raven's help finding Werner. It would be safer to go it alone. But no matter how smart that idea was, she found she couldn't look away from Nero and stepped closer to the bathroom door.

15

Nero ground his fists against the smooth-tiled shower wall and let the cold water rush over his skin and soak into his pants. If he'd been able to force himself back to his bathroom, attached to his bedroom, he would have been able to strip down and let the water run over more flesh, drawing more of its power into his soul, but he hadn't—and he hadn't wanted to risk Raven barging in on him naked if something went wrong with Becca, so he'd kept his pants on. As it was, even if he was completely bare, he doubted the running water would have its full effect. He'd just hoped—

But hoping wouldn't help anything.

Mother!

He growled and pressed his first two knuckles into the seam between the tiles. He'd only intended to wipe his dried blood from his torso, but the turmoil in his soul squeezed his chest so tight it was hard to breathe, so he'd stepped into the shower. Just for a minute, to think. But he was pretty sure more than a minute had passed, and his thoughts still whirled, always jumping back to *protect*. He had to protect her, had to save her, had to be with her. If she was soul sick, he had to find a way to mend her soul—and she wasn't a water drake, like him, so running water wouldn't help.

Human lives were so short.

A drake couldn't be inamorated twice.

God damn it. He had to regain his focus. First question: what to do about Becca? A dragon with the ability to make a gatelock knew she had a mental connection to the dugga—he could only hope that dragon didn't know he was the dugga.

That meant he had to keep her here, no matter what he'd said to Diablo about not restraining her. She couldn't fall into the wrong hands. She had to fall into his hands—

Wait, no, there wouldn't be any hands involved in anything, because she wasn't inamorated back, and he wasn't going to consummate their soul bond. That would only make a bad situation worse.

Another growl curled in his throat. If he really was inamorated, he wouldn't be able to resist her, no matter what he wanted. He didn't doubt Hunter and Capri, probably even Grey, had tried to fight their soul bonds. All three of them were inamorated out of species or out of coterie. That was a problem none of them had gone looking for, and Nero knew from the first time around that resisting was pointless.

Please let the sensation come from our mental connection and not a true soul bond. He could survive that. He could work with that. It made more sense than being inamorated again.

Sure.

Right.

Okay.

Now, get back to the problems at hand: the dragon who's going after you, the problems at Court, and how to protect the kids.

Something shifted at the edge of his senses. He wasn't sure what and couldn't explain how it caught his attention, but his gaze jumped from the shower floor to the door, and his heart froze.

Becca stood in the doorway, her expression worried, her hair a mess, and the hospital gown stained with his blood from when she'd stabbed him and he'd captured her against his body to escape. Even bedraggled and filthy, she was breathtaking, and the thought of her body against his drew a heat within him that his combat adrenalin had overridden during the fight.

She caught his gaze with a strength in her expression he already knew she possessed, from their mental connection. If anyone could conquer the soul sickness that resulted from having mind and body invaded by a powerful dragon spirit, she could.

"Sorry." She didn't sound sorry, and she didn't look away.

He shut off the water and reached for a towel, her gaze churning what little calm he'd managed to find in the shower into howling primal instinct. He belonged to her whether she accepted him or not. If she told him to leave her forever, he'd respect that. It would break his heart, but he couldn't make her life miserable just to be with her. There would never be another—

Except that wasn't true. She *was* another, a second one. Which meant this sensation wasn't true. His soul was confused. The dugga's magic was broken and making him feel this way. His unnatural Handmaiden-imbued telepathy had somehow locked with whatever earth magic Becca possessed. That was all.

And yet knowing the truth didn't change how he felt, how he irrationally craved her, had to be near her, wanted to draw her close, wrap his arms around her, feel her body pressed against his, fully seal the bond between their souls. Forever.

Jeez. He clenched his jaw and draped the towel over his head to dry his hair. Maybe if he couldn't see her—

But the loss of sight only made him hyperaware of her, standing a few feet away with her blazing red aura, half as brilliant as when he'd first seen her, but still squintingly bright and cutting through the towel's fabric. Her power crackled against his aura, shivering over his senses, making him hard—

Who was he kidding? Harder. He could barely tell she was human, even with his enhanced ability to sense auras. Half of the members of the Asar Nergal might not be able to tell she was human, but he had no idea if that was the power of her earth magic, her soul magic, a result of being inamorated—which God damn he wasn't—or something else.

"Did you use all the hot water?" she asked, her husky alto sliding, warm and sensual, over him.

Mine. Protect.

He growled and yanked the towel from his head. *Get your shit together.*

Fear flickered in her eyes for a second, then her gaze hardened and she squared her shoulders, which only turned him on more. "I mean, that's not a problem."

It should be. She should have all the hot water in the world—

Stop it. Not inamorated, remember?

A shiver swept over her, making him cold just looking at her. Soul mate or definitely not, she'd been through an ordeal. For the moment, he wasn't trapped in her head, but that didn't mean he couldn't imagine her pain and confusion. Right now, she wasn't trying to escape. He'd assume that was because of a conversation with Raven, but Becca's mental state was unstable, and she could change her mind at any time.

"I'll get you some clean clothes."

"That woman, Raven, said she already got me some."

Of course she did. "Okay, then." He should go. Give Becca a chance to clean up. Alone. Putting some space between them might help him regain his bearings.

But he couldn't make himself summon a gate, let alone walk out of the room. Walking out would just bring him closer to her. And he really wanted to get closer.

"She said I could use the bathroom next door." Except Becca didn't turn away from him, didn't even glance in the direction of the other room. He didn't think it was possible that she was just as captivated as he was. That was desperate hope, begging for something that wasn't real. She had to be in shock.

Even if she wasn't strapped to a bed or running for her life, and even if Raven hadn't told her the truth, this new situation was still a lot to process. He couldn't afford to make the wrong move here. He couldn't scare her away, not because of his messed-up emotions, but because if that other drake got her again, everyone he was certain he cared about would be killed. Really.

Focus on the situation. Shut everything else down. That was what made him an effective dugga and doyen. He hadn't survived more than two thousand years in a society of predators by letting his emotions get the better of him.

But he couldn't get his mind to work past the thought of her, standing before him, her gaze locked on him, capturing his soul. Her. There was only her.

No, there wasn't. He had a house full of teens, a whole network of natural human mages throughout the world who'd *graduated* from his program, and dragons who depended on him. They were his family. Their love and friendship had carried his shattered soul through all these years, patching it together enough that he'd survived the death of his inamorata. Focus on that. Whichever drake had captured Becca, he endangered all that, and to stop him, he needed more information.

Nero opened his mouth to demand details from Becca about the facility, but the words froze in his throat. At the moment, she might look mentally stable, but she couldn't be. Not enough time had passed for her to even fully get her bearings. Interrogating her wouldn't help. He needed to ease into the conversation.

"I'll arrange for food."

"Raven said that, too."

Son of a— "Did Raven offer medical help, too? How's your shoulder and ribs?" Hadn't he thought she had a broken collarbone and cracked ribs? But she wasn't showing any sign of pain.

Becca frowned and rolled her shoulders. Confusion flickered over her expression. "I thought—" Another shiver swept over her, and she gripped the doorframe as if to steady herself. The confusion deepened into panic and her breath turned into sharp gasps. She pressed one hand to her ribs but didn't wince in pain. "They were— This isn't... real?"

Shit. With one quick question, he'd managed to ruin everything.

He rushed toward her, every instinct screaming to comfort her. "You're all right."

"You tried to kill me." She jerked away, stumbled, and fell onto her butt on the concrete bedroom floor.

He dropped to his knees but managed to keep from reaching out to her. "I was wrong." *Please, let me hold you. I'll make this right. I'll kill the monsters. I'll—*

"You're a monster." She squeezed her eyes shut. "No, you're a dragon."

"And this is real," Raven said from the doorway. She crouched where she was and didn't approach. "Just take a breath."

"But my ribs were broken."

And they should still be. Only human sorcerers had healing like a dragon. And it was too much to hope that his soul had picked a sorcerer. They were so rare. He was still kind of shocked he had one living under his roof.

"Does not having broken ribs put you in danger?" Raven asked.

Becca frowned. "No, but—"

"If it's not a danger, maybe you shouldn't worry about it right now."

Mother, he had to do something, but this was Raven's specialty. He and his team brought the human mages to her and, of those she could save, she somehow just knew how to get them to accept reality.

"I don't understand." Becca hugged herself, her jaw clenched tight.

Except none of them had gone through what Becca had. Three dragon souls, each tearing into her, trying to awaken a magic that was now screwing up his life. She had to still be determined to hold onto her mind, and a part of that for humans involved clinging to their perceived reality.

"You do understand. You just don't want to." The muscles in Raven's jaw tightened, adding to the evidence of what Nero had suspected for years but had no proof—that Raven had some kind of earth magic that influenced humans. "You know what I'm thinking. You know I'm telling you the truth."

His mind lurched and he grabbed onto that detail. "Telepath?" Nero mouthed to Raven, and she gave a tight nod.

Well, that confirmed how Becca had managed to highjack his dugga's mental connection. She had one of her own. Here was hoping it was still sporadic and wasn't always on, like the only other telepath he knew about. Always on would create problems. It meant he couldn't hide anything from her, and he certainly couldn't lie.

Wonderful. That just made everything more challenging.

"One thing at a time," Raven said.

Becca nodded and hugged herself, as if she could physically hold her mind together. "Baby steps."

"Yeah. Let's get you cleaned up."

Becca's gaze lifted to Nero, making his soul tremble with the need to comfort her, even though his logical mind knew drawing closer would only terrify her. "He used up all the hot water."

Raven cocked an eyebrow, and her gaze dipped to his soaked pants and the puddle around his bare feet.

"I didn't use all the hot water." He hadn't even turned on the hot water. He'd just desperately needed to think. Not that the soak had helped, and now Raven knew something was wrong. She was a water drake, too. She knew what running water meant to their kind, now that they were trapped in human vessels.

"There's a casserole in the oven." Raven straightened and swept her ponytail over her shoulder, radiating a confidence he was starting to see more often in the young dragon. The strain in her jaw, however, remained. "Nero, why don't you get changed and meet us in the kitchenette?"

"Yeah." It was a good idea, but he couldn't make himself say his power word to summon a gate and get a change of clothes from his bedroom.

The strain tightened around her eyes.

God damn it, just summon a gate. Raven had this. She was more qualified to help than he was, and even if she wasn't, his very presence seemed to make Becca unstable.

He bit back a growl. Do it. Summon. He hissed his power word, making Becca jump. His chest ache at her fear, and he pressed his hand to the bathroom door. A black vortex appeared, and he staggered through before it had completely formed and before his emotions stopped him.

16

I vette stood in her office on the top floor of her research facility and stared out the bank of windows at the city lights beyond. Her office tower wasn't the tallest in the Newgate city center, but it sat on the edge of a high rise cluster and offered her a spectacular view of the original century-old business district and half of the state university's campus, which looked more like a park than an educational facility. This high up, with the ground covered in snow in a typical February freeze and early evening darkness creating shadows hiding the hustle of pedestrians on the street, she could almost forget that her facility was in chaos.

Almost.

The red light at the top of her computer screen—reflected in the office windows—indicated Rebecca Scott's tracker had been deactivated, and Ivette's computer techs claimed they had no idea what had gone wrong. Their best guess was that Rebecca had been somehow hit with a violent surge of electricity that had fried the tracker, or it had been cut out and deactivated. Given the device's location, Ivette doubted Rebecca had removed it, and the last time the tracker had worked, she'd been halfway across town from the other subject who'd escaped with her, so he couldn't have cut it out, either. But the electric surge was also doubtful.

Which left magic.

Ivette turned to her computer, reran the security video of the fight outside, and paused it on a clean image of the dragon. Nero Tassinari. Given how private the black dragon was, there was a surprising amount of information on him. Of course, that might be due to his age, and the fact that her association had been gathering information on dragons since the Dark Ages. Capturing and torturing a few dragons over the years had also helped gather more details.

It shocked her a dragon as old and powerful as Tassinari would get involved with anything relating to humans. He was a known leader of one of the dragon clans and believed to be a dragon Traditionalist—which meant he approved of slaughtering humans who possessed magic.

She hit play and ran the video to the part where Nero grabbed Rebecca and dragged her into the street and out of sight. He'd gone straight for her. He hadn't tried to kill her or Werner Scholtz, which was surprising, given Werner had clearly demonstrated his magic to consume someone's life force with a touch and had taken out more of her men than she'd like to admit. Her head of security would need to be replaced. He hadn't imparted to his men the importance of not letting Scholtz touch them.

She started the video from the beginning again. Tassinari went straight for Rebecca. According to the tracker, he'd gated her twenty blocks over and then gated her away again when the facility's men went to pick her up. This had to confirm he was a high-level member of the Asar Nergal, someone the dugga trusted to apprehend the human listening to all his telepathic communications. And while killing Rebecca outright would have been more efficient, the dugga had proven once again he was a cautious dragon and chose to investigate Rebecca's power before ending her. That was what Ivette would do. Find the reason, the cause, and a way to prevent it in the future, then eliminate it.

Her office door opened and Dinah Koehn stormed in. "Didn't you warn the men about Werner Scholtz? Security is your purview."

Ivette fought to not roll her eyes. Dinah cared too much about their employees and especially about the subjects. Yes, they walked a fine line between gathering the necessary information about humans with unnaturally acquired magic and endangering those humans, but lives were on the line.

"The head of security was appropriately briefed. He'd even witnessed a demonstration of Scholtz's abilities, so he was fully aware of the danger."

"Werner outright killed three of them, two more are in comas, and five sustained injuries that will put them out of commission for weeks."

But those injuries had more likely come from Tassinari's wind magic. "So you're saying we need to hire more men."

"I'm saying you should have let me fully sedate Rebecca."

Ivette hit stop on the video—it landed on a blurry image of Tassinari—and turned the screen. "But the facility just got a surprise lead on the dugga."

Dinah crossed her arms. "Which beast is that?"

"Nero Tassinari."

"The Major Black Coterie's doyen?"

"Indeed."

"What is he doing in Newgate?" Dinah inched closer to Ivette's desk. "All reports indicate he's usually at his home in Rome. He's been there exclusively for the last sixty years."

"I think the dugga sent him to grab Ms. Scott."

"You think the dugga is more powerful than an ancient dragon? Maybe *he's* the dugga."

"The dugga wouldn't be so stupid as to grab Scott himself." Ivette turned her monitor back into proper position. "We need to find out if Tassinari has returned to Rome."

"We need to activate the elimination protocol and destroy the facility before Nero returns," Dinah said with a grimace, her expression clear that she didn't like the idea.

Ivette didn't like the idea, either. She might not like Dinah, and they might not have the same goals, but they'd been running this facility and overseeing this research for years. If they followed the required elimination protocol, they'd lose everything.

"Do we think Tassinari would return here so soon?" Yes, he'd return, but—if he was as smart as all information they'd gathered suggested—he wouldn't rush back. Besides, he was the only lead Ivette had ever gotten in identifying the dugga, and she was damned if she was going to waste her time following protocol and let him slip away. Dinah might want to research the unnatural magic and the degrees of insanity developed by those forced to have a dragon soul invade their body, but Ivette wanted every dragon dead, and she was starting with those who reveled in murdering humans with a naturally born magical ability.

Dinah's eyes narrowed. "Protocol clearly states if the facility is compromised, everything must be destroyed."

"I know what the protocol is. I'm in charge of security." Ivette gripped the back of her desk chair. "I also know your life's work is in this facility. We have a secondary location…" A location Tassinari didn't know about. If they moved, she might not be able to justify keeping a full security force here for when the dragon returned—and he, or someone else just as significant, would return to find out what was going on here—but if she slowed the transfer down, she could have at least a partial force.

"I could arrange to have the servers and the most important experiments moved while the suppression magic on the new cells is activated," Dinah said.

"We could turn the elimination priority list into a moving priority list. The most sensitive information first. If Tassinari or anyone else shows up, we can always switch to the elimination protocol."

"I wouldn't lose everything, and we wouldn't have to euthanize all the subjects." Relief flashed across Dinah's face before she schooled her features back to stern superiority. "We still need to get Rebecca Scott back and put Werner Scholtz down."

Ivette raised an eyebrow. That kind of bloodthirstiness wasn't like Dinah at all.

"All the unnaturals are mentally unstable. We've known that for hundreds of years now," Dinah said. "Even if Scholtz hasn't been demonstrating the same degree of insanity as previous subjects, his power has only grown in strength since we detained him and that was only two days ago. He's a danger to society."

And she must have had a thing for one of the guys he'd killed.

"Killing Scholtz won't help us," Stanbury said. Dinah might share the leadership of the facility, but she wasn't the brains behind the operation. She possessed the medical education and scientific curiosity to further the facility's knowledge about dragons and unnaturals, but she couldn't envision a master plan nor set one into motion. That was Ivette's job.

Like her father and mother, and theirs before them for generations, she—and Dinah as well—had been born into a select class of humans who knew the truth about the universe and possessed its true power. And like the generations before, she had been told of the terror of the Asar Nergal, the dragon death squad.

Her ancestors had tried to destroy the ferocious beasts but had only managed to force the creatures into hiding in humans, and for generations they had worked to finish the job. Having a direct link to the dugga's communication would be a major success, something her association hadn't seen in centuries. Captured members of the Asar Nergal or any dragon would be a feather in her career cap, and while killing the dugga was believed to be the ultimate goal by many of her peers, that wouldn't solve the main problem. Ivette had confirmed from multiple sources over the years that the dugga was a position with power, not a dragon. Killing the dugga would alert the dragons' sorcerer, and another dragon would be given the power.

But *take* the dugga's magic, and Ivette was willing to bet the dragon sorcerer wouldn't notice. She'd researched imbued spells for most of her adult life. The magic was always linked to the bearer's life force, but not the bearer's essence. One life force worked the same as another. Once she took the dugga's power, she'd have a telepathic link to every member of the Asar Nergal. She could find and kill them all.

But to do that, she needed Rebecca Scott to lead her to the dugga.

"How does not apprehending Werner and keeping him alive help us?" Dinah asked.

"Scott's tracker has gone dead. His hasn't. He risked recapture to help her escape, and she hesitated to leave him behind. If the dugga doesn't kill her, she's going to contact Scholtz. And when she does, we can grab her and then the dugga."

17

Tobias sat on a stone bench at the mouth of the royal archives. No matter what he yearned for, he didn't have time to wander the massive maze of papers and books containing the history and activities of the Dragon Court since the Handmaiden had created it — Okay, maybe it didn't hold the *entire* history and activities. The previous chamberlain hadn't been as fastidious as Tobias about recordkeeping, probably because the paperwork hadn't been his hoard. But for Tobias, this was his hoard, even if he knew it wasn't actually his.

Yes, he journaled every day and kept those pages in a vault in his suite, and that was his real hoard, but the records from the Chamberlain's Office had somehow become an extension of his collection. It didn't matter that they weren't really his. His impulse to collect records, keep a history, surround himself with truths, facts, and minute details, made him crave them. He'd been chamberlain for over eight hundred years, had handled millions of records and reports during his tenure, and he had no intention of stepping down. They were his.

The problem, however, lay with his intention of remaining Court Chamberlain. It was becoming increasingly dangerous to stay in the

Royal Coterie's employ, and that included danger—perhaps the biggest danger—from his doyen, Prince Regis.

"Thinking that again?" Ophelia eased from the shadows of the farthest passage, one of five connecting this modest entrance, with its three simple benches, to the maze beyond. With her dark skin, hair, and clothes, she could have been standing in that shadow for as long as he'd been sitting on the bench and he wouldn't have noticed her. She'd even confessed that she possessed the ability to mute her aura, making her harder to detect and appear younger and weaker—not that he could see auras and prove her claim. But no doubt that kind of ability gave her an advantage in her position as head of Internal Inspection.

She sat on the bench opposite him and met his gaze, a hint of a challenge in her eyes, but not the kind that said she wanted his job... or him. "If you leave, the rest of us will be in danger."

And while his second-in-command could manage the day-to-day business of running Court—finances, food, maintenance, etc—he had no experience with Tobias's responsibilities with maintaining dragon security—liaising with all the doyens and their heads of coterie security, handling disputes, arranging replacement vessels and new identities, as well as top-level dragon security. No other dragon was capable of handling the chamberlain's responsibilities, and the Dragon Court would fall into disarray if he left without preparing a successor.

Except Court was already in disarray, and there wasn't anything he could do to fix it. Even sitting near his unofficial hoard wasn't helping to ease his worry or inspire a solution.

"I doubt you'll be in danger," he said.

"No one really likes to think about Internal Investigations." She offered a half shrug. "I'm sure I'll be the last to be noticed. No, I was thinking about Vessel Appropriations, Security, Maintenance, that new secretary... what is his name?"

"Xiphos." A young yellow drake who'd recently changed allegiance to the royal coterie from the Minor Yellow in hopes of advancing his position in Court. Too bad he'd made the switch a mere fifty years before things started going south.

"What about your Clean Teams? Capri won't be able to keep her change of allegiance a secret forever."

"Capri hasn't changed coteries." Although he'd been suspecting she had for a few weeks now. He just didn't know who her new doyen was or why the change.

Ophelia cocked an eyebrow, reminding him with one simple action that it was foolish to deny anything to a drake who could always, whether she wanted to or not, hear peoples' thoughts.

"Has she thrown in with Hunter?" If Hunter raised his banner as doyen of a new coterie, that might solve all of Tobias's problems. He didn't need Ophelia's reports to guess that dragons of all colors would leave their coteries to support the only dragon able to take dragon form. Only the Traditionalists would stand against him because of his human sorcerer inamorata.

"Hunter will never proclaim himself a doyen and take the throne."

"A dragon can hope, can't he?" He'd liked working with Hunter, even if the red drake had been terse with all his reports and paperwork. As prince's assassin, he'd gotten the job done with as little fuss as possible and hadn't gotten involved in politics—which, with the enormous power of the rebirth medallion in his possession, he could have. It had only been recently that Hunter had created problems, and even then, he'd been in reaction to Zenobia's attempt to oust Regis.

"Hoping Hunter will change his color won't solve the immediate problem." Ophelia sat forward. "I've searched all of Court. There's nothing to indicate what happened to King Constantine and no one's thinking about having disposed of his body."

"And you're still getting mixed messages from Regis?" Last time they'd talked, Ophelia hadn't been able to tell if Regis had murdered his father or had just wanted to.

"I still can't confirm anything from Regis. His thoughts are getting worse. His soul sickness is progressing faster than his father's."

"I'd hoped we'd have more time." Tobias slid his gaze to the aisle behind Ophelia. "More time to convince Hunter to step up, and get at least one Traditionalist to change his mind about him and add in support."

"After Zenobia's coup, getting any Traditionalist to change his or her mind in the next hundred or so years about a human sorcerer, even if she's somehow inamorated to a dragon, is going to be tough." Ophelia rubbed her temples. "We don't have that kind of time."

"I know." Mother, he needed to come up with a solution fast or more dragon souls would be forever lost to the universal ether. "Pike's report about the Major Green Coterie might have indicated everything is under control, but even I can see factions forming in his membership. If he doesn't step up and regain control, or step down and give leadership to a stronger drake, fighting will begin."

"It already has."

"Shit. Why haven't I been told about this?"

"Pike's coterie security got to the scene of the assassination and cleaned up before anyone noticed. The Asian Clean Team wasn't notified. What I can garner from Pike's Second is that five green drakes who were suspected of starting a faction against Pike were murdered."

"Just great." Not only was his prince torturing dragons indiscriminately, doyens were murdering their own coterie members in their determination to maintain control.

"It gets better. I'm hearing whispers that members of the Sect of the Divine Mother are planning something, but so far I don't know any of the specifics."

"Wonderful. We need more information on that. If drakes are angry now, they're going to get furious when Regis starts enforcing his decree that all dragons return to Court. I've been instructed to assemble a retrieval squad, using the most powerful dragons from royal security, and have been given authority to use any force necessary, even if that means losing dragon souls."

Ophelia swore. "We can't wait for the Handmaiden's return.

We're going to have to do something, pick someone, and force them to take the throne."

Mother of All, why had she left? Except what his soul really wanted the answer to was why she'd left *him*? He'd thought— No, it had merely been a hope that they'd been friends. He had no proof either way.

If he was honest with himself, he wasn't sure he'd ever seen the real Handmaiden, even when he'd stopped by her chambers to fill her in on the happenings at Court and she'd invited him in for tea. Perhaps all he'd ever seen was a slightly softer version of the mask she wore in public.

Sure, he believed she didn't invite many dragons into her inner chambers, but that didn't mean his invitation had meant something different or that his information about her habits were correct. What did he really know about her? Clearly not enough, since he had no idea she'd planned to leave.

"And now you're thinking that," Ophelia said, the concern in her gaze belying the boredom of her tone.

"Well, I'm pissed."

"Doesn't sound like it to me."

"You're not listening right. She had to have known Regis was soul sick. She has a full sorcerer's power and can cast an auger spell." Maybe if he focused on being abandoned, that would ignite his missing fury. He wasn't some child abandoned by a parent. He was an ancient black dragon. He'd seen things, done things. A colleague leaving without notice when the situation was about to become dire shouldn't make him worried. It should make him furious.

Ophelia pursed her lips.

"Yeah, I know," he said. "That's the root of the problem."

"You're not furious at her."

"I'm scared for her."

"She's disappeared before. When Regis took the throne from Constantine."

"There was a clear line of succession. The kind of upheaval happening then is nothing to what we're facing now. And knowing what we went through with her absence during that, I doubt she'd willingly leave now." There had to be a good reason for the Handmaiden to just up and leave, and if she was in trouble, then who ruled the dragon throne was insignificant to what was coming. With Grey and Ivy having recovered the rebirth coin and Hunter inamorated to a full sorcerer likely able to cast the rebirth spell, dragonkind might be able to survive without the Handmaiden, but it wouldn't be easy, and many drakes would rebel.

"She'll come back."

"Mother, I hope so." And it was his job to hold it all together until she did... if he didn't get caught in the political crossfire.

18

Nero changed into dry clothes and paced his bedroom, furious at his lack of control, at the Handmaiden for not being around to fix his dugga's magic—because he wouldn't be feeling this way if his magic was under control—and at fate, on the slim chance he really was inamorated.

Whatever the situation, he had more important things to worry about. And as much as he knew keeping his distance from Becca was the best solution to his situation, he needed information about the dragon who ran the facility who'd been holding her prisoner.

He gated into the transition suites' kitchenette, determined to keep his focus. The warm, comforting smell of the creamy chicken and pasta casserole heating in the oven made his stomach growl, reminding him that, even if he did have reasonably fast healing, he still got hungry and he hadn't eaten in a day. Because Becca had hijacked his dugga's magic. Mother, this was such a mess.

Raven stepped out of Becca's room, glanced into the other room where the new intake lay, then glared at him. "I don't know what you said to her, but that's got to stop if she has any chance of conquering the soul sickness."

"I asked her about her injuries."

Raven frowned and strode toward him. "More than the cut Diablo had given her?"

"Cracked ribs and a broken collarbone."

"She didn't look physically hurt when I talked with her."

"That's the problem." And it was more proof toward the truthful reality, which Becca's mind just couldn't handle. Mother, she was going to go insane and take him down with her, and he couldn't even order her death to save himself. Even the idea whirled in his mind and made his stomach roil. "If she's a sorcerer—"

"Her mental state is even more tenuous. I've changed my mind," Raven said. "You can't be here."

"I have to be here." To protect her—

No, God damn it, to get necessary information.

"You endanger the very tentative balance I've managed to create in her mind." She crouched before the oven and gazed inside. Had she just admitted to having an earth magic that helped her deal with human mages? She was a young drake. She might not have even realized until recently that she possessed the power, until she'd been faced with all of Zenobia's soul-sick mages. "Did you really try to kill her?"

"She endangers the *puzur*," he growled. Even if Becca did conquer her soul sickness and join the *puzur*, she still endangered everyone he cared about. If the wrong dragon got his hands on her, she could be used to expose his secrets. If the wrong dragon had her, Nero would sacrifice everything to protect her. Killing her would never be an option, which left him with removing himself from the *puzur*—and in effect giving up his hoard—as well as leaving his coterie and the Asar Nergal.

"So why didn't you?" Raven asked, her gaze still locked inside the oven. She'd encountered unnaturally created mages before and knew the most likely outcome. Since she'd joined the *puzur*, she'd dealt with over a dozen and had only managed to save two. But in the last three weeks, there'd been dozens more, and she hadn't been able to save any of them.

What Zenobia had done to those humans was more than just a dragon desperately needing to transfer into a vessel and ending up in one already occupied. No, for the last hundred years, Zenobia had stolen people, mostly homeless soldiers already struggling with psychological conditions from their combat experiences. The dragons who'd been assigned to awaken the humans' soul magic hadn't tried to hide their presence. They'd barged in, taken over, and clawed at the humans' mental essence—until magic was awakened, they'd gone crazy, or the dragon had given up and moved on to another victim.

There was nothing delicate or discreet about their actions, and what made it worse, those taken at the beginning of Zenobia's plan and who'd managed to escape discovered themselves decades ahead in time. The dragon souls in their bodies had slowed their aging and extended their lives, but also made them lose sense of the time when they'd been trapped in their own heads.

God, Becca could be dealing with that, too. Sure, he knew she was a soldier, but he didn't know much of anything else about her. How many years had she lost? There'd been that horrible event in Afghanistan. How long ago had that happened? Had that forced her into a life of living on the streets?

"Why didn't you kill her?" Raven asked again.

He jerked his attention back to her, his gaze having dropped to the floor. He had no good answer. And no way in hell was he telling her the truth, because *that* wasn't the truth. He wasn't inamorated, and soon enough he'd stop craving the feel of her aura against his. "We need to convince her to stay here."

"And by *we*, you mean me, because you're leaving before she gets out of the shower."

"No. I need information from her. She's the leak in the Asar Nergal. Her telepathy connected to my dugga's magic, and she's been eavesdropping on all my orders."

"She's the one who's been passing that information to the other mages? No wonder the last handful have been so hard to apprehend." Raven grabbed the oven mitts, opened the oven, and pulled out the casserole. "But that would mean she knew who you were."

"She didn't know who, but certainly what. Zenobia's drakes didn't care if their vessels were soul sick. One of her drakes had the earth magic ability to control their minds, so I doubt they tried to hide their essence or knowledge from their victims."

"That explains why the soul sickness has progressed so far by the time we get to them," Raven said. "It also means Rebecca knows more about dragons and the world than she wants to admit."

"And if she knows what the dugga is and his job…"

"It also explains why she thought Diablo really was the devil. She thinks he and you have to kill her." She got two plates out from the cupboard.

"I said I'm staying."

"And I said you can't. Maybe tomorrow she'll be stable enough to talk."

"No, I got her from a facility with a gatelock on it." Nero reached around her and pulled out another plate. "They'd been interrogating her about me."

"She told you that? Was that before or after you tried to kill her?"

"She didn't have to tell me. When her magic seizes mine, I see and hear what she does."

"The seizures." Realization flashed across Raven's expression. "Her magic causes them. So your dugga's magic isn't failing?"

"I don't know. It could be, and that's why Becca can affect me."

"Becca?" Raven cocked an eyebrow.

"That's how she thinks of herself… some of the time." It was how he thought of her— because of their close mental connection… not because he was inamorated. "I know this will make her recovery harder on you, but I need to know about the facility and any leads on the dragon in charge." Hell, he wasn't even sure he knew where the building was. Yeah, for all the high rises around it, it was somewhere in the heart of the city and had that weird piece of art in front of it, but that was all he knew. Dealing with Becca in his head had been such a distraction, he'd neglected the common sense that had kept him alive for over two thousand years.

"Pushing her now means we could lose her forever."

He knew that, but with the kind of tactical support the facility possessed, he had to assume it had security cameras as well, which meant the drake in charge already knew he'd gone after Becca and that put him at a serious disadvantage.

"It's a risk I have to take," he forced out, his stomach churning and soul screaming in protest.

"And I suppose I don't get a say in this?" Becca asked from her doorway, her gaze on Nero, making his pulse race. She wore black athletic leggings that accentuated her lean, muscled legs and a black hoodie that skimmed her hips and hid the rest of her figure. She'd tied her dark hair back in a ponytail, a practical move, but that emphasized her gaunt facial features and drew a small growl—irrational as it was—from deep within him at the reminder of her mistreatment.

"Of course you get a say." Raven pointed at the small kitchen table. "Let's eat."

Becca glanced at the table then back at Nero. Heat throbbed in his chest. He couldn't ask her questions. That endangered her.

He clenched his jaw. Not asking questions endangered everyone else. He had to keep his focus long enough to determine which drake ran the facility and for the Handmaiden to return and fix his magic... or give it to someone else.

"I need to ask you about that facility," he said before he could change his mind.

"If you're up for it." Raven spooned a scoopful of casserole on a plate and shoved it into Nero's hands. "For Becca," she said.

Nero slid into the closest chair and set the plate on the opposite side of the table from him.

The muscles in Becca's jaw tensed, her gaze still locked on him, appraising, judging his very soul, making his heart pound. She didn't draw closer and didn't sit, and all he wanted was their mental connection to renew so he could find out what she was thinking. If he knew that, he'd know how to approach her without hurting her more than he already had. And that only made the churning need to protect her stronger.

Mother of All, he wasn't going to get anything done if he kept feeling like this.

He jerked his thumb at the chair across from him. "Just sit already."

Raven set a plate in front of him with a low growl.

Crap. That wasn't what he'd meant to say, and he certainly hadn't intended such a sharp tone.

"If you can, I'd like to know about the facility, and then I'll leave you alone," he said.

Becca raised her chin and still stood her ground. "I'm not sure I can tell you much."

"Any little thing will help." Help him avenge what they'd done to her.

"You don't have to talk about it if you don't want to." Raven sat with her own plate and three forks.

Steam curled from the plate in front of him, and his stomach released a loud growl.

Becca snorted. "So the devil's master gets hungry."

"I'm still a person." He should eat, get the information he needed, and move on, but he couldn't bring himself to look away from her long enough to grab a fork.

She cocked an eyebrow. "Except you're not a person."

"You probably shouldn't think about that," he said.

A shiver swept through her and her hands fisted at her sides, but she didn't hug herself like she had before, as if while in the shower she'd come to a decision.

"I don't want to think about that hospital, either."

"Tell me what you remember, and you never have to think about it again." He knew trauma didn't work that way, but he vowed he'd never ask her about her experiences again. Not about her time as Zenobia's prisoner nor the facility.

"Only if you feel you can," Raven said.

Becca's gaze jumped to Raven. "Oh, I'm sure you'll know when I lose it."

Raven pursed her lips, and Becca blew out a heavy breath. "You didn't say that out loud, did you?"

"No."

"Sorry."

"Sit." Raven gestured to the chair across from her. "Eat."

"And let's get this information about the hospital out of the way," Nero said. Just get the information and go. Please. He could leave her alone. He could. If she was safe with Raven, he could leave and not return until Raven told him he could— or not return at all.

Riiight. Who was he kidding? Even just thinking that made his insides squirm and only confirmed how much he needed to stay away for good.

Raven shot him a glare, but Becca's attention dipped to the plate of food.

"I want two things first," she said, her voice low.

Desire churned in his gut, his soul straining to agree, and his mind fought to lock away the urge. A smart drake knew the terms first before he agreed to anything.

"There's a GPS tracker in my body. I want it taken out."

"It's been disabled. You don't have to worry about it," he said.

"I want it out." She squared her shoulders. "If magic exists, then you can't say it won't ever be activated again."

"It's a valid point," Raven said.

"There's only one drake who could reactivate it, and he won't." Because Nero would kill Gig if he did.

"Only one drake that we know of." Raven speared a piece of pasta and chicken with her fork. "We know roughly where the tracker is embedded. If we can safely take it out, we will."

"Raven, I want you to do it." Becca crossed her arms, as if standing her ground and making her demand gave her power. And it probably did. She hadn't had control of her life since Zenobia had kidnapped her, and as a captain in the army, she'd been used to having at least a bit of control.

"Fine. Raven will remove the tracker." He glared at Becca, trying to will her to sit and start eating since, knowing Raven, she wouldn't do anything until after dinner.

"And your second request?" Raven asked.

Becca slid into the chair and picked up her fork. "I need to look for Werner and any of the others who might have escaped and warn them about the tracker."

There was no way in hell he was letting her out of the transition suites, not until he'd dealt with the drake who ran the facility. And while he could use his dugga's magic to find her friends, there was no way he was going to activate it until the Handmaiden had returned and fixed whatever was wrong with it. For all he knew, just summoning his dugga's magic would send him into seizures again.

"If they have trackers embedded in them, they'll have been picked up already."

"That's an assumption," she said.

"A good assumption," Nero growled.

"I'm not denying it isn't true, only that until we have confirmation either way, it's still just an assumption." She took a small bite of casserole.

"I can follow up on them," he said, "but the facility and the dragon running it is the pressing issue."

"And I'm not a fool. I won't tell you what I remember about the facility until we confirm my friends are still captured."

For the love of—

"It's dangerous out there."

"I've dealt with worse." Her expression darkened. "I can always leave and look for my friends myself."

"No, you can't." The hell he was letting her leave.

"Am I a prisoner?"

"No." *Never.*

"So I can leave," Becca said.

Raven shoved a forkful of food into her mouth.

"We both know why you can't." Because his Mother-forsaken soul didn't want her out of his sight. God, he couldn't even bring himself to go and let Raven—who was better equipped and clearly preferred by Becca—handle the situation.

"I'm willing to risk losing my shit to confirm the whereabouts of my friends."

God damn it. "I'm not." He growled and slammed his fork down on the table.

Becca jumped, her body tensed, and her expression hardened. No sign of soul sickness or fear, just ferocious determination to stand her ground. "I'm going, and Raven can come with me. After that, I'll tell you about the hospital. Those are my terms."

"I don't accept them." Even if he let her go with Raven, if something happened, Raven couldn't free gate. They'd be stuck wherever they were until he could get there to help.

The determination in Becca's gaze darkened, and a hint of something—was that fear?—flickered through him. As soon as he turned his back, she would leave. The only way to keep her safe was to prove she could trust him.

"You're just like the others," she said.

His soul howled at the accusation. *I would die for you. I'm going to give up everything for you, if only to keep everyone I care about safe.* Zenobia would never have done anything like that for anyone. Not many drakes would. "I'm nothing like them."

"Prove it."

"Fine. We'll go confirm your friends are still imprisoned at the facility, and then you'll tell me everything so I can break them the hell out of there." He jerked to his feet, the need to take action propelling him up. Except he didn't know what to do or where to go. His gaze jumped to Becca's, and his soul ached with a need he didn't want to acknowledge.

He forced his attention behind her to the hall and the two open doors. *There. Go there. Just get away from her.* He stormed past her, heading to the room with the unconscious mage. Except he could still feel her aura crackling against his even as he rushed away, and sense her determination and fear in his soul. She was going to destroy everything he cared about. Without a doubt he had to leave everyone to protect them, and denying it wouldn't change the truth.

19

B ecca watched Nero storm into the room where the unconscious man lay, her insides churning with fear and determination and—if she was being fully honest with herself—desire. Now that the voices were a whisper and the panic of reality had eased—albeit not entirely—all that power, mental and magical, in his deliciously muscular body that she'd seen half naked, called to something primal within her. An attraction that she knew was a bad idea, but one she had nevertheless. She doubted he was attracted back and, with her making demands, was probably pissed at her. But the demands were necessary. He needed to prove his claim that he was different from the other mon— dragons.

And he had. Sort of. Clearly he hadn't liked the idea of looking for Werner before getting the information about the hospital, and there was no guarantee he wouldn't just kill her once she'd told him what he wanted to know—also a good reason to ignore her irrational attraction—but he had agreed to her terms. It was a surprising start. Even Raven—if Becca had heard her thoughts correctly—had been surprised at Nero's response. Raven, however, had only been partly surprised at him storming off. Him storming away had been expected. Him not summoning a gate to leave faster? That was a surprise... and a worry.

His emotions are usually better controlled than this.

Becca bit the inside of her cheek before responding to Raven's thoughts. At least this time she recognized it was a thought and not said out loud.

A hint of a shiver threatened to sweep through Becca, but she managed to hold herself together, not the least in part because of Raven's magical warmth in her head. Raven's magic had faded when Becca had been in the shower, but returned when she'd walked in on Raven and Nero talking in the kitchen. Which suggested the woman's— damn it, *dragon's* magic only worked in close proximity or line of sight. And while Becca had managed to keep the terror that was curled tight within her soul in check while showering and making demands of Nero, she had no idea how she was going to manage while looking for Werner. Which meant she had to get out there, find Werner, and return as fast as possible, or escape Nero... or something.

"You should probably eat that before it gets cold," Raven said, pointing her fork at Becca's plate.

"Or before Nero loses his patience and changes his mind?"

"He's given his word. Unless you betray him, he won't change his mind." *Although he isn't himself right now.*

"That works both ways, you know." Trusting him *and* not being herself—that had to explain her attraction to him... because it certainly wasn't his smoking hot physique... no way. A part of her still wanted to run. If she was smart, once she had a coat and boots and was out of wherever this was, she should flee. Except nothing had changed with her previous arguments against running. Nero had found her before, he could find her again, and now—if he kept his word—he was going to help her find Werner and anyone else who'd escaped Stanbury's hospital, as well as help her free the others. Of course, had Nero agreed to help to save her friends or to kill them?

If Raven's thoughts had been correct, none of the people the dragon had encountered who'd been imprisoned in the cave had been sane.

Except Werner and Glenn and the few others who'd stuck

together from the beginning didn't seem crazy. Or was it just because Becca was crazy and couldn't see it in them as well?

Her fork scraped against her plate, and she realized she was done and trying to get the last of the cheesy sauce. She hadn't even realized she'd been eating. Her body had gone through the actions while her thoughts had whirled… while, if she was being honest with herself, other people's thoughts whirled within her as well, not just Raven's. Thankfully, everyone's thoughts but Raven's were still a whisper, and she suspected Raven's thoughts were louder because she was easing magic into Becca's head and had created a connection between them.

But there was no telling how long the whispers would stay whispers, and while she could have gone for a second helping of dinner, it was best to take care of business first. She could fall apart after she knew everyone was safe.

"Let's get this tracker out of me."

"Absolutely. What's your shoe size?"

"My shoe size? Eight."

Raven pulled out her phone and sent a text.

A chime sounded down the hall.

"Fine," Nero growled, and a whoosh of air swept into the kitchen.

"What was that?" Becca asked, except a part of her knew. The knowledge tickled at the back of her mind. She'd felt that wind before and knew from the monsters who'd been in her head that the wind came from the black vortex Nero—and Werner—had used to move around.

Raven pursed her lips, and the heat in Becca's head swelled.

"Yeah, I know," Becca said. "I know already. I just don't want to think about it."

"That's fair." Raven cleared their plates and set them in the sink. "If I'm getting the tracker out, Nero can grab you a pair of boots and a coat."

"I'm sure he loves doing errands." From the moment he'd started talking in her head, she'd known he was the monst— *man* in charge. He had more important things to worry about than chores. Which begged the question— "Why isn't he sending the devil to go with me? Why is he going himself?"

Because D has been upset lately and is just as likely to kill you as protect you. "If that facility where he found you is being run by a dragon, he can't afford to have second-hand information. It's too dangerous."

"Because?"

Raven met Becca's gaze. "Because he's supposed to kill you and all the others like you, regardless of your intention toward our kind."

Becca could feel the truth in her words... and her fear.

"Dragon law demands all humans with magical abilities be killed." Raven strode past Becca to the cabinet in the hall and pulled out a sealed medical kit.

"That seems a little extreme." And highly prejudiced.

"Those who made the law didn't know at the time how many humans could naturally develop a magical ability." *Or they didn't care.*

Becca shifted, a shiver threatening to sweep through her. She knew this and could have only known it because of the dragons who'd been in her body.

"We were afraid," Raven said.

"Because we— us humans with magic had tried to kill you."

"Yes."

"You were left in this... state." Spirits trapped in humans. It actually surprised her Raven wasn't furious about that.

"Yes. When dragons fell, they didn't realize our souls awakened powerful magic in roughly twenty percent of humans, and initially most dragons had to share a body with an occupied... vessel."

"And that created more of the people you feared."

"Yes, and they were dangerous, most falling soul sick and going crazy."

"So that law was made."

"Yes, and the Asar Nergal was formed." Raven set the medical kit on the table and pulled a chair to Becca's side. "A handful of centuries later, Nero took over leadership, because he realized the law was making him kill innocent children who were naturally developing earth magic, and he started hiding them instead. Dragon society wasn't ready to accept humans with natural magical abilities. The Great Scourge, that's what we call what happened, was still too raw." *Even after two thousand years, it's still raw.*

Becca glanced at the room where Nero had been, with the young man in the bed. The other dragons feared him. They didn't know Nero was the dugga, but they feared that position. Dragon law was absolute. If any one of those dragons had known Nero was protecting mages instead of killing them, he'd be sentenced to death — no, that wasn't right. He'd be sentenced to *rebirth*, something akin to death, without a second thought—and she wasn't going to think too hard about what that rebirth thing was. It wasn't important to the conversation.

"So he risks everything to save humans, defying his own peoples' law."

"And if the dragon who runs that facility learns he's the dugga, Nero could be challenged for his position—" *Or politically forced out of his position.* "—and then everything he's built here would be in danger." *They would kill our kids and rebirth every dragon involved.*

"I can see why he wanted to kill me." When they'd been connected, his thoughts had told her that. She endangered everyone he held dear. And yet his thoughts had changed the moment he'd tried to kill her. She'd become a part of that *everyone* even though he didn't know her. It had scared the crap out of him.

And it scared the crap out of her.

She'd been alone since leaving the army. Her grandmother was gone, she had no other family—Lord only knew why she'd moved back into her grandmother's house in Toronto. All her friends were either dead, deployed, or living closer to Petawawa. To be a part of an *everyone* again—

The loneliness of those months back made her heart ache, and made her terrified of how much she needed to be part of a unit again. Military or family. It didn't matter.

But Stanbury had known Becca was psychically connected to the dugga, which made her a target. Which in turn made him and his family a target. Nero had been in her head while she was being questioned. He had to know she'd been pressed for information about him. It was actually a wonder he hadn't killed her, and even more of one that he'd agreed to her terms and was going to let her leave wherever they were.

Raven peeled back the top of the medical tray, revealing an incision kit complete with surgical blade, gauze, self-adhesive bandages, and sterile wipes. "Let's get this tracker out. Shift to the side on the chair, so I can get to your back and expose your right shoulder."

Becca unzipped her hoodie and slid it and the strap of her tank-top off her shoulder, revealing the rose and thorn tattoo licking the bottom of her neck, dipping across her collar bone and curling down her biceps and shoulder blade. The ink swept in and around her scars, the jagged ones from the shrapnel from the explosion and the rounder one from the sniper's bullet.

"This is lovely," Raven said. *But those scars. She's seen things.*

"I got it for my grandmother. She raised me and died while I was on my second tour in Afghanistan." Becca wasn't going to acknowledge Raven's other thought. Yeah, she'd seen things, but the worst of it hadn't been in Afghanistan and hadn't left a physical scar.

"I'm sorry."

"So am I." Her grandmother hadn't wanted her to go back, but Becca hadn't been able to retire. There were too many people who needed help and friends who were going back who she wanted to protect. She'd thought her whole life had been with the army. So she'd gone and had been unconscious in an army hospital in Germany when her grandmother had taken ill and died.

"I think I see something." Raven ran cold fingers over Becca's shoulder, drawing a shiver. "And I certainly feel it. Just under the skin here. Hand me the scalpel and grab a piece of gauze."

Becca handed her the knife and picked up the gauze.

"Take a breath in."

She did.

"And out."

The blade pinched the back of her shoulder, and Raven took the gauze. "Got it. Want to unwrap a bandage?" She pressed the gauze to

Raven's back and set the scalpel and tracker on the table. "It wasn't deep, so you shouldn't need stitches." She took the unwrapped bandage. "Which is good because I'm terrible at stitches."

"Dragon healing and all that." The words jumped out before Becca realized what she was saying. It came from one of her captor's memories. Dragon's souls had magic that healed them at an accelerated rate. It also stopped their bodies from aging, making them immortal.

Another shiver threatened to rush over her, and she drew in another breath, steadying herself before Raven eased more warmth into her head.

"You got it?" Raven asked. *She's so strong. Maybe she can do this.*

"I'm okay. Been through worse." Becca shrugged her scarred and tattooed shoulder. Although she wasn't sure whether how her last tour had ended was really worse than what had happened in the cave.

A black vortex formed on the wall beside them and with a whoosh, Nero stepped into the kitchenette. He wore a winter jacket and held a pair of boots and another jacket. His gaze landed on her as if instinctively drawn to her, and a hint of something heated in his eyes. It drew another shiver within Becca, but one of craving, not of fear.

Jeez. What was wrong with her?

The terror threatening to overwhelm her should have frozen her libido, not turned her on. But that fear wasn't why she was drawn to him. It also had nothing to do with the fact that she'd been pretty much celibate for a year... years, if the memory from the cave was right. No, it was the knowledge that his core value to protect those who couldn't protect themselves resonated with her. She'd become a soldier because people were being terrorized. He was defying his people's law because he couldn't murder innocent children. And— the memory of him in the shower flashed into her mind's eye—she just had to face it, he was sexy as hell.

To think, less than an hour ago he'd tried to kill her, but that made perfect sense. What didn't make sense was why he'd let her live. No matter what she'd told Raven, her odds of staying sane were slim. Even with the other woman's magical help, she could feel her mind trembling, on the verge of splintering.

The only thing she could do was hold it together long enough to contact Werner and free the others. After that... well, she had no idea what would happen after that, but in the very least, she couldn't allow herself to endanger other people.

20

Nero knew where Becca was the instant he gated into the kitchenette. His gaze leapt to her, and he couldn't make himself look anywhere else. Something in her expression had changed, the wariness she'd had moments before had softened... a bit, and it could have only been because of something Raven had said. He could tell from the strain around the younger drake's eyes that she desperately wanted to save Becca, and he hoped to the Mother of All for all their sakes that she could.

"You ready?" he asked.

Raven applied a self-adhesive bandage to the back of Becca's shoulder.

"The first place I want to check out is on Liberty, across from the train station." She zipped up her hoodie, her gaze locked on his, making him want to flash his teeth at her in sexual invitation.

"Good location to meet," he forced out, keeping his jaw tight. Becca wouldn't understand what showing his teeth meant but Raven certainly would.

Stay focused on the job.

Keeping Becca safe—

Keeping *everyone* safe, God damn it.

He dragged his thoughts to the train station. It was in the heart of town, with lots of people coming and going, so someone could easily hide among them. It also had easy access to public transit and taxies, as well as a number of side streets nearby if escape was necessary.

He hung the coat he'd grabbed for Becca on the back of his abandoned chair and set the boots on the floor beside her, then made himself step away and pull out his phone. He opened up the map app and searched the street view of the location for a place to put his gate. Using his car would have been less noticeable and therefore less risky, but he didn't want to waste time driving around Newgate and potentially searching for parking if something happened to Becca—not that he wouldn't just abandon his car without a second thought, but he couldn't do that if stuck on a road without a place to pull over—that would draw even more unwanted attention from humans and dragons.

"There are two spots I want to go to before we surveil Stanbury's hospital," Becca said, drawing his attention inexorably back to her.

She slid her feet into the boots he'd taken from the supply room. There were used, a man's size six, and had been worn by a teen he'd rescued thirty years ago who now ran Nero's center for troubled youth in London, England. Nero had a room full of outgrown shoes and clothes, ready for a youth coming in off the streets in need of help, but it was also a room full of memories of those he'd saved and welcomed into his house.

And now he endangered all of them.

That was what he had to concentrate on.

Not Becca.

Even if not killing those kids was the right thing to do, Regis and many other drakes would see saving human mages as unforgivable. If that information got out—

And with Becca connected to his dugga's magic and another drake after her, that would happen sooner rather than later.

It was time for Raven to review the protection plan and notify the coterie's second in command, Hunain, in case it needed to be activated. Mother, the idea of giving it all up hurt—that was the danger with having a living hoard—but he'd always known it might be necessary.

"While we're gone, and you're keeping a watch on—" He jerked his chin toward the new intake's bedroom, not certain what to call him in front of Becca.

"The new guy?" Becca asked, making him wonder if she'd read his thoughts even though he couldn't feel her in his head.

"Yes, the new guy," he said. "While you're watching him, you need to review the protection plan. Also, call Hunain and tell him of the review and—" He couldn't believe he was going to say this, but times had changed in the last month. "—bring Hunter and Grey in on it, and Capri if she's returned from her shift at work." The two ancient drakes and the head of the North American Clean team would be assets in helping the *puzur* disappear and, knowing all three of them, they'd know something was up anyway and stick their noses in, causing trouble until someone told them what was happening.

Raven's eyes narrowed. "It's too soon for such a drastic measure."

"That's why I said review. But if anything goes wrong, I need you to enact it." His gaze jumped to Becca, and he wrenched his attention back to Raven, who narrowed her eyes, not even trying to hide that she knew something was wrong.

"I understand," Raven said.

Becca shrugged into the also-used winter coat. "Protection plan?"

"Just a precaution. Also, get Diablo to search for metal umbrella art in the downtown core. That will help narrow down where this facility is and perhaps who owns the property." He pressed his hand to the wall, subvocalized his power word, and summoned a gate before Raven could question him further. "Let's look for your friend." Even though he doubted anyone else had managed to escape.

Becca shuddered and crossed her arms. The strain of standing in front of the gate made her body stiff, and the muscles in her jaw and neck flexed. Another good reason he should have chosen a motor vehicle as their means of transportation.

No. Speed over comfort. That was the best choice, even if it did make his insides squirm seeing her strain.

Mother of All, he was a stronger drake than this.

"Take a breath." He held out his hand. "You've done gate travel before." *Guess this would be the test if she can keep it together or not.*

Please let her keep it together. He didn't know what he'd do if she succumbed to the soul sickness. His only option would be to suffer with her until she died of old age, accident, or, Mother help him, suicide. Or until the Handmaiden returned and he could beg her for help—although, with a dragon's sense of time, her return could be in a few centuries and that wouldn't help him.

Her hug around her body tightened, her expression turned determined, and her brilliant red aura flared, as if she were gathering her power around herself and strengthening her will. Mother, she was breathtaking.

The sense within him that claimed he belonged to her howled with certainty and desire. *Hers. Always hers.*

Not hers. Because that was impossible and a distraction he couldn't afford to have. It was his broken dugga's magic. That was all.

"All right," she said, but it sounded more to herself than to him, and she stepped into the gate.

He followed. The black woolly nothingness surrounded him. Up and down vanished, so too did light and darkness, and then he stepped into the dimly lit alley he'd picked from the map app. Only a hint of streetlight cut this deep into the passage between the towering high rises, and cold air nipped his face and hands.

Becca staggered beside him, unsteady after stepping out of the gate, and he grabbed her to help her balance. His bare hand touched hers, and heated desire sizzled up his arm at the sudden contact. She gasped and jerked free of his grip, pressing that hand to the concrete wall beside her.

Here, in the darkness, her aura blazed. The force of her power slid against his senses and stole his breath, even more compelling than that brief touch. He'd felt the same sense of awe and surety of his bond with his first inamorata.

Damn it, his *only* inamorata.

He tried to step back and put some distance between them, but his body didn't move, as if the thought had gotten stuck in his head.

Her gaze lifted to his, her red power shimmering in the depths of her dark eyes, with not even a hint of a flicker in her aura indicating she was human. So much power. Her expression tightened, forming tiny lines at the edges of her eyes. So much pain. He had to take the pain, carry it for her, hold her, give her the strength to kill her demons—

"Nero," she said, her husky alto shivering through him and making his heart skip a beat.

Her hand landed flat against his chest, sending another shock of attraction zinging through him, and he realized he'd stepped toward her, not back.

God damn it. It was as if his body and soul had a mind of their own, and that only added more evidence to the *being inamorated* side of the argument. If he wasn't careful, it was going to be him having the breakdown and not Becca.

He forced himself back a step. Surely he could control himself long enough to fulfill the terms of their deal and get her back to Raven. Then he'd make himself leave her and not return.

That thought made his insides squirm, and he clenched his jaw. *Finish what you promised. Leave her. Don't return.* It was the only way.

"Where's this meeting place?" he asked, with more growl than he'd intended.

She pursed her lips and looked ready to argue—probably about his tone—but glanced up and down the alley instead. "Which way is Liberty?"

"That way." He pointed behind her. A step closer and he'd be able to touch her again, brush a hand through her hair, caress her cheek—

Jeez.

"There's a greenspace across from the train station." She headed to the alley's mouth.

Nero followed, determined to keep his distance, no matter what his churning insides were saying. If he gave in and did anything, he was going to feel like an idiot once the Handmaiden fixed his dugga's magic. Not to mention it wasn't fair to Becca. She had to have a mess of complicated emotions racing through her. He didn't need their mental connection to know that. He'd also tried to kill her, and he doubted she'd forgotten. Besides, she'd stabbed him, which meant she wasn't inamorated back.

A shiver shook her, and he clenched his hands into fists at his sides before he could wrap her in an embrace to steady her. Mother, all he wanted to do was hold her and never let go.

"If Werner's around, he'll be near the greenspace," she said, reaching the alley's mouth and turning onto the street.

It was only nine at night, and there were still a few pedestrians and enough traffic that Nero was glad he'd picked the middle of the alley to form his gate and avoid notice. The streetlights glimmered off ice patches on the sidewalk and along the gutters on the road, while a frozen wind gusted, caught between the high rises. Ahead of them sat the greenspace, with half a dozen trees and boxy shrubs, their branches naked for the winter, along with a couple of benches and no one around.

Nero glanced across the street to the train station. On this side, all he could see was a multi-story parking garage and a big sign indicating an entrance solely for buses. No one with Werner's yellow aura loitered there, either. And there was no way Nero was going to activate his dugga's magic to find the mage, not until the Handmaiden had returned and fixed him. A seizure right now not only endangered him, but Becca as well.

"There's a twenty-four-hour coffee shop over there. With this cold, he might be there." She headed past the trees and shrubs to a towering white and gray building. The front windows on the left side of the main entrance were lit, revealing a cozy café in browns, burgundy, and chrome, and half a dozen people seated inside.

"I don't see him." And Nero didn't see a glimmer of yellow aura inside, either. "Let's check out the other location." Then get back to the transition suites so they could finish their deal, and he could get the hell away from her.

"He wouldn't be sitting in a window seat. He could also be nearby watching. I want—" She rubbed her temples, and another shiver swept through her.

His muscles twitched. *Just hold her. Comfort her.*

"I want to get my bearings. Last time I was here, I thought it was a nightmare."

The other location will be worse. Her words were a whisper, and her essence flickered through his head and disappeared before he'd realized she was there.

He strained to hear anything else, but she was gone, making him ache from the absence and reminding him of the quiet in his head and the terror trembling at the edge of her mental essence. All he wanted to do was whisk her home, to hell with their deal, but he couldn't risk her refusing to share what she knew about the facility.

"How about a coffee and—" *And you can tell me about the facility.*

"And we talk?" She raised her eyebrow, her expression dry.

"It's rude to read someone's thoughts."

"So Raven has told me. But I didn't read your thoughts." She headed toward the coffee shop's door. "You're just that obvious."

"Then I can assume Raven also told you why I need information on that facility, and the sooner, the better." He held the door for her, the hot air blasting from a vent above ruffling a lock of hair that had escaped her ponytail. His chest tightened as he followed her inside.

The aroma of brewed coffee and pastries enveloped him, along with warmth and soft jazz. A quick scan confirmed no auras among the seven patrons and one employee inside—so no human mages or dragons—and no one gave off any predatory vibes, which would indicate bad intentions or a trained combatant.

She paused only a few steps in, leaving him just enough space to let the door shut behind him if he stood close to her. Within embracing-distance close. Just wrap his arms around her and—

"Raven told me what you do," she said, her voice low, "and why you tried to kill me."

"That was a mistake."

"You think that now."

"So you *are* reading my mind?"

She frowned. "No, I mean you thought that when Stanbury's men tried to grab me after we'd gated—" She pressed her palms to her temples again.

"You don't have to say it. Just let it slip out of your mind. Don't think about it." If he could embrace her, he could take her pain. Except being inamorated didn't work that way—and he was *not* inamorated. He also didn't have an earth magic that could help her, so all he could do was watch, helpless. And Mother of All, he hated being helpless.

"After we'd gated," she said between clenched teeth.

The twenty-something guy behind the counter smiled and waved. Yeah, they were being weird, standing in the doorway, and everyone in the café had more than likely noticed them.

"A drink to get warmed up? What do you want?" Nero strode past her, hoping his movement would spur her into action without him having to touch her—even if he desperately needed to.

"Coffee. Black."

He ordered two medium black coffees to go, and they sat at a table by the wall, close enough to the window to see out but not be easily noticed from those passing by on the street.

Her aura pulsed against his, sensually sliding and crackling, as a whisper of words and pain bled into his head. And stayed. He could feel her mentally holding herself together and caught a flickering glimpse of himself through her eyes.

He looked hard and... angry, with an aura—that he wasn't sure she recognized as an aura—that made her insides squirm. He wasn't as powerful as Hunter was now, or had ever been, but he was as old. That age radiated from him like it did from Hunter, Grey, and Tobias. Even if he tried to hide it, an astute drake would eventually notice, and she recognized what it meant. Her life was the blink of his eye, a mere few breaths or heartbeats. Even the drakes who'd possessed her hadn't been close to his age. They'd been children, foolish to think the dugga wouldn't notice them, and she'd believed they'd been old. The thought stole her breath, filled her with an awe she didn't want to recognize—and in part hoped was still a dream.

How could she have thought to make a deal with him? All he had to do was wait her out. An hour, a day, hell, ten years, were nothing to him, while she—

His throat tightened.

Too soon. It would come too soon, and he'd suffer like he had after the Scourge.

No. It would be worse. With this connection, he'd feel her die.

21

Becca wrenched her gaze from Nero to the lid of her coffee cup, but the lack of eye contact did nothing to ease the attraction sizzling through her veins, the weight of his ancient masculine presence, or his fear whispering in her head. Somehow, insignificant little her terrified him. But his thoughts weren't clear, muddled with the other voices, and she couldn't figure out what someone so powerful could fear, especially about her.

"So, ah…" He drew his coffee cup to his lips, his hand trembling. *Shit*, he hissed in her head, and captured the cup in both hands. The muscles in his jaw flexed, and he visibly steadied himself. "You take your coffee black, hunh?"

Guess he wasn't going to talk about it. Not that she'd expected he would. Even if he seemed determined to help her—and that was clearly for Raven's sake, not hers—she and Nero weren't friends. They barely knew each other, and they certainly didn't talk to each other about things that bothered them. "I found it easier to drink it black than needing cream and sugar and stuff when I was in the army."

"The army?"

"You know I'm a captain. You were in my head." The heat of embarrassment seeped up her neck. "You heard it all, didn't you?" All her thoughts and determination to hold onto herself. It had been all she'd had.

"I heard enough."

"Do you know about Afghanistan?"

He gave a tight nod, his expression dark.

"And you know what they did in the cave." Her pulse stuttered and a shiver swept through her, jostling her hand and making her coffee spill out the opening in the lid. She set the cup on the table and pressed her palms on either side of it, as if that could somehow steady the panic whirling through her. "You know—"

"Just take a breath."

She swallowed at the lump in her throat. Just breathe. Think of Raven's warmth. But it was so hard to focus, and the whispers turned to hisses. *She's strange. Look at her. What's wrong with her?* Everyone was staring at her. They could see her falling apart, they knew pieces of her soul and mind were snapping away, and she was going to go crazy.

Nero laid his hand over hers. *Please, Mother, just breathe.*

The hisses vanished, as if someone had flicked a switch. All of them but Nero.

This was a mistake. I pushed too fast. The puzur *will still be in danger, my kids will be in danger, and I'll lose her, too, way too soon.* An overwhelming fear and yearning rushed over her, and she jerked her hand away.

Nero's voice in her head disappeared, but the whispers returned. His eyes flashed wide for a second as if he hadn't realized he'd grabbed her hand, then his gaze hardened as he leaned back and cupped his paper coffee cup between both palms. "Tell me where this second location is, and I'll get you back to Raven, then look for Werner myself. You can tell me about the facility when I get back."

That sounded like the best idea ever.

And yet if she wanted to help Werner—and help herself—she needed to pull her shit together and deal with this. If Stanbury still had him, there was no telling how long she'd keep him imprisoned, and without a doubt when she was done with him, she'd lock him in some sub-basement cell or kill him. There was also Nero. If Stanbury didn't know who or what Nero was, she would soon. Becca didn't doubt the hospital had security cameras, which meant Stanbury had a picture of Nero's face. If Stanbury was after humans with magic—and it was looking like she was—those kids Nero ferociously wanted to protect were in danger.

"Tell me about your kids." Maybe she could use that to anchor herself. When she'd returned to Afghanistan, she'd known who she was fighting for, and it had given her a strength she hadn't known she possessed. It had helped her drag two of her men from their burning light tactical transport vehicles and a dozen feet away to cover while she'd been injured—although at the time, adrenaline had disguised how injured she'd been. Werner was a good reason to hold herself together, but he was still capable of defending himself. Nero's kids, however, were innocents in danger. Maybe knowing about them would help her to hold it together long enough to see this through.

"You need to return to the transition suites."

"I need to do this." Seeing it through would mean she'd managed to hold onto a part of herself. It would mean she wasn't lost or crazy or helpless. God, she couldn't be helpless while knowing she'd put people in danger.

The hardness in his eyes softened, and his hand slipped from his cup and started to ease across the tabletop toward her fingers again, before he stiffened and stopped himself.

Ah, crap. "You heard that, about being helpless, didn't you?" she asked.

"Yeah."

"Well, now you know what drives me." She had a feeling protecting those around him drove Nero, as well. "Please, tell me about your kids."

He pursed his lips, his gaze holding her captive and sizzling through her nerves. What would it be like to feel all that power, that strength, focused on her, wrapped around her... inside her?

Jeez. What was wrong with her? *Please don't let him have heard that.*

But his gaze remained steady, intense, and didn't indicate he'd heard that embarrassing thought at all.

He took a sip of coffee, his attention still locked on her. "There've been a lot of kids over a lot of years."

"Raven said you started saving them instead of killing them." *Concentrate on that. Not him.* But her pulse still beat too fast for just sitting in a café drinking coffee.

"Yeah. That was a long time ago. Right now, there are just over a dozen in my house who I discovered in almost every corner of the world, and there are three dozen more, adults now, who are happily living their lives on whatever continent they want. Some nearing the end of their lives, some newly adults." He took another sip and somehow, even though he never looked away, his posture and expression softened, as if talking about his unorthodox family changed him. He no longer seemed as powerful, ancient, and intimidating. His power had turned ferociously protective, and, if she looked closely, he also seemed fearful and fragile. "Naturals—a human who naturally develops a magical ability—are rare, so given the size of the human population, my family is small."

Although it's gotten bigger with Grey, Anaea, Capri, and the others.

"When you're ready, you might want to talk with Anaea," he said. "Her circumstances were different, but she's not a Natural, either." *But not too soon. Not until Raven thinks it's safe. Mother, anything could break her and— Stay on topic. Give her purpose. Keep her together, achieve her goal, get her information, then get the hell away from her.*

Her throat tightened at his thoughts. The reaction was stupid. They weren't friends. They weren't anything. She had to remember that. She'd just thought, when he'd touched her hand, that something was changing between them. She yearned for something to have changed between them. But clearly, he wanted nothing to do with her.

"Mia is one of our youngest. She's fourteen. A few years ago, she started having strange dreams. Some good, most bad. Those dreams started coming true. When she tried to warn her parents and anyone else who would listen about a terrible car accident, they started sending her to psychologists. When her parents were killed in that car crash, the rest of her family feared she'd been involved and, even though they had no proof, they put her in a strict disciplinary boarding school for troubled youths." *No one wanted the girl who'd murdered her parents.*

"That's terrible."

"Almost all of my kids are like that. Their families don't understand and are afraid of them. They may not know why they fear the kids, but they do. These kids end up in fights, or disciplinary facilities, or mental institutions, or on the streets. They think no one loves them, that they're so damaged no one could love them."

"But you do." She could feel it radiating from him, and now all she wanted was to be a part of his ferocious protection, for her and with her. To be a part of a family, even if it was an unusual one, again.

Every single one. "I try to give them a fighting chance." *I need you to fight for your chance.*

"Well, if you want me to fight for my chance, why the hell do you want to get away from me?" The words blurted out before she could stop them.

His eyes widened and his aura flared.

"I know, it's rude. But you keep giving me mixed messages."

"If you didn't listen to my thoughts, you wouldn't get mixed messages." He sat back, his body tense, and his thoughts snapped to a barely there whisper, while the other whispers grew louder.

"You want to help me, but you want nothing to do with me?" She strained to hear what he was thinking, his thoughts not even a whisper within her anymore.

"It has nothing to do with you."

"Yeah, right, because you wanting to get away from me has nothing to do with me?" The people in the café were starting to stare at her again. A shiver shuddered through her, and she fought the urge to hug herself.

His eyes narrowed, as if he could sense her strain. Maybe he could. He'd been in her head before. Just because she couldn't hear his thoughts didn't mean he couldn't hear hers.

"Oh, my God," she said, "are you eavesdropping on my thoughts?"

"Only when you yell them in my head," he growled. His left arm twitched, and he hissed. "If I can put some distance between us, perhaps I can sever our connection."

Someone in her head screamed, then another and another. She shoved at the voices, desperate to put them back on low volume, but only managed to turn them down to a roar. She clenched teeth and concentrated, wrenching them back to a normal conversational level. Pain sliced through her skull, and Nero gasped as the pain cut into her.

"You felt that?" she asked.

His expression tightened. "I was hoping we were done with that. We're going to this other location and then I'm getting you back to Raven."

"But you felt that?"

He stood and glared at her.

Well, that would explain why he wanted to get away from her.

"I don't know much about telepathy, but maybe think about being in a soundproof room or turning the volume down or something. See if that helps."

"Just tried the volume thing. That's what made you wince."

"Lovely." *Mother, if I could just take her pain.* "Here's the short of it. I'm worried that whatever connects us will get worse." *Except if I'm inamorated, it's already as bad as it gets.* "Things are happening in my world that have raised the danger level for my kids, and it was pretty dangerous for them before." *But I'm not inamorated because it isn't possible.* "If there's a drake out there who knows you're connected to the dugga and is after me, and that drake discovers my kids—"

"They'll be killed. Yeah, Raven said that." The thought made her pulse race, and the memory of the kids screaming in the school tent flooded her. She couldn't let more children die. Even if stopping whatever was happening was impossible, she had to try.

Nero dropped his coffee cup into the nearby garbage can and headed to the door. Becca followed.

"I can't afford to be distracted." He held the door for her, and she stepped onto the cold dark street. "And I can't afford to be incapacitated."

She shivered but couldn't tell if it was from the voices in her head or the winter wind... or how close she stood to Nero. "You think the connection is that strong?"

"I know it is." *And it terrifies me.* "If I just felt the pain in your head, imagine what I'd feel if you were shot or killed. If that happened when I needed to protect my kids—" *Mother, don't let that happen.*

Another shiver swept through her, and the voices grew louder again.

"So what do we do?" she asked, struggling to ignore the voices, but afraid if she pushed at them again she'd hurt Nero.

"First I fulfill the terms of our deal and look for your friend," he said as they headed back to the alley where they'd first arrived.

"I appreciate that." Although she was surprised, given what she now knew, that he'd carry on with their agreement. She wouldn't have, not until she'd figured out how to separate their minds. "We can make it fast, then get back to your place."

"Thank you."

They walked to the middle of the alley, and he placed his hand against the concrete high rise wall.

"I'm sure it'll be a relief to get me out of your head." He didn't sound as if it would be for him, and a mix of confused emotions swelled through her. *Just get some distance. That's all I need.* "Where are we going?"

"There's an abandoned warehouse on Battle Ridge Road. You're aware of it. You sent the dev— Sorry. You sent Diablo there a few days...? No, closer to a week ago."

"I remember it. Would your friend really return there?" With a whoosh of wind, a churning void of darkness formed around his hand and grew until it was large enough to engulf them.

She clenched her arms tight around herself and fought another shiver. "We had hoped you wouldn't think we'd double back. At least long enough for us to regroup and move on. But that plan wouldn't have worked, would it? You aren't looking for us in any traditional way."

He held his free hand out to her, an invitation to take it and step through his gate. Not anything more. Not the surety and comfort she irrationally wanted from him, a stranger. Yet a part of her knew he wasn't a stranger. She recognized a fellow soldier who strove to protect innocent lives, a kindred spirit, a match she hadn't realized she'd been looking for.

"No, I have... an ability that lets me hone in on a... person—"

"Jeez, you can say it." She squared her shoulders and took his hand. "Magic. You have magic that lets you find humans with magic." A shiver threatened to shake her, but she managed to keep steady. "See, I'm holding my shit together even while looking at that black hole."

"Oh, yeah, you're not affected at all," he said, his tone sarcastic. "I'm stuck in your head, remember?"

But please, not hearing everything. Oh, man. That would be embarrassing.

He didn't respond to that, so perhaps—thank God—her confused emotions weren't bleeding through the connection.

"Fine," she forced out. She'd carry on as if he didn't know. When she got herself fully together, she'd consider her emotions. Until then, not feeling anything and moving forward was the only way to get through this. "Given the circumstances, I'm holding enough of my shit together to function."

"I'll give you that." He pulled her into the gate, and the stomach-churning, mind-burning darkness enveloped her.

The tremor she'd been fighting rushed through her, and with a gust of wind, the world returned. She staggered forward, her legs wobbly, her pulse racing, and the people yelling and hissing in her head grew louder than before.

Nero's grip on her hand tightened, and he tugged her to his chest, giving her something to steady herself against. Warmth flooded her body and the voices vanished. For a moment—a few seconds that she yearned would last longer—she felt safe and steady, as if just being in contact with Nero anchored her. There was a surety in his presence. One she craved and wasn't going to think about, for fear she'd break down and take him with her. So much fear and determination radiated from him. And so much certainty from the depths of his being. He had a purpose, just like she'd had in Afghanistan, to protect those who couldn't protect themselves. Except, as much as she feared and hoped she was part of his purpose, his family, a part of her was disappointed she was lumped into the same category as his children.

Nero forced himself to relax his embrace around Becca. She'd stumbled coming out of the gate, and he'd instinctually drawn her close to steady her. Now that she was tucked perfectly against his body, he didn't want to let her go. This was where she belonged. This was right.

Except it wasn't right. It was his dugga's magic making him feel that way, and even if he was impossibly inamorated, she wasn't.

The only saving grace to the physical contact was that the voices in her head—now also yelling in Nero's—had gone silent. The pain, however, had returned to radiate through his skull, although he wasn't certain if it was hers or just his.

She eased out of his arms and cleared her throat. "Thanks," she said in her soft alto, making him yearn to draw her back into his embrace.

The voices rushed back into her head and swelled through him. His temples pounded, but she didn't try to turn their volume down, afraid she'd hurt him again.

A fact he wasn't going to put too much significance on. It didn't mean she was inamorated back. It meant she cared about hurting other people. That was all.

He forced his attention away from her and scanned the area. They stood beside an open door at an abandoned 19th century brown brick three-story factory. Before him lay the parking lot, covered with undisturbed hardened snow that sparkled in the moonlight, indicating no one had come in from the road since the snowfall, melt, and then freeze a few days ago. Beyond stretched the road coming from the bend around one hill and disappearing down the slope of another.

There wasn't another building in sight, only tree-covered snowy hills. He remembered the place well. He'd been hit with a flash of the location with almost a dozen mages inside and had sent Diablo to check it out, only to have the drake discover the building was empty.

"Doesn't look like anyone is here," he said. "No tracks." Although lack of tracks in the parking lot didn't necessarily mean the building was empty.

"Werner had already thought about that. After you sent Diablo here and we all fled, we agreed if we returned, we would approach from the hills and enter at the back."

Becca's aura brushed his. She'd turned to the door, inadvertently stepping closer to him—he didn't even need to see her to know she'd moved—and he ached with the need to hold her again. His gaze slid to her, drawn of its own volition, and he was too tired to fight it.

"That's smart."

"He was a soldier, too... if his story is true... which I guess it is." Her essence trembled in his head. "I guess he really is a German World War II soldier who was picked up in Berlin... East Berlin... in 1949 and speaks English because of the dragon who'd possessed him. I guess—" Her mental shaking grew stronger.

Pain sliced through Nero's skull. He needed to distract her before she incapacitated him.

"Take a breath and tell me where your friend might be. The place is pretty big." And if he recalled correctly, it was a maze of shelves and machinery on the first floor and then a warren of offices on the second and third floors.

"Right." She drew in a ragged breath, but the roar in her head and the pain remained, and she hugged herself tighter. Last time she'd been there, she'd thought it was all a nightmare. It still felt like one. She'd lost years of her life, was in a foreign country without a passport or any kind of identification, and now the voices— God, the voices just kept getting louder, but there were so many she couldn't understand any of them.

She shifted her weight from one foot to the other.

He could feel her thoughts whirling through his head, and her determination to enter, but also the fear of what would happen if she did.

She'd been cold and starving and confused. She hadn't been able to stop thinking about the monsters and the cave. She'd wanted to go home, but didn't know where home was anymore. Where was up or down, left or right, or anything? Nothing had been real, and yet it had all been too real.

Her will clenched around her essence, catching him up with it and slicing more pain through his head.

I can do this. I have to do this.

A tremor raced through her, and her panic tightened her grip on him even more.

But is it worth it? Really? This might be a demon she wanted to face, but it wasn't necessary to face it right now. She could come back when she was ready. "Perhaps you should use your magic to find Werner," she said.

"Yeah." Except he didn't know if using his dugga's magic would send him into convulsions. And if he was convulsing, he couldn't protect Becca or summon a gate to get back home if anything happened to her, as well.

"I see." She squared her shoulders. "You're right. If using your magic could incapacitate you or both of us, then don't."

"I can go in myself and search." He raised his hand to brush her arm, steal a whisper of contact, but managed to shove it into his coat pocket instead. "You don't have to go in. I could also gate you back to Raven and return to search alone."

Something thumped inside, and two crows flew out a broken

second-story window, screaming their complaint. Nero tensed and jerked his attention to the doorway. So did Becca.

"Werner," she said. *Except it might not be him.* Her thought was so strong, Nero almost mistook it for having been said out loud.

"But it might be him." From this angle, he could only see a few feet inside, even with his night sight. "If I can get within spotting distance, I'll be able to tell if it's him from his aura."

"It could also be anyone." *It could be Stanbury's men, and we don't have sidearms. Except if it was Stanbury's men, how did they learn about this place?*

"It doesn't matter. I'm hardly unarmed."

"You've done that twice now." She leveled a glare at him that made his pulse rush with desire, likely the opposite of her intended effect.

If she flashed a little teeth and growled, he might not be able to control himself.

"Didn't Raven say that was rude?" she asked.

"Didn't Raven what?" *What was she talking about again?*

Listening to my thoughts, she thought, so loudly he wasn't sure if she'd meant to think that at him or say that to him.

"Yeah, well, you responded to mine as well. Or didn't you notice?" But he pulled his essence back into a tight ball in hopes that would dim the connection between them. He'd done it back in the café. He'd just gotten distracted when they'd arrived here. Holy hell, had he gotten distracted. Jeez, this was embarrassing. "You okay to wait here?"

She glared at him again. "I'm not waiting here. If it's Werner, you'll need me to convince him you're not going to kill him. If it's anyone other than Werner or a homeless person, you might need backup. In the very least, it'll be easier to get out of here if we're together." She glanced through the doorway, then grabbed an arm-length piece of pipe and a flashlight that had been tucked tight against the frame on the floor.

But if it's a drag—

"I can't hear you," she said, glaring at him, "but I *know* you're thinking something. Your expression turned moody." She flicked on the flashlight, stepped inside, and made room for Nero to move past and take the lead.

"I was thinking if it's a dragon, that pipe isn't going to be much help."

"If it's one of Stanbury's men, it'll do fine enough. At least until I can upgrade to a sidearm."

"When we get back to the house, you're going to tell me about this Stanbury." He strode past her, his night sight giving him a clear view of the debris and garbage littering the open area just inside the door. "You should also stick close."

"Yeah. I've always been pretty good at seeing in the dark, but this flashlight isn't very bright and I don't have magical night vision like some drakes." She shuddered. "I just said that, didn't I?"

"You did, and yes, I do." *And please don't let that overwhelm you.* That was the second slip of knowledge she shouldn't have. First was the likely truth about her friend's impossible story and now this. Whatever mental barrier she'd created to protect herself was starting to come down and soon she'd be forced to fully face reality. Here was hoping it came slowly, not in a great overwhelming wave.

"Good," she said. "Lead the way. Those crows came from the second floor. There's a set of stairs at the back. If you keep to the left, that'll take you straight there."

He followed a narrow passage between the wall, towering shelves, and massive machinery to an open area at the back, where a rickety wooden staircase led up to the second floor. Pain still radiated through his skull, and the voices in Becca's head were getting louder, making it impossible to listen for sounds of someone above.

As much as he wanted whoever was there to be Becca's friend, the odds weren't in their favor. It was more likely the wind had knocked something over, and that was what had disturbed the crows. And once he'd confirmed that, he could take her back to the transition suites and hold her tight—

No, leave her.

His chest ached at the thought.

God damn it. Concentrate. He had to get the hell away from her and regain his bearings.

He stepped onto the first rickety stair as something tingled across his senses and made him pause. It was just a flicker. He wasn't sure what. It felt like a human mage's aura. Probably Becca's. Except it didn't feel like Becca's.

Movement at the edge of his vision caught his attention, and he jerked off the step into Becca. Taser barbs clattered against the cinderblock wall behind him, and half a dozen men in black tactical gear, helmets, and night vision goggles rushed into the open area with weapons drawn—two with Tasers, the rest with Glocks.

Above, someone screamed, and Becca's friend shoved another man in tactical gear through the railing at the top of the stairs. He landed with a sickening crunch on the concrete floor and didn't move.

"Werner," Becca said.

Werner's gaze leapt to her then jumped to Nero, and his expression hardened. "Get away from her."

Two of the men with Glocks fired at Werner, forcing him to jerk back into the second story hall. More gunfire exploded from above, and someone screamed.

Becca grabbed Nero's arm—the voices vanished but pain roared in his skull. She wrenched him aside as two more Taser barbs hit the wall beside him.

"We need cover."

"No." He hissed his power word, sending more pain lancing into him, then slammed a gust of wind at the three closest men, crashing them into the side of a massive machine. "We need to get to your friend and get out of here." On a good day, he could probably take all of them in a fight, but with the pain in his head and his soul howling to ensure Becca's safety, he couldn't afford to risk it. Retreat was the best option.

"We'll be sitting ducks running up those stairs," she said.

Another man in tactical gear staggered onto the second story landing. Werner kicked him in the gut and shoved him over the edge.

Nero blasted more wind at the other two men on their level, but they'd tucked themselves behind more machinery and he couldn't get in a good strike. He also couldn't see the sixth man and was damned sure there'd been six before.

"Werner, back door." Becca turned away from the stairs and headed to a doorway half hidden behind a toppled shelf, her flashlight beam jumping over the floor before her as she ran. "This way."

A tremor swept through Nero's left arm as he sent another gust at the men, forcing them to stay behind their cover, and raced after her. They scrambled into a cramped boiler room with enormous octopus boilers and tangles of pipes.

There's a second door into the two-story addition at the back, through here. She twisted to the side and slipped between a set of heavy pipes and another toppled metal shelving unit.

The light from her flashlight vanished for a second, and Nero's pulse sped faster.

He snapped a lasso of wind around the shelf. His magic stuttered, dropped the shelf, then strengthened and reconnected. He ground his teeth and shoved the shelf aside to make room for him. Now wasn't the time for his magic to fail. But the voices in Becca's head had increased, as if the immediate needs of the fight had distracted her and she'd lost her concentration on keeping them quiet—or at least to a dull roar.

Her will clenched tight as she rounded a concrete pillar lined with more snaking pipes. The voices dimmed, but the pain in Nero's head increased and so did the tremor in his muscles. Her flashlight jerked up to shine on a closed door, thirty feet ahead of them, with a foggy glass window. She stumbled on something, her light dipped, and a man-sized shadow rushed up behind the glass.

Werner? Becca caught her balance and raised her pipe.

The door flew open, and a man in tactical gear aimed a Glock at her.

23

Nero's pulse froze at the sight of the Glock pointed at Becca's head. One shot and she'd be dead. But Becca lunged at the guy in the doorway before he could fire and cracked the pipe against his sidearm. A bang roared through the cramped room and debris on the floor jumped away from their feet as the bullet impacted the floor. She wrenched the pipe up and smashed it against the side of his head.

The man staggered back, and Nero seized him with a wind whip and slammed him into the concrete pillar they'd just passed. Behind him, something crashed, and someone yelled. The rest of the tactical team was still after them.

Becca leapt back from the doorway. "There's more coming from this way." *That makes what? Nine or ten?*

"I'd say, with the two your friend took out, at least a team of twelve."

"For me?"

"Might be for your friend." The earth magic he'd displayed during the fight outside the facility had looked dangerous. Probably some form of energy or soul consumption. But if he was that dangerous and they knew where to find him, it didn't make sense to have waited so long to grab him.

"This is a trap for me." *So I can end up being a trap for you.* Her will tightened even more around him.

Two men rushed toward them from around one of the boilers. The first guy knelt to help the man Nero had tossed into the pillar. The other raised his Taser.

Nero sent a lurching gust at them, then jerked his attention to the office doorway, where three men had taken cover, one behind a pillar, the other two behind toppled filing cabinets. He and Becca were surrounded, and while he could summon a gate, he still needed a good few seconds to make it large enough for them to pass through. His gates didn't rapidly form like Diablo's, and that opened them up to an attack. He needed to get them some place safe.

A gunshot exploded behind him and pain sliced through his chest. Becca screamed, and Nero blasted wind at the guys behind him. Someone yelled, and two more gunshots roared from the office in front of him while pain sliced his shoulder and thigh.

Oh, God, he's hit.

"I'm fine. It'll be healed in a few seconds." *And any internal injuries will heal within the hour, but we still have to get the hell out of here for me to summon a gate.*

The men in the boiler room scrambled closer. He swept another gust of wind, but it sputtered out before it hit them.

Shit. "Tell me there's another way out of here." He ground his teeth, fighting past the pain, and willed his wind back into a gust that forced the men to take cover.

"No." *But they want me alive.* Becca lunged through the door into the office.

God damn it. Nero bolted after her, sending his wind behind them to cover their backs.

She slid over a debris-strewn desk and dove for the closest guy, who jerked his weapon down and scrambled to draw his Taser.

I was right. She grabbed the barrel of his gun, smashed the pipe against the man's face, and yanked the weapon from his grip.

The other two men aimed, ready to fire at Nero, but he sent a blast at them and heaved their hands up, throwing off their aim.

More gunfire exploded behind him. Another bullet pounded into his back, cutting through the almost-healed wound in his chest with searing pain. His knees buckled, and he swept wind around himself to catch his balance.

Nero? Becca's fear and pain flooded him, making his wind waver.

He staggered, re-caught his balance, and rushed around the desk. *I'm fine. Just keep going.*

The back door is straight ahead. She smashed the pipe against her guy's head a second time then dropped the pipe, switched her grip on the gun, and fired at the other two men in the office, forcing them to tuck tighter behind their cabinets.

The back door stood partially ajar, with a toppled shelf and a fallen I-beam between them and escape. Nero gusted wind at the cabinets and smashed them into the men ahead of them, while Becca fired behind him into the boiler room. It was as if she'd known who he was going after and acted to cover his back. Of course, she *could* have known. She was in his head, an agonizing presence squeezing his essence so tight it was hard to keep his wind activated. Hell, it was hard to even breathe.

Get the door, she said, and he knew she meant with his wind.

Duck.

She dropped to one knee as he seized the rusted metal security door with his magic, wrenched it off its rusted hinges, and tossed it behind him at the men coming from the boiler room. Someone screamed. More gunfire exploded.

"I said don't hit the girl!" someone yelled.

Pain burned through Nero's skull and his wind faltered. Even if they got out of the building, they still needed to get away long enough for Nero to summon a gate. What he needed was for them to get out and for his wind to have enough power to pull the roof down behind them.

He hissed his power word, hoping to build up more magic, but it flickered, a whisper of wind trailing around his hands, and the agony in his head grew. Becca's hold was too tight. She had to let go. Just for a second.

But the voices. They're so loud. I can't—

Please. Just get out the door and let go for a second.

She gave a tight nod and ducked under the angled I-beam. Nero raced after her and yelled his power word, praying the force of the call would help him summon and hold onto his magic.

Just a few more feet. Becca was now framed in the doorway with a pale snowy yard beyond that sparkling in the moonlight.

The cabinet closest to him heaved aside, and one of the men jerked his Glock up and fired.

Becca gasped as searing agony shot through her chest and Nero's.

She stumbled. *Oh, God.* And collapsed in the snow just outside the door.

No. Mother, no. Nero's pulse skipped a beat. She'd been shot. She was down. He was going to lose another inamorata and before he'd even had a chance to get to know her.

Rage roared through him, and his wind erupted over his hands with a ferocity he hadn't known was possible. He bolted out the door, grabbed Becca, and slammed his magic into the office. It hit like a tornado into the two-story addition on the back of the factory, sweeping debris and furniture and broken glass into a slicing, piercing, crushing vortex.

The men inside screamed, tossed with the furniture, slammed into the walls and ceiling like toys, until a deafening crack cut through the roar of the wind and the outside wall of the addition collapsed, pulling it down along with part of the main brick wall.

Nero dropped to the ground and ripped open Becca's bloody coat. Blood stained the front of her hoodie, the tear above her left breast ragged. He pressed his hands to the wound but knew applying pressure wouldn't stop the bleeding if the wound was a through-and-through.

She gasped for breath, her eyes wide, her thoughts an incoherent whirl in his head.

"Hold on." *Please, Mother. Hold on.*

But they both knew the shot was fatal. Blood already pooled beneath her, seeping a wide swath over the hardened snow, dark against its brilliant white. She was losing too much too fast. The bullet had to have severed an artery. If she was a dragon, she'd survive. If she was a true human mage, she'd survive. But she wasn't either, despite what her miraculously healed bones suggested. He had to have been mistaken about that... or it was the new intake's magic... or something.

Right now, all he knew was that she was human, with a bit of magic. Not nearly enough magic. And in the flash of a heartbeat, a split second of knowing her, his soul had picked hers for eternity. He could try to deny it all he wanted, but that wouldn't change the truth. She was his inamorata.

The myth about there only ever being one might be a lie, but it had taken him almost two thousand years to find another. He couldn't go through that again. *Mother, please. I can't.*

Cold seeped through their mental connection. Becca's breath gurgled, and blood bubbled over her lips.

There had to be a way to save her. There had to.

Now you'll be safe, she thought. *It can mean something.* "I die, your kids are safe."

But the price was too high. His soul was already shattering, howling with desperation. If he lost it, his *puzur* wouldn't be safe. He wouldn't be able to protect them. He couldn't even protect his inamorata.

A scream tore from him. He couldn't face the desolation of losing an inamorata again. His chest burned, and his heart and soul squeezed in anguish. There was no purpose without her. And yes, it didn't make sense, he didn't know her, and she didn't love him back. But being inamorated didn't make sense. It wouldn't matter if she despised him. His soul had picked. She was his match, his destiny. And she was dying in a frozen parking lot, her blood oozing hot between his fingers.

She didn't deserve this. Not with everything she'd already survived. Mother, if he'd just gotten shot instead. He could heal this. Hell, even if the impossible happened and his soul magic couldn't heal the wound, at least she'd be alive. At least she could have had the life Zenobia's dragons had tried to take from her. If she could just survive this, she'd overcome the soul sickness. Raven would help her. The *puzur* would take her in. She'd be all right. They had to get back to the house. Anaea could rebirth Becca, like she'd done with Ryan.

He pressed a hand to the ground beside him, hissed his power word, and summoned a gate.

More blood bubbled over Becca's lips and her thoughts shuddered, turning to fog in his head. He could feel her soul weakening.

Come on. Come on. The gate was forming so slowly. Each second drew into an agonizing eternity.

She wasn't going to make it. And even if they could get to the house, there was no guarantee help would arrive in time. He was going to lose her. Mother. This wasn't going to work. There had to be something else he could do. Some way he could save her. Some way he could take her suffering.

An inferno erupted in his chest. Agony screamed through every cell in his body as the flesh and sinew in his back and chest over his heart burst, as if a bullet had torn through his body, but no one had fired. White lightning shot through him, stealing all thought and breath. There was no up or down, no frozen parking lot, no cold. Only agony, and Becca screaming in his head.

24

Darkness surrounded Becca, thick and consuming, but still the voices howled in her head, Nero's strongest of all. He was going to lose her. He couldn't lose her. He—

She jerked, and her back hit something hard as heat enveloped her. Except her back couldn't have *hit* something. She was already lying on the ground. Outside. In the cold.

No. Not outside. There was a ceiling with a light fixture above her. Her thoughts stuttered, her mind and body filled with a searing agony, while the voices howled.

Nero screamed and collapsed unconscious on top of her. Someone yelled.

She had to protect them. Get them out of wherever the hell they were. She heaved him over and yanked up her stolen gun. Raven, Diablo, and another man—God, he was huge and looked like a Viking, but was dressed in a well-tailored suit—sat around the table in the kitchenette in Nero's transition suites.

Diablo stood and his chair clattered over. "What the hell?"

"Oh, my God." Raven scrambled toward them. "What happened?"

"We—" *Shot. I was shot. But—* Becca could breathe, when moments before she couldn't. The pain in her chest wasn't the agonizing fire of before, either.

Nero gasped and blood pooled beneath him and around her knees.

"How—?" It didn't make sense. But he'd been shot. "He said he could heal it. He said—" She ripped open his coat. Blood soaked his dress shirt. She ripped that, too, revealing a gaping wound over his left pec. "Why isn't he healing?"

"He should be. He shouldn't be unconscious." Raven grabbed a fistful of napkins from the table and pressed them against Nero's chest. Just like how Nero had applied pressure on Becca's chest.

Her thoughts snapped, sending shards of agony slicing into her head.

She'd been shot.

In the chest. Above the heart.

Her pulse beat faster, and the voices in her head roared louder.

"Diablo? Why isn't he healing?" Raven asked.

"I don't know." Diablo vanished with a whoosh. A fraction of a second later with another whoosh, he reappeared in the hall and pulled a medical kit and an armful of towels from the cabinet.

Becca couldn't catch her breath. She couldn't focus her thoughts.

Right above the heart.

She clawed at her hoodie. There was blood on her clothes. There was a hole. There was—

"I was shot," she gasped.

"She's human," Raven said.

"Let me look," the big blond guy said. He knelt beside her, but she hadn't seen him move. Had he gated liked Diablo? She hadn't felt the air gust. No, time had jumped. Darkness flashed in her head. More thoughts snapped into shards and more voices clamored to be heard.

Another whoosh and Diablo was back, kneeling beside Raven. "He's barely breathing. He should have healed enough to be conscious."

"But I was shot."

The blond guy grabbed her hands and drew her focus. Grey. His name was Grey, but she had no idea how she knew that.

"Where?" he asked.

"Above the heart."

His gaze dipped to the hole and the blood soaking the front of her hoodie. *She's a sorcerer?*

"Nero said I wasn't." No, that wasn't right. "He thought that? I can't—" God, it was so hard to think.

"What happened?" Grey's grip tightened and his eyes narrowed. He was dangerous. A dragon. A monster... not a monster... not—

"I—"

"Tell me." *Tell me. Now.*

"Grey." Raven replaced the napkins against Nero's chest with a towel. "Stop."

A tremor shook Becca and the voices turned to hisses. *Something is wrong. I don't know how to save him. I can't lose him. I have to know what happened. She's done something to him. She's killed him. She—*

"I didn't. He said he could heal. He was fine. Then I was shot, and he started screaming about losing another one." She rammed her foot into Grey's side, wrenched free from his grip, and scrambled to her feet.

Another what? Raven asked. "Lose another mage?"

"I don't know." It hurt to think.

Grey stood, and Becca's pulse beat faster. The pulse she wasn't supposed to have.

"I won't let you take me back. I'm not going back." The gun lay a few feet away.

"You're not going back," Raven said.

"Lose another what?" Grey tensed, his muscle bunching and straining against his dress shirt.

More tremors clawed through her and agony sliced in her skull. It hurt to think. Everything hurt. Her chest burned and everything within her was screaming. "He's supposed to be healing."

"Lose another what?" Grey asked again.

"An inamorata," Diablo said. *He's God damned inamorated with a soul-sick human.*

"A what?" Raven's gaze leapt to him. *Holy Mother.*

An inamorata? "He's taken on her injuries," Grey said.

"You can do that if you're inamorated?" Raven jerked her chin at Diablo. "Help me roll him. I want to check his back."

Another tremor shook Becca and she hugged herself. Somehow he'd taken it from her. The hole in her chest. Certain death. God, he was going to die, and it was her fault.

"How the hell can a soul bond transfer an injury?" Diablo growled as he helped Raven roll Nero on his side.

"As far as I know, it's only happened once, and that was before the Scourge." Grey shifted closer to Becca.

She jerked back. "I didn't know. He shouldn't have. I—" The shakes increased, making her teeth chatter. Magic. He'd saved her with magic. Impossible magic. And now she was going to be the reason someone else died.

"If he's inamorated and you were shot, he wouldn't have been able to stop himself." Raven shoved Nero's jacket off his shoulders to expose his back. *He would have died for her. I would have lost him. Mother, please. Why hasn't he healed this?*

"I didn't do this. I didn't make him—" He didn't know her, but he'd die for her? That didn't make any sense. Magic didn't make sense. But the monsters had possessed magic.

Fucking soul bond. Something like this was bound to happen sooner rather than later. The thought sliced through her, but she couldn't tell who thought it.

"Will he heal this?" Raven asked. She grabbed a pair of scissors from the first aid kit and cut open the back of Nero's shirt.

"He will," Grey said. "But because it's a magical transfer, it'll be slower than normal."

"As slow as you?" Diablo asked. *We have to keep her here. Ensure Nero's safety.*

"Does anyone heal as slowly as I do?" Grey rolled his eyes. "His soul magic is working double time, first to keep the wound from reforming in her and then to heal the injury."

"I think the bleeding might be slowing down." Raven ripped open a sterile wipe and dabbed at Nero's back.

"He'll be okay?" *Please, he had to be okay.* Becca had no idea what she'd do if he wasn't.

He won't be fucking okay. He's inamorated, Diablo growled.

"I don't know what that means!" More pain sliced through Becca's head and her legs buckled. Grey grabbed for her, but she wrenched out of reach. "He shouldn't have saved me. I endanger everything." It was like Afghanistan all over again. The Taliban had learned she'd been meeting with the village elders. She'd put all those people in danger, killed all those people in the market and all those children in the school tent, and had murdered Scott and Johnson and paralyzed Keller. All by taking her unit back to that village. Nero had children in his house, people he had to protect. She was broken and hunted. She'd made him go with her to find Werner, and it had been another ambush.

The muscles in her chest and arms seized and stole her breath. Nero gasped, and his thoughts blasted into a scream of pain and desperation.

Her knees gave out, and she didn't have the strength to catch her balance. She fell to her hands and knees. His agony overwhelmed her and his thoughts howled, devouring all the other voices. She had to live. She was everything. He couldn't lose another. Please, Mother, not another.

"I didn't ask you to save me," she screamed at him. "You should have let me die." Then she wouldn't have to fight the voices and the memories and the terror. Her throat tightened. This wasn't real. It was a nightmare. It couldn't be real. It couldn't be happening.

"Ah, fuck, she's losing it." Diablo vanished with the whoosh.

Grey grabbed her shoulders. She tried to jerk away, but he held tight. "I won't let you take me again. I won't. You can't." She clawed at his hands. "Stay out of my head. It's my body. My soul."

Grey heaved her around, planting her back against his chest, and wrapped her in a bear hug. *Holy Mother, she's soul sick.* "Raven, what do we do?"

Air gusted, and Diablo appeared beside her and jammed a needle in her shoulder. "Sedate her."

"No. I won't go back. I won't—" Weight rushed through her limbs.

Another pinch in her shoulder.

"A double dose?" Grey asked, his voice rumbling into her back, making the drug's weight billow to her extremities.

"Trust me," Diablo said.

Becca dragged her gaze to Nero. He groaned, opened one eye, and stared at her as if he instantly knew where she was.

It'll be all right, he thought. *I've got you. You'll be okay.*

But she could feel the insanity threatening to overwhelm her. He'd saved her with magic. Impossible magic. Those monsters in the cave had been real. Stanbury and her facility were real. It hurt to think about it. It would have been easier if it was just a nightmare and she could wake up. Please. She just wanted to wake up... or never wake up. Then he wouldn't be in danger, and his kids would be safe.

"You shouldn't have saved me. You don't know me." *I endanger everything. I don't deserve to be saved.*

Yes, you do.

Diablo turned to Nero and slid a third syringe into his shoulder.

Just take a breath. You can handle this.

I can't. God. I can't.

Yes, Nero said, his thought soft and sure as unconsciousness started to flood through her. *Just breathe.*

25

Becca collapsed in Grey's arms and Nero went lax in Raven's. Diablo wrenched himself away from them to the far side of the kitchenette, his beast roaring and clawing at his insides. He needed to scream, fight someone, break something, anything to ease the raging emotions. For a second, when Becca and Nero had first appeared, there'd been a frozen moment of nothing, then a massive wave had exploded through him carrying her panic and desperation and pain. So much pain. It had only gotten worse when Nero had regained consciousness. More agony and heart-rending terror.

"Okay," Raven said, her voice breathy.

Diablo ground his teeth. Her and Grey's fear remained the only emotions in the room—and, thank the Mother, at a fraction of the force of Nero's and his human's—but it still set his beast on edge.

"Okay." She tossed the sterile wipe to the floor beside her, grabbed a towel, and dabbed at Nero's back. "Okay."

Her fear didn't diminish.

"Okay.

Mother of All. "Stop saying okay," Diablo snapped.

"She's just trying to get her bearings." Grey adjusted his grip on Becca and hooked his forearm under her legs, holding her cradled against his chest. "It's all just a little shocking."

"You God damn think? The dugga of the Asar Nergal is fucking inamorated with a human mage." *And your fear is making me want to punch someone.* He glared at Grey. "How long will he be hurt?"

"I have no idea," Grey said. "I only read about it in one of the Handmaiden's books. She'd been wondering if, in our new human state, being inamorated was even possible."

"Fucking wonderful." The longer Nero was out of commission, the greater the chance the problems at Court would make an appearance. That's what they'd been doing down there in the first place. Raven had needed to stay near the new intake, who had yet to regain consciousness even long enough to give her his name, and he and Grey had joined her to figure out what the hell to do about everything.

"At least we can still soul bond." Raven rolled Nero onto his back, the towel still in place behind him, and checked the hole in his chest.

"That's not a good thing," Diablo growled. It was a fucking mental illness and everyone around him was falling victim.

"It is what it is," Grey said.

Diablo's beast snarled. "It is what it is?" He jerked toward Grey, but managed to wrench himself into stillness instead of crossing the remaining feet to the silver drake. "She's soul sick. She's one of Zenobia's broken toys, and she's going to destroy this *puzur.*"

"You don't know that." Raven glared at him.

"You're willing to bet Mia and Jeff and Tyler and all the others' lives on that?" Was she willing to bet her own life on that, because he sure as hell wasn't.

"He's inamorated. He doesn't have a choice." Grey's expression turned fierce, and his love for his inamorata flooded Diablo. Grey would do anything, including sacrifice himself, to protect his soul mate. The emotion defied logic. It really was a mental illness.

"We need a plan," Diablo said. A way out. Mother, a way to save Nero when his human succumbed fully to the soul sickness.

"I agree," Grey said. "First, let's get these two in a bed. Is there anything big enough down here for two?"

"Because they're in luuuuv?" Diablo's beast shuddered.

The muscles in Grey's jaw twitched, but his emotions softened toward Diablo—not the response the beast wanted.

How the hell was he going to get a fight if he couldn't rile anyone up?

Not fucking now, he hissed at himself. *Just hold your shit together long enough to figure out how to deal with Nero being inamorated.*

"They should be together so it's easier for Nero's soul magic to deal with taking on her injury. If either one of them was conscious, I'd suggest getting him into a bath."

"Running water is better for water drakes," Raven said.

"I'm sure Nero has a tub with jets," Grey said. "But again. Both unconscious. It'll be easier to just put them in a bed while we figure out what we're going to do about this… development."

"And by development, you mean fucking insanity," Diablo said.

"For the love of—" Raven sat back on her heels. "Pick up Nero and gate him to the room with the queen bed. I want him down here so I can keep an eye on everyone."

"Fine. Whatever." Diablo picked Nero up, making sure to also hold the towel against his doyen's back, and gated to the room at the end of the hall. It had a queen bed because sixty years before, they'd rescued twins with a linked earth magic and there had been separation issues when their earth magic had first awakened.

He set Nero on the bed and forced himself to the far side of the room before he could grab the black drake and shake him. What was he thinking, letting himself get inamorated? It put everyone at risk. Except Becca knew that. She probably knew a whole lot of things, including all of Nero's secrets. As a telepath and with the bond of being inamorated, she was probably in Nero's head. No, she was *stuck* in his head.

That had been clear from the emotions pouring from her. She'd been terrified she couldn't control her magic. She'd been terrified of magic. But nothing had been more terrifying than realizing Nero was willing to sacrifice himself and everything he held dear for her. And with all that fear, Diablo couldn't tell if Becca was inamorated back. That would just suck, since Nero's emotions had been clear.

His soul had chosen her. But he'd also been confused, as if there'd been something wrong about being inamorated with Becca.

Yeah, well, there was everything wrong with being inamorated with the human. Especially if the human wasn't inamorated back. Even worse if that human went crazy.

Grey strode through the doorway and laid Becca on the bed beside Nero. Raven followed with the towels and the first aid kit.

"At least her aura is strong," Grey said, setting Becca's hand on Nero's.

A wave of calm from Nero washed through Diablo, as if just that simple contact was enough to ease some of the turmoil.

"Strong aura means strong magic." Diablo shifted, uncomfortable with Nero's comfort. "She's not a natural. That means it'll be harder for her to accept reality."

"Strong aura might also mean that even dragons with the ability to see the difference between humans and drakes might not be able to tell she's human," Grey said.

Raven set the extra towels on the bed beside Nero and put the first aid kit on the bedside table. "I didn't know you could see the difference."

"I can't." Grey tapped his temple. "Read that in one of the Handmaiden's books, as well."

"Was there anything in those books about how to uninamorate a dragon?" That would solve all their problems.

Raven glared at Diablo. "You'd really take this away from him?"

"To save him and all of us when she loses it? Hell, yes."

Grey's expression darkened, and a wave of danger and sadness billowed from him. "You don't understand what you're talking about."

"I understand that if any dragon sees Nero with that woman and realizes she's human, he's dead. Regis won't care about saving his soul. He'll send whoever his assassin of the week is and kill him."

"I doubt Nero will be taking her to Court." Raven checked the wound on Nero's chest, and her emotions turned to relief. Guess the wound was finally sealing shut. It wouldn't be long before the internal injuries were taken care of and his soul magic had burned through the sedative keeping him unconscious. Which only brought them back to their original problem.

"Dragons don't just live at Court," Diablo said. "Is he going to take her to his home in Rome? Sure, a third of our coterie knows about the *puzur*, but another third thinks he's a Traditionalist and has given Regis his full support."

"If Regis gets his way, there'll be very few dragons living in the human world," Grey said.

"That's a whole other problem, and we aren't going to figure anything out right now." Raven squared her shoulders. Now that Nero was out of immediate danger, her relief was being overwhelmed with exhaustion. She'd been helping Anaea with her out-of-control magic for almost two weeks now, which had to be stressful enough, but yesterday she'd had an all-day vigil with the new intake who, for some reason, wasn't waking up. And now she had one of Zenobia's victims to save because their doyen was inamorated with her. And there wasn't a damned thing Diablo could do to fix any of that.

His beast growled and churned.

And no, killing Becca wouldn't really solve anything, as much as that seemed like the easiest answer.

Mother, he really needed to hit something.

26

B ecca woke to silence. Glorious, peaceful silence. The pain in her head and chest was gone, and so were the voices... voices she shouldn't have been able to hear in the first place.

A hint of panic squeezed around her heart. She stiffened, and the person beside her—no, it wasn't just some person, it was Nero—shifted in his sleep, sliding his arm around her and drawing her against him, her back to his chest. His warmth seeped into her body and spread to every cell, easing the panic and filling her with a calm certainty and—if she was being honest with herself—a sizzling desire she wasn't sure she wanted to keep ignoring. It churned her insides, made her breath hitch, and charged the calm warmth into sudden sultry need.

The panic over her insane reality and the fear she wouldn't be strong enough to fight for herself and her friends vanished. All that remained was the alluring feel of his body tucked tight against her back and his arm holding her secure.

His warm breath feathered over the back of her neck, scorching need through her veins to her core. There were no voices, no fear, only him, and his essence magically anchoring her within herself.

Yes. Magic. *He* was magic and not just in how she craved him.

There was something about him and his soul that, if she accepted it, steadied her. Told her that she was all right.

Except the memory of them appearing in the kitchenette flashed into her mind. He'd been willing to sacrifice himself and everything he held dear just to save her. That wasn't all right. He barely knew her, and just existing with her mental connection to him put lives in danger. The devil had said... thought?... jeez, did it matter? He'd said that Nero was inamorated, but she didn't know what that meant—

And yet, a part of her did know.

Soul bound. Forever.

The thought drew another shiver, and God help her, it wasn't one of fear.

She eased from his embrace, not wanting to face the truth about his *condition,* and the whisper of voices flooded her head again. She concentrated on turning her mental volume knob down. Nero groaned but didn't wake, and the voices dimmed.

What were the odds she was getting better at that?

She bit back a sigh. She could only hope. It had been agonizing, back at the abandoned factory. She'd fought to stay focused on her thoughts while everyone else had screamed at her, but she'd been afraid if she tried to shut them up she'd hurt Nero. The sooner she figured out how to disconnect herself from him, the better.

But that thought made her chest ache. He'd been the one steady voice inside her when everything else had gone crazy. He was the calm in the middle of her storm, and she didn't want to lose that. Except she had to. She endangered everything he cared about, and she now had proof he'd sacrifice it all to save her. She just had no idea if she'd be able to keep it together without him.

She slid out of bed and hugged herself, her hoodie stiff and crusty with her blood.

Some soldier she was. She needed to stand on her own. Only then could she be an asset to a partnership... which they didn't have... because they barely knew each other... and because she had to get as far away from him as possible to protect his family. She might not have a family anymore, but she knew what it was like to have one. It was precious and deserved to be safe. She could do that for him, and them... and for herself.

She had to. She also had to get her shit together, returned to the factory and find Werner... and if he hadn't escaped from Stanbury's men, she had to return to the facility for him, Glenn, and the others —she wasn't even going to contemplate the possibility that Werner was dead. That would mean she'd failed at everything and she couldn't accept that.

A soft feminine voice said something from down the hall. Raven. She had to be talking to the guy in the bed again. Maybe she'd have some insight into how to control this—God, Becca couldn't believe she was going to think it—this magic. In the very least, maybe Raven had a way to not break down in a panic when magic reared its dangerous head and things got stressful, something Becca could use when she headed out on her own to find Werner.

A shudder swept through Becca, but the certainty from Nero's presence within her billowed and soothed it. Even the other voices softened a bit. She mentally clung to his presence, a lifeline she needed but knew eventually she'd have to give up. Sooner would probably be better for everyone.

Who was she kidding? Being on her own made her even more of a danger to his family. Which only made everything more compli-cated. As much as she wanted to belong, she didn't and didn't know if she ever would.

She headed into the hall. It was the same one as before, just this room was a few doors down from her previous one.

Raven said something else and another feminine voice responded. Guess she wasn't talking to the guy in the bed. A hint of Raven's presence flickered into Becca's head. Raven sat at the table in the kitchenette, talking to another woman, still terrified for Nero's sanity and that she wouldn't be able to save Becca. The other woman, also afraid but holding herself together with a fierce determination, was trying to calm Raven but wasn't certain what to say.

Becca ducked into the closest room—the one with the uncon-scious guy in it—not ready to face anyone other than Raven. This other woman might not understand that Becca hadn't meant to inamorate Nero. Hell, Becca had no idea how it had even happened, and she had no idea how to make him uninamorated. Everyone was afraid and angry over the situation, and it was all Becca's fault, and God, all she wanted was to fix it, ensure his kids were safe, and rescue her friends.

The guy in the bed groaned and jerked in his sleep. Light billowed around him, and sweat slicked his forehead.

I'm sorry. This new voice—the guy in the bed's voice—was a soft tenor, filled with pain.

"It's all right," Becca said. And it might be for him, if she could just fix the situation with Nero so he wouldn't risk his life for her.

It's not. I failed. I'm sorry. Please, he begged. *End it.*

Becca's throat tightened. His pain was overwhelming, a mix of physical agony and soul-deep grief, and she shifted toward him, drawn by his plea. She knew that grief. The pain in his body was nothing compared to the agony of his soul. She still saw that kid with the backpack, still heard that baby's wail, and now felt the monsters clawing under her skin, tearing into her. She fully understood the pain that might drive someone to suicide. If Werner hadn't taken her with him when he'd escaped, she'd have succumbed to her demons. But even if she'd been sure it was a nightmare, he'd given her a purpose.

Please. End me.

More light flared from the guy, and his body arched off the bed with convulsions. *I'm sorry. So sorry. I deserve this.*

"No." *No one deserves this.*

But I made so many mistakes.

We all make mistakes. Horrible mistakes. Mistakes that got people killed. Mistakes that could never be forgiven. She'd been awarded a medal for her mistake when all she'd been trying to do was save as many of her men as she could.

We were so afraid. I was afraid. Another blast of light radiated from him, stronger than the last. *I'm still afraid.*

So am I. Even if he wasn't an unnaturally created mage like her, discovering the truth about the world had to be terrifying. *Maybe together we won't be so afraid.*

You don't understand.

Do I need to?

The guy's eyelids flew open, and his attention jumped to her as a ferocious power filled her mind. The weight of hundreds of years flooded her, and her pulse leapt. He wasn't human. He wasn't a naturally created mage, as Raven thought. He wasn't even unnaturally created like Becca.

He was a dragon.

"You're a—"

I'm not! he roared. *Not anymore. I'm not—!* He screamed, the gut-wrenching cry in her ears and in her head, and brilliant yellow light exploded around him, ten times more powerful than before. His body jerked, his back arching off the bed again for an agonizing heartbeat, then he started thrashing.

I've got you. Becca scrambled to him and grabbed his shoulders. *I've—*

White lightning slammed through her body, searing into every cell with a power stronger than the first time his magic had shot through her. Her breath caught in her throat and every muscle jerked taut. The dragon screamed, and so did she. Everyone in the building screamed. Everyone in the city started yelling— no, the country— no — more, so many more.

27

There were too many voices in Becca's head. All of them shocked and confused, raging into a fire that was burning her up from the inside. Her legs gave out and she collapsed to the floor beside the guy— no, dragon in the bed, unable to breathe or move or think.

Becca! Nero's consciousness slammed to the forefront. He was jumping from the bed and burning with her.

Someone yelled… in her head? Not in her head? She couldn't tell. There was only the inferno consuming her and Nero's desperation to get to her.

I'm sorry, the dragon in the bed said. *I'm so sorry. I didn't mean—*

A hand grabbed her shoulder, and Raven's thoughts exploded into Becca. The inferno leapt into the other woman. She screamed and a vortex of wind erupted around her.

My magic— Raven gasped as she strained to yank it back, but it tossed the lamp and book off the nightstand and whirled them into the air. *It just— All that power—*

More light flared from the dragon in the bed, and the voices in Becca's head roared louder while the fire blazed hotter.

Not a dragon, he sobbed. *Not anymore. Never again.*

So much— Raven howled. *Too much. He's—*

The other woman, the one Raven had been talking to, of similar height and build to Raven with a pixie cut and pale eyes, scrambled into the room. A brilliant white aura blazed around her, and her thoughts sliced into Becca in a wild yell of determination, confusion, panic, and pain. She had to help. *But how? All that wind.* She didn't have control of her magic. *The guy in the bed— The woman on the floor weeping. Raven—*

Raven.

The woman's thoughts jerked to a stop. *I'm helping Raven. She'll know how to fix this.* She reached for Raven, who slammed a gust of wind into her and threw her into the room across the hall.

Mother, no! "I'm sorry, Anaea," Raven gasped, and her wind wavered than blasted stronger into a tornado. *I can't control it.* Her wind seized the lounge chair and nightstand and smashed them against the wall, whipping the pieces into dangerous projectiles.

Anaea rushed to her feet and back into the hall as Nero barreled through the doorway, shirtless, his muscular chest crusted with dried blood. He stopped midstep, his dark gaze flashing over the room then landing on Becca. For a second the voices dimmed. There was only him. No wind. No guy in the bed with his body on fire and a wild magic she didn't understand, and no roaring mob in her head. Only the agony of the blaze consuming her essence.

Protect. Nero had to protect her. There was only her, there would only ever be her, except—

A piece of something sliced Becca's cheek and shot over Nero's shoulder, heading for the other woman, Anaea. Becca screamed, but she had no idea if it was all in her head or not. Raven's thoughts fought to control her wind and turned horrified when she couldn't. Anaea's thoughts stuttered, then she dropped to the floor, and the spike of metal whizzed past her and embedded in the concrete wall.

Raven is the immediate danger. Help her. Except Becca had no idea if that was her thought or his.

More agony sliced through her skull and the fire in her body burned hotter. "Help. Raven." *Then, if you can, you can help me. Please, God. Help me. End this.*

Raven screamed again and more wind tore from her. "He's a surge." *Please, Mother.*

"What's a surge?" Anaea asked.

Nero swore. "He amplifies earth and soul magic, even awakens dormant powers, and depending on the force behind the power he surges into you, it's permanent." He had to get this situation under control and help Becca.

Becca's heart contracted— or was that Nero's? All her pain, all those voices. It could be permanent. It could—

Nero barked a guttural word and slapped his palm to the wall just inside the door. The black vortex of a gate flared to life and his thoughts tightened, shooting more blazing agony into Becca's head.

Got to control this.

He said his other power word and his wind roared from his hands. "Anaea, call—"

Diablo slipped past him into the room. "I'm here."

"Get Raven," Nero gasped. "Calm her down, knock her out. I don't care. Just end her power." He flexed his hand, and his wind swelled into Raven's and yanked it toward the gate.

"Surge," Raven gasped. "Please." *No one else could touch him. It's bad enough Becca had.*

The pain in Becca's body flared. God, she didn't think it could get worse. Her muscles trembled and she gasped for breath. Between one blink and the next, Diablo vanished from the doorway and appeared at Raven's side. Her wind surged, and the top of the night-stand bashed into him. He staggered against the bed, a slice of white lightning shooting from his thoughts into Becca. He howled, but he caught his balance and heaved into the wind.

"Hurry up," Nero growled. He couldn't keep fighting Raven's wind and holding the gate open while his body was still healing Becca's gunshot wound.

"I'm trying," Diablo yelled back. But it was hard to concentrate, hard to hold it together. Hard not to rip everything apart. "It would help if pieces of chair weren't slamming into my face."

Another thread of wind joined Nero's, not as strong but enough to keep the flying shrapnel from Diablo, and Anaea's thoughts, her need to concentrate on her magic, cut through the roar in Becca's head.

The guy in the bed screamed again, then his thoughts vanished, along with the light blazing around him. But everyone else's thoughts remained. Clamoring, in pain, desperate, needing, cajoling, consuming. She was losing herself, uncertain which were her thoughts and which weren't.

All because of magic. Impossible, nightmare magic. This wasn't real. It couldn't be real. This couldn't be her life. She didn't have a life. There was no life. There was nothing—

The muscles in Becca's chest jerked taut, and the fire in her body turned to ragged, slicing shards. It wasn't real. She wasn't real. She—

Nero howled, but she had no idea if it was in her head or not.

Not. It had to be not. Hearing voices was impossible. This wasn't possible.

Her throat tightened. She couldn't breathe, couldn't think past the pain.

"Mother, help," someone gasped.

Nero dropped to his knees, his wind still tangling with Raven's. His chest heaved, and his body was tight with agony. "Get Raven under control."

"What do you think I'm doing?" Diablo grabbed the front of Raven's shirt, but her wind sliced deep into his forearms. His grip tightened as the wind whipped his blood into the tornado, and he roared.

Come on, Raven. Snap out of it. Please. I can't fight it for much longer. Becca is losing her shit and taking me with her. Nero is about—

White light blazed behind Nero and Anaea stepped closer. Her wind raced around Raven and Diablo, pinning them to the far wall.

"Knock me out," Raven gasped.

"Control your God damned magic," Diablo hissed at her.

Both of their thoughts sliced into Becca. Raven couldn't hold it together. Diablo was going to kill her, all of them, everyone. And it wasn't real. It couldn't be real.

A seizure slammed into Becca and she screamed. All thoughts turned to her. Even the hundreds— no, hundreds of thousands of others in her head froze and concentrated on her. They were captured in her agony, their thoughts shattering with her, and she didn't know how to save them... because it wasn't real.

Oh, Mother, someone whispered, the voice soft, feminine. Raven.

Sudden warmth flooded Becca, easing the inferno consuming her and the agony slicing into her brain. This *was* real, and she could handle it. She was strong. She could heal. And she could learn to control her power. Yes, the universe wasn't what she'd expected, but that was all right. She was strong enough to handle the truth. She had people who loved her and would help her.

The wind in the room vanished. Nero groaned and Anaea's blazing white aura dimmed. The guy in the bed sobbed and Raven sagged into Diablo's arms.

"What was that?" Anaea asked.

"The effect of a surge on a wind power," Nero said. "Diablo, call Grey and get him down here."

"Fucking call him yourself." Diablo shifted his grip on Raven and cradled her in his arms. With a whoosh, he vanished and reappeared in the room across the hall. He laid her on the mattress and then vanished again. But his fear and rage remained in Becca's head. He was terrified, but she couldn't tell about what. They were all scared, Anaea because she'd barely managed to keep her magic in check, Raven—only semi-conscious—because she could have hurt her family, and Nero because Becca could have died. Even all the hundreds of thousands of others were terrified. With the force of Becca's power, she could have shattered their minds. All those voices she'd captured in her head didn't know exactly what had happened, only understood on a primal level they'd been in danger. They didn't even know how, but they, like her, knew that she could have hurt all of them.

Nero eased to her side and grabbed her hand. All the voices but his disappeared, and she slumped against him in relief. He was scared he'd lose her. He was scared they had a chance at forever now. He was scared of how scared he was. And he was furious. Dragons weren't scared. Dragons killed the things that scared them.

She shifted, drawing his arms around her. "Just hold me." *Just let me be with you without the pain and the other voices.* Everything else… she could figure out later.

The whoosh of air from a gate swept down the hall. Grey strode into view and his gaze leapt over the shattered furniture, knocked-over cabinet in the hall, and strewn medical supplies, towels, and sheets. "Holy Mother. What happened?"

"The new intake is a surge," Nero said, his voice rumbling into Becca. "Raven touched him." *Becca, too. Mother, how are we going to fix this?*

One step at a time, she thought back at him, knowing the calm had come from Raven before she'd passed out.

"I need you to watch him and Raven until—"

"No problem," Grey said. *Nero looks like shit. Probably hasn't fully healed that gunshot and now—* Grey's gaze slid to Anaea. "Probably best if you keep your distance. You barely have control of your earth magics as it is. One new power awakening every week is the most we can handle. We don't want you to be at full power for everything all at once."

Anaea shuddered. "Agreed. Will you be all right?"

Grey shrugged. "Not going to touch him." *I'm having enough trouble with the earth magic I have. I don't want another one.* "Although hey, maybe he'll give my soul magic a spark and I'll get faster healing."

"Not a risk I'm willing to take," Nero said, his grip around Becca tightening. *She could have full soul magic now. Permanently.*

Grey's expression darkened. "Me, neither." His gaze turned to the room with Raven. "I'm going to sit with her, just to be safe. You—" He turned to Nero. "You should probably get into some running water and finish dealing with that gunshot and…" *Your inamorated problem.*

And it's one hell of problem—

Shit, did I just hear that because of Becca? Nero tensed, his grip around her tightening.

Sorry. She tried to focus on her magic and turn it to a dimmer setting, but couldn't seem to concentrate on anything other than her body against his, his arms around her, and his thoughts muddling in her head.

"Don't think I'm not dealing with it," Nero said. "All of it."

"I know. It's just—" Grey rubbed his face. "I don't know how much time we have. Regis could start enforcing his proclamation for all drakes to return to Court at any point and there's still the issue of Becca and her circumstances. If even half of what Raven told me was true, you need to be as close to a hundred percent as possible, and fast. With all our current troubles, everyone is in danger until you get back to fighting form." He rubbed his face again and sighed. "The rest of us can only cover for so long. Hell, I can't even cover for you because I'm on the prince's most wanted list."

"Ivy will be safe." Nero drew Becca closer, and the thought of something happening to her and not being able to save her made his heart race. "She's part of the *puzur*. You're part of the *puzur*."

"So are you." Grey glared at Nero. *Raven also fears you might leave because of Becca. I won't let that happen. None of us will.*

I might not have a choice. Nero's sadness filled Becca, and her throat tightened.

"So you better take care of yourself, especially with what I know about soul magic."

"And what's that?" Nero wasn't sure he wanted to know, but Grey wouldn't be saying anything if it wasn't important.

"Taking on someone's injuries takes more out of soul magic than any other kind of injury. I'm assuming what you did is similar to spells mentioned in the Handmaiden's book, so we have to assume, even if your injuries are healed, your soul magic is still diminished."

Becca shivered, and Nero inched her closer. "Get to the point."

"Your healing will be slower than before until your soul magic can recover. Taking on any more of her injuries anytime soon would likely kill you, and I'm pretty sure your soul magic wouldn't let you do it, even if she is your inamorata." Grey strode into the other room to the lounge chair beside Raven. "Get him in water, Becca, and see he stays there until his internal injuries are healed and his soul magic is back on the mend."

"Right. Sure." Why not. Magic existed, so why not knowing when internal injuries were healed without any medical equipment? Sudden realization swept through her. Water meant little or no clothes. Hopefully less clothes than Nero wore now. And a part of her—and not just the part that was mentally linked to Nero—liked that idea. Really liked that idea.

28

Nero summoned a gate underneath them and moved them from the concrete floor in the transition suites to the rug in the middle of his bedroom. His mind whirled with a confusing mix of thoughts, his, Becca's, Grey's, and Anaea's, while his heart pounded, half with Becca's fear and half with his own. She could have been killed, and he had no idea if he'd have been able to take on her injuries again. He had no idea how he'd done it the first time, and Grey had warned him he might not be able to do it again.

As it was, he still hadn't fully healed from the gunshot wound, and Grey had been right. He needed to get into fighting form as fast as possible. Except with the strain of having held open a gate while battling Raven's wind and funneling it out over the Arctic, he didn't think he'd have the power to stand. Certainly not for the time it would take to heal while being in the shower. No, he needed submersion in water, and the best place for that was the whirlpool tub in his en suite, so he'd gated them to his bedroom. He wasn't going to think about how Becca felt in his arms, a perfect fit, held tight against his body, making him hard in anticipation. Or how the sight of his king bed made him imagine how she'd look, naked and spread on his sheets.

No, he needed to figure out what to do with her—

And it shouldn't be making love and sealing his soul bond to her.

No matter what he craved.

Besides, she wasn't inamorated back, not to mention she was human.

His pulse stuttered. Connecting with the surge's magic could have fully awakened her soul magic. The first time she'd touched the new intake explained how her broken ribs and collarbone had healed so quickly. A second blast and… she could be immortal like—

He clamped down on that thought.

"I've already heard it," she said, her voice trembling, her palm pressed against his bare chest.

Please, Mother, not the thoughts about the bed.

"Your soul magic—" he said, unable to keep his desire from making his voice gruff. "It's just a hope." An unfair one, as well. Not inamorated back, remember? When she figured out how to control her telepathy, she'd want her life back and would want to go home. "The new guy is just coming into his magic. It probably isn't at full strength, which means any effects he might have caused will fade."

"That would be good for Raven." Becca shuddered and drew Nero's arms tighter around her, hugging her body against his and making him harder.

He bit back a groan and fought to focus on the situation, not the woman, not how she felt, or the electric sear of attraction burning through his every cell. Becca had touched the new guy as well, and Nero had felt the agony of her magic scorching inside her. Having the strength of her telepathy fade would be good for her, too.

He pressed his cheek to the top of her head, unable to stop himself from savoring the feel of her against him, and breathing in her scent of vanilla from the shampoo in the transition suites' showers. He wouldn't get much more of this. Even if, hope beyond hope, she was inamorated back, he'd at best get sixty or seventy more years.

Unless her soul magic had been fully awakened.

God, he couldn't seem to stop himself from going back to that impossible thought.

"I promise it'll fade soon," he forced out. *All of it.*

Except you're not sure that's true, she thought, her words clear in his mind. "I'm getting mixed messages again."

"Because I don't know what the truth is, and I'm too tired to ignore being—" *Being inamorated.* "—in this situation." No matter how impossible it was to be inamorated a second time.

Now his chest really ached. Mother of All, he needed to pull himself together. Grey was right. He was doyen and dugga and the members of his coterie, *puzur,* and the Asar Nergal needed him to protect them. He had to regroup and to do that, he had to finish healing the wound he'd taken from Becca—because, Mother of All, he really was inamorated—and figure out what to do with her.

Inamorated. Again. As impossible as it was.

The thought settled around his heart, solid and strong and right. He belonged to her. His dugga's magic had nothing to do with this, and, good or bad, his soul knew she'd make him a better, stronger drake.

Which still didn't help him figure out what to do with her. And taking her to bed wasn't one of those options.

"You know I can still hear your thoughts." She shifted to look him in the eyes, her body still trembling, the strain of her magic tightening her jaw, but her expression hard with determination. A hint of blush crept up her neck. "*All* of your thoughts."

"Right." *Jeez.* "Sorry."

I'm not. Except he could feel that a part of her wasn't certain if her attraction to him originated from her, or if the emotion came from him because he was inamorated. But her desire shoved that away. It didn't care. She yearned for him with a core-deep need that was both thrilling, confusing, and terrifying.

"This is my fault. I should get into the tub to finish healing and, if we're being honest, to think straight. Then—" *The bed. No. Figure this mess out. Focus.* "You can stay here, watch TV or sleep. I don't know how long I'll be." He didn't want to leave her but knew he should, and made himself shift away.

The moment they separated, searing agony and the roar of voices slammed into him. Becca gasped and grabbed her head. A tremor swept through her body then another, stronger than the first, each shake slicing white lightning into Nero.

He seized her hand and the voices and pain vanished, leaving only Becca with her lurching thoughts, gasping against the pain.

Holy Mother! This wasn't good. They wouldn't be able to do anything if her telepathy didn't ease up.

"Please tell me the new guy's magic will wear off soon." Her eyes were too big and her fear cut into her determination, making his chest ache even more.

"I don't know." And Mother, he never wanted to feel that again.

"Agreed." She drew in a ragged breath then another, and her thoughts squeezed around his essence until it was hard to breathe.

One thing at a time. Baby steps. Don't lean into him. Don't kiss him. Make a list, prioritize, break the problem into manageable pieces. Her will tightened even more as she focused on the problem, pushing everything else aside. This was the woman who'd led men into battle, who'd kept calm under sniper fire while injured.

"Our first priority is your healing," she said, her brusque tone belying her whirling thoughts and emotions. "We should get you in the tub and then start to figure everything else out. If we have to be in contact to keep the voices under control, then I'm going in the tub with you." *And I won't get distracted, no matter how hot he is with his shirt off...* or how much she wanted to see the rest of him... touch the rest of him—

He'd be flattered if the situation wasn't so awkward. "You can sit on the edge. Fully clothed." Surely he could control himself if they just held hands.

Disappointment flooded her, and his grip on her hand instinctually tightened. Her gaze jumped to his, realization flashed in her eyes, and a blush swept over her cheeks. "Wow, you heard that. I have no idea what's wrong with me." *But I do. I want you.*

"It's me. It's my fault." He rose, his legs trembling for a second before he steadied himself then helped her stand. "It has to be my soul bond influencing you." But a part of him hoped it was more than that.

She met his gaze.

Shit. She'd heard that.

"I'm not thinking straight," he said.

Maybe you are, and right now it doesn't matter. Maybe I shouldn't take advantage of your condition.

"Maybe we're both confused." But he knew he wasn't confused. His soul knew exactly what it wanted, and it wanted her. However he could get her... preferably in his bed.

Becca raised an eyebrow.

And she heard that, too. Wonderful. "Let's get me in the tub and figure out what we need to do next." *We can be adults about this.*

"Adults. Yes." *Sex is off the table.* Her gaze jumped to his antique writing desk by the window. *Not sturdy enough.* Her attention shot back to him, and her face turned red. "Oh, my God! Sorry." *Stop teasing him... and yourself.*

"Okay." He grabbed her by both shoulders and met her gaze as a shiver of need churned in his gut. *Not going to think about the counter in the bathroom or the desk in my office—* "Moratorium on apologies. I'm influencing how you feel. I won't take any of your thoughts personally, and I'll try to keep a leash on mine."

Not sure your thoughts are the problem. Her gaze slipped behind him to the bed. "You think you can do that?"

"Probably not, but if I don't try, we're going to end up stuck in the middle of my bedroom apologizing to each other for who knows how long until the surge's power wears off."

Or we could satisfy the problem. "Sorry."

"Not taking it personally, remember?" No matter how much his inner drake wanted to purr.

Mother, now he really knew he was inamorated. Purring was the one sure sign a dragon soul had picked its mate. If he hadn't known before, he certainly knew now.

And not something he was supposed to be thinking about.

He switched his grip to her hand and led her into his en suite bathroom. It was a modest-sized space, clean and masculine, with black tiles around the walk-in shower and two-person tub, white everything else, and chrome fixtures. He turned on the hot and cold taps on the tub all the way, to fill as fast as possible, but then paused, his mind stuck on the next step: his pants.

Becca's gaze slid to his fly, and his heart skipped a beat.

"I should keep these on." Even if the bath would be more effective without them. He wasn't shy. He just didn't want to make an awkward situation worse.

"How about I not look." *Yes, please. Take them off.* Her grip around his hand tightened, and he couldn't tell if it was her pulse racing or his.

Her other hand brushed across his abs to his heart, drawing a shiver of need, and a purr bubbled in his throat.

"I think it's best if they stay on," he forced out. *I'm not going to take advantage of her.*

"Will it achieve the goal of healing you as fast as possible?" she asked, her voice husky. She knew from his thoughts it wouldn't.

"I think we need to find a balance between healing and—" *Succumbing to the soul bond.* He wasn't going to survive this. The inamoration was too new, the need to seal the bond too strong. If he could just get some distance, perhaps she'd know for certain if her desire was his or hers.

"No."

His thoughts stuttered. He had no idea what she was saying no to.

"You wouldn't be taking advantage of me."

But my thoughts? Our connection? She couldn't be thinking straight.

"My thoughts are straight enough. I don't know if I'm inamorated back." She released his hand and pressed her other palm beside the first, the heat from her body flooding him and making his pulse roar. "I don't know if a human can be inamorated. But I do know, at this moment, there's something between us and as much as it's a bad idea, I want it." She pursed her lips. *I need it.*

"You don't know what you're saying. Our bond— *my* bond has to be influencing you."

"Yes… maybe? I don't know. God, this is such a bad idea." Her gaze locked with his and her body leaned closer, belying her refusal. "If I'm not inamorated back, you're going to get hurt."

"You're confused," he growled, forcing his hands to stay at his sides and not wrap her in an embrace.

Not about wanting the peace I get from being with you. I'm steady with you.

You weren't earlier this evening when I asked you about your injuries.

My magic is steady. The voices are quiet. Sadness crept into her expression. "It's selfish, I know." *I want you to help me forget everything that's happened, to not hear all those voices, and, if only for a moment, just be.* "You're the only one who's been able to quiet the voices. But this will hurt you. I know from the memories I got from the monsters— I know this will hurt you." *I can be strong and prevent his grief.*

His heart aching with hers, he gave in and wrapped an arm around her back, drew her tight against his body, and pressed his forehead against hers. "Giving you what you want will never hurt me."

Liar. You're terrified I'll leave.

I am. "I'm also terrified you're in pain, that I won't be able to help you, that you won't have the life you deserve." *With or without me at your side.* "If you're not inamorated back, I will fight to win you. If you reject me, I will respect that decision." A purr rumbled in his chest. Every cell in his being burned with the need to fulfill her request. Now. Anything else past this moment didn't matter. He'd deal with it when the time came. At the moment, he could ease her pain and remind her that she was loved and worthy and whole.

29

Becca's heart swelled with his love and desire. "You don't deserve to have your heart broken again." Every time he'd thought about being inamorated, she'd always sensed grief. It was muted, as if years had passed, but the grief was still there... except she wasn't sure if the grief was for what had been or what could be between them.

Which only made her more certain that giving in to her craving, to use Nero to forget herself and everything that had happened, was a bad idea. No matter how much her insides squirmed for more than just his embrace.

A mix of emotions tightened his eyes and swept through their mental connection, grief and resignation, but also awe and yearning.

"This isn't something you can control. It's not like a human infatuation." His gaze dipped to her lips, and her pulse skipped a beat. "Even if you left me right now, my soul would crave you. I would never move on. There would never be another." *Not, at least, for two thousand years.* Except she sensed even that wouldn't happen now.

"This is stronger than before, isn't it?"

"Yes." His dark gaze grew intense, boring into her as if he could see her soul and feeding the flames of her desire. All that power, wrapping around her, filling her, anchoring her within herself.

It's like lava burning through my veins, he said, his mental voice thick with need. *My soul has chosen. Even if you're not inamorated back, giving you what you crave won't cause a greater hurt. It will satisfy your desires.* "Let me satisfy you."

Her pulse skipped a beat and her mouth went dry. His gaze held her essence, and she trembled with a need that was mirrored in his eyes. The heat from his flesh under her palms seeped over her arms and pooled low in her body, and the crackle of invisible energy, his impossible magic, tingled over her skin.

"Yes," she breathed, and the word zinged like lightning through her and him, heightened by their mental connection.

He hissed, a whip of wind gusted to life and turned off the tub's taps, then his mouth crushed against hers with a hunger that fueled her longing. This was right, what she needed, what he needed as well.

A growl— no, a purr rumbled in his chest, vibrating into her hands and resonating with the core of her soul. His grip on her back tightened and his other hand tangled in her hair as he deepened the kiss.

Heat seared through her. His mouth plundered hers, his lips hungry with the ferocious passion that had radiated around him from the first time she'd seen him. She was on fire, her skin blazing, the magic in his soul sparking over her.

Her back hit the counter, his hand left her hair, and he captured her hips. Without breaking the kiss, he lifted her up. She grabbed the waistband of his pants, tugged him between her thighs, and wrapped her legs around him, sliding herself against his erection. A shudder of need swept through him and into her. His hands slipped under her hoodie and tank top and brushed an agonizingly slow whisper of fingers against her skin, over her waist and up her ribs.

Too gentle. Too slow. She wanted hot, fast, hard. Needed it to burn through the memories haunting her, as well as to scorch away her fear and his. Yes, he was inamorated, and this was what he craved —she felt that sure and solid from their connection—but she also felt the fear he fought to acknowledge. A fear about the truth that, even if by some kind of miracle she was inamorated back, she still had a human lifespan.

She arched into him, drawing a groan from him.

"Too much thinking," she said against his lips.

"What if I was thinking that you're wearing too much clothing?" His fingers splayed over her ribs as his thumbs grazed her nipples with another teasing whisper of a touch.

Her breath hitched, and he trailed his lips down her neck to her collarbone as his thumbs teased her again.

"What if I said I wanted my mouth here." Another graze, sending electricity zinging from her breasts straight to her core.

Yes. God, yes.

But his hands slipped out from under her hoodie.

"Did I not make myself clear?" She clenched her legs tighter, pressing him to her.

"You did." He unzipped her hoodie.

She shrugged out of it, and he grabbed the bottom of her tank top and pulled it off over her head. His gaze trailed up her naked chest, but his mouth tightened when his eyes reached her shoulder where her tattoo trailed over and among her scars.

I'm sorry for that.

You didn't shoot me or blow up my tactical transport. But the memory made her shiver, and her stomach tightened. She didn't want to remember. For the love of God, all she wanted was a moment to be herself again, to forget everything that had happened, to bathe in the ferocity of this man's passion. It didn't matter that he wasn't actually a man. It was his spirit that counted, and he was driven by the same things that drove her: a need to protect those who couldn't protect themselves.

She met his gaze, letting his dark eyes and ferocious energy capture her. *You promised satisfaction.*

I did. He captured her lips again in a hungry kiss, his hands sliding over her ribs, his thumbs tortuously skimming the edges of her breasts, then his lips followed. They trailed a blazing line down her skin to one nipple then the other, laving, sucking, fueling the fire within her that burned all memory and thought away.

He tugged at her leggings. She lifted so he could pull them and her panties off, then captured him again between her legs, needing the hard heat of him against her, but he slipped a hand between them and stroked her. Glorious lightning snapped through her and stole her breath.

She gripped the counter to keep her balance, tipped her head back, and closed her eyes, letting the sensation flood her. *Yes, oh, yes.* This was what she needed.

Another purr rumbled through him, and he slid two fingers inside her, drawing another moan. His thumb brushed her clit, sending more lightning shuddering through her. Her breath hitched, and he tangled his free hand in her hair and captured her lips again with a scorching kiss. His fingers drove inside, and his thumb rubbed her, the movement growing faster and harder, driving her closer and closer to orgasm.

His need filled her, mind and soul, and she wrapped herself in it, letting their desire fuel each other. They shared breath, thought, and glorious sensation, building, surging into a powerful eruption. Her muscles clenched, his soul's magic seared over her skin, and bliss exploded within her in a great wave that sent sparks flashing across her sight.

Oh, yes. Oh, God, yes.

He deepened his kiss, riding her wave of pleasure through their mental connection, and purred.

Hers. Only. Ever. Hers.

His certainty flooded her, and a flash of regret—that he knew she was using him and wasn't inamorated back—swept through her.

Her throat tightened, and her pleasure turned bittersweet. No matter what he said, he deserved better than this. Being with her endangered those he cared about most. And yet she couldn't stop herself, didn't want him to move his hands from her body, and, no matter how desperately she knew it was wrong, couldn't even begin to try severing the mental connection between them. He was her anchor, the missing piece within her that steadied the truth of her soul. And that terrified her more than the idea of just using him.

He stilled and pressed his forehead to hers, his warm breath teasing across her cheeks and sending shivers of need sliding over her. Even now, against everything she knew was right for him, she wanted more.

Say the word and I'll stop. He would. He'd do anything for her. Sacrifice everything.

And still—

"I don't want you to stop." *That's what scares me.* She didn't want to have his life in her hands. She didn't want anyone's life. Not after Afghanistan. People had trusted her, and they'd died. Nero's soul, his fellow dragons, and his children— God, his children! That was too much responsibility. Too many people who would get hurt because she wasn't strong enough to resist.

"It's okay." He cupped her face between his strong palms and met her gaze. "It'll be okay."

"No, it won't. You don't know me, and you'll sacrifice everything for me."

"It's the way being inamorated works." A hint of sadness crept into his eyes.

See, you don't even like it. And that broke her heart more. A part of her wanted him to be happy to be with her, needed him to love her back—

His eyes widened, and she froze.

She needed him to love her back, not because some magical soul bond was forcing him, but because he wanted to.

Except that didn't make sense. She barely knew him... and yet they were sharing thoughts and connecting on a level more intimate and revealing than anything she'd experienced before. She *knew* him. Core deep. The heart of his essence. He was a kindred spirit, a match to her soul.

A mental wall within her cracked. Magic was real. He was magic... and so was she.

Light and heat flooded her body, and Nero's grip tightened, his hands having moved to her hips to steady her. Her skin burned where he held her, fueling an ache for more, for everything. The mental wall shattered and an electric shock snapped through her. This was her. The real her. And she belonged with him. She couldn't put it into words. She just knew, like a key finding its lock and clicking open.

30

Nero felt her shudder, an aftershock of her orgasm, followed by a renewed flood of aching need and a certainty in her soul toward him that terrified her. Their connection might just be mental, not a proper two-way soul bond, but it was strong, and it went both ways.

You'll be okay. I promise. I'll keep you safe.

It's not me I'm worried about. But he could sense that the depth of her feelings after knowing him for so short a time frightened her.

And exhilarates. The memory of her orgasm shuddered across their connection. Her head tipped back and she groaned, making a purr bubble in his throat.

If he didn't think too hard about it, he could imagine the burn of a soul bond flooding her as much as it filled him. Swelling in her mind and body and making her pulse race. No. Don't hope. She wasn't inamorated. That was his desire playing tricks on him. Only heartache lay with that thought. But he couldn't deny there was more to this moment than just temporarily searing away bad memories. This was a joining to heal a part of her she hadn't fully realized was broken, a way for her to wrap herself in glorious sensations that were all her own.

Her gaze captured his, and her pupils dilated with need. Right now, in this moment, there was only him. No horrifying past. No uncertain future. Just him and how they made each other feel. *More.*

The thought shot straight to his erection, making him throb. *Mother, yes! More.* Whatever she desired. He knew he'd never get enough of her, of how she felt, strong and soft against him, of the sounds she made when he brought her to climax. He wanted to make her cry with satisfaction again and again.

He captured her mouth in a quick kiss then tugged her to the edge of the counter, and pressed his hands along the inside of her thighs, opening her wide. Her chest rose and fell in rapid breaths, still riding the tail end of her climax, and a shudder swept through her as he trailed a hand and his gaze down her body to the curls and swollen folds damp from her first orgasm.

Her yearning whirled with his, her erotic thoughts fueling his. Yes, she wanted him there. Filling her. Driving into her.

Not yet. He knew she was planning on leaving as a way to protect him and his *puzur.* If she was leaving, he was going to savor every second he had with her.

She leaned forward, but he ducked her lips and grazed his tongue over her nipple instead. A shudder trembled through her, drawing a moan. Another flick of his tongue, then he drew her into his mouth, sucking and laving until her breath came in quick gasps. He switched to the other nipple and ran his hands from her knees up the inside of her thighs.

Another tremor shook her, bringing her close to climax again. Her thoughts jumped to how he'd made her come with his hand moments before, and she moaned his name. He was so hard it hurt. He needed to be in her, feel her hot slick tightness clamp around him, and Mother, she wanted that, too, burned for it. But if this was the only night he was going to get with her, he was going to make it one she'd never forget.

He kissed down her belly, circling his thumbs on her inner thighs, closer and closer to her core. Her trembling increased, and she gasped when he flicked his tongue over her clit.

The heat of her thoughts turned to molten lava. He spread her with his thumbs, slid two fingers inside her, and drew her clit into his mouth, sucking and flicking, driving her back to climax. Her grip tightened around the edge of the counter and she writhed against him, her breath coming faster, her thoughts splintering on the verge of orgasm again, and he teased her there, easing off and building again, keeping her on the edge until she was gasping and moaning.

She tangled her fingers into his hair and urged him to look at her. Another shudder swept through her. "Tell me you have protection."

He glanced up at her. Her eyes were half closed. Her breasts rose in rapid shuddering breaths.

I need you in me.

Dragons are infertile.

Oh. A flash of sadness chilled her craving.

It's okay. It's just the way it is. And he wasn't going to think about that. Right now, this moment was for her and her pleasure. He flicked his tongue over her clit and drove his fingers deeper inside her, burning away the sadness with the tremor of climax. She was so hot, so sensual. Everything about her was amazing, and he strained to control himself and fulfill her need to forget everything but the here and now.

God, Nero. Her trembling grew stronger and her nails dug into his scalp. She bucked against him, her climax on the edge again. *Want you in me. Need you—*

Yes. With one hand, he released the button on his pants and shoved them and his briefs off his hips, while still working his fingers inside her.

Her gaze dropped to his erection, and her tongue darted across her lips. A half-purr, half-growl filled his chest. *Hers. Whatever she desired.*

He grabbed her ass and aligned himself with her, bringing his tip to rest against her slick folds.

I desire this. She clenched his erection at the base and drew her hand up to the tip, keeping it pressed at her entrance, teasing him back.

His muscles clenched, the strain to keep in position and not drive into her making him shake.

She pumped her hand back down to his base, her grip tight, a promise of what she'd feel like. Her hips inched forward, drawing his tip inside her, and a tremor of climax swept through her. Her breath came heavy and her gaze locked with his, capturing his soul. If her essence hadn't been seared there already, it would be now.

He brushed his thumb over her clit. She gasped, and he pushed deep within her. Her grip switched back to the countertop as he slid out then plunged back into her tight sheath. Her muscles tightened further around him, and he fought to control himself and bring her to climax first. Her first. Always her. He slid out and drove back in. Faster. Harder. Out and back in. Lifting her hips to meet him, driving deep. Her breath came faster, a match to his. Her pleasure spiraled tighter and flooded through their mental connection until he was whirling out of control.

She screamed his name. Her climax tore through her and pounded into him. Lightning shot up his spine with a ferocious release, and he roared.

Hers. Forever.

Deny it all he wanted, his soul had chosen, and when she left this house without him—and he knew she would to protect him and his kids—it was going to shatter him.

I vette clenched the back of her office chair, fighting the desire to break another annoying protocol, summon her most powerful magic, and turn Dinah into a heap of smoking flesh.

The other woman leaned back in the chair across from Ivette's desk and raised an eyebrow, her expression cocky. "Do you need me to repeat that?"

"Do we honestly think anything Werner Scholtz says is reliable? His magic is unnatural. He probably sees the dugga everywhere he looks. Nero Tassinari might be a high-ranking member of the Asar Nergal, but he's not the dugga. Everything we know about the dugga says he wouldn't go after a human himself." But Ivette knew the moment she'd said it, Dinah would have a defense for Scholtz's sanity. This was the woman's chance to prove Ivette had screwed up by letting Rebecca Scott escape and using Scholtz as bait. She was aiming to take Ivette's job and was smart enough to know she needed something solid, not just the hearsay of a crazy man.

"He's far from crazy. Final analysis of Glenn Lewis's shielding magic indicates he's been putting barriers in his mind and the minds of those closest to him to protect them from going insane. It explains why Glenn has been so cooperative and forthcoming about Becca

Scott's connection to the dugga. He's sane enough to know he should be terrified of the Asar Nergal."

"That doesn't confirm Nero is the dugga, and it doesn't explain why Scott was clearly losing touch with reality." There were holes in Dinah's argument, and Ivette was going to find all of them before her backstabbing co-worker took control of the facility.

"Glenn claims his power doesn't— *didn't* work on Rebecca, but was working on Werner."

"Still, doesn't prove anything." Which meant Ivette hadn't lost control and wouldn't. Dinah had no proof of anything, and even if she was right, Ivette just needed to be smart about this, keep in control, especially when they'd completed the evacuation and transition to the new facility. If Dinah was going to make her move, that was when it would happen, during the peak of the chaos incited by an ancient black dragon showing up on their doorstep.

She relaxed her grip on the chair and turned her back on Dinah, keeping an eye on the woman in the reflection in the floor-to-ceiling windows. The facility move was almost complete. The servers had been loaded into a van and were in transit to the new location, all of Dinah's precious experiments had been transferred, more than half the facility had been wiped clean, and the highest priority subjects were about to be sedated and moved to cells with newly activated null magic to secure them.

Outside, the city was blanketed in darkness, dawn still a few hours away, but traffic was returning to the streets. In February, the workday didn't start with dawn. It started when the alarm clock blared. And for Ivette, yesterday's workday hadn't ended. The last twelve hours had been a disaster she was determined to turn around, and a part of her grudgingly hoped Dinah's information was correct and Tassinari was the dugga of the Asar Nergal.

If he wasn't, she was almost back where she'd started before learning about Becca's direct mental connection with the dugga. Her incompetent security team had killed Scott and failed to capture Tassinari, and while they had Scholtz back in custody, that didn't get her any closer to achieving her goal of taking the dugga's magic so she could hunt down and kill every last member of the Asar Nergal.

The only positive thing to the situation was that Tassinari knew about the facility. Without a doubt, he'd return. The fight with her security team outside the building, along with the presence of two human mages, would be enough to force the dugga to send someone, likely more than one dragon, to investigate, depending on what Becca Scott had revealed—and Ivette wasn't going to start trying to figure out why Tassinari had been with Scott when she'd gone to meet Scholtz. All Ivette needed to do was wait, maybe slow the move to the new facility to ensure she had a reason to keep a full security squad here, and she'd have her opportunity to apprehend one or more of the dragons tasked with murdering humans.

Her gaze slid back to Dinah's reflection in the window. She couldn't let the other woman know what she planned. In fact, it would be best if Dinah left and plotted her futile takeover at the new facility.

"If Tassinari is the dugga, then it's imperative we keep security high until we've completed the move to the new facility," Ivette said. "We've almost managed to save everything. Just a little longer and you can continue your work."

A hint of relief flashed across Dinah's face. "We should also requisition surveillance teams for Tassinari's Newgate and Rome residences."

"Of course." Requisitioning men was Ivette's purview. Dinah was the medical and experimental researcher. Ivette turned to her computer. "You should get back to overseeing the move or disposal of the remaining subjects."

"I'm just waiting on word that the null magic on the cells has been fully activated." Dinah stood. "I'll also want a security team to move Scholtz."

"I won't be able to spare extra bodies until we're cleared out. We can't risk Tassinari or other dragons arriving before the move is complete."

"Let's hope that doesn't happen. I don't want to try to explain why we chose to move instead of destroying the facility."

"It won't come to that." A message popped up on her screen. "The subject transport van is standing by. I suggest you take this load and make sure everything at the new location is ready."

"This trip shouldn't take more than an hour. Make sure the next batch to go are sedated in thirty minutes." Dinah strode to the door. "I want to make sure they're fully unconscious by the time we need to move them."

"Everything will be ready."

"Let's just hope we can get out of here before Tassinari returns," Dinah said, and she left.

"Let's hope." *Not.* Ivette opened the top desk drawer and drew out the folder containing the spells she'd spent the last two decades building. The first, a series of many pages, designed to take the dugga's magic and give it to her, and the second—actually many copies of the second—small sheets the size of her palm with a spell to recognize the dugga. If Tassinari was the dugga, she'd know, take his power, and then kill the monsters who'd been terrorizing her family and friends for centuries.

Nero woke in blissful, painless quiet, with his arms wrapped around Becca. Her back was tucked against his chest, her breath slow and heavy with sleep, and her thoughts—dreams most likely—were gentle whispers across his consciousness. The feel of her skin against his made him harden, and his thoughts jumped back to the bathroom, where he'd made love to her on the countertop, and then to the bed, where they'd made love again before falling asleep.

His inamorated bond with her had been well and truly solidified and sat whole and dense around his heart. The sensation was stronger than he'd ever experienced with his first inamorata. Maybe it was because his soul magic had become stronger when the Great Scourge had sentenced dragonkind into their spirit state, or maybe it was because they both possessed a form of telepathy and the mental bond enhanced the inamorated connection.

He didn't know. All he knew was that he was hers. He wanted—no, *needed* to bring her shinies and meat, needed to add to the hoard she didn't have because she was human, and needed to convince her when she said she was going to leave—and he knew she would—to stay.

Becca sighed, still asleep, and shifted, rubbing against him and forcing him to suck in a slow breath and calm his arousal. If he didn't, he'd wake her and bring her to climax again. Surely so soon after sealing the bond, he'd be able to convince her they were stronger together.

But that didn't address the danger she presented to his *puzur*, one she was determined to protect him from. She knew he'd abandon everything to be with her, and he knew she wouldn't let him. Except if he let her walk out on him, she'd be a target for the drake who'd captured her before, the one who knew she had a direct connection to the dugga.

She shifted again, sending an electric shock of desire zinging through him.

He bit back a moan and made himself ease to the edge of the bed and get up, instead of sliding his hands over her soft skin and waking her. Too much had happened in such a short time. He needed to think, regain his focus, and figure out what he was going to do... about everything. In the very least, he had to find a way to make it safe for Becca to have what she wanted, even if that was to head out on her own.

He forced his attention through his partially closed drapes and out his bedroom window. Darkness still veiled his property, with the moon sparkling on the stretch of snowy garden between his house and the woodlot. The clock by his bed said 4:32. A few hours until dawn.

Mother, he couldn't believe his world had irrevocably changed in less than twelve hours.

He pulled on a clean pair of pants and a Henley, his attention returning to Becca again and again. Every time he looked away, his gaze was drawn back to her. Her dark hair, still in its ponytail, was splayed on the pillow, a splash of darkness against the white sheets, just like the rose and thorn tattoo curling over her biceps and shoulder. Black ink in pale skin. Her complexion still held a sallow hint, and her figure was too thin, revealing the ravages of her captivity, but a sense of peaceful satisfaction radiated from her, a calm he knew she'd never thought she'd have again.

A soft purr slid up his throat, and he didn't fight it. He was hers. Forever.

The purr turned to a growl.

And he damn well would figure out how to protect her and give her everything she wanted. He could only hope that also involved staying and not just because staying was the logical answer to all their problems.

He made himself step into the bathroom and not return to her in his bed. If he woke her now, he wouldn't have the self-control necessary to carry on a serious conversation about what she wanted. The soul bond would take over, and all he'd want would be to lose himself in her pleasure. No, the best thing he could do was take care of what problems he could and give Becca time to process how she felt about everything.

With a hiss, he summoned a gate, then grabbed his phone from his discarded pants on the bathroom floor as it formed. As much as he didn't want to put any distance between them, he wouldn't be able to think straight until he forced himself into a room where he couldn't just open the door and watch her sleep.

The gate finished forming, and he stepped through into the kitchenette of his transition suites, not too far from Becca, but hopefully far enough away. No one sat at the kitchen table, but the coffee maker was gurgling its announcement of an almost-ready pot.

He grabbed a mug from the cabinet, poured himself a half cup, and headed down the hall. Raven and the new intake were the easiest of the problems on his list. He might not be able to do much for them, but he could at least make sure things weren't worse. A part of him was also hoping Grey was still around and would remember some precedent that might help him deal with Regis and the decree that all dragons return to Court's interdimensional sphere. That kind of proclamation could incite war between the Royal coterie—and its supporters—against all the other coteries. And while he'd backed Regis in the Council session—because he'd had no idea what Regis had been ranting about—he needed to find a way to get the prince to change his mind.

Inside the new intake's room, Raven was curled up in the lounge chair, asleep, with whispers of wind dancing around her making her hair flutter. The magical enhancement of her earth magic had yet to diminish, which meant the new guy's power was strong.

On the bed beside her, a blanket tucked around him, lay the new guy, also asleep. His aura was now a muted yellow and no longer angry and pulsing, indicating the flare of his magic that had roared through Becca and Raven had eased. Nero, however, wasn't foolish enough to hope the young man's power had completed the first, painful awakening stage. For now, it looked like he'd at least been given a reprieve from the anguished state they'd found him in. It also helped to know—as bad as it was that Becca and Raven had to have been accidentally in contact with him to learn—that he was a surge. While Nero hadn't ever had a surge, dragon or human, in his *puzur* or coterie, knowing what the problem was gave Raven a direction to work in, and with Grey around, perhaps he'd read something somewhere that might help her deal with the new human's magic.

Raven's expression grew pinched, and a hint of wind swept through the room. The new guy mumbled something, but neither of them woke. Still at peace. For now. That moved them to the bottom of the *things he should be worried about* list. If Nero was thinking straight, the top of that list should be Regis. But it wasn't. It was Becca, and if he was smart, the sooner he solved the question of her safety, the easier it would be to focus on the dragon problems.

Of course, Becca's biggest problem was a dragon problem. Some drake out there, with the ability—or connected to another drake with the ability—to cast a gatelock, knew Becca had a direct link into the dugga's communications. Every drake but Regis and Tobias would want to get their hands on her. And Regis and Tobias would want her if they knew the truth about how Nero had *modified* the Asar Nergal's only directive.

He took a sip of his coffee and headed back to the kitchenette to focus on that, but found Grey standing in front of the open fridge putting away a carton of cream.

"Raven is asleep," Nero said.

"She was when I went to ask her if she wanted coffee. She only woke and took over watching the surge half an hour ago." Grey grabbed a spoon from the drawer and stirred his coffee. "She said she'd already been zapped and it would be better if she got zapped again than if I did."

"I'm not sure I agree with that. If the surge's magic floods her again, what might not have been permanent before could become permanent."

"Only if his earth magic is powerful enough."

Nero raised an eyebrow and sat in a chair at the kitchen table. A flicker of hope trembled in his chest. "You saw his aura."

"Hey, a drake can hope. I don't know how you begin to teach a surge with that kind of power how to control it. He made Raven's magic rage out of control without a power word or a gesture and while unconscious. Just living in this house with all the kids… one wrong touch…"

"One problem at a time. For now, he's isolated. We've dealt with a fifteen-year-old with uncontrolled disintegrating touch. We can deal with a surge."

"But disintegrating touch is just touch." Grey slid into the chair across from Nero. "With a surge, even an accidental brush against his arm or leg, heck, his hair, could set off someone's earth magic. The kids will need to be wary of more than just his hands."

"I didn't say it would be easy." The kid with the disintegrating touch hadn't been easy, either. Raven had spent two months feeding him because every time he picked up a fork or a glass he destroyed it.

"So." Grey took a long swig of coffee. "Did you get some quality water time?"

"I'm back to fighting form." Or as back to fighting form as he could get, without the help of a soak but with sealing his soul bond.

"And your inamorata?"

Just the thought of her made his insides squirm with the need to summon a gate and return to her. "Asleep."

"Did you... you know?" Grey asked, his tone clear. He meant sex.

"Not your business," Nero growled.

Grey raised his hands in defense. "It's not, but sealing the bond might solve your dugga problem."

"Except my dugga's magic isn't an earth magic. I'm not sure being inamorated would affect it like it affected your earth magic." Both Grey and Capri's earth magics had become unpredictable—and both were still struggling to control their newfound magical strength.

"I don't know, either, but it couldn't hurt." Grey's expression darkened. "I'm also hoping sealing the bond will help her overcome the soul sickness."

"Even if she's not inamorated back?"

"You know for a fact she's not?" A hint of pity flashed across Grey's expression. The silver drake was newly inamorated, as well. Nero knew how that felt and knew even just the thought of his inamorata not being inamorated back would make his soul ache.

And now it was aching, a heavy, painful throb at the knowledge that, no matter what he'd thought he'd felt when they'd made love, she probably wasn't. "She's human. Can they even be inamorated?"

Grey shrugged. "I'm pretty sure Anaea is. You should have seen it. The moment Hunter showed up, she managed to lock down all her empathy, or at least all of it until you gated in from that fight. Even then, there wasn't a hint of smoke, and you know the first two things she releases when she's shocked are her fire and telekinesis."

"So my drapes are finally safe, but my small pieces of furniture are still in danger. Wonderful."

"If she wasn't inamorated back, having Hunter return wouldn't have affected her magic like that. I'm pretty sure Ryan is also affected by Capri. It just isn't as obvious."

But both Anaea and Ryan were magically different. Anaea was a true sorcerer and immortal, and Ryan had been reborn and was now immortal as well. Becca...

Could be immortal, if the surge's powers had affected her soul magic and was strong enough to make it permanent. But that was a hope beyond hope, and it would be Nero going insane if he continued to cling to that. Even an immortal inamorata didn't guarantee forever. The time he had with her was the time he had with her. He was just going to have to accept that.

"She's stable for now." It was the best he could hope for, and with there being nothing he could do about that, he was best to concentrate on things he could change. "Did Raven mention the drake who'd abducted her?"

"The one after Zenobia?" Grey asked, his tone dark.

"Yeah. There was a gatelock on that dragon's building."

"She mentioned that as well, and I've been trying to figure out who it could be. There's only a small number of drakes capable of casting a gatelock."

"That we know of. I didn't even know my cousin, Servius, had any sorcerer's magic." Nero's gaze slid to the black depths of his coffee. "It could be anyone. A smart drake keeps an ability that powerful a secret."

"And more so now, with Regis seeing traitors everywhere."

"Another drake on my list of worries." Nero tightened his grip around his mug. "If I'm forced to abandon the *puzur*, promise me you and Hunter will protect it?"

"It won't come to that."

"It might. If I or one of the other doyens of the Counseling Coteries can't find a way around Regis's proclamation that all drakes return to Court, the kids will certainly lose Raven and the dozen others not part of the Asar Nergal." And if he couldn't figure out who the drake was who'd captured Becca, he might be forced to abandon everyone just to keep them safe.

Mother! Just focus on one problem at a time. Becca was the priority. Even if her issue wasn't as pressing as it was, she'd always be the priority. *So satisfy the soul bond, and protect her.*

He raised his gaze from the mug and met Grey's, fighting the growl bubbling in his throat at the look of concern in the silver drake's eyes. "Did Raven also tell you about the umbrella art outside the facility? Do you remember it?"

"I haven't really spent any time in Newgate in the last seventy or so years." From Grey's tight expression, it wasn't a conversation he wanted to have, and Nero wasn't going to ask. He'd known the silver drake had kept to Court, and Nero had heard the rumors that something had happened, and that Tobias had reprimanded Hunter for using the Royal Coterie's medallion to take the souls of two drakes without permission, but that was all Nero knew.

"Raven did ask me about it," Grey said. "She mentioned Diablo was supposed to be doing a search for it."

"He was." But given his reaction to Raven getting hit with the surge's magic, Nero doubted Diablo was going to pop by the house anytime soon. At least the younger black drake hadn't decided to challenge Nero for the doyenship of the coterie and instead had just gated away.

"I did my own search, just in case."

"Thank you." If anyone knew what Diablo was thinking, it was Grey. Not that the two were particularly close, certainly not anywhere as close as Diablo had been with Andy, but with Andy's murder, Nero feared Diablo would shut himself off like he'd been when he'd first joined the coterie, only fulfilling his duties because of his sister, Raven. But for some reason, he and Grey had started an albeit tentative friendship.

"It helped kill the time while I was sitting in a chair watching your new human mage sleep and hoping I wouldn't have to touch him."

"Did you find anything?"

"I did. Five years ago, the square at Fourth and Ross was redeveloped and a local artist's sculpture, *Up, Up, and Away*, was installed."

Nero pulled out his phone, and entered the installation's name and Newgate into his internet browser's search box. The image of the umbrella art was the first thing on the list and behind it was the familiar set of stairs leading to the front doors of the building where Becca had been held captive.

He opened a map of the area. The best place to gate into was the alley where he'd first accidentally arrived. The rest of the nearby buildings only had street access at the back or wide walkways with picnic tables and cement planter boxes. The only other good place to form a gate without being noticed was the loading bay of the building owned by the mystery dragon, but that wouldn't work because of the gatelock.

"Not a lot of places to gate close." He supposed he could also send a gate to one of the rooftops, but if he wanted to change locations, he'd still be forced to send a gate to that original alley.

"You're not planning on going alone?"

"For initial surveillance, it would be easier." Usually, he sent Diablo. With the black drake's rapid free gating ability, he could pop in and out of just about anywhere, and if things went south, he could get out fast so long as he wasn't trapped within a gatelock.

"We know nothing about this dragon."

"Hence the need for surveillance." The sooner he scoped the place out, the sooner he could ensure Becca's safety. "Any idea as to who might own the place?"

"Of the buildings in the area, there's only one with uncertain ownership, and by that I mean it's owned by a shell company within a shell company within a shell company."

"So most likely an elder dragon."

"Or an ancient one," Grey said.

"Not sure I want to consider that. An elder dragon with a thousand years of resources and earth magic training is bad enough." An ancient one would be even harder to capture and stop. Even an elder dragon had enough experience to know not to hang around the incriminating evidence. Hell, for all Nero knew, that facility had been cleared out the moment he and Becca had gated away.

Shit. He should have thought of that. There might not be any evidence left of anything, and he'd have no clue who wanted to abduct Becca.

Grey pulled out his phone. "Why don't I call Hunter and the three of us will make a hunting party?"

"I really like that idea, but for the purpose of just checking the place out and seeing what I can learn, it's best if the three of us aren't accidentally caught together on video surveillance." That would instantly send everything crashing down, as opposed to the teetering edge he was currently on. Yes, Regis was going to eventually learn the truth. Now would be a terrible time for that to happen.

"I see your point. Why don't Hunter and I check it out."

"That might still alert the dragon in charge about our connection. I show up, and less than twelve hours later you and Hunter come sniffing around." Nero finished his coffee and pocketed his phone. "No. It's better if I do the initial surveillance. I'll be in and out within an hour, and hopefully I'll have a better idea of who's in charge."

"That's a terrible plan."

"You got one that's better?" Nero stood and pressed his hand against the wall to summon a gate.

"No."

"Then keep an eye on things until I get back." He hissed his power word. The gate flared to life and he stepped through, coming out in the alley in the same place where he'd first arrived. He slipped past the rusted fire escape bolted to the brick wall and eased to the alley's mouth. A car drove past, its exhaust a white plume and its lights adding illumination to the filthy snow banks. Its engine rumbled, growing fainter as it drove away, and no other engine sounds drew close. The side street was even quieter than before, without even the hint of anyone around. Good for noticing anything out of place. Bad for offering any kind of cover if he wanted to wander closer.

Jeez. There wasn't any way he was going to get close to the building without being noticed, which meant he wasn't going to get much information right now. If he'd been thinking, he would have waited until the workday had started and more people were about. Except he hadn't been thinking, not about proper surveillance, only about Becca and ensuring her safety.

He scanned the high rises on either side of the facility's building. Maybe if he snuck into one of those from the other side, he could get a closer look at his primary goal, and hopefully this outing wouldn't be a complete waste of time.

He turned, intending to head to the other end of the alley and work his way around the block to the other side of the left-hand neighboring high rise, when something sharp dug into the back of his shoulder.

What the—

He pulled it out and had just enough time to recognize a large animal tranquilizer dart before the weight of the drug slammed into him. His limbs grew heavy, his breath slow, and his thoughts stuttered.

Trap.

This was a trap.

And the dart had enough tranquilizer in it to compensate for his dragon's enhanced healing, or he would have burned it out of his system between one breath and the next.

Someone yelled, and men in full tactical gear rushed from the nearby buildings as well as across the square toward him. More than a dozen. More than enough to take him down with the drug dragging at his senses.

He growled his power word, summoned his wind, and blasted the guys straight ahead, then turned and bolted deeper into the alley without waiting to see if he'd slowed any of them down. He needed time to summon a gate, and for that he needed distance.

A gunshot exploded behind him and pain bit his shoulder.

He sent another gust of wind behind him without looking. His foot hit an uneven patch of asphalt. He stumbled and caught his balance as more gunfire erupted and pain sliced into his chest.

Ahead lay the end of the alley and, if he could build up the strength of his wind for a blast that kept them at bay long enough, a chance for him to get out of sight.

He gasped, trying to catch his breath through the pain and the limb-numbing weight of the tranquilizer.

Twenty more feet.

He concentrated on his wind, drawing his power tight to release it in a gust that would buy him the time he needed.

Five feet.

Now.

He released the gust into whoever was behind him, and bolted out of the alley right into the line of fire of another group of armed men.

B ecca jerked awake. Someone had screamed? Roared? Been in pain? She couldn't remember. It had felt like a dream, and yet...

Nero howled in her head and she scrambled from the bed, adrenaline racing through her, ready for—

She had no idea for what. He wasn't in the bedroom. The drapes were only partially drawn, and in the dim moonlight, she couldn't see anyone in the bed or the lounge chair by the window or at the antique writing desk. The bathroom door was partially closed, but the light wasn't on, indicating he wasn't there, either. Not that Nero couldn't see in the dark, but—

Another howl, and the mental connection seared through her, locking her thoughts with Nero's. He was in trouble. He was surrounded. Men. Guns. Drugs.

The weight of a sedative crushed her and dragged at her thoughts and limbs— no, *his* thoughts and limbs. He'd been tranquilized. He'd been shot.

Where are you? She had to get to him, get help. God damn it, she needed a gun.

She rushed to the bedroom door, grabbed the knob, then realized she was naked.

Shit.

Another howl. The cry tore into her soul. He had to escape. Get back to her. Get—

Agony sliced through her chest— *his* chest. He gathered his wind, a ferocious gust that swept from the core of Becca's being and exploded from her hands—

No, damn it. *His* hands.

The bedroom darkened, and the bite of cold air stung her cheeks. Men surrounded her— *him.*

It was so hard to concentrate.

His thoughts whirled, louder than any other voice in her head. He stood on a side street lined with tall brown-bricked buildings, an alley behind and to his right, and almost a dozen men in tactical gear with weapons ranging from Tasers and Glocks to M4 assault rifles. And there were more in the alley and likely in the buildings and on the rooftops.

He lunged at a man in tactical gear while shooting a blast of wind behind him and fought past the tranquilizer to slam his fist into the man's face. He needed to cover his back, get to a wall, buy himself enough time for his soul magic to deal with the tranquilizer. Better yet, somehow summon a gate and get the hell out of there.

But there were too many of them. His wind would only hold them off for so long, and he wouldn't have enough time to summon a gate.

Where are you? she asked again, focusing her thoughts on him, willing him to hear her.

He gasped, and pain snapped through their heads. *Becca?* He couldn't let anything happen to her, had to protect her, had to—

Someone yelled. The guy he'd punched jerked around to attack him, but Nero wrenched the guy's arm back into a joint lock and, with another gust of wind, tossed the two men standing between him and a brick wall a dozen feet away.

Where? she barked.

At the facility. Ambushed. Get Grey.

The facility? God damn it. She needed clothes, but she didn't have any here except for the bloody ones she'd been wearing. *What is wrong with you? Why would you go there without backup? Why would you go there without me?*

To protect you, of course.

Of course, because I'm incapable of taking care of myself. Did I ask you to take care of my problems without me?

Well—

No. She scrambled to the bathroom and pulled on her filthy leggings and tank top. *And I'm guessing you didn't go with a plan.*

Someone yelled and gunfire exploded. The man in Nero's grasp jerked—they didn't even care if their own men were caught in the crossfire—and more pain slammed into Nero's chest.

This was supposed to be reconnaissance, he growled. *Find Grey.*

Did she even know who Grey was? Yes. He was the big blond guy who'd been in the kitchenette when she'd been shot. Still, how the hell was she going to find Grey?

He's in the transition suites… I think.

You think? She couldn't go running through the house. Hell, she didn't even know where she was.

Something flickered at the edge of her senses. Nero yanked his attention beside him to the mouth of an alley, but no one was racing out. It wasn't his senses, but hers, the whisper and rush of the other voices in her head threatening to overwhelm both of them.

Someone behind him grabbed his arm. He sent a blast of wind into them and staggered to catch his balance, his limbs numb from the tranquilizer but gaining strength.

I just need a few minutes, he said.

I'm not willing to bet your life on a few minutes. She was finding Grey and extracting Nero from this mess.

Can't send Grey, but he'll know who can help.

You're going to be picky about who saves your ass?

Need to protect the puzur.

Shit. He was right. She didn't know half of the complicated details around dragons. Forcing Grey to join a rescue team might create more problems. Still, if Grey knew what the hell was going on, she needed to find him. She just had no idea how.

The voices in her head grew louder, drowning out Nero's essence, and she fought to tune them down and get them quiet. Not now. She needed to find Grey.

Coffee? a voice asked, the words clear unlike all the other voices in her head. The tone was masculine but different than Nero's and familiar, like—

Nero ducked a punch at his face, stumbled, and swept a whip of wind at the M4 in the hands of another man, wrenching part of Becca's essence back to him.

Nero is out, the voice said. *He'll be back in a bit.*

Thanks, Grey, Raven said.

Yes! Her concentration stuttered, and the other voices flooded her again.

No! If they'd just shut up for a minute, maybe she could communicate with him like she could with Nero. She strained to focus on Grey and only Grey. She could sense he was close, below her and… out beyond the window… in the yard? But that didn't make sense. It felt as if he was lower than that. Below the ground. *Where are you?*

Grey was silent, and the voices grew louder.

Crap.

Come on.

Please.

Where are you?

Maybe she could only overhear what others were thinking and could communicate with Nero because he was inamorated with her.

But if that was the case, she needed to be physically searching for Grey as well.

She scrambled across the bedroom and out the door, into a hall with classic dark wood paneling and floorboards, a thick rug running up the center, and half a dozen other doors. She still didn't know if Grey was in the transition suites, only that he was with Raven, and had no idea how to get to wherever he was.

She banged on the first door. No answer. Same with the next. Halfway down the hall, it opened up into a stairwell landing, revealing another story above and one below.

She raced down the stairs. Pain sliced through her chest. Her vision wavered back to the dark street and the men surrounding Nero.

A fist cracked against his cheek. He snapped the elbow of one man then shoved him into the one who'd hit him. Two more men lunged at him, and he knew they were keeping tight to prevent him from summoning a gate. They knew he was a dragon, and knew how to take him down.

Not going to happen. She was getting him out of there. No one else was going to die because of her, and she was God damned going to find Grey.

Grey's consciousness flashed to the forefront of her mind. *Who the—?*

She seized at his thoughts and held tight. *Becca. Nero's in—*

Nero growled, wrenching Becca's attention back to him. He jerked a dart from his arm, and a massive wave of exhaustion swept through him.

Hold on. God, he just had to hold on. *I'm coming.*

What's going on? Grey's confusion snapped through her. She stumbled over the last step into a wider hall with similar dark wood floorboards and paneling, but no rug.

Nero needs—

Another blast of pain in her chest. Nero clutched the front of the tactical vest of the guy in front of him, his legs weak. The man sneered, yanked his three-inch knife from Nero's chest, and slammed it back into Nero's gut.

Becca's knees buckled and she staggered, fighting to keep her balance. Nero howled. He shoved the man—helped by his wind—into another, but the weight of the second tranquilizer dose dragged at him, turning his thoughts muddy and filling Becca with a heavy fog.

He was going down. His panic clutched around his heart and hers. He had to protect his kids, and above all, he had to protect Becca.

You God damn stupid drake. I'm not helpless.

He dropped to one knee, and two men rushed to grab his arms.

Stand up, she barked at him. She was going to get him out of there. He just needed to hold on.

He struggled to rise. The closest man seized his wrist. If both of them got him, he wouldn't be able to break free.

I said stand the hell up and fight, she roared.

He jerked up and slashed a whip of wind at the man holding his wrists. The guy released him with a yelp, and the other man lunged in. Nero wrenched out of reach. Gunfire roared beside him and more agony sliced into his chest.

He dropped to his knees again.

No. Stand.

He heaved himself up but couldn't catch his balance. His breath burned. He'd taken too many shots to the chest, and with the second tranquilizer dose, he could barely think.

She was running out of time and still hadn't come across anyone in the house. Where the hell was Grey? Where the hell was anyone? She had to get to Nero but had no idea how. Even if she knew where the facility was, she wouldn't be able to drive there in time. She needed someone who could make a gate, but the house was massive and no one was awake at this hour.

A roar filled her, and she screamed her helplessness into the dark hall. She didn't know what she had with Nero, they'd barely met, but she knew him more intimately than she'd ever known anyone else and she couldn't lose him. Not now. Not when he was the only one who made her feel stable and sane.

Somebody. Please. Anyone who can make a gate.

Becca. That was Grey, but he sounded far away, caught on the other side of Nero's desperate thoughts and woolly sedation.

I need a gate. Now. She rushed through a dark kitchen and down another hall. *Please. I have to get to him. I need a gate.*

The world shuddered and blackness enveloped her. Darkness, deeper but not as bone-weary as the tranquilizer, swept around her. For a second, less than two rapid pounds of her heart, up and down vanished and she was surrounded by nothing. Then her foot hit something solid and slippery—

She tumbled backward as cold bit her bare skin and her gaze darted over surprised men in tactical gear, standing on an empty nighttime street surrounded by brown-brick buildings.

Nero roared, and she heard it in her head and with her ears. Her butt hit icy asphalt and her attention leapt across the street to him. He was on his knees, two men holding him down, his gaze locked on her, his eyes wide.

She scrambled to her feet, lunged at the man closest to her, and grabbed the top of the handguard of his M4. There wasn't time to think about how she'd gotten there. What was important was gaining a weapon, getting out from the middle of the enemy, and getting Nero to safety. The man yelped, wrenched his M4 from her grip, and staggered back. She heaved forward, determined to keep him off balance and to stay moving, to make herself a harder target to shoot.

He jerked the butt of his gun at her face. She heaved back and a tranquilizer dart embedded into the front of his vest. She dove to capture his M4 as another dart bit into her shoulder.

Nero screamed. She hit the quick release catch on the M4's sling and wrenched around as the tranquilizer's weight flooded her. Darkness swarmed her vision and her knees buckled. Nero roared again, but she couldn't tell if she heard it or if it had just been in her head.

Nero woke on his side, with his heart racing and his wrists on a short chain attached to a ring in the center of a stainless steel floor in a stainless steel room. All four walls—no window—the door, and the ceiling were steel, with every inch covered in hieroglyphics. Inside his head, Becca was silent, but he didn't know if that meant she was unconscious or dead—

No, not dead. He'd feel it in his soul if she were dead.

So, one plus. And yet so many negatives as well. She was captive again by the same drake who'd had her before, and now so was he.

A heavy lock on the door *thunked*, and it swung open.

Wonderful. No windows and a solid bolt on the outside, not to mention he could still feel the tingle of the gatelock and the weight of something else, most likely the lingering effects of the tranquilizer.

The woman with the dark-rimmed glasses, the physician's coat, and the clipboard, who'd been interrogating Becca before, stepped inside and shut the door behind her with another heavy *thunk*. A hint of flickering aura glowed around her. It indicated she was a human but didn't have enough magical strength for any kind of power, probably not even enough for the development of an earth magic ability. Which meant she wasn't the dragon in charge.

She stayed by the door, pulled a pen from her breast pocket, and tapped it against the clipboard.

He shifted, but the chain securing him to the floor was too short to get his knees under him without forcing him into a scrunched, bowed position, so he gave up and subvocalized his power word instead, hoping she wouldn't notice his discomfort or his magic. Nothing. Not even a hint of the surge of power within him indicated he'd summoned his wind.

She cocked an eyebrow, but he couldn't tell if she knew he'd tried to summon his earth magic or not. Given she didn't have any magic herself, probably not. But that meant whichever drake had him was a powerful sorcerer, if not a true power, then close enough. It also meant the weight inside him wasn't just the last of the tranquilizer. It was the feel of a null magic spell—most likely coming from the hieroglyphics—which would explain why Becca wasn't in his head.

His gaze slid to the figures in the floor at his knee. There were a lot of glyphs. Grey had said Servius had only had a few symbols on his arms, and he could control the earth and wind as well as gate through a gatelock. How many glyphs were needed for a permanent null magic spell and how many other spells were in this room?

"Not going to try the chain?" the woman asked.

"And then? I'm in the middle of a secure facility. I suppose I could break free and threaten to tear your throat out until you release me." But that wouldn't help Becca, and he couldn't demand her freedom as well, because that would reveal to the dragon in charge that she meant something to him.

"Or do you not have enhanced strength?" The woman pursed her lips, her gaze steady on him.

He didn't, but that wasn't the point. Even if he did, the odds weren't good for escaping from this room. Biding his time and hoping she'd eventually move him someplace less secure was his best bet. Except with a dragon in charge, that could take a lot of time, and the more time Becca spent here, the greater the danger.

"Why don't we cut to the chase and you introduce me to your boss."

"What makes you think I have a boss?" the woman asked. "Because I don't have any magical strength or because I'm not a dragon?"

That would be a yes to all of the above. He met her gaze and held it.

"I expected arrogance from an ancient dragon." She jotted something on the clipboard. "So far you've only partially disappointed."

"Oh?"

"I wanted to see how long it would take you to figure out that, even with enhanced strength, you couldn't break the chains."

"You can put me down for five seconds."

She rolled her eyes. "You didn't have a clue until I told you."

"And you'll never really know." *Come on. Slip up and mention the dragon in charge.*

"You're right. I never really will." She flipped over the page she was writing on and drew out a slip of paper the size of her palm, clipped to the top of the next page. "But let's find out for certain if you're the dugga of the Asar Nergal."

She sauntered toward him, confident in the magic on the chain securing him to the floor, and crouched opposite him, his hands and the ring on the floor between them.

"No growl? No sneer?" She flipped the first page back and made another note. "I wish I'd had an ancient dragon to study sooner."

Which suggested her boss wasn't an ancient dragon. "You've studied a lot of dragons?"

"A few."

"Because your boss won't allow more?"

"Back to the boss again." She clicked her tongue. "Are you hoping to make a deal?"

He was hoping to find a way out of there and take Becca with him. "Just trying to fully understand the situation."

"Understandable. You wouldn't have survived as long as you have by being an idiot."

Even if right now he felt like an idiot for having been caught by a human with only two dozen men and a sniper with a tranq gun.

"The problem is that you won't be able to figure it out." She raised the small piece of paper to eye level, drawing his attention to the four black hieroglyphics on it. "The others never did."

"I'm sure just about any dragon, including a hatchling, could recognize a sorcerer." He let a hint of a sneer seep across his expression. Maybe if he got her riled up, she'd reveal something. "It isn't even the most powerful kind of sorcery if it needs glyphs."

"It's powerful enough for what I need." She pressed the paper to the back of his hands and lightning exploded through his body, jerking his muscles taut, as if he'd been hit with a Taser's current.

Mother of All, that hurt! And he wouldn't have thought it possible with the null magic spell on the room. But whoever had cast it must have woven in an exception for this woman, since the only way she could have cast a spell would have been an exception to the null magic, or if she'd cast the original null spell herself.

The woman gasped and her eyes widened with dark delight. "It's true. You're the dugga."

The paper turned to ash, the blast released him, and his muscles went limp. If he'd been standing, he would have crumpled to the floor. Black and white specks flashed across his vision and he fought to catch his breath.

"What the hell was that?"

"A little spell I wrote. You know, nothing overly powerful, just a way to know if you possess the dugga's magic."

"Well, now you know." And she could take her confirmation to her boss and destroy everyone he was trying to protect.

She pulled more pages from her clipboard, the sheets bigger and covered with more hieroglyphics. "And I'm going to take it."

"You're what—?" If she took the dugga's magic, she'd have a mental connection with every member of the Asar Nergal, as well as every human mage he'd let live. She'd know who they were and where they were. He couldn't let her do that, except he had no idea how to get out of there. "Wouldn't your boss rather have the magic, or is this an attempt to unseat him?"

Buy time. Just buy time, and he could figure a way out of this.

The woman tipped her head back and laughed. "Really. You have to stop thinking about my boss." She set the papers on the floor beside her—out of reach—and held up her hand, wiggling her index finger and drawing his attention to a gold ring.

With a wicked grin, she slipped off the ring, and her aura blazed white around her with a ferocious magical strength. The flicker was still there, indicating she was human and not a dragon in disguise, but the promise of her magic was revealed in full. She was a sorcerer. Not as powerful as Anaea, but more powerful than most drakes—since dragons only had one or two earth magic abilities or at most a moderate sorcerer's magic.

"I am the boss, and when I have the dugga's magic, I'll be able to hunt down every one of your assassins and kill them." She slipped the ring in her pocket, pressed her palm to the center of the top paper with the hieroglyphics, and hissed, "So it be done," in ancient Egyptian.

Light exploded from the glyphs, consuming the black ink into a blazing white brilliance that poured over the papers and ignited the glyphs on the floor. It raced around Nero, shooting from the floor as if cracks had formed and light was bleeding through, then rushed up the walls and over the ceiling.

"So it be done," the woman hissed again.

The light around Nero blazed stronger, writhing up from the glyphs in strands that strained and stretched and latched around his wrists and ankles.

The woman stood and stretched out her arms. "So it be done."

The light snapped tight, cut into his skin, and shot straight to his heart. Fire exploded within him, a mix of Taser-convulsing lightning and heart-of-the-sun searing. He couldn't catch his breath, couldn't move, and could barely think, his thoughts locked on how he had to stop her and how he had to save Becca.

Through the haze of white, the light swept around the woman's ankles, dug into her skin, and raced like glowing veins through her body.

She gasped and turned a wide-eyed, wild look at Nero. "I will hunt the hunters and your reign of terror will finally be over."

The light surged, consuming Nero's vision with a blinding white nothing and filling him with blazing agony, freezing him in a torturous convulsion and stealing even his thoughts of escape. There was no escape. Even if he could move, he wouldn't be able to break the chain, and he wouldn't be able to stand.

"So. It. Be. Done," the woman screamed.

Darkness slammed over him, taking the light but not the agony. His muscles trembled and he still couldn't catch his breath. Every inhalation and exhalation sawed through his chest and throat.

"So it *is* done." The woman chuckled, sending shivers racing over Nero, sparking a blast of pain that shuddered through him.

"And I can feel them in my head." A hand grabbed his chin and jerked his head up. "There are more than I expected," she said, her hot breath burning against his face. Even his clothes, set off by every shift and shiver, chafed against every sensitive nerve.

The darkness turned to a haze, and he could make out the woman's face inches from his. He should attack her, somehow, fight to take back what she'd stolen, but just the thought of moving made agony roar through him. The only saving grace was that if she didn't kill him, he had about an hour to figure out what he was going to do. The power wouldn't fully lock with her soul. She'd know how many members there were of the Asar Nergal, but not who or where. At least until the hour was up.

She cocked her head to the side, her gaze turned inward. "No, they're not all dragons."

A flash of ice swept through the blaze.

"They're humans. More than I expected." Her focus returned to him. "Saving up your next victims for something special?"

Except they weren't his next victims. There weren't that many human mages out there that weren't part of his *puzur*, and Mother, what would she do if she discovered his kids were a part of his family? What would she do if she thought that meant they were traitors to humankind?

35

Becca paced the barren white cell, her attention locked on the hall beyond the heavy Plexiglas front wall and the solid steel door. She couldn't feel Nero in her head, or anyone else for that matter. There was only silence, and the sensation made her skin crawl. Funny how just a handful of hours ago, she would have given anything for pure silence. It made her realize the quiet she'd had before hadn't been complete silence. It had merely been everyone at the dimmest setting she could get. She knew now that was the way it was supposed to be, not this unnerving emptiness.

"You know pacing like that won't get you out of here faster," Werner said from his perch on the slab protruding from the wall that was supposed to be a bed. He had a black eye and a nasty welt along the side of his neck. He also held himself a little too stiffly, as if he had cracked ribs.

"But it might make me feel better." Even though the pacing wasn't. She just couldn't sit there and wait. She had no idea what she was waiting for and didn't like any of the options she could imagine.

"If you don't stop, you're going to use up everything you have before we get our chance to escape."

"A few laps around this cell isn't going to exhaust me." She had to find Nero and—

What? A part of her wanted to flee, along with everyone else held captive here. And even though the two cells across from her were empty, that didn't mean there weren't others here. There had been others before. Werner had said most of them hadn't managed to escape, and she didn't want to think about what would have happened to them if they weren't here now.

But another part of her, a bigger part—the part that was the real her fully awakened and no longer terrified—wanted to take the fight to Stanbury. She wanted to toss the crazy doctor at the feet of the Newgate police or the FBI or whoever in this country Becca could get to arrest the bitch and ensure the safety of Nero and his family.

"Fine. Sit for me. I still don't know how you're standing. I saw you get shot. I saw the blood after that snake gated you away from the abandoned factory." He ran a hand over his wild, unkempt locks. "You should be dead."

She should be, but she wasn't because of Nero. "That snake has a name."

"Yeah, and I'm pretty sure it's dugga. Does he also possess mind control like the one from the cave?"

"No."

"Then why the hell were you running around with him?" Werner balled his hands into fists. "The only reason I can think of is that you were playing it up for him, waiting for the right moment to escape and had somehow managed to convince him not to kill you."

Movement at the far end of the hall caught Becca's eye, and she turned to face whoever was coming. Two men in tactical gear, each with a shoulder under Nero's armpits, half-helped and half-dragged the semi-conscious dragon toward the cell, while two more men, one with a Taser and the other with an M4, followed behind.

The guy with the M4 entered a code into the digital lock and opened the door without taking his hand away from the trigger of his rifle. The guy with the Taser aimed inside and jerked his chin at Becca, indicating she should back up. She did, and the other two shoved Nero inside.

He stumbled and collapsed to his knees as the door was locked and the men marched away.

Becca dropped to the floor in front of him. "What did she do? Why aren't you healing?" *And why can't I hear you in my head yet?*

"I am healing, but this magic is harder to deal with than a gunshot," he said, his voice gruff.

"Jeez. You can stop playing your game. We're all captives. Pretending you care about him won't help you now," Werner growled. "We should kill the snake and use it as leverage to get out of here."

"You honestly think Stanbury will release us if we kill Nero?"

"You mean the dugga?" Werner asked.

"I'm not right now," Nero gasped. "And I'm still your best bet of getting out of here."

Werner huffed and crossed his arms. "Oh, yeah, how?"

"What do you mean, you're not right now?" Becca cupped his cheeks in her palms and drew a pained gasp. She yanked her hands back, afraid the contact would continue to hurt him. *Talk to me. Hear me.* If he'd just meet her gaze, surely their mental connection would come back. She needed it to come back— no, she didn't *need* it, she wanted it. She could survive without him in her head, but she didn't want to.

A shudder swept through Nero. His jaw tightened on a groan, and her heart squeezed at his agony.

"There's null magic in the cell but not the hall," he said, lifting his gaze to her, and something in her soul steadied. Even though he wasn't in her head, he was still hers, always hers, and she would take care of that responsibility.

"That's why—?" She tapped her temple and glanced at Werner, not wanting to reveal she had a mental connection with Nero. She knew how Werner felt about dragons. She'd felt that way, too, until she'd met Nero. If she couldn't convince him Nero wasn't the monster they'd feared, she was going to have to get him away from Nero.

"Yes." Nero gave a tight nod, and she knew it was also in answer to her unspoken request to keep their mental connection a secret.

"I already know that," Werner said. "And thanks to your friends, I also know it means whatever magic *you* have won't work in here, either."

"Friends? Because all drakes know each other?" Nero rolled his eyes. "If you know anything about me, you know what my directive is regarding those *friends*."

Werner jerked from the bed and shoved Becca aside. He grabbed the front of Nero's shirt and heaved him to his feet. "Do you know how long they held me?" He slammed Nero against the Plexiglas wall.

Nero gasped, and his eyes rolled back.

"Put him down. He's going to pass out."

"No, he won't." Werner grabbed Nero's chin, forcing him to look at him. "If you were following your directive, you should have stopped them. They would have never kidnapped Becca or Glenn or more than half of the others."

"But I wouldn't have caught the main drake responsible. She would have started again."

"And you fucking would have stopped her again. Isn't that what your magic does?" Werner leaned close and sneered. "Except you wanted the big fish. You didn't care about how many humans were tortured or for how long, so you waited."

Becca grabbed Werner's shoulder and yanked him back, but he held tight to the front of Nero's shirt. "Werner, let him go."

"Sure. When he's dead."

"Damage this vessel beyond repair, and I'll just take yours," Nero growled. He matched Werner's sneer, but a feral menace filled his eyes, his true dragon nature revealed. "I haven't been alive for over two thousand years because some infant managed to kill me."

Werner's eyes widened. "You'd break your own laws."

"To survive—" Nero's gaze jumped over Werner's shoulder to Becca, and she didn't need a mental connection to know he was thinking, *and to protect my inamorata,* "I'd do anything. So don't press your luck, infant." With a roar, Nero seized Werner's hand holding his shirt, broke his grip, and shoved him back. "I haven't ripped out your throat because Becca seems to care about you, but endanger her and you'll wish all I did was kill you."

"With what magic?" Werner squared his shoulders.

Nero's sneer turned into a snarl, and a hint of wind shuddered through the room.

Werner's eyes widened in surprise again. "But the null magic?"

"Not strong enough in this cell to completely stop an ancient drake about to lose his temper," Nero said.

The two men glared at each other.

Becca's heart pounded. Nero shuddered but kept standing, his expression ferocious, while Werner glared back, not looking nearly as intimidating.

Werner raised his chin.

Nero growled.

Jeez. Were they going to stare at each other all day? This wasn't helping anything. She wanted answers, and she wanted the hell out of there.

"Good Lord! Have you figured out which is longer?" They both looked at her, and she rolled her eyes at them. "Even if you can summon wind, that doesn't help us out of this cell."

"Yeah," Werner said. "This one has a keypad on it. It's not like the previous ones we were in, with a deadbolt on the outside."

Nero glanced back at Werner, snarled, then sagged to the floor, his expression pinched with pain. "I also made a point of watching the guard enter the code." He settled his gaze on Becca, drawing a heated attraction fluttering in her chest. "I'm not just a pretty face, you know."

"Oh, my God, are you flirting with her?" Werner stalked to the slab and sat. "Guess playing along with your captor also involved seducing him. I didn't think you were the type."

"There was no playing along." And the seduction had been mutual and very satisfying. She sat beside Nero, her shoulder brushing his, needing to be near him and not caring what Werner thought of that.

Nero slid his hand down and intertwined his fingers between

hers, out of Werner's sight. Thank goodness he wasn't going to continue the pissing contest and show off how close he and Becca had become. Just the feel of his skin against hers, a complete hold, not the gentle brush when she'd tried to cup his face, steadied her. She hadn't realized how unsteady she'd been, and, after a few seconds, a hint of his thoughts fluttered into her, along with the whisper of searing agony. Guess the null magic also wasn't strong enough to silence their mental connection when they were in physical contact for any length of time.

Thank the Mother she's safe.

And so are you, she thought at him.

He squeezed her hand and tipped his head back, his expression still tight with the pain she now felt at the edge of her senses.

"Nero isn't who we thought he was," she said.

"He's not the dugga?" Werner asked, his tone sarcastic.

Nero groaned. "Not right now."

"What does that mean?" Becca tightened her grip on his hand. A sinking feeling filled her stomach, and she feared she did know what that meant.

"The dugga is a position, not a person," Nero said.

"We know that," Werner said.

"That woman with the glasses—"

"Stanbury," Becca said.

"She's figured out a way, a rather painful way, to take the magic that comes with the dugga's position."

"How'd she do that?" The need to take the fight to Stanbury and see her arrested swarmed through Becca. To hell with even the idea of running. Someone had to stop her.

"Turns out she's a pretty powerful sorcerer," Nero said.

"Did you decide to *wait and see* with her as well?" Werner snorted. "You're a pretty shitty dugga. Can't even seem to do the most basic part of your job."

"Trust me, he's the drake you want as the dugga," Becca said. Enough was enough. She couldn't afford to have Werner and Nero at odds if they were even going to try escaping. "He's been breaking the rules to keep human mages alive and hidden from the other dragons for centuries."

"And now that Stanbury has the dugga's magic, she can sense all of them." Nero caught Becca's gaze. "If she accidentally reveals them to another dragon—"

"All your kids will be in danger." Becca's pulse stuttered. She didn't know those kids, but a part of her hoped one day she would. They meant everything to Nero. He risked his life every day to keep them safe, and if she hadn't come into his life, they wouldn't be in danger. "We have to stop her."

"No. I'm getting you and Werner and anyone else we can find out of here, and then *I'm* stopping her," he said.

"Don't be an idiot." There was no way Becca was letting him face Stanbury alone. "We've already established you can't go after her alone. That's how we ended up in this mess."

"And you believe this load of crap?" Werner asked.

"I do, so either get with the program and agree to help or sit there and shut the hell up."

Werner's eyes narrowed.

"I have less than an hour to reclaim the dugga's magic. I'm not willing to put you or anyone else in danger."

"And you can't make me leave without you." Becca tightened her grip on his hand. "These are your kids we're talking about." *You know about Afghanistan. You think I'd ever turn my back on a child?*

But you're my inamorata.

And a female drake is just as ferocious as a male.

You're not a dragon. His heartache and terror at losing her flooded their mental link. He knew what it would feel like, and he didn't want to lose another.

Like it or not, I'm a soldier. You can't stop me from protecting those who can't protect themselves. As hard as that truth was, she couldn't deny it. Protecting the innocent was her core value. Just like it was Nero's.

God damn it, he growled. "Fine. Werner is put in charge of evacuating any other mages who are here, and we deal with Stanbury."

"Now all we need is a plan."

36

Nero shifted and realized his butt had fallen asleep while sitting on the cell floor. The agony searing through his body had changed to a soul-deep ache in his chest that he knew was his spirit trying to adjust to the loss of the dugga's magic. Soon the ache would be gone and so would any possibility of regaining his power.

The three of them had spent the last twenty minutes brain-storming ideas for a plan, and it had taken everything in Nero's power to concentrate on coming up with something and not wrap his arms around Becca and hold her close. She was alive, and even though he'd known in his soul that she was, he'd still been terrified he was wrong. She was also unhurt, and he couldn't thank the Mother enough for that.

Unfortunately, that probably wouldn't last. With their limited time and resources, the best plan they could come up with was to move fast, strike hard, and hope like hell.

According to Werner, there was access to a stairwell at the end of the hall to the left, and a bank of elevators down the hall and around the corner to the right. He also said there was another stairwell on the other side of the building, but it would be hard to get to. Becca had been unconscious when they'd brought her in, so she couldn't confirm anything, and Nero could only confirm the location of the elevators, which meant he was going to have to trust that Werner's sense of self-preservation was stronger than his hate for all things dragon.

Nero also knew there were security cameras in the elevators and the halls, but a quick glance proved there were none in the cell. That suggested the security system might be tight, but it wasn't over the top. There were also most likely cameras in the stairwell, and if Stanbury was smart—and he'd be smart to assume she was—her security probably had remote access to the elevator controls. So if they were going anywhere, they'd have to take the stairs.

He still didn't like the idea of Becca coming with him, but he recognized a losing battle when he saw one. And really, as if his soul would pick some pushover. She might be human, but she still needed to be ferocious enough to stand up against his dragon spirit. There was no way she was going to leave the facility without him. Hell, she'd accidentally gated to him when he'd been ambushed—no doubt thanks to having all her earth magic awakened by the surge. That determination to get to him had to explain why she'd been able to rapid free gate before she even knew she could gate, and that spoke to a fierce determination.

The other thing he found shocking was Werner's state of sanity. The human didn't seem to be struggling with soul sickness, and if— no, *when* Nero got his dugga's magic back and Becca to safety, he was going to look into the cause for Werner's sanity. With luck, it was due to something Raven could use to help the remaining few of Zenobia's victims he had yet to bring in.

"Okay." He glanced at Becca, but he didn't need to look at her to know she was ready. He could feel it in the re-established mental connection between them. It was faint, and when she spoke mind to mind with him she sounded like she was at the end of a long hall, but their mental connection was back. And thank the Mother! He never wanted to feel that kind of emptiness again.

"Let's do this," Becca said. *As soon as I'm free of the null spell, I'll try to pinpoint Stanbury.* She'd assured him she could figure out how to do this and wouldn't let the other voices overwhelm her.

You get two minutes. No more. And any sign the voices are too strong, you stop.

We have to confirm where she is or we could waste all our time searching for her.

He wanted to disagree but he couldn't. Werner had suggested Stanbury might be in her office, but he really didn't know.

Werner squared his shoulders. "Let's not and we just get the hell out of here, Becca."

"No." She matched his stance and raised an eyebrow, her expression daring him to keep pressing. "I'm helping Nero. You get the others to safety."

"This is a terrible plan," he grumbled.

"It is." And as much as Nero wanted to argue with that, he couldn't. "But I have less than half an hour to stop Stanbury from permanently gaining the dugga's magic, so it's now or never." It didn't matter that he wasn't fully healed from having his magic ripped from his essence. If he was going to get it back, or in the very least, prevent Stanbury from learning about the members of the Asar Nergal and the *puzur*, he needed to act now.

"I still don't trust you."

"You don't have to." The ache in Nero's chest billowed and he ground his teeth. "You just have to get everyone we find in this hall out of the building and some place safe. I'll find you when we're done."

"A part of me hopes you don't." Werner pressed his cheek against the Plexiglas and glanced down the hall. "Looks clear."

"Good." Nero crouched in front of the door and hissed his power word. A yell would have been better to bolster his will against the weight of the null magic, but he didn't want to alert anyone they might not have seen farther down the hall about what he was doing.

His magic, a tiny ball within the core of his being, strained against the null magic. The spell wasn't as strong as the one in the room where Stanbury had taken his dugga's magic. A different sorcerer had cast it, or she hadn't put in the same amount of time creating the glyphs to maintain its strength. But still, Mother of All, it had been easier to summon his wind when he'd been pissed and had all that emotion to add power to his magic.

He clenched his jaw, fighting to bring a small breath of wind forward. He didn't need much, just enough to slip under the door and depress five buttons on the keypad.

"Any day now," Werner hissed.

"I'm trying."

Werner checked the other direction of the hall. "I thought you said your ancient dragon magic was more powerful than the null spell on the cell?"

"It was more powerful when I was about to lose my temper." Nero's pulse pounded in agonizing beats through his head, and the ache in his chest billowed again.

"Well, Stanbury is going to find and torture all of your kids if you don't get that door open," Becca said. "Get pissed about that."

"I am." But his wind still wasn't breaking through the spell.

"Come on," Werner growled. "You promised me a great escape." He seized Nero's shoulder and shoved him against the door. "I'm tired of waiting." He rammed his fist into Nero's gut, and the force stole his breath.

"Werner." Becca grabbed his arm, but he wrenched from her grip and jerked his elbow toward her face.

Power erupted in Nero's soul and exploded from his hands in a wild gale. He snapped it into a whip and seized Werner's arm before he could hit Becca, slamming the other man against the Plexiglas.

Werner raised his other hand, palm up in submission. "Now use that wind to unlock the door."

Nero wrenched his wind from Werner and shoved it under the door. He didn't like Werner's style, but it had gotten the job done, and fast. Lucky for Werner, Nero had just enough self-control not to break his neck when he'd threatened Becca.

"Get ready to move." Becca glared at Werner and shifted closer to Nero. He could feel her tension, a quiet far-off ripple at the edge of his senses, mixed with determination and exhilaration. They didn't know if unlocking the door would set off an alert and security would know right away they'd escaped, or if they had a few seconds before being spotted in the hall on a monitor.

"Was before and still am," Werner said.

Nero pressed his face against the Plexiglas to get the best view he could of the panel. He could perform any number of amazing fine-detailed things with his wind, but what he didn't have was a sense of touch, which meant he had to use the memory of his quick glance at the keypad to assume where the numbers were. He should have tried to rip the bolts out of the hinges but that required brute force, and he didn't know if he'd be able to summon enough wind against the null magic spell for that. Guess that was plan B, since he was pretty sure a failed code would alert someone monitoring security about their escape attempt.

You've got this, Becca whispered in his head, her essence warming his soul.

He had to have this. For her.

For your kids.

For all of you. He drew in a quick breath, created a square of wind the size of the security panel and aligned the two. With the image of the keypad in his mind's eye, he extended a knob of wind aligned with the first number of the code and depressed the button, then the next and the next until all five digits had been entered.

The lock clicked, and Becca eased the door open. No one came running and no alarms sounded. Which didn't mean their escape hadn't been noticed.

Nero released his wind and ran out, followed by Becca and Werner. The weight of the null magic spell vanished, and Becca's presence rushed into his head, solid and sure, where she was supposed to be, along with a sudden blast of voices all clamoring for her attention. His own magic, the promise of his magical wind, tickled over his forearms, as if it hadn't been fully released or he was a young drake again and not in full control. Not ideal, and he wasn't a hundred percent, but he was determined to put up one hell of a fight.

The ache in his chest swelled again, the pulsing coming faster and stronger than before. He didn't know if that was because he was free of the null magic and whether the spell had somehow also been affecting his soul. And he wasn't going to spend a lot of time thinking about it. Stop Stanbury. Get his dugga's magic back. That was the plan.

He called his wind again, savoring the feel of its strength surging through his limbs and gusting around him, and turned his attention toward the elevators to cover Werner—who was checking the other cells—and Becca—while she tried to focus inward and find Stanbury.

Werner ran to the next cell over and staggered to a stop. "Another keypad."

Inside, a man stood with one hand pressed against the glass and pointing into the hall with the other. His hair and beard were matted like Werner's, and his expression was wild.

"Get the others. Theirs is just a deadbolt," he yelled through the glass.

Becca jerked toward him, and Nero felt her concentration on her magic vanish. "Glenn."

"Get the others." Glenn pointed again, his movements shaky and desperate.

Five people in the other cell hurried forward. They all wore hospital gowns, like Becca had when Nero had first found her, and while their hands and faces were clean, their hair was unkempt and they were all undernourished. They also all had the flickering aura of human mages, none as powerful as Becca or even Werner, but all had fully developed magic.

"I'm not leaving you," Becca said to the guy with the beard.

"Neither am I." Werner glared at the keypad.

"Becca, get back and find Stanbury." Nero gathered his wind. "Werner, get the others in the cell. I've got this."

You don't know the code. But she rushed out of the way toward the stairs.

I don't need the code. "I'm going with plan B."

Werner frowned. "What's plan B?"

"Get the others and get them clear," Nero growled. "Now."

Werner unlocked the door and hurried the five others toward Becca as Nero surged his wind into the door's hinges. He yanked out the bolts then wrenched the door free and tossed it down the hall toward the elevators. Two men in tactical gear with Tasers scrambled out of the way, one of them screaming for backup with M4s and a tranq gun.

"Crap. I was hoping it would take them longer to get to us," Becca said. Nero couldn't tell if she'd begun to focus her magic again or not.

"Focus." *Please.* Nero didn't want to end up running all around the building looking for Stanbury, and he could only hope Becca could control her earth magic long enough to find her. She'd said before she'd gated to help him that she'd almost found Grey with her telepathy. She was certain she could do it now.

I have to. I won't let Stanbury hurt your family. She wouldn't be responsible for anyone losing their family again.

I know you won't. With his wind, Nero heaved the door up and slammed it into the two men again, ramming them against the wall at the end of the hall.

"Becca. Location?" He didn't want to make her run and concentrate at the same time, but they were going to have to get moving soon or switch to the plan where they captured one of the security guards and hoped he knew Stanbury's location.

The ache in his chest billowed again, and the searing pain from Stanbury's spell flared with it. His wind stuttered. Mother of All. He squeezed his will into his magic, fighting to keep it activated.

"Come on, Becca," Werner said, ushering the escapees to the stairwell at the end of the hall. "Let's get the hell out of here, for good this time."

"Not without stopping Stanbury first." Her mind squeezed around Nero's essence like it had before when she'd been clinging to her sanity, making it hard to breathe and concentrate.

The men in the hall shoved the door aside and staggered to their feet.

Where is she? Where? The force of Becca's will tightened.

Nero blasted a wall of wind into the security guards. His heart raced— no, *her* heart. There were so many voices, yelling, screaming, filling him— *her*.

"I've almost got it."

But he could sense she was barely holding on to herself among all the voices, let alone able to find one specific mind, and he was barely holding on to himself, too. This wasn't going to work. If she didn't shut her magic off, she was going to lose her essence to the force of her power and never get it back.

37

Becca's mind reeled, caught in a tornado of thoughts, whispering, screaming, happy, sad, hundreds upon hundreds of them, all clamoring for attention, all threatening to drown her essence and sweep her away.

Stop. "You have to stop." Nero's desperation cut through the roar, a tiny anchor in the whirling chaos.

"I've almost found her." If she could just focus, she was sure she'd be able to find Stanbury's mind out of all the others. She'd found Grey. Except she hadn't really found him, only known he'd been close.

Becca, please. Nero's essence— no, his physical body jerked away from her, and he blasted more wind at the men in the hall. Men with howling fear, their thoughts panicked. They didn't have the right weapons. They needed help. They—

"Come on, Becca. Let's get out of here." Werner, Glenn, and the others were almost at the end of the hall, and a part of her just wanted to flee with them. But a stronger part couldn't leave Nero. This was her chance to save kids instead of helplessly listening to them scream. And God damn it, there was something about Nero, something she couldn't explain, that wouldn't let her abandon him. She barely knew him and didn't know his kids at all, but he needed help, and she could help. That was it. He needed help. But in her heart, she knew the reason was more than that, soul-deeper than that.

"Let it go and get to the stairs." Nero grabbed her arm. *Your power is too strong, and you're untrained. You'll lose yourself. I can't lose my dugga's magic and them and you, too.*

You won't. She wasn't going to let that happen.

She wrenched free of his grip. "I'm finding her, and we're getting your power back."

Stanbury had to be close. Nero had said she'd taken his magic in a room in the building. Of course, Stanbury could have left in the twenty minutes they were locked in the cell. But—

Mother of All. She was as stubborn as a dragon— Nero's thoughts. Not hers. It was even becoming hard to separate him from her and everyone else.

She strained to keep her essence within her. He'd cursed her for being stubborn as a dragon. Well, she'd be stubborn and make her magic do what she wanted.

She mentally shoved at any of the voices that she sensed weren't nearby, but there were still too many. *Come on, Stanbury. I know you're here.* She'd heard the other woman's thoughts before she'd first escaped. Surely that would help her make a connection now. They were running out of time. Maybe if she thought about how that first connection had felt, her subconscious would be able to recognize Stanbury's thoughts again.

But that sent a shiver racing through her and the terrifying thought that magic was real seized her heart. Her pulse raced faster, and she clamped down on that thought.

"Becca?"

Yes, magic was real, and she had magic. She'd already dealt with this and had no intention of going back.

"Becca," Nero growled, his tone tense, his thoughts heavy with worry.

Wind gusted past her and someone yelled, but she didn't dare break her concentration to check what was going on. Their plan wouldn't work if they couldn't find Stanbury, and it certainly wouldn't work if they couldn't find her quickly. Nero was running out of time.

Nero grabbed her arm again. "You need to move. I can defend you better in the stairwell." *As well as ensure Werner gets the others to safety.*

I don't want to lose my concentration. She tried to pull away again, but Nero tightened his grip.

"Do you have her?"

"No."

"Then haul ass to the stairwell and try again." *Since I can't convince you to stop.* He blasted more wind at three men between them and the stairwell door and shoved her into action.

She didn't want to lose what she had, but he was right. If the stairwell was a better position for him, then that was where she needed to be.

"We're running out of time," she said as she bolted to the door.

One of the men clambered to his feet. She punched him in the head, knocking him back to the floor, and took his Glock.

Nero's wind seized the other two men and tossed them down the hall into the first two.

"Then find her." Nero jerked his chin at Werner, who was holding the door open. "You guys get out of here and don't stop for anything."

"Stating the obvious, snake," Werner said. He turned to Becca. "Don't let him mind-control you."

"Clearly not my magic." Nero swept a gust of wind around them. "But I've got her back."

"And I trust him." Becca squeezed Werner's hand. "I'll find you when this is done."

"You better." Werner wrapped an arm around Glenn's back, taking some of his weight, and they hurried down the stairs with the others.

She prayed they'd finally escape. It had been a nightmare, a real nightmare, for all of them for too long, and it needed to end. And to do that, she needed to find Stanbury. She grabbed Nero's shoulder, and all the other voices disappeared, as they had before in the coffee shop and back in his house. Something steadied within her, and a new hope blossomed. Maybe if there was just Nero's voice to ignore—

I'm trying something new.

Work fast.

His muscles bunched underneath her hand, and the howl of a wind blast roared through the stairwell.

She closed her eyes, savoring the feel of just him, solid and sure within her, then imagined a wisp of smoke unfurling. Stanbury. The woman was cocky and demanding. She hadn't cared if she killed Becca. She had wanted to find the dugga at all costs.

The smoke shuddered. Becca tightened her grip on Nero's shoulder. He was still in pain, the searing agony from the spell and a growing ache from the part of his soul that had been damaged by the spell. His internal injuries from the bullet wound in his chest, that he'd taken from Becca, still had not completely healed, as well as more recent wounds from when Stanbury's men had captured him.

And none of that was important right now. He needed to protect his inamorata and his *puzur*.

And she needed to find Stanbury.

The wisp of smoke jerked taut and shot up the stairwell. A voice hissed something, angry about something— no, furious about Nero and Becca's escape. The voice— *she* had wanted to keep them, study them, find out how Becca could be connected to the dugga, and if Becca was now mentally connected to her, Stanbury, now that she was the dugga.

Yes. Stanbury.

The voice paused, listening, as if she thought she'd heard something but wasn't sure.

Becca held her breath.

Someone yelled and wind swept around her.

Running out of time, Nero growled.

She shoved him aside—feeling his flash of shock, which quickly turned to understanding at her dismissal—and she focused on Stanbury. She needed a location, a clue, anything to tell her where the woman was.

"Send more men to the stairwell," Stanbury said.

"Protocol also requires men to your position."

"Do you honestly think they're going to make it to my office? It's on the top floor."

Got her. Becca wrenched her focus from Stanbury and released Nero's shoulder. The voices roared around her with a force that made her knees buckle. She grabbed the railing and fought to turn the volume down.

"I know where she is," she said, realizing the moment she'd said it that Nero knew, too. A part of his consciousness had been with her, helping to keep her steady and control her magic.

"She'd have to be ten flights up, wouldn't she?" His wind wrapped around them and swept them up three sets of stairs before sputtering out and dropping them on the landing.

Nero's pain burned through her head, and his breath was ragged. Moving them like that required too much control. He could get them to the top, but he'd be spent before even confronting Stanbury, and if she was as powerful a sorcerer as he feared, he was going to need as much as he could hold back to defeat her.

The men he'd been keeping at bay in the doorway three flights down rushed into the stairwell and started firing. Nero shoved Becca against the wall, covering her with his body. She would have been pissed if she hadn't known he could heal from a gunshot wound in a matter of minutes. Even then, though, that would take more out of him, making it harder to fight.

"You've got to watch how much magic you're using. If Stanbury is powerful, I'm not sure how much help I'll be in a fight. It's going to be up to you to get your magic back."

"And if we don't get to her office soon, none of this will matter."

His thoughts turned to wrapping his wind around them and flying them up more landings.

"Don't," she said, aiming her stolen Glock at the stairs to cover their backs. "You'll tire yourself out. We're three flights ahead of them, and I can run seven flights."

Something banged above them, someone yelled, and heavy foot-falls pounded down the stairs toward them. So much for that.

"Fast and hard." She hadn't been in a situation like this before, she'd never been on a breach team, and all her combat experience had been outside in the desert or among buildings, but she'd still been trained for it. "Don't waste your strength on these guys. We can manage."

"Agreed." Even if she could tell he didn't like it.

Five men appeared at the top of the stairs. Nero whipped a lasso of wind at the closest guy and yanked him over the railing. The others jerked back and fired. Becca returned their fire but only managed to hit one in the shoulder.

The voices in her head yelled, the men in the stairwell yelled—and she couldn't tell if that was in her head as well or not. She strained to concentrate. Focus on the shot. Focus on the situation. Nothing else mattered.

Depending on how many men Stanbury has, it won't make a difference if I weaken my magic or not. We're going to be exhausted by the time we get to the top. Nero yanked another man over the railing.

Behind them, more footsteps pounded up the stairs.

38

W*e need a new plan,* Nero said in Becca's head as he shoved the security door open with a blast of wind and Becca scrambled through. "We're taking that other stairwell."

He followed her and slammed the door shut. A flicker of thought from Nero, hoping for something to bar the door, flashed through Becca, louder than everyone else, and she scanned the hall— no, they were in a partitioned office area. Nothing to block the door, but a maze of partitions and desks to hide among as they made their way to the stairwell on the other side of the building.

"This way." She bolted into the first narrow aisle between partitions, heading toward the stairs. "That stairwell will also be monitored."

Nero followed. "I know, but maybe everyone is on the other side of the building. Then at least we'll just be racing up seven flights, instead of fighting as well."

The security door behind them banged open and someone growled a command. The new hires were useless. They didn't have enough men. And both stairwells should be covered.

There isn't anyone at the other stairwell.

Well, that's good, Nero said. *Now to get there.*

They rushed down another aisle and were about to turn a corner when questioning surprise from Nero flashed through Becca, and he grabbed her wrist.

Do you see any security cameras? he asked.

She glanced at the ceiling and along its edges and corners. *No.*

I have another plan.

Does that make this plan C or plan D? Not that it mattered. The situation was fluid, and she was willing to change tactics in a split second.

Plan 'hopefully it will help us sneak around instead of exhausting us.'

Well, I hope it's fast.

Nero grimaced, and pain shuddered in his chest and into her. Yeah, she didn't need to remind him that they were running out of time, but couldn't help herself. Everything counted on them getting to Stanbury before the dugga's magic became permanently hers.

He straightened and glanced over the partition, back the way they'd come. *They've split up.*

That's how I'd have searched this floor.

Me, too. He jerked his chin to the passage beside her. *There's a door against that wall and two men heading in that general direction.*

And in a flash, she knew what Nero was planning, as if she'd thought of the idea herself. Check the door, see if it was unlocked— or make it unlocked with a little wind to push open the pins in the lock—then drag the two unsuspecting men inside and take their equipment. Dressed in their gear, they might be able to slip up the other hallway without drawing notice, or in the very least delaying that notice until they were closer to Stanbury's office.

Becca scurried down the aisle with Nero close behind and took up position beside the door, the Glock raised as she scanned the adjoining aisles.

Nero checked the door. Unlocked. *Finally, something is going our way.*

And the door even opens in the direction the men are coming, so we can hide inside and watch through a crack. The voices in her head swelled, those she'd dismissed as too far away breaking through her control and adding to the noise.

Just turn it down. You can do it, Nero said as he slipped into the room.

Sure, just turn it down. No problem. She followed him inside. The space, a janitor's closet, was narrow and dark. With the door cracked open, Becca could make out wide metal racks on either side, packed with cleaning and office supplies, but couldn't determine other details.

Nero eased inside as well, held the door open a crack, and waited for the men to come their way. *We'll need to make this fast. Chances are we won't be able to subdue them without one of them making a noise.*

Which means we'll need to get into their gear and sound convincing when someone comes our way wondering what happened. If Werner had thought their previous plan was bad, he'd think this was terrible.

So please, turn your volume down. It's so loud it makes my head hurt.

I'm trying.

I know you are. Take a breath.

She drew in a breath, but the voices didn't quiet. They didn't even dim a little. She took another. If they were going to get through this, she had to hold it together. They didn't have much time left. Surely she could keep the noise down for a little while longer.

She imagined a volume knob, concentrated on it, then turned it all the way to minimum.

The voices dimmed a bit, but it was enough. The pressure in her head eased and Nero's pain lessened.

Thank you, he said, but the muscles in his back and shoulders tensed and a hint of wind billowed around his hand. *And right in time. Just a few more steps.*

Becca's heart pounded. Once... twice—

Nero shoved open the door and stepped into the aisle. A lasso of wind seized the front guy and jerked him into the closet, while Nero wrapped the other guy in a head lock, his hand over the guy's mouth, and yanked him inside as well.

With a flick of wind, Nero closed the door and turned on the light. Becca grabbed the first man, twisted his arm back into a shoulder lock, and rammed his head against the cinderblock back wall. The man gasped and staggered, stunned.

She punched him in the face and knocked him out. He crumpled to the floor, bumping two bottles of bleach from the rack beside him. She scrambled to catch them but wasn't fast enough, and they hit the floor with a thump.

Leave them. Nero released the headlock from around his guy's neck and eased the unconscious man to the floor. *We need to get changed. Fast.*

Right. They stripped the guys of their clothes, Nero even taking his guy's boots for Becca, since hers were still somewhere in Nero's house and no footwear would give her away faster than ill-fitting footwear. Her guy was the bigger of the two, so she swapped with Nero, taking his guy's slightly smaller pants, shirt, and tactical vest. It wasn't a perfect fit, and she was grateful her guy had a second belt for his pants and not just his duty belt for his holster and equipment pouches. These guys were each armed with a Glock and had extra magazines of ammo.

Somehow their luck held and both of the men had helmets. She secured the strap under her chin then checked her duty belt. She didn't think she'd stripped someone and thrown on their clothes— including elbow and kneepads—so fast in her life.

Ready? Nero asked.

As ready as I'll ever be.

He cracked open the door and glanced out. *All clear.* He eased into the aisle and checked both ways as Becca stepped up behind him and shut the door. If their luck held, the men wouldn't wake up—and no one would find them—until everything was said and done.

Nero paused at an intersection, looking every bit a soldier in their stolen gear, until a shudder rushed over him and the ache in his chest made both him and Becca gasp together.

That's the loss of your magic, isn't it?

And that ache is coming more frequently.

They didn't have much time left. He jerked his chin, and they hurried across the intersection to the next one, with Becca covering their rear. The action was second nature. Even after everything that had happened and after all the years that had passed—even though she hadn't been aware of most of it passing—all of her training returned in a flash. This was who she was. A soldier who helped those who couldn't help themselves.

Almost there.

Movement in the aisle behind them caught her eye. She tapped Nero's arm, the action instinctual when she could have just as easily communicated mentally with him.

They started to duck into a cubby with a desk and filing cabinet but weren't fast enough. Two guys in tactical gear rounded the corner, and their surprise flashed through Becca. They'd been seen.

The guy on the left, a short, stocky man with dark eyes, raised his hand in hello. "Hey—"

His thoughts stuttered. He'd thought he knew who they were, but didn't recognize them. They had to be part of the new guys brought in last minute after the first escape attempt earlier that evening.

His partner frowned, his thoughts startled at the other guy's sudden stop in speech.

"Finished checking the northwest quadrant," Nero said, his voice soft and indistinct.

"Dalton said to wrap around and meet at the elevators," the first guy said.

"I doubt they're stupid enough to get in one of those," the other guy said, his thoughts clear that he disagreed with their squad leader's assessment. "They went right for the stairs the moment they escaped their cells."

"But what Dalton says goes," Becca said, pitching her voice as low and gruff as she could make it.

The first guy frowned again. She hadn't sounded right. Shit. Being disguised wasn't going to work. She was a soldier, not an actor. Her pulse sped up. She'd be much happier in a gunfight than trying to trick someone.

"So let's prove him wrong," Nero said. *Just keep scowling.* "You check those aisles, we'll go that way—" He jerked his chin at the aisle in the opposite direction, the one they needed to take to get to the other stairwell. "They have to be here somewhere."

"God damned freaks," the second guy said as they hustled down the aisle Nero had suggested.

Let's go. Fear flashed through their mental connection. That had been closer than he'd liked, and she couldn't have agreed more. Yes, they could have fought their way off the floor, but that would have lost them any advantage they'd gained by stealing the clothes and gear.

Keeping low, beneath the top of the partitions, they hurried to the door with an EXIT sign above it. Becca strained to listen to the thoughts of those in the area while trying not to let anyone get loud, but could only make out a few clear thoughts among the whispers of everyone else and didn't want to try harder for fear she wouldn't be able to get them quiet again.

Nero reached the end of their aisle. Ahead stood the door to the stairwell and on either side stretched a wider aisle. He glanced in both directions then rose and scanned the area behind them.

Clear. You get the door. I'll enter first. First through was dangerous. If they were stepping into an ambush, Nero could be attacked before he could fully realize he was in trouble. But he could also heal from that injury and she couldn't.

Deal. She hurried to the door, laid one hand on the crash bar, and waited for Nero to get into position beside it.

A nod from Nero and she pushed it open.

He rushed inside, his stolen Glock held ready, and a hint of wind fluttered around him. *Clear.*

She entered as well, eased the door shut behind her, and without waiting for his thoughts on the matter, started up the stairs. She kept it quick, but not too fast. If someone was watching the security feed, they needed to look like they were doing what they were supposed to be doing. Which, because she hadn't gotten the sense that an emergency had been sounded, meant they couldn't look like they were racing to the top.

Somehow the stairwell remained quiet, and she could only hope that didn't mean Stanbury's security team were busy with Werner and the others.

At the top landing, Nero drew up to the side of the doorway to enter first again, and Becca squeezed the door handle.

She had no idea what was on the other side of the door, and there wasn't time to think about it. The longer they stood in position, looking like they were going to breach a doorway that Stanbury's security team wouldn't be breaching, the sooner someone would notice they weren't security. Not to mention time was running out for Nero.

Now or never.

She yanked the door open. Nero hurried inside. Becca followed. They were at the end of a dimly lit hall with three closed doors, but light bled from under the door to the left.

"What do you mean, you've lost them?" a woman yelled on the other side of the door with the illumination. It sounded like Stanbury and she sounded pissed.

Okay, shoot to disable, not kill, Nero said as he grabbed the door handle. *If you kill her, it's over.* A hint of wind whispered around his hand, and Becca knew he'd unlocked the door. They switched position so he could enter first. *But still, shoot and shoot fast. Everything gets harder if she has a chance to cast something.*

Is that everything? She'd been a pretty good shot, but shooting to disable was a lot harder in a combat situation than just shooting for center of mass.

Don't die.

Right back at you. She opened the door. Nero went through and she followed.

Stanbury stood behind a large desk, a floor-to-ceiling bank of windows behind her giving a spectacular view of the city below. Her eyes flashed wide.

Becca fired. So did Nero.

Stanbury slapped one hand to her chest and yelled, and the bullets slammed into an invisible barrier surrounding Stanbury. *Holy shit. The woman is bulletproof.*

Nero fired again. Mother, how had that woman cast something so fast? His only hope was that the spell, being cast so fast, wouldn't last long. But his second shot slammed into the magic protecting her and the bullet clattered to the floor.

Shit.

He had no idea if that was his thought or Becca's.

The barrier was strong enough to buy Stanbury time to cast something else more dangerous.

He had to do something.

Now.

He hissed his power word and summoned his wind, but the woman slapped her hand to her hip pocket, yelled again, and the weight of a null magic spell swept around him. It snuffed out his wind and made Becca's essence in his head vanish. A chill shuddered through him at the sudden loss of her presence, and the ache of his missing dugga's magic swelled.

Son of a— In only a few seconds, Stanbury had eliminated their sidearms and his wind as if she had experience battling dragons... or in the very least, other magic.

"God damn it." Becca holstered her Glock, drew the tactical knife from her hip sheath, and lunged at Stanbury.

With a growl, Nero did the same. Stanbury might have magic, but it was still two against one. Surely between them, they could grab her long enough for Nero to take the dugga's magic back. Here was hoping the barrier spell was limited to projectiles and not everything else. He couldn't imagine casting it so quickly if it was for everything.

Stanbury bolted to the other side of her desk, pulled two cards from her pocket, held up one, and yelled another power word. A bolt of lightning shot from the card and raced toward Becca.

Nero seized the back of Becca's tactical vest and yanked her to the floor. The lightning exploded into the wall behind them, tearing through the dry wall and sending sparks flying when it hit the metal wall frame.

Another bolt streaked their way. Becca rolled to the side and wrenched Nero on top of her as the lightning exploded into the floor where he'd been.

Stanbury's card blackened and crumbled, but she held up the other card. Nero scrambled off Becca as Stanbury drew breath to yell again. He rammed his shoulder into the desk and shoved it into Stanbury. With a gasp that didn't activate the card, the woman staggered back.

Becca leapt onto the desk and dove for her, making Stanbury jerk back another step. Becca swiped at the hand holding the card with her knife. The tip caught the back of Stanbury's hand—thank the Mother the blade got through the barrier spell—making her scream, and the card fluttered to the floor.

Stanbury's gaze jumped to it, and for a split second, Nero prayed the woman would try and grab it. With it so close to Becca, that would give her the opportunity to grab her. But Stanbury jumped back instead and reached into her pocket again.

Nero bolted toward her as Becca dove at her from atop the desk. Stanbury screamed and pulled out another card. A gust of wind hit Becca, tossing her across the room and into the wall. She hit with a bone-breaking crunch and fell to the floor.

Pain sliced through Nero's head, strong enough to cut through Stanbury's null magic spell.

"Becca." He jerked toward her. He couldn't help himself, even if all his centuries of combat experience told him to stay focused on the enemy. Instinct overrode everything, and his inamorata was hurt.

"Eyes on the target," Becca gasped, rising to her hands and knees. "I'm all right."

He couldn't believe that. His chest was on fire and it had to be her agony. But she was right. Stanbury was the danger, and he wrenched his attention back to her as another blast of wind shot from the card. Nero dove to the side. The wind slammed into the desk and tossed it toward Becca, who scrambled out of the way.

More pain burned into Nero, stealing his breath and dragging his attention back to Becca. She'd probably broken her ribs. Maybe punctured a lung.

But he knew this hadn't been the first time, and from her memory of the attack in Afghanistan, she'd been through worse. Not to mention they were running out of time.

Becca staggered to her feet.

Stanbury shot a third blast of wind at Nero. He leapt to the side, but it caught his shoulder and jerked him around, back, and down to his hands and knees.

The card crumbled, the pieces fluttering to the floor, and Stanbury pulled another card from her pocket.

"Jeez. How many cards do you have?" Becca asked, her voice tight with pain.

"More than enough to deal with you and that monster."

Which meant he had to get up and move. Now. Before Stanbury could cast anything else.

With a roar, he lunged at Stanbury. She jerked back, but he caught her wrist and yanked her hand from her pocket. She held four cards, and he twisted her wrist, forcing her to drop them instead of trying to stab her.

The cards tumbled to the floor and Nero plunged his knife toward her gut. She twisted, blocked his strike with the wrist of her free arm, and rammed her heel into the inside of his knee. The joint crunched and his leg buckled. He seized her free wrist and tightened his grip on the other one as he fought to regain his balance.

A wicked grin curled Stanbury's lips. "I don't need to hold one of my cards to activate it." She pressed her elbow against her side and yelled another power word. "Now drop."

A weight swept over Nero, everything went numb, and he collapsed. He fought to stand, to move, to do anything, but he could barely feel his body and couldn't get even the smallest muscle to move.

"You honestly think you could win a fight against me?" Stanbury pressed her heel against his chest and leaned in. He fought to breathe. "You dragons think you're so superior, that your very nature makes you special, but you're not. You're just beasts disguised as people."

The weight on his chest increased, building with the aching loss of his dugga's magic. Black specks danced across his vision and searing pain lanced through his head.

From above and behind him, Becca yelled.

Stanbury yanked a card from her pocket, barked her power word, and a gust of wind shot from the card. "I'm not ready for you."

Nero strained to turn his head to see, but still couldn't. There was only the weight and Becca's pain, blazing through him. He didn't even know if she was conscious.

I'm all right, she said, her mental voice pained and sounding far off, but still there along with a hint of her presence in his head.

A flash of relief flooded him. Thank the Mother, it looked like the null magic spell was starting to fade. That had to be the catch with the paper. The spell was fast to cast but didn't last.

Except that didn't help anything. Becca was still in danger, and Stanbury still had who-knew-how-many spell cards left.

You have to get out of here, he thought with as much force as he could, in hope of getting through the null magic. *I'll distract her, or something, but you have to run.*

For the love of— Becca growled, and Stanbury's gaze leapt from

Nero back across the room again. *We're getting your magic back and protecting your kids. Now get off your ass and fight.*

Except he couldn't move and could barely breathe. All he could feel was Becca's burning agony and little sharp bites in his arms and legs.

"You should stay down," Stanbury said, crouching beside him. Another gust of wind exploded from the card.

Something crunched, Becca screamed, and more of her pain swept through him, their connection growing stronger. Mother, Stanbury was going to kill Becca, and there was nothing he could do about it.

He mentally wrenched against the paralysis spell. He had to get up. Help Becca. More agonizing bites sliced into him, as if his muscles were being stabbed with a thin blade.

Stanbury shot another blast of wind, and Nero jerked his head to follow it.

Becca scrambled from beside the desk, over a chair, and dove out of the way.

Stanbury swore. Nero heaved his attention back to her as the card crumbled. If she was going to cast again, she needed to activate another card. This was his chance to strike. He'd moved his head. He could move other muscles.

He heaved at his arm, willing himself to grab her wrist and stop her from drawing a card long enough for Becca to attack.

Stanbury sneered. "Please. Keep trying. I have more than enough time to kill Rebecca before my spell on you wears off."

His hand twitched.

Stanbury's eyes flashed wide as he forced his hand to her wrist and seized it. With a yelp, she fell back onto her butt.

About time, Becca said. She lunged at Stanbury, but the other woman wrenched free of Nero's grasp and got out of the way. She scrambled to her feet, bolted to the back wall, and pressed a button. Half hidden by a tall leafy plant, a pair of elevator doors slid open, revealing a waiting car, and she rushed inside.

Becca raced after her and drew her Glock. Nero heaved to his hands and knees and drew his sidearm, as well. Stanbury yanked another card from her pocket, said the power word, and a wave of power slammed into them. Becca was thrown back, flying past Nero and tumbling across the floor into the broken desk. Nero managed to hug low to the floor and was shoved back, the force stealing his breath. His still partially paralyzed muscles trembled, and the force ripped the sidearm from his numb fingers, tossing the weapon into the broken furniture at the back of the room.

Pain radiated through him. He couldn't tell if it was Becca's agony or his, but it didn't matter. Everything coming from Becca screamed. Whatever her injuries, they didn't matter. He couldn't let Stanbury get away. Becca wouldn't be responsible for the deaths of any more children.

Nero glanced at her. She climbed to her feet, no longer holding her Glock—it must have been ripped from her hand like his—and ran toward him. But Stanbury sneered, and the elevator doors slid shut.

Nero groaned and the ache in his chest shuddered, swept along his limbs, and made his muscles seize.

"Get up." Becca offered him her hand, even though she didn't look as if she'd be able to stay standing if she helped him up. Her essence flooded him, and he mentally clung to it to give him strength. Either Stanbury was too far away now, or her null magic spell had finally run its course. "We need to figure out where that elevator is going."

There wasn't enough time for that. He ignored her hand, stood—his muscles shaking even more with the effort—staggered to the elevator doors, and forced them open. His adrenaline burned through the rest of the paralysis spell and his determination—along with Becca's—gave him extra strength.

Below them, the elevator car rushed away, more than four floors between them already.

"Climbing after her will be slower than taking the stairs."

"We're taking the fast route." He summoned his wind, wrapped it around them, and half-dropped, half-lowered them to the elevator's roof.

They landed with a thunk, harder than he would have liked, but not because of the null magic—that felt as if it were completely gone

—but because of the ache in his chest and Becca's overwhelming pain.

Lightning exploded through the top of the elevator. Nero shoved Becca back and the electricity sliced through his leg and side. Agony screamed over him, his blood splattered to the elevator's steel top, but his soul magic sealed the wound shut before he could bleed out.

Stanbury glared at him through the hole. She raised her card and sent another blast of lightning toward him. He leapt out of the way this time and the bolt shot past him, sputtering out before hitting the top of the shaft and raining down stinging sparks.

The ache of his missing dugga's magic billowed again, stealing his breath for a second, and Becca gasped. The pain was so strong, it was now only a matter of minutes before Stanbury permanently took his magic.

Stanbury reached into her pocket to get another card even as the lightning card was still crumbling away, but Becca dropped to her knees and heaved open the hatch. Nero jumped inside the car, but it stopped and the doors swept open. Stanbury scrambled out of his reach into a cold, dark loading dock, and yanked out another card.

Son of a— Nero snapped a whip of wind at it, slicing it in half. If her magic was like other glyph-based magics, when the symbols were damaged, the spell wouldn't work. He didn't wait to see if it worked and bolted toward her, focusing his wind into a lasso to bind her.

His wind lashed around her, caught her hand and jerked it up, but she slapped her other hand to her hip pocket, barked a power word, and vanished with the whoosh of a rapid free gate portal.

Becca yelled, her surprise snapping through him, and he wrenched around.

Stanbury held a knife against Becca's neck. Becca had both hands around Stanbury's wrist, but she didn't shove the blade away, and the weight of a paralysis spell flooded from her into him— no, not a paralysis spell. That wasn't what Stanbury had cast on him before. It was more like a muscle control spell, forcing the spell caster's will on the body of the unsuspecting victim.

The cards also don't let her gate far away, Becca said, *or she would have fled.*

"Back up, dragon, or I'll kill the human." Stanbury shoved Becca out of the elevator.

"What makes you think I care?"

"Really?" Stanbury snorted and pushed Becca forward another step, the knife still tight against her throat. "You're the dugga. You're supposed to have killed her, and yet you haven't. You obviously have a use for her."

"And you're betting that use outweighs stopping you?"

"You've protected her from my lightning twice in this fight." Stanbury's gaze raked over his charred and bloody clothes. "At your physical expense. Now back up."

Don't you dare. Becca glared at him.

He inched back a step and subvocalized his power word, drawing the magic to summon his wind to just under his skin, ready to burst forth.

Stanbury rolled her eyes, drew a card from her pocket, and the weight of another null magic spell swept around him. His wind vanished, but Becca's essence didn't, not completely this time. "How dumb do you think I am?"

Becca's eyes narrowed, her expression tight and her will—a sensation that felt as if she was far away—straining to make her body move against Stanbury's magic. Bites of pain nipped through Nero's legs— no, not his legs. Becca's. Surely that meant this null magic spell wasn't as strong as the others, which meant it wouldn't last as long.

That's it. Keep straining. We just need to buy time until the spell ends.

And by that time your dugga's magic will be hers, she said, her mental voice barely discernible. *There isn't enough time.*

It's okay. It would be all right. He didn't know how, but he and Becca and the *puzur* would survive. He just needed Becca safe. That was all that mattered.

It's not all that matters. When the heat of whatever this is between us dies down, you'll want your family.

What I feel will never die down. That's what it meant to be inamorated.

It doesn't have to just be us. It can be us and them.

It will be. Mother, he wanted that, wanted Becca as part of his *puzur*. But if he had to pick, he'd pick her.

And I won't let you make that choice. Fear bled from Becca into Nero, small and weak through the null magic spell, but clearly fear. *If you sacrifice your dugga's magic, Stanbury will know about the* puzur. *She could kidnap your kids and torture them like she did me and the other mages she kidnapped.*

Nero's heart stuttered. He couldn't let her do that to his children, to anyone's children. It was the reason he'd taken the dugga's magic from his predecessor and secretly changed the Asar Nergal's only directive. Stanbury's torture would be worse than the quick death they'd get at the hands of Regis. Except Regis was soul sick. He might not just kill his kids, either. He might torture them, as well.

He couldn't pick between Becca and the *puzur*, no matter what his soul bond was screaming. *Mother, please, don't make me pick.*

A hint of wind whispered around Nero's hands.

It's not a choice. You can't let Stanbury torture your kids. Summon your wind and end this bitch.

But I can't endanger you. More wind whispered up his arms. He couldn't lose another inamorata.

You can't lose your kids, either. I won't see your family hurt because of me. I won't have more children die.

"Back up," Stanbury growled.

Nero backed up another step. He couldn't do anything else. The soul bond was too strong. *That bombing wasn't your fault.* His throat tightened. Her pain over all those deaths was still so raw, cutting even through the null magic spell.

I know. Her expression grew sad. *But if your kids die now, it will be my fault.*

No. I wasn't strong enough. I—

You are strong. Stronger than this null magic. Our connection is proof of that. She felt so far away, a ghost of what she should have been, but a determination was building within her. If Stanbury didn't have a hostage, Nero could attack.

"I said back up," Stanbury yelled.

Mother, no.

The ache of his lost dugga's magic surged and he bit back a gasp. Time was almost up.

I won't be able to control the blade. I won't be able to fight her. Becca's determination turned fierce.

But I won't be able to save you. My soul magic hasn't recovered.

I know. She screamed, the yell helping her fight past the control spell on her body.

Her grip on the knife tightened. Stanbury tensed. Becca wrenched to the side and the blade sliced across her neck.

Agony screamed through Nero across his throat, through his chest, and from his soul. Becca gasped, blood rushing over her shoulder and chest, and went limp. Stanbury barked a harsh laugh and sneered, and with a howl, Nero's wind exploded from his hands. He shot it at Stanbury, slamming her into the cinderblock wall beside the elevator doors.

Stanbury slapped a hand to her hip pocket, but Nero, roaring, his soul wailing, shot another blast at her. Bones crunched. Stanbury shrieked.

He shot another blast. This one tightened, with all his will and soul-rending agony, into a deadly wind blade. It speared into her chest with a force he'd never been able to summon before and exposed her heart. She shrieked again, her eyes wide, blood gushing from the wound.

The ache of his dugga's magic flared, but it was nothing to the agony of Becca's essence draining away from him. He had to save her, somehow—

Get your God damned magic back, she gasped.

He shoved his hand into Stanbury's chest, ripped out her beating heart and took a bite.

She howled, her hands ineffectually pressing against the gaping wound in her body and crumpled to the floor, blood rushing around her.

He took another bite of her heart. The ache of the dugga's magic flared again, making his pulse roar with it. He was too late. He hadn't been able to get the magic back, and he was going to lose his inamorata as well.

Then lightning shot through him, a burning white agony, scorching every cell in his body. Thoughts and essences flashed through him. Every member of the Asar Nergal, all the members of the *puzur*, and half a dozen human mages twenty blocks away. There were more human mages, a few in the city he hadn't found yet, a few more in the country, and a few more of each, not yet fully into their power, on the other continents.

He fought to control the power and tear his focus away from the mages. He needed to save Becca. If his soul magic wouldn't let him take on her injuries again, he needed to get her past the gatelock and get her to help.

She gasped, her hands on her throat as if that could somehow save her, and he dropped to his knees beside her.

"Hold on. I'm getting you out of here." He pulled her into his arms and cradled her against his chest.

They're safe?

He stood, staggering at the burn of her agony, but kept his balance. "Yes, they're safe." *Everyone is but you.*

It's okay. Just hold me. I know this wound. I'm not going to make it past the gatelock, let alone out the door.

"It's not okay." Mother, it was never going to be okay. His soul was already shattering. He wasn't going to survive the death of another inamorata. She had to make it past the lock.

You know I won't, and you will survive this. For your kids. A ghost of a smile pulled at her lips. *That's the deal.*

"I didn't agree to that."

And I didn't agree to you giving up everything because of me.

"How many times do I have to tell you before you'll believe it? That's how being inamorated works." He would sacrifice anything for her. His soul had picked. He'd never thought he'd have the solid strength of a soul bond again, and he couldn't lose it. He could barely stand to see her in pain, to feel her pain—

Her thoughts stuttered at that. *Except I'm not in pain. Not anymore.* Her gaze captured his, her eyes wide. *I should be dead. I should—*

Sudden hope flooded him. "You were hit with the surge's magic." *Oh, Mother, please.* "Ease your hand away."

But I—

"If the surge is powerful enough, your soul magic could still be heightened." It was too much to hope that the effects were permanent. It might have been hours, but the surge's aura had been blindingly bright.

She peeled her fingers back. Blood didn't gush over her neck, and the wound had sealed up into an angry red slash across her throat.

"Oh, Mother." *Thank you. Thank you.* His kids were safe, and so was Becca.

He bent to kiss her, but she put a hand on his chest and held him back. Her gaze jumped to Stanbury's body and the growing pool of blood on the floor then back to him. "You just ate a woman's heart. That's disgusting."

"It was the only sure way to get my magic back." If the Handmaiden didn't bestow the job, a dragon with a strong enough soul and within the first hour of the magic being transferred to someone could still take it—and he'd taken it all those years ago to protect those innocent kids the Asar Nergal's directive said he needed to murder. "And it wasn't the *whole* heart. Just a few bites."

"Still disgusting."

"We are predators."

"Yeah, and I'm not kissing you until you've polished off a bottle of mouthwash." Except she was surprised at how much she'd just accepted it.

The thought sent mixed emotions churning him. Her acceptance had to be in part because of the influence of the dragon souls who'd invaded her when she'd been Zenobia's prisoner. A part of her was forever changed. She'd never be the same.

And I'm okay with that. "I'm still not kissing you until you've thoroughly cleaned your mouth."

"Jeez, can't you be happy with not being dead?"

"I'm raising my expectations. Alive, sane, and with a boyfriend who doesn't have bloody-heart breath."

"Boyfriend, hunh?" He liked the sound of that. It meant she was thinking of staying.

"You're going to have to work hard to convince me," she said, but he could hear the flirtation in her voice and felt her yearning to have a family again. *We never did make it into your whirlpool tub.*

"That's our first stop."

"After mouthwash."

He flashed his teeth at her in a dragon's sexual invitation, unable to help himself. "After mouthwash."

A black miasma pressed around Constantine, filled with agony and screaming voices. He was on fire and frozen at the same time. The Mother of All…? the Handmaiden…? He didn't know who had said this wasn't his punishment, but it had to be. He'd failed dragonkind… except he couldn't remember how. He'd been sick— yes, his soul hadn't been strong enough to survive changing between so many vessels, and pieces of himself had started to break away. He hadn't known what was real. Demons, human-monsters, with the power to wipe every last dragon from existence, had haunted him, asleep or awake. And then—

Then there'd been pain and—

The cold… no. Frozen ground digging into his side. A dragon had appeared, his aura writhing darkness, crackling with anger and fear and… the potential for all emotions, separately and together at the same time.

There'd been screaming.

But he didn't know if that had been the black drake, or him, or his soul.

Then, for a moment, there'd been nothing. A dark emptiness that had been soothing and terrifying. No light, no pain, and no Mother.

Except there hadn't been the Mother before. Not since the Great

Scourge. The spell had been cast, they'd fallen from the sky, and She had sacrificed everything to save what few of them She could. And even then it had just been their souls, the core of their essence, forever changed, trapped in fragile human vessels.

The emptiness didn't last, shocked out of existence with blazing agony and blinding light. It roared through Constantine, burning and slicing, filled with the screams of his soul for not being able to protect dragonkind. Who would have thought he'd need to protect them from himself?

Everyone did, his soul hissed. *Everyone knew, and they stopped you.*

And now this was his deserved punishment.

Except the Mother...? Handmaiden...? a part of his soul he still thought was good...? had said it wasn't. But that meant this suffering had no reason. It was just suffering, and he couldn't live with that. He didn't want to live at all. He didn't deserve life. He'd mistreated fellow drakes, imprisoned them, tortured them, all in an attempt to control their wild souls and keep them hidden from humanity. If the humans knew about dragons, they'd finish what they'd started. But he also saw drakes accepting life in the human realm, making human friends, taking human lovers, slowly letting the nature of their human vessels transform their souls and erase their feral dragon natures. All the humans needed to do was wait until the influence of their bodies transformed all dragon souls, and dragonkind would be gone.

Or if that wasn't enough, just wait for proper extinction. Without their original physical forms, dragons couldn't beget new dragons. Accidents always happened. Every decade a few souls were forever lost to the universal ether. Eventually dragons would just cease to exist and that which had terrified those humans all those centuries ago would be gone.

Someone screamed, a piercing howl in his head, and he heaved against the darkness.

The someone screamed again—

No, not a someone, the woman from before, who'd somehow

gotten into his head and knew he was a dragon. She was in trouble and pain and—

And he didn't want to know. He was probably responsible for that, as well, and he couldn't carry the burden. Mother, he wasn't strong enough. There wasn't any room left in his crumbling essence. The guilt was crushing him, and all he wanted was for the darkness to consume his soul and be done with it.

"You're almost through," a soft feminine voice said.

The Mother? Handmaiden?

It didn't sound like either. And it didn't sound like the woman who'd been in his head.

"It's almost over."

And then? Would he get what he deserved? Dragons were paying for his mistakes, and he deserved to suffer. They didn't.

The scream came again and agony sliced through him. She needed help. He had to do something. He couldn't explain it. It didn't matter that she wasn't a dragon, or that he didn't know her. This new agony and fear seared through his previous guilt and wrenched him from the darkness.

He jerked up— half up, unable to rise more than midway with his wrists bound to the sides of his bed. A dragon with a blazing black aura sitting in a lounge chair beside him jumped, her eyes wide with surprise.

"You're awake." The surprise in her dark eyes softened to kindness with a hint of worry. She dropped her book and pulled the chair closer to him. A hint of wind whispered around her and made the locks of hair that had fallen out of her ponytail flutter around her face.

The power of her aura suggested she was an ancient drake, but he didn't recognize her essence, and he'd known every remaining ancient dragon. He squinted without trying to look like he was squinting, except he couldn't see the minute differences in her aura he used to be able to see. Something was wrong with his aura sight, but he was soul sick and had only just managed to pull his consciousness from the darkness. Not being able to read slight differences in a dragon's aura didn't mean anything, and he didn't have time to figure it out. The woman in his head was in trouble.

"You're okay. You're safe," she said.

"I—" The woman's essence vanished. He strained to sense her, but she was gone. Yet another one he couldn't save. Perhaps this was the real torture, knowing he'd failed, knowing he needed to do better, and not being able to do anything. Losing the connection with her was probably for the best. She'd be safer without him. Everyone would be safer without him.

"Can I get you anything?" The woman unhooked the restraint around his wrist. Now he got the sense that she was young, but that would mean her aura wasn't indicating age but an enormous earth magic power, stronger than any he'd seen before save for the Hand-maiden—who was the exception to everything. "You were having seizures. We were afraid you'd hurt yourself."

"Or others," he said, his voice gruff, different from what he remembered.

The woman flashed a hint of teeth— no, that wasn't right. She smiled. A gentle, sad smile, more human than dragon, proving his fear that dragons were slowly becoming human. Except he didn't sense that from her. The smile felt more like she was fighting her dragon nature, softening her expression for him.

"But you didn't," she said. "Everyone is okay, and so are you."

Mother, he wanted to believe her, wanted to forget who he was and the things he'd done.

She leaned over him to unhook the restraint of the far side of the bed, and her body brushed over the blanket. The movement slid his clothes against his skin, suddenly too sensitive, making his pulse leap.

His breath hitched as she drew back, and he hugged his arms against his chest to resist reaching for her. It had been too long since anyone had been close. He'd had centuries of confinement in his chambers, his thoughts broken and whirling, no one daring to approach.

Because he deserved it.

He didn't deserve her kindness now.

Why couldn't he just forget?

"I'm Raven." She picked up a glass of water from the bedside table. "Can you sit up? Do you know your name?"

He frowned. That seemed a weird question. "Would I not know my name?" Except she didn't recognize him. Maybe this was his chance. He could become someone different. Start over. Atone for his mistakes.

"You've been through a trauma. Your memory might be a little shaky."

But his memory hadn't been clearer. Not for centuries. He knew and felt every mistake he'd made, and his soul ached with all the things he'd done for fear dragonkind would be destroyed.

"What's the last thing you remember?"

"I was—" Screaming? Shattering? Crushed by darkness? There'd been a voice, the Mother of All who wasn't the Mother but the Handmaiden... or was that the woman who had thought he was a human but discovered he was really a dragon? Why would she have thought he was human?

Because you are now. The Mother's voice swept through him. They'd had this conversation before, when the darkness had first devoured him.

But I'm a dragon. I'm king. His pulse leapt again, this time in fear. *They need me. They don't understand how dangerous humans are.* No. That wasn't right. Everyone he was responsible for had gotten hurt. Because of him.

They do understand and they don't. The miasma shuddered within him, threatening to consume him. *Nothing of the king, the elder of the last two gold dragons, remains.*

What does that mean? Could he really start over? Could he become an insignificant nothing, with only the responsibility to do and be better?

The darkness flooded his vision. He gasped, fighting to keep Raven in sight and hear the Mother's answer, but all he could hear was the roar of his pulse.

What does that mean?

Thu-thump. Thu-thump.

Answer me. Please. His pulse raced faster, the beats pounding through him, rattling into his essence. *What does that mean?* "What does that mean?"

A hand settled on his, lightning snapped across his skin, and Raven jumped back into focus.

She clenched her jaw, her body tight, and more wind rushed through the room. "Stay with me."

The lightning, a crackling gold energy, danced over his skin and up her arm.

"Just stay with me this time," she said again, her expression tightening even more with pain.

He jerked his hand away, taking the lightning with him, and her body sagged with relief for just a second in an unguarded moment. She'd felt the pain, too, and it had come from him—it always came from him—but somehow she'd kept the darkness from consuming him again.

"I know this is confusing, but I also know you're aware that you're different." She held out the glass of water, a hint of the pain still in her eyes confirming she wasn't an ancient dragon and not even close to an elder drake. "You might not know how or understand why, but you feel it deep within you that you are."

He sat up and took the offered glass.

And yet, there was also a maturity to her, an understanding of loss and responsibility that he usually saw in drakes who remembered the Scourge.

"I'm here to help you understand what happened and what your magic is."

I'm getting a second chance, a chance to just be me, not King Constantine. He wasn't even sure he knew who that was. He couldn't even pronounce the name he'd had before he'd killed the Zhongguo empress and joined all the dragon clans.

"Let's start with hopefully something simple. Your name?"

Except it wasn't simple. He was Constantine... had been Constantine. Who was he now? Who did he want to be?

You're still Constantine. You'll always be Constantine.

But what if he didn't want to be *him* anymore?

You think you can run from who you are? You were hiding from yourself as king. The king is dead. You're Constantine again. You can't run from that.

He was damned well going to try. And that started with a new name. John, or Henry, or Sam?

"I'm S—" The name stuck in his throat. Maybe he was Charles... Chuck?... Cole?... Coleridge? "I'm Co—"

"It's okay if you don't know. It might take some time for things to come back to you." Except her hint of a frown indicated she was worried about him not knowing his name.

And Mother of All, he just had to pick a name. Coleridge. Perfectly good name. Say it fast, and it'll come out. "I'm Con—"

Wait. What? That wasn't what he meant to say, and he could feel the press of the miasma billowing and tugging within him.

"Con?"

Shit. "Yeah. Con." Nothing more. Nothing again.

"Pleased to meet you." Raven gave him her human smile again with a little more teeth.

He flashed his teeth back, realized what he was doing, and pressed his lips closed. If what the memory of the Handmaiden—or whoever it was in his head—was right, Raven thought he was a human—

His stomach bottomed out as horrified realization flashed through him. This black drake thought he was a human with magic, and she was trying to help him. Now he knew how to save dragonkind. Find out why this dragon was helping human mages and bring the wrath of the Asar Nergal down on her and her mages.

Except—

The miasma billowed again.

She thought he was human. The only one who knew he was a dragon was that woman, that human woman, and he'd said he wasn't one anymore... and she hadn't been afraid of him. Not like any of the other humans he'd encountered.

His heart skipped a beat. She was in trouble and pain, and there was nothing he could do to help her—

Which didn't make sense, either. He was supposed to be terrified of her, and a part of him was. She was a human with earth magic. It had only taken a handful of them to rip dragons from their physical forms and sentence them to eternity in a parasitic spirit state. That was the root of the law banning body hopping into human vessels with a human soul. It was the birth of the Asar Nergal with its only directive to kill all human mages.

The gold lightning snapped across his skin and fear tightened in his gut. His own dragons were sworn to kill him. They were sworn to kill this drake, with her human smile and kind eyes, who was defying royal decree. The Asar Nergal would come after her. They wouldn't ask questions, that wasn't their job, and they'd kill her.

Tobias shifted on the bench at the mouth of the royal archives. He'd thought about leaving many times—and not just the archives, but his position at Court and dragon society altogether. A small part of him hoped it would be easier if he just left, but the rest of him knew—having intimate knowledge of what happened to drakes who abandoned their coterie, especially the Royal coterie—that his tough problems would just change to other tough problems. A drake didn't just leave his coterie without the protection of another doyen. And a drake of Tobias's position didn't leave. Period.

The only drake who'd managed to escape was Hunter, and Regis was still demanding his head. Tobias was certain that was what Regis had pulled Nero aside to talk about after the Counseling Coteries meeting.

It had been eighteen days since Hunter and his sorcerer inamorata had left Court and Nero had yet to report anything about their location. Of course, given how magically powerful that woman had been, it wouldn't surprise Tobias if Nero knew where they were and was trying to figure out the best way to deal with her and Hunter without losing any members of the Asar Nergal.

"Or maybe he's decided Hunter and his inamorata aren't a threat,"

Ophelia said, easing from the shadows just like she'd done earlier that day... or late last night? He'd lost track of how long he'd been sitting there.

"He's the dugga." Tobias bit back a growl. Ophelia wasn't the source of his frustration and didn't deserve his short temper. "His job is to eliminate all human sorcerers."

"Technically, if Grey's thoughts are correct, the wording is 'all human sorcerer *threats*'." She leaned against the wall and raised a dark sculpted eyebrow. "If that human sorcerer is inamorated back to Hunter, then she's only a threat to those who would hurt Hunter."

"I'm not sure Regis would agree with an argument of semantics." Tobias rubbed his temples. He'd been sitting there for hours, his mind whirling from one problem to the next, determined to have solved at least one issue before returning to his office.

He didn't want to organize a retrieval squad, but he had to. Which meant he needed to pick the squad leader carefully. He wanted to replace Regis on the throne with someone sane, but the divide between coteries as well as Traditionalists and non-Traditionalist made finding a candidate impossible. And Mother of All! Where the hell was the Handmaiden? She could solve all of this by proclaiming someone king, and most of the factions would bow to her revered status and accept her choice.

"Regis doesn't agree with much of anything anymore, even when it's in his best interest," she said. "Don't tell me you've been sitting here all this time trying to figure things out. People are going to start wondering where you are."

"Let them wonder." Getting through the situation with as few casualties as possible was more important than the day-to-day functions of the Dragon Court.

"Not sure that's the attitude you want. Regis sees betrayal at every turn. If you don't stick to your routine, he'll suspect you of something."

"Even if I stay on routine, he'll suspect me. I need answers and now." He ran his hands through his hair, not caring that the habit had returned. "There just isn't a good replacement. Hunter won't raise a banner and even if he did, the Traditionalists will fight him. Nero, as a grandchild of the Zhongguo Empress, has a legitimate claim."

"But he's a Traditionalist, and anyone who supports Hunter will see Nero as another Regis." Ophelia pinched the bridge of her nose, a sign the voices in her head were getting hard to control. "Although if Nero isn't actively going after Hunter, he might not be as much of a Traditionalist as we think."

"Do you know for certain?"

"No. He doesn't spend a lot of time at Court, and I was chasing down thoughts of an attack from the Sect of the Divine Mother when Regis called the Counseling Coteries meeting, so I couldn't eavesdrop on anyone's thoughts."

"I wish you'd been there. I really want to know what the other doyens are thinking." Then at least he might have a clue if any of them would be better candidates for king. Although at a quick glance, none of them were great.

Pike, who had the largest coterie, was too young and could barely control his members. He wouldn't be able to control all of Court. Barna at least was an elder drake, but was heavily invested in the human realm and wouldn't gain the support of any of the Traditionalists. And while Lothair and Maize were also elder drakes and in control of their coteries, their coteries weren't as big, neither had a powerful earth magic, and they didn't have any claim to the throne, making it difficult for either one to legitimately take it.

The only other candidate could be Grey. He was an ancient drake, the Handmaiden's servant, and most considered him the second in command in her coterie of two. But as Hunter's friend, he'd run into the same problem as Hunter. Support from non-Traditionalists and rejection from Traditionalists.

"There's another ancient dragon you're not considering," Ophelia said with a pointed stare, clearly indicating he should consider himself in the running.

"Yeah, no." It was bad enough he was the chamberlain. He didn't want the throne.

"You know how to run Court. You have connections with every doyen, their Seconds, and their heads of security."

"Drakes see me as a servant to the Court. Nothing more."

"People respect you."

"Not enough. I'd need a powerful earth magic to maintain control, and I have nothing. I can't even make a gate to leave." One of his other worries, because if he wanted to get the hell out of Court, he'd have to go to a gatekeeper, and then Regis would know he'd left.

Ophelia eased away from the wall. "You're going to have to come up with someone."

"Why do you think I've been sitting here?" If Regis remained in power, dragons would die. If Tobias backed the wrong drake, dragons would die. And if Tobias approached the wrong dragon, he'd be charged with treason, and he'd be tortured for who knew how long until the Handmaiden returned and rebirthed him, essentially killing him.

"How about picking a leader for the retrieval squad? You have a short list, even if you don't like any of them."

"I don't like the idea of a retrieval squad."

"Regis will expect one. And soon."

"You're telling me something I already know."

"I know." Ophelia sighed. "I just can't help myself. I don't like the position you're in."

"That makes two of us."

"You just think the word, and I'll gate you out of here."

"And then what will happen to all the dragons in the Royal Coterie you say I'm protecting?" he asked, throwing her words from earlier back at her.

"Then, Mother of All, make a choice for king and do something." She flashed her teeth at him, her expression all aggression. "Stop wallowing."

"Fine. Find out where Barna stands in this mess." The doyen of the Major Brown coterie wasn't ideal, but he was probably the best of all the bad choices. With Zenobia in prison, he could—most of the time—exert dominance over everyone on the council now, other than Nero, and he had the next largest coterie after the Major Green. There were more non-Traditionalists than Traditionalists—

"I wouldn't bet on that," Ophelia said. "Zenobia's coup with human mages has swung the pendulum for those drakes on the fence."

"Then also do a little eavesdropping on Nero. Find out if he really isn't going after Hunter and his sorcerer." Nero really was the best choice. He might be a Traditionalist, but he had royal heritage, he was an ancient dragon with a powerful earth magic—and, unlike Barna, had clear dominance over the other Counseling Coterie doyens. If he could somehow be convinced to form an alliance with Hunter, it would still alienate some of the Traditionalists, but with any luck not all of them.

"Especially if Hunter's inamorata can demonstrate she has dragon interests in mind," Ophelia said, finishing Tobias's thought, again. "The Handmaiden could be gone for a few hundred years. A sorcerer to help dragonkind during this transition, even if she is a human, would be a valuable asset to a new king."

"True, and I hate when you do that."

"You didn't say that out loud?" Ophelia asked, blinking her lashes in mock innocence.

"You know I didn't. Now go eavesdrop on Nero and find out how much of a staunch Traditionalist he really is." Mother, here was hoping he wasn't. An alliance with Hunter would be everything he needed—and Tobias wasn't going to think too hard about how difficult it would be to get Hunter and Nero to form an alliance. One step at a time.

"Nero and Barna are second on my list." Ophelia headed to the hall leading up to the main passages in Court. "The Sect of the Divine Mother is planning something, and soon. Whatever that is, it takes priority."

"Report as soon as you know something." If she thought it was more important than finding a replacement for Regis and stabilizing Court, it had to be serious.

"Deadly serious," she said as she left.

Ice churned in Tobias's gut. Too much was happening too fast and too many dragon souls were being lost. If the Handmaiden didn't come back soon, he feared there wouldn't be a Dragon Court left for her to return to.

D iablo reached the front of his apartment building and jogged past the door for the fifth time. Mother, the beast still raged within him, and thanks to the God damned surge, other peoples' emotions flooded him, as well. So much so, he thought he'd burst into flames or explode. With the luck he'd been having lately, it would probably be both.

Six fights in the illegal dragon fighting ring and still nothing had eased. He'd even held his beast back for as long as possible, letting his opponents beat the shit out of him, drawing blood and breaking bones, before his control shattered and the beast went berserk. After his last fight, where the fighter's manager had to hold his heart back in his chest to speed up his healing, Diablo left. That was one bridge burned. They were never going to let him fight there again. That dragon almost hadn't survived, and he'd left one hell of a mess to clean up.

He reached the alley between two apartment towers, three blocks from his, picked up his pace, and roared as he hit the shadows, desperate to release the pressure building within him. So many people *feeling* things. So many things. And he felt all of them. What control he had over his empathy was gone. The ability to just think about shutting it off or turning it down was gone, vanished by the brush of a knuckle against the back of his jeans.

Through his God damned jeans!

It was a miracle the surge's power hadn't materialized before Diablo had found him in that parking lot. Mother, he couldn't imagine trying to control all that emotion when Grey had been going crazy about Servius kidnapping Ivy. Dealing with Grey's emotions had been hard enough with what little empathy he'd had to begin with.

Now it felt like he'd grabbed a high voltage power line, and his beast was going insane. It needed to attack the danger, be in control, be the strongest baddest mother-fucking drake around. And while it might be—it would certainly fight dirty to win—being at the top meant dealing with politics. Something he didn't have the skills or patience to deal with, and was smart enough to rein the beast in long enough to not get involved.

Except he was involved in everything right now. That's how he got zapped by the surge. Nero had lost control, was barely holding it together, and was inamorated with a soul-sick human. That had put Raven in danger.

But a part of him couldn't accept that. Raven had been in danger by the surge's massive, uncontrolled power because she cared about these humans and wanted to help. Even if he let his beast scream at her, she wouldn't back down from that. And he would never let his beast do that. She was the only true thing in his life. His rock. His sister. They'd been twins. Before the Scourge. And even though they'd both been reborn with new names and new interests, that knowledge, that connection formed in conception, always remained. He would die for her again and again if he had to, and he'd follow her wherever she went.

The last time she'd been reborn, she'd gone to Nero. So had he. Nero had been good for her.

Diablo passed his front door again.

If he was honest with himself, Nero had been good for him, too.

He'd met Andy, who'd proven to him that he could control the beast. The beast wasn't in charge. Diablo was... *had* been. Now it took everything he had to keep from destroying his furniture in a rage that would only satisfy the beast for a moment.

Grief swept over him in a massive wave and dragged at his control. Rage burned in after it.

The beast slammed his fist against the side of a dumpster, crashing it against the building's side with his enhanced strength and making a thunderous boom roar through the alley.

He punched the dumpster again, crushing in its side.

The beast howled, and the rage and grief burned hotter.

Another punch. Another boom.

He grabbed the lip of the opening, heaved, and swung it to the other side of the alley. It hit with another boom, toppled over, and spewed garbage bags over the broken asphalt.

With a roar, he ripped off the lid and tossed it deeper into the alley. It ricocheted off the wall and crashed into another dumpster.

Yes. More.

He had to let it out. Release the pressure.

But there was no end to it. All the beast did was rage. It was always ferocious. Letting it break and tear and howl didn't release anything, it only made it stronger.

A gust of confusion and fear swept through the rage. More fear, boredom, lust, craving, joy, all clawed past the beast. The apartment buildings were filled with people, and too many of them were awake at this hour. Except that wasn't the truth. He wasn't being overwhelmed by just the people in his vicinity. The magic the surge had flooded into him hadn't just increased his ability to sense, but also his range. This was his earth magic at its strongest. It was crushing him, and the beast's only survival instinct was to fight and kill.

Destroy.

The beast rushed toward the other dumpster.

No.

He staggered to a stop halfway down the alley. Trashing the trash bins wouldn't solve anything. It wouldn't make the emotions go away. And Mother, it had been hours since he'd been zapped by the surge. That meant it wasn't going to go away at all. The effects were permanent.

The beast screamed. It couldn't live like this. Not with all that fear and desire and rage and even joy. It was too much. He was going to lose who he was, and the beast wouldn't allow that.

He clenched his fists. If he was smart, he'd gate to his apartment—

Bad idea, the neighbors would hear him breaking his furniture— Nero's? His room was too close to the kids' rooms, and the transition suites were occupied.

The beast screamed at that. He grabbed the lid of the broken dumpster and slammed it against the wall.

Damn it. No.

He tossed the lid behind him.

His only option was some place remote. But he didn't have a satellite phone. If Raven woke and needed him, no one would be able to get ahold of him. He couldn't risk it. Too much was happening at Nero's house, first with Anaea, then Capri and Grey, and now Nero himself. He had to stay close to ensure Raven and the kids were safe.

God damn it. That meant there was no safe place to go where he could scream the beast into submission without endangering anyone. He was just going to have to suck it up and control it.

He drew in a ragged breath and ran past the dumpster, out of the alley and along the deserted block.

Andy had taught him control.

Mother, Andy would have understood this overwhelming buffet of emotions, too. When he'd first joined the *puzur,* he'd been a teen with an out-of-control empathic ability, so strong Raven hadn't been sure if he'd ever be able to fully know which emotions were his and which weren't. That kid had grown into an amazing man and had taught Diablo so much about empathic earth magic, what it meant to really be a part of a family, and about friendship.

Diablo growled.

No way in hell was he going to ruin his friend's memory by

letting the beast loose. He could control this. The running wasn't burning the beast's energy away, so perhaps concentration on the calmer emotions within him might help.

He reached his apartment building's front door. If he was going to gate into his apartment, he'd need to run back to the alley to hide his gate from prying eyes. But the beast really wanted to smash that other dumpster, so he decided just to take the three flights up.

Even taking the stairs three at a time did nothing to wear the beast out. Not that he'd expected it would. He'd spent the last few hours fighting and then running around. Physical exercise wasn't going to do anything to bring the beast under control.

Except he doubted concentration would, either, and feared nothing would.

He reached the third-floor landing, yanked open the fire door—managing at the last minute to not rip the door off its hinges—and stormed toward his apartment.

Just get inside and do that meditation thing Andy had taught him. Surely that would help.

But his beast wrenched him to a halt before reaching his apartment, and his gaze leapt to the number on the closest door.

306.

Eva's apartment. The new neighbor he'd been spending— and *wanting* to spend a lot of time with. The *girlfriend* Raven had been teasing him about. The one he didn't want to accidentally hurt or scare with his beast.

The lock on the door clicked, heard with crystal clarity in the quiet of the hall with his enhanced hearing.

His pulse pounded. She couldn't catch him here. Not like this. He had to get to his apartment, now.

He drew his power to rapid free gate into his apartment, but the beast jerked him a step closer to her door and the power to gate vanished.

The door opened, framing Eva in a simple red wrap dress that accentuated all her curves. His pulse, his whole essence, including the beast, stuttered. There was something about her that stunned him every time he looked at her.

In that moment all he wanted, and all he feared, was for her to invite him in. Just ask. He'd say yes. Right now, he had no control over anything, including his beast.

And that was what terrified him the most.

Nero pocketed his phone and let his gaze slide over his office. Dawn had yet to lighten the sky outside and only an hour had passed since he'd cradled Becca in his arms, strode beyond the edge of the gatelock, and returned home. It was hard to believe everything had changed just over twelve hours ago. The shelf where Diablo had slammed Grey last night was still broken, the books a tumbled mess on the floor, and the half-empty bottle of scotch still sat on the corner of his desk with the dirty glass beside it.

Only twelve hours and his life had twisted out of joint, throwing everything in chaos, then wrenched back together in a new, stronger configuration.

Inamorated.

Again.

He still couldn't quite believe it, but the weight and surety pulsing around his heart couldn't be denied. And he didn't want to deny it. For whatever reason, he'd been gifted a second soul bond. A single soul bond was rare enough. A second one had never been heard of... and only a select few would ever know the truth.

Not because he didn't want to roar about his love to the world, but because she was human with magic and there was still a complicated mess at Court, inciting fearful dragons to want to kill her without question.

His pulse raced at the thought.

Not helpless, silly dragon, she said in his head, louder than the other voices still whispering at the edge of her—and his—senses. *I'm working on keeping the chatter down, too.*

Didn't say you weren't. And he didn't really care. The voices meant he could feel her presence. He couldn't hear her thoughts—he might be able to if he concentrated, but he wasn't going to—but just knowing she was there and sensing the strength of her spirit helped to calm his fears. He also felt—though he was afraid he was mistaken —a certainty in her soul about him... and them. The certainty had been a whisper when she'd realized she had healed a fatal injury and had been growing stronger as the hour progressed.

Are you coming? I'm waiting, she said, her mental voice edged with a mirth he didn't understand. *Oh, you'll see.*

What do you mean, I'll see? His thoughts jumped to earlier that evening, when they'd made love in his bathroom. *We're having breakfast, right? It's morning. My kids will be down soon.*

Don't tempt me. Heated desire rushed through the mental connection, adding to his hope that he could convince her to stay with him. *And yes, we're having breakfast. Then...* The desire turned to scorching need.

Breakfast couldn't come soon enough, because after—

After, he'd take a moment to catch his breath with Becca, but a moment was all he could allow. Things were still dangerous and complicated, and now Becca, not just his *puzur*, was at risk. He wasn't going to mentally add her to the *puzur*, not until he knew for certain she wanted to stay—

Mother, he wanted her to stay, hoped what he sensed from her meant she would.

Their relationship was still young, barely embryonic even by the standards of short-lived humans. It wouldn't be fair to assume anything about what she wanted. He could be feeling from her what he wanted to feel and ignoring everything else.

Besides, his day might have been stressful, but hers had been a nightmare. Even if he hadn't had the experience of helping his kids deal with the horrors of awakened magic and family abandonment, he'd known that what Becca had to deal with would take time to emotionally recover from. All he could do was be there for her, in whatever way she wanted him, and take one day at a time.

For his part, he still had to deal with Regis's decree demanding all dragons return to Court, as well as giving the prince the heads of Hunter and Anaea within the week.

Problems he didn't even have answers for, and ones he feared would finally force his hand against the Royal Coterie. He didn't want to be the latest dragon to attempt a coup against Regis, but he would if it was the only way to protect the people he cared about.

He stepped into the hall, and his phone buzzed, indicating a text message. Terry—a member of the *puzur* and a human graduate of Nero's program—had Werner and the other mages settled in a motel. Until Nero could trust them, he wasn't inviting them home, but he also wasn't going to leave them to the streets. It would be a long road for many of them, and a lot of work for Raven, but he was hopeful they could be saved. They hadn't deserved what Zenobia or Stanbury had done to them, and while he couldn't—and wasn't going to try to —atone for someone else's sins, he could try to do right by these people.

Of those sins, though, it was Stanbury who concerned him the most. Yes, the woman was dead, but she'd been a strong enough sorcerer that she'd been able to rip his dugga's magic from his soul. That kind of magic didn't just naturally or quickly manifest. Not with the level of control and knowledge about hieroglyphs that she possessed. He should have been aware of her years ago and that re-raised the question about his failing dugga's magic.

Except he was positive now it hadn't been failing. Grey had been right, and it had been Nero's sudden soul bond with Becca that had surged his dugga's magic out of control. Without much thought and without any seizures, he could pinpoint Werner in his motel room and watch him from above—and not from within him, like how he'd connected with Becca. Nero had also sent a quick message to Diablo using the dugga's mental connection without any problems, either.

Well, without problems from his magic. The younger black drake had been strung tight about something and had jumped at the idea of the potentially dangerous investigation of Stanbury's facility.

Nero hadn't really expected a yes, or even an answer to his mental call, what with how Diablo had vanished from the house after the surge had zapped Raven. And if there'd been any other drake who was as good an option, he would have asked him or her. But Diablo already knew about Becca, the facility with the gatelock, and could rapid free gate. Also, as much as Nero hated to admit it, Diablo was his most reliable and best hunter. The younger black drake took the responsibility to save human mages seriously—probably because it was something his sister held dear.

Voices carried down the hall, Becca's husky alto and a reedy tenor.

"Sometimes he gets distracted in his office," a young soprano said. Mia. His fourteen-year-old auger who, while still shy and sweet, was starting to show signs of feisty independence—a far cry from the terrified girl he'd rescued.

"I'm sure he'll appreciate this," Becca said. *Your children really care for you.* Awe and affection and familial love swept through their connection, along with a flash of surprise.

He rounded the corner and stepped into the kitchen—a large space with granite countertops, a massive island, three fridges, and two stoves. Mia sat with Becca, giving her a warm, welcoming smile, and across from them sat Tyler. All were on stools at the island, while Jeff—in his workout sweats—stood at the stove, frying bacon in a pan.

Mia, her petite fourteen-year-old frame still in her pajamas and her mousey brown curls pulled into a ponytail at the top of her head, hopped from her stool, rushed to Nero, and wrapped her arms around him. "I'm glad you're okay."

"Bad dream?" Nero hugged her back. He couldn't imagine how terrifying it was to be able to see the future and not be able to do anything about it. And while he'd called it a dream, they both knew it had been a vision of the future.

"She was screaming." Jeff jerked his thumb at Tyler. "Woke the new guy."

"So you decided to make breakfast?" Nero asked.

Jeff shrugged and cracked an egg into a second frying pan. "Mia suggested it." And, according to Raven, Jeff would do just about anything for Mia. "For Becca here."

And for you, Becca said.

He met her gaze over Mia's head and warmth swelled around his heart. She looked like she was right where she belonged, among his family, as part of his family.

"She said Becca needed the welcome," Tyler said.

Mia sat back on her stool beside Becca. "And Ivy, too."

Air whooshed from down the hall, and Hunter, Anaea, Grey, and Ivy walked into the kitchen.

Your unusual and unique family. Becca flashed him a wide smile, showing more than enough teeth to make him hard.

"Checking in before we head to the Handmaiden's residence," Hunter said, his gaze sweeping over the occupants of the kitchen. "You're Rebecca?"

"Grey and Raven mentioned you," Anaea said.

"You didn't mention they'd all be here." Jeff opened the closest fridge and pulled out another package of bacon. "Should I cook enough for Capri and Ryan, too?"

"I don't know," Mia said with a mischievous smile.

She does know. She's teasing him. She thinks Capri and Ryan will be down in a few minutes.

Nero pulled out the stool on Becca's other side and sat. "Welcome to my family."

She laced her fingers into his, the action feeling—from her as well —natural, as if they'd always been holding hands.

Grey pulled out the stool beside Tyler and offered Ivy the seat. "Do you still need us to find information about the dugga's magic? Or has that been figured out?" His gaze slid to Becca. Nero didn't need Becca's telepathy to know Grey was wondering if sealing his soul bond with Becca had stabilized his magic as predicted.

Nero rolled his eyes. "Real subtle. I'm sure everyone here but the kids know what you're talking about."

"Oh, we know as well." Jeff added more eggs to the frying pan.

"I had *that* dream last night, but then tonight, you were in danger." Mia shivered and hugged herself.

Hunter raised an eyebrow.

Nero squeezed Becca's hand. "Long story."

"We're okay," Becca said.

"And you're staying." Mia said it as if it were a fact.

"Well, she's staying for breakfast," Jeff said.

Becca locked gazes with Nero and her affection for him filled her. *I can't explain it. This, being here with you, with your friends and family, feels right.* It was something she'd been missing and longing for since she'd left the army. *I've never been more scared than when I couldn't sense you in my head, when I thought I'd lost you. What I want— how I feel—* "It doesn't make sense."

"Welcome to the world of dragons," Anaea said.

"Things here are dangerous and complicated." With every fiber of his being, Nero wanted her to stay, even if she didn't fully return his affection, but being with him put her in danger.

Becca rolled her shoulder, the one with the tattoo and the scars. "Dangerous and complicated doesn't scare me." *Even feeling what I feel for you doesn't scare me.* "That bacon does, though."

"Hey!" Jeff scooped the over-crispy bacon onto a paper towel to sop up the extra grease. "My bacon is perfect."

"Looks good to me," Hunter said.

Grey snorted. "And of course the fire drake likes his bacon fried to a crisp."

Nero raised Becca's hand to his lips and kissed her knuckles.

"Oh, Jeez," Tyler groaned. "Tell me now if there's another part of the house I need to avoid. Catching Ryan and Capri was bad enough."

"What's bad enough?" Capri asked as she and Ryan entered the kitchen.

Jeff threw his hands up in mock disgust. "Mia!"

"I am yours, my inamorata," Nero said. "Heart and soul, if you'll have me and my crazy family."

Her emotions swelled through him. Love, awe, and desire. This was a connection of souls that he never thought he'd have again, with a woman who amazed and inspired him. "I wouldn't have you without your crazy family."

OTHER BOOKS BY C.I. BLACK

ABOUT C.I. BLACK

C.I. Black has always lived in a world of imagination. When she's not daydreaming, she puts her flights of fancy down on paper writing urban fantasy, paranormal romance, and romantic suspense books.

She's the author of The Dragon Spirit series and The Medusa Files series. You can find a complete list of C.I.'s books at www.ciblack.com.

I hop from my coffin, zip up the stairs, and go to the front door, giving it a hard yank to yell at whatever merchant is peddling their wares at such an ungodly hour. "What the devil do you…" My voice trails off.

Standing before me is the woman I saw through my window earlier. Her potent, sweet floral scent slams into me like a mallet to the face. It is painfully delicious.

I step back and pinch my nose. Otherwise, I will have to pull her inside and devour her—not the wisest decision when I am now a stranger in a strange land. Killing so close to home in such unfamiliar surroundings may prove problematic, if I am to heed Neli's warnings.

The young beauty with her silky dark hair and wide inquisitive eyes looks up at my face. Her gaze then begins the journey south until she realizes I am in my nightclothes. "Oh! Oh, God! You're naked!"

"Yes. As you can see," I say, still holding my nose, "I am a man, and real men do not wear garments to bed. Now what may I do for you?"

Cheeks red, she closes her eyes and holds out an odd-looking container of pastries. "I, uh…uh…just came by to introduce myself. I'm your neighbor from across the road, Stella Baker. I brought homemade cupcakes."

A baker at a vineyard? "I do not eat sugar, but I thank you all the same." Suddenly, I realize two things. One, pinching my nose is completely useless. Her sweet, virginal scent is still entering my lungs and calling to me. And second, I am nude, which is normally no concern of mine—I am a man and modesty is for women—but for some odd reason my shaft is beginning to thicken.

OTHER WORKS BY MIMI JEAN PAMFILOFF

COMING SOON!

The Librarian's Vampire Assistant (Book 5) ← I can't wait to hear from Miriam.

The Dead King (King Series, Book 6) ← Dark stuff.

THE ACCIDENTALLY YOURS SERIES
(Paranormal Romance/Humor)
Accidentally in Love with…a God? (Book 1)
Accidentally Married to…a Vampire? (Book 2)
Sun God Seeks…Surrogate? (Book 3)
Accidentally…Evil? (a Novella) (Book 3.5)
Vampires Need Not…Apply? (Book 4)
Accidentally…Cimil? (a Novella) (Book 4.5)
Accidentally…Over? (Series Finale) (Book 5)

THE BOYFRIEND COLLECTOR DUET
(New Adult/Suspense)
The Boyfriend Collector, Part 1
The Boyfriend Collector, Part 2

FANGED LOVE ← You are here. ☺
(Standalones/Paranormal/Humor)

THE FATE BOOK DUET
(New Adult/Humor)
Fate Book
Fate Book Two

The Librarian's Vampire Assistant (Book 2)
The Librarian's Vampire Assistant (Book 3)
The Librarian's Vampire Assistant (Book 4)

THE MERMEN TRILOGY
(Dark Fantasy/Suspense)
Mermen (Part 1)
MerMadmen (Part 2)
MerCiless (Part 3)

MR. ROOK'S ISLAND TRILOGY
(Contemporary/Suspense)
Mr. Rook (Part 1)
Pawn (Part 2)
Check (Part 3)

THE OHELLNO SERIES
(Standalones/New Adult/Romantic Comedy)
Smart Tass (Book 1)
Oh Henry (Book 2)
Digging A Hole (Book 3)
Battle of the Bulge (Book 4)
My Pen is Huge (Book 5)
Wine Hard, Baby (Book 6)

WISH, a Standalone Novel
(Romantic Comedy)

OTHER WORKS BY KYLIE GILMORE

THE CLOVER PARK SERIES ← brothers who
put family first!
The Opposite of Wild (Book 1) ← Mimi's favorite.
Daisy Does It All (Book 2)
Bad Taste in Men (Book 3)
Kissing Santa (Book 4)
Restless Harmony (Book 5)
Not My Romeo (Book 6)
Rev Me Up (Book 7)
An Ambitious Engagement (Book 8)
Clutch Player (Book 9)
A Tempting Friendship (Book 10)
Clover Park Bride: Nico and Lily's Wedding
A Valentine's Day Gift (Book 11)
Maggie Meets Her Match (Book 12)

THE CLOVER PARK STUDS SERIES ← hawt
geeks who unleash into studs!
Almost Over It (Book 1)
Almost Married (Book 2)
Almost Fate (Book 3)
Almost in Love (Book 4)
Almost Romance (Book 5)
Almost Hitched (Book 6)